Killing Aquila

Harriet Carlton

Copyright © 2023 by Harriet Carlton

All rights reserved.

No portion of this book may be reproduced in any form without written permission from the publisher or author, except as permitted by U.S. copyright law.

To my beta readers both on Discord and in person; Kelly, Natalie, Autumn, Crow, Emily, Maggie, Nadia, Nikki, October, Sonya, Val – thank you for putting up with my 3AM moments of "So I had this thought." This book wouldn't be what it is without you.

Gail – you've truly brought out the best in this book. For that, I'm more grateful than words can express.

To my grandmother, "Jumbo" – the idea for this book was scribbled down by hand in your living room. I still have the original notebook.

Finally, to Susan, who first told me that this idea was worth its salt. Without you this book would not exist.

Chapter 1

If anyone asked Zoey Blackmore about the first time she'd gotten someone killed, she would have told them it happened by accident. She would have said it was something she'd never meant to happen. She'd panicked. Been desperate. She'd never meant for anyone to get hurt. She would have said it was a collision of events that had started on a rainy night in June.

~ ~ ~ ~ ~ ~

June had no right to be this chilly. Low-bellied rainclouds obscured the stars, giving the night a strange reddish hue, city lights reflecting off the bottoms of the clouds. A steady, cold drizzle soaked Hereford's streets. The small English city, though, was not bothered by the rain – it was an almost daily occurrence. The summertime Saturday night continued without regard for the weather. Restaurants, bars, and nightclubs bustled with activity.

Zoey pushed a few strands of dark hair out of her eyes and straightened her shirt. She had bought it earlier that day while shopping with her sister, Rona, and wasn't sure how much she liked it. It had looked great on the hanger, but on her, it didn't quite fit her shoulders, slipping askew at every possible opportunity. It wasn't quite holding up to the nighttime chill either. Then again, she hadn't expected it to be quite this cold. She wished she'd listened to her gut and brought an umbrella or a jacket.

Standing on her toes and waiting for Rona to return, Zoey stretched to see how many people were in line ahead of them. All anxious to get into the nightclub. Zoey glanced up at the sign showing the name of the place. *Morceau*, she said silently to herself. How French. She dropped back down to her heels as Rona returned in line beside her.

"Okay, the sign at the entrance says there's a cover charge," Rona sighed, taking some cash out of her pocket. "I'm *much* too pretty to pay a cover fee. Honestly."

"Rona," said Zoey, grinning. "You mean *we're* too pretty, right? Do I need to remind you that we're identical twins? Besides, I don't think looks have anything to do with it."

Rona laughed, sweeping some of her hair off her shoulders. "If this new place wasn't the talk of the town right now, I'd say we should just go on to the next club. In any case, it's so rare for you to come out. I'm determined to keep you out for as long as I can."

Zoey sighed and shook her head. "I don't know how you talk me into these things, Ro. You know I hate nightclubs as much as you hated my ballet recitals."

"But I still went to them, dear sister. And as payment for my loyalty, I now drag you out for a good time."

Zoey laughed and brushed some imaginary dirt off her leggings. "You have a point. Hey, did you end up using your debit card to withdraw money for the cover fees or did you use mine?"

Rona scoffed. "Neither. You think I've got money? I used the card that our absentee father-of-the-year left with us."

Zoey's blood ran cold, and her good mood vanished. "Rona, absentee father-of-the-year or not, Maxwell will murder *me* when he finds out. You know he will! We're not supposed to use his money unless it's an emergency."

"Well, he can kill me instead of you when he gets back from London. He might not even notice the money's gone, anyway."

"Oh, he'll notice," sighed Zoey. She lifted a hand and anxiously rubbed the ballet slipper pendant on her necklace. "And *I'm* always the one he shouts at, not you, when this kind of thing happens."

"That's the cost you pay for being 'the good child'. I think he just expects me to be a delinquent at this point," replied Rona. She nudged Zoey's shoulder. "Don't worry. I'll be sure to take the brunt of his anger when he gets back. It's next week, isn't it?"

"Allegedly," sighed Zoey. "But you know how he is about giving us a time frame for coming back."

"Then stop your fussing," said Rona. "It'll be alright. It can't be any worse than last month when he went to Spain for two weeks and came back to find that I'd blown up the microwave."

"I seem to remember I got blamed that time, too," grinned Zoey, letting the gold pendant fall back against her chest. "In hindsight, it *was* funny."

"See? Whatever happens, we'll be laughing about it in a few months."

"Provided he never finds out that we leave Hailee alone when we go out clubbing, I think we'll both live to see our twenty-first birthday."

"Please." Rona rolled her eyes. "She's almost fifteen. She'll be fine. Our dear old Dad, aka Maxwell, was leaving us alone when we were eleven and Hailee was six."

"That's not fair, Rona. He didn't exactly have a choice. Mom had vanished by then, and he had to work. He could hardly have quit his job to take care of us."

"Could have hired a nanny," muttered Rona.

"I won't argue with you there," replied Zoey.

She fell silent and shuffled forward as the line moved, Rona half a step ahead of her. For June, it was cool, and the rain made the air feel just that much colder.

One bouncer stood at the doorway, looking bored. The white club logo of Morceau stood out on his shirt against the night. A tiny dash of color on black fabric. Zoey heard the thump of a pounding bass coming from inside the club doors. It seemed to shake the building's walls, and she could feel the vibrations inside her chest. Every now and again, she spotted a flash of neon against an interior wall.

"I still don't understand how you enjoy this," Zoey said, glancing at Rona.

"You need to live a little, Zoey. I'm sure you'd get to like it if you came out with me a bit more. You can't find this sort of excitement in any of those stuffy ballet lessons you take. This is good for you. Healthy."

"Loud music and flashing lights. Different kind of excitement, for sure."

"Look on the bright side. At least this is a type of dancing. Maybe it'll get you back in the mood to start training again. When did you last dance?"

"It's been a while. Too long," muttered Zoey, glancing up at the white club sign.

The line shuffled on, and Zoey took half a step forward. Finally, it felt like they were getting close to the front. It wouldn't be long now.

"Got your phone on you?" asked Rona.

"Of course," grinned Zoey. "I guess that means I'm in charge of calling the taxi?"

"I have about twenty percent battery left on mine. It'll be a miracle if it doesn't die before they close the place for the night."

"Rona, you practically live next to a charger. *How* is your phone about to die?"

"Hailee stole my charger before we left. What kind of sister would I be if I didn't let her steal my things? Oh! Finally!"

Zoey shook her head as Rona darted ahead, not a second after the bouncer waved them on. She swallowed and tried to shake off the wave of nerves that rose inside her as Rona handed over the cover charge. It wasn't a lot of money.

~ ~ ~ ~ ~ ~

There was something disconcerting about the arrhythmic movements of everyone on Morceau's dance floor. No rhyme. No reason. Just movement. It was what had driven Zoey away from the center of the floor where Rona had dragged her at the start of the night.

She rested an arm on the glass bar top. She fiddled with the straw in her drink. A vodka-soda. Her third. Rona was still in the melee, hidden for the moment by the masses of people. Zoey took a sip of her drink. This one was stronger than her last, but by no means less enjoyable.

How Rona enjoyed the clubbing scene, she didn't think she would ever understand. She wasn't sure she wanted to. Zoey rolled her shoulders. The close proximity of so many people in such a small space had always unsettled her. At least the drinks, while expensive, were really good and helped her feel less on edge. She took another sip, grinning around the straw as Rona emerged from the crowds, face flushed and make-up running slightly.

"One more song! You have to come out for just one more!" she shouted.

Zoey blinked, struggling to lip-read what Rona said.

Rona tucked her dark hair behind her ear and hopped up onto an empty bar stool, while pointing at Zoey, then at herself. "You! Me! Dance!"

"Buy me another one of these, and I'll come!" shouted Zoey. "Or rather, have our dear father buy me another!"

"You're expensive! Oh well! Not my money!"

"Such is the price of getting me on the dance floor, Ro," replied Zoey. There was a lull in the music, and she breathed a sigh of relief, glad to be able to lower her voice.

"Alright, might as well get myself a drink, too. By the way, how many have you had, so far?" asked Rona.

Zoey set her empty cup back on the bar and made eye contact with a bartender. "*That* was number three."

"God, Zoey. I'll be pouring you into the taxi when we leave this place!"

"Hey, what was it you said earlier? 'Live a little'?" Zoey grinned and leaned over the bar as the bartender approached. "Another vodka-soda for me, and what for you, Rona?"

"A rum and Coke, please. This round's on me, Zo. Well, actually it's on Maxwell."

"Rum and Coke?" asked Zoey. "I thought you swore off that combination."

"Well, since you'll be going home drunk, I figured I'd join the party," replied Rona, taking her drink.

Zoey laughed and picked up her fourth drink. Already, everything started to haze into pleasant fuzz. Even the blaring music seemed more bearable now.

"Ah!" shouted Rona. "My favorite song! Come on!"

Zoey yelped as Rona grabbed her wrist and pulled her off her stool, weaving them back to the center of the dance floor. Zoey swallowed. Three vodka-sodas in, clutching a fourth, which she miraculously hadn't dropped, and she was still wary of going into this crowd. She shook herself. It was just the club scene making her feel more jittery. That was all. She glanced over her shoulder. Her barstool of solitude had already been claimed. She took a long sip of her drink and stood close to Rona. She relaxed, her younger twin already dancing in time with the music. Rhythm to club music was something Zoey had never quite mastered. Classical dance routines were one thing. This bass-dropping chaos was something else. She did her best to copy Rona's movements. Her sister seemed to be dancing ten beats to her two, or was it the other way around? Perhaps there *was* something a little hypnotic about the thumping club music. Zoey took a deep breath and tried to shed her nerves – the drinks helped, but only so much. There was nothing to be afraid of here. She was with her sister. They were in a large crowd in a controlled environment. There was no reason to be worried – aside from the fact that Rona had used their father's card for something she wasn't supposed to. Zoey swallowed. She needed to stop fixating on that. They'd sort it out in the morning.

The bass dropped, neon lights flashed as more people crushed in. A burst of artificial fog shot down from the ceiling. Rona raised her cup toward the ceiling, and Zoey copied her movement. Why they were raising their cups, she didn't know, but why should she care?

She grinned as the music lulled again. Another new song began as more people pushed their way to the middle of the dance floor. People swapped positions. Zoey glanced at the new faces around them. A young man had maneuvered his way toward Zoey and her sister. Zoey shrugged. He wasn't unattractive. Even with the strobe lights, she could tell he had dark hair and even darker eyes. Taller than her and built like an athlete. Had it been quieter, she might have asked his name. But this was a loud nightclub, and names were not important, much less audible.

The young man grinned at her, and Zoey flashed him a smile back. A careless flirtation, nothing more.

The music picked up again. Neon lights flashed brighter. Bodies swarmed. Then something settled on Zoey's jawline. She looked up and froze. The young man had moved closer. Too close. He was in her space. She didn't want him here. Zoey stiffened, tension seizing her as he reached out in seemingly slow motion. Beside her, she felt Rona hesitate. His hand ghosted lower, down her neck and paused on her collarbone, fingers pausing on her necklace's gold chain, then lower. Zoey's blood flashed hot. No thought. Just action. She dropped her drink and swung, open palm slapping him across his cheek.

"Zoey!" shouted Rona.

"Get off!" Zoey shouted, drowning out Rona.

A few people glanced toward them, but for the most part the rhythm of the club had hardly even been disrupted. Zoey sneered at the young man as he turned and pushed his way off the dance floor.

"What were you thinking?" cried Rona.

"He shouldn't have touched me!" snapped Zoey. Rona balked, and Zoey felt a sudden rush of guilt, unsure herself why she'd snapped at Rona.

"Come on," said Rona, grabbing Zoey's wrist.

Zoey fell into step behind Rona, stumbling over a few other patrons' feet as she struggled to keep up. Maybe the vodka was hitting harder than she'd realized. Rona headed straight to the women's bathroom, Zoey following her inside. The reprive from the pounding music and flashing lights felt heavenly. Surprisingly, no one else was in the bathroom. She drew a deep breath, shocked to feel her chest tremble.

"Christ, Zoey, you didn't have to slap him," said Rona, as they both went into stalls beside each other, slamming the doors. "They'll probably chuck us out when we go back out there."

Somehow, Rona's tone made Zoey angrier. "I'm alright. Thanks for asking," she spat as she flushed the toilet.

"I could tell," huffed Rona. "What would you have done if he'd hit you back?"

Zoey, washing her hands at the sink, opened her mouth, venom on the tip of her tongue.

"And don't say something stupid like you would have fought him," snapped Rona, as she walked out of the stall. "We both know you wouldn't."

"I was angry, that's all!" shouted Zoey, her own temper rising. Outside the bathroom door, the constant *thump, thump* of the bass seemed to rattle the walls of the ladies room. "You would have been, too!"

"I wouldn't have hit him!"

Zoey fumed silently, one hand balling into a fist and trembling at her side. Rona hadn't been the one who'd been touched. She couldn't know what she would or wouldn't have done. What a stupid thing to say.

"Whatever you say," snapped Zoey. She glanced at herself in the mirror. Her face was flushed, and she knew it wasn't from heat. "Ro, can you close our bar tab? I need some air. I'll meet you outside the exit door in five?"

"Zoey, just *wait* for me! I'll be out in a minute!"

"I'm fine! I just need some air."

Rona hesitated, looking at her sister. "Zoey, *are* you okay?"

"I'm fine!" shouted Zoey. She just wanted to be back home. Back in her quiet bedroom. Away from this thumping club with its shaking walls and handsy men.

She yanked open the bathroom door and stumbled, just barely missing the bathroom doorframe.

Zoey stopped outside the door and took a moment to get her bearings before heading off to find the exit. Her steps felt heavy. She blinked, eyes unfocused. The exit door was somewhere across from the entrance. She remembered that much. But where, exactly? Ah. There. She spotted a few patrons making their way out a glass door, onto a patio, and through a gate beyond.

Zoey drew a deep breath as she weaved her way through the crowd toward it. Her heart thumped a little too hard in her chest. Her legs felt so heavy. She was so hot. Now that the idea of 'outside' was in her head, she was desperate to leave the club. This was definitely the vodka-sodas affecting her. She should have been more careful. This was reckless. She knew better than this.

A bouncer stood just inside the exit door as she walked up to it. Probably to guard against anyone sneaking in without paying. Zoey half-nodded at him as she walked past and stepped out onto the patio. Cold air hit her in the face, sobering her slightly. Her ears were still humming though. Numbly, she opened her phone and started scrolling through the internet for a taxi. She wanted to go *home*, not to another club. She pinched the bridge of her nose and stopped looking. She'd wait for Rona before she called a taxi. Taking a deep breath, she clicked her phone screen off, making her way toward the patio gate.

Looking over her shoulder at the glass exit door she'd just come out of, a rush of nerves settled in her stomach. She moved away from it. She didn't really want to be seen alone – particularly if the person who'd touched her on the dance floor caught sight of her. She walked over to wait outside the back gate of the club. There would be no problem with waiting for Rona on the other side. She could easily listen for Rona coming out of the back door. Then she'd talk to her about going home and calling it a night. At least this would give a bit more space between her and the pounding music, too. Maybe she'd be able to get herself together a bit more out there, too.

The gate swung shut behind her, and Zoey leaned back on the exterior fencing. Not another soul in sight. Perfect. Quiet. It was exactly what she needed. The world swam before her eyes. She was a lot more drunk than she'd thought. Maybe that had been the catalyst for slapping someone. She had *never* smacked anyone before – much as she may have wanted to. It felt as though it had been warranted though. Closing her eyes, Zoey pressed her palms flat against the wood slats, tilting her head back against the fence.

"You look like you could use a cigarette."

Zoey jumped and straightened. A man stepped out of a shadow a short distance away, a pack of cigarettes and a lighter in his hands. The club logo was embroidered on the front of his shirt. A club employee. Probably taking his break He looked like he might be a bouncer, built broad and strong. There was a cold look in his eyes. Zoey mentally shook off any wariness.

"I don't smoke," she replied.

"Does wonders for the nerves," he replied, striking the lighter.

"I've heard. I've also heard it causes cancer."

He breathed a quiet laugh. "You're the girl who smacked that guy just a minute ago, aren't you?"

Zoey pinched the bridge of her nose and sighed. "I am. Don't worry about booting me out. Me and my sister are already leaving."

The employee shrugged. "Seen it happen before. It's not unusual. You alright?"

"I'm fine," replied Zoey, taking a deep breath. "Thanks for asking."

"That's my job," he replied. "Club much?"

"No. No, not really," Zoey replied, her body starting to relax at last. "I hate it, actually. This is my first time here, and I think it's going to be my last. Now, my sister? She loves it. She's the one who dragged me out here tonight."

"Makes sense. Any other siblings?"

"Yeah. One other younger sister. She's fourteen." For a moment, Zoey was tempted to bite her tongue, but why? These were innocent questions. Small talk. He was probably just trying to get her mind off everything.

"What's your name?" he asked, blowing a puff of smoke.

"Zoey. Zoey Blackmore. You?"

"Ed." The bouncer stuck out a hand. "Ed Smith."

Zoey hesitated for a second, then shook his hand in return. Her fingers felt numb and clumsy. "Nice to meet you."

"Said Rona's with you?" asked Ed, still shaking her hand.

"She is. She should be right behind me," said Zoey, half turning as she tried to pull her hand from his grip.

He held her fast.

Zoey laughed nervously and tried again to pull loose. She glanced at his face as he gripped tighter. She stiffened. Instinct reared its slow, drunken head and blinked blearily. *Wrong*, it slurred. Something was wrong. Even through her alcoholic fog, she knew that beyond certainty. Then it clicked. Rona. When had she mentioned Rona's name? She hadn't.

Swallowing, Zoey pulled back again, looking up at Ed. His face had gone hard. An aggressive look gathered in his eyes. Zoey cried out as his grip tightened painfully, and he spun her around. Her back pressed flush against his chest. Too fast. She couldn't process what was happening. Her legs refused to work properly. One of his arms snapped tight around her neck, pressure. Intense pressure.

Zoey could feel her pulse racing. In a mist, she frantically fumbled through her pocket for her phone. Call Rona. Call the police. Call *someone*. She clawed at his arm with one hand, trying desperately to enter her password with the other. *Smack!* Zoey let out a strangled, airless cry as her phone was knocked out of her hand. She watched in horror as it smashed against the asphalt, screen shattered and completely useless. She opened her mouth, fighting to force a scream.

"Make a sound, and we'll go in there and get your sister," came the hissed threat in her ear.

Rona. Not Rona. Keep Rona out of danger. Zoey closed her mouth. A damp cloth pressed against her nose and clamped over her lips. It didn't smell or taste. But gray overtook what little vision she had left. The arm around her throat tightened. Everything turned foggy. She fumbled with both hands, her nails scratched weakly at his arm. The world faltered. Breath tore ragged at the back of her throat. *Rona. Rona. Rona.* Black appeared, and Zoey felt her legs go weak. The gate *had* to open ... but it didn't. From the corner of her vision, she caught the sight of a car's reversing lights. Doors slammed and Zoey felt herself slip. The pavement rushed up, and blackness crushed inward.

Chapter 2

Rona pushed open Morceau's back gate. This was where Zoey had said she was going to wait. But the patio was empty. Where was she? Beyond the patio was a gate, then a dead-end alley. There was nowhere she could have gone, except back onto the main street. Would she have done that?

Rona leaned on the wall and pulled out her phone to call Zoey, grimacing at the low battery warning. Maybe she'd wandered off? Maybe she was waiting just beyond the alley on the main street? It was worth a try.

Pushing the alley gate open, Rona kept her phone pressed to her ear. A screen on the ground lit up. Rona's heart dropped as she froze, the sound of her phone ringing going deaf in her ear. She recognized that phone. She recognized that contact ID. Zoey's phone. Her own contact ID. No. Zoey never went anywhere without her phone. This wasn't right. This *couldn't* be right.

"Zoey?" Rona called, taken aback by the shakiness in her voice. "Zoey, are you out here?"

There was no response, save for the fluttering of a few trash bin bags. Rona made a small sound of concern in the back of her throat. Zoey never did this. She was always where she said she was going to be. What was she supposed to do? Who was she supposed to call? Zoey was her go-to person when things went wrong. Their father almost never answered his phone – not even when he was needed – and Hailee couldn't possibly help.

A sob clung to her throat. What should she do? Call the police? Emergency services? Had something horrible happened? Was this even an emergency? Rona took a sharp, shuddering breath and snatched Zoey's phone from the ground. She turned and ran to the alley entrance. Desperation cracked in her chest. The street was empty. No one. No cars. Certainly, no Zoey. No sign of her anywhere. Rona gasped as she saw hairline cracks splintering Zoey's phone screen. Zoey would never let this get damaged. No matter how impaired she was. *Never.*

"Zoey!" shouted Rona, fear constricting her throat.

No response. Nothing. Who did she call? She drew in a shuddering breath, and pressed *Maxwell Blackmore* in her contact list.

"Come on, Maxwell," whispered Rona, their father's first name slipping from her mouth. She, Zoey, and Hailee had always called Maxwell by his first name. 'Dad' had always felt too familiar.

The call went straight to voicemail.

Rona whined in the back of her throat and dialed again.

It rang twice. Voicemail.

"Please, please," whimpered Rona, pressing his contact number a third time. It rang once, twice. "Come on. Pick up your phone, you useless excuse for a –"

"Useless excuse for a what, Rona?" asked Maxwell, his voice low and groggy.

Rona's breath jammed in her throat. She pressed one knuckle to her mouth. Behind his obvious tiredness, she could hear carefully restrained anger.

"Do you have any idea what time it is?" he asked. His tone hadn't changed, nor had his inflection, but there was something horribly glacial in his words.

"M-Maxwell," said Rona, her heart sinking as her voice broke. "Something's happened to Zoey. I need help. We were out at a nightclub, and I can't find her. Something bad happened, I know it. Her phone – I have her phone. She dropped it. I don't know –"

There was a shuffle from the other side of the phone, and Maxwell groaned quietly. "Go home, Rona."

An awful chill swept over Rona, as though she'd been dunked in cold water. "What? What about Zoey?"

"Go home. I'll be there in the morning."

Nausea swept over Rona, and she sat down heavily on the curb. "Do I call the police? You're supposed to call the police when people go missing."

"No. I'll be there in the morning."

"But what if someone took her? What if she's hurt? What if –"

"Get a taxi and go home. I'm on my way back as we speak."

"Maxwell, I'm scared. I don't know where she is. This isn't like Zoey."

"She may have gone home. Or gone home with someone."

"She wouldn't do that without telling me!" Rona shouted, her voice trembling uncontrollably. "Please. I don't know what to do."

"I've already told you what to do. Have you called a taxi yet?"

"No. I've been on the phone with you."

"Well, get off the phone with me and call a taxi," said Maxwell. "I'll be there in the morning."

"Maxwell –"

The line beeped three times, and Rona pulled her phone away from her ear. *Call ended.*

Rona wiped away the tears stinging her eyes and bit down hard on a knuckle. Absently, she scrolled through her phone and called a taxi. Go home. Wait. Sit and wait. Don't call the police. Wait until morning.

It went against everything Rona wanted to do. Everything she thought she should do. And yet, she waited, alone, on the roadside for the taxi to arrive. Time crawled by in a strange haze. One second, she was connected to the taxi service. The next, the taxi was simply *there*, like a being from another world. Movement felt slow, stilted as Rona slid into the taxi, glancing up and down the street one last time for Zoey. Nothing. Zoey wouldn't do this. Zoey would never have left her if the situation had been reversed. But she didn't know what else to do, so she pulled the taxi door closed and told the driver her address in a voice that didn't even sound like her own.

~ ~ ~ ~ ~ ~

Morning came slowly. Gray. Like a wash of despair. Rona raised her head and looked out of the living room window to the back garden. It was raining. A relentless, misting kind of rain that settled in for days, chilling everything and everyone to the bone. This rain, though, seemed cold. More dour than usual. A manifestation of what had happened the night before.

Resting her chin in her hand, Rona swallowed and drew a deep breath. These had been the worst few hours of her life. No reprieve. The only hope, her father's impending arrival with, she hoped, a plan to find Zoey. Rona had hardly slept all night – only for minutes at a time. Her eyes ached. The sides of her face felt dry and tracked with salt from all the tears she'd cried. Zoey's phone had stayed dormant on the table all night. Not a single notification. Nothing. As though she had vanished from the planet.

There was one thing Rona knew without a doubt. If it was possible for Zoey to come home, she would have been here by now. At the very least, she would have called. Taken a taxi. She would have done *something*.

Rona leaned forward and pressed her palms against her eyes. What was she going to tell Hailee? Where was Maxwell? He said he'd be here in the morning. So where was he?

A mug of cold tea stood on the coffee table in front of her. She couldn't drink it. Her stomach had turned against her. She should have called the police. She should have done something.

She grabbed the mug and stood up, walking back to the kitchen. More for something to do than anything else. She pushed the door open and froze. Hailee was already awake, pouring her own cup of tea. Rona stood stock still as Hailee half turned and looked her up and down.

"You look half dead. Where's Zoey? Too hungover to get out of bed?" Hailee asked, laughing as she set the teapot back on the counter.

Rona dropped her mug, porcelain shattering across the tile floor. Avoiding the broken shards, she crossed the kitchen and pulled Hailee into a tight, trembling hug.

"Ro?" asked Hailee, as she pulled back, looking her sister in the eye. "Are you okay?"

Rona shook her head and opened her eyes, not realizing she'd closed them. "Hailee, I – something happened last night."

"Well, tell me. You're going to make me more worried if you don't," said Hailee, stepping out of Rona's hold.

Rona heaved a deep breath as she took a step backward and pressed her hand to her mouth. How did she say this? How did she tell Hailee that their oldest sister was *gone*? Missing. And there were no traces of her. Tears welled up in her eyes, and she looked away from Hailee, shaking her head and letting them fall. Desperate for something to do with her hands, Rona spun, frantically grabbing paper towels and starting to clean up the mess from the shattered mug.

"Ro?"

Hands shaking, Rona tipped the shards of ceramic into the trash bin. "It's Zoey. She's –"

Rona cut herself off at the sound of the front door opening and turned, sprinting from the kitchen into the foyer.

Zoey. Zoey. Zoey.

Let it be Zoey.

But it wasn't Zoey.

Closing the front door was Maxwell Blackmore. His black hair was tousled, as though he'd driven with the windows down. A livid, red scratch ran from his temple, disappearing into his hairline. Even from across the foyer, Rona could see how bloodshot his gray eyes were. Their gazes met, and Rona's mouth ran dry as he inhaled and exhaled heavily. In spite of him being across the room, she couldn't keep herself from taking a step back. Maxwell was by no means a large man – Rona was only a few inches shorter than him these days – but there was something horribly imposing about him. This morning particularly.

"Rona, what in the –" Hailee stopped herself as she stepped around Rona. "H-Hi, Maxwell. I thought you weren't back until next week?"

"I wasn't supposed to be," he replied, setting his laptop case down by the door. He straightened and took off his jacket, then indicated with one finger to the living room. "Make us a cup of tea, Hailee, then come and sit down. You'll want to hear this, too."

Rona swallowed hard and tried to take a steadying breath. She felt sick. She didn't want tea. She wanted a hug, but she knew better than to ask for one. She dropped her gaze to the floor and walked to the living room, fighting the tears that threatened the backs of her eyes. She mustn't, she *mustn't*, cry in front of Maxwell. As she collapsed heavily back onto the couch where she'd been earlier, her eyes focused on the beige carpet. Beige. The memory of Zoey spilling coffee on it earlier in the year surfaced in her mind. She remembered Zoey's terror well. Had he ever found out, Rona was sure Maxwell would have been incensed. The carpets had been new then – just replaced. Why was she thinking about that *now*? Now when her sister was missing. But here she was, thinking about coffee on pale carpets.

A new teacup with freshly hot tea clunked on the table in front of her, and Rona felt the couch dip as Hailee sat next to her. Her sister's confusion was almost tangible, filling the room. Rona finally lifted her eyes back to their father.

"What happened, Rona?" asked Maxwell, one hand clutching a cup of tea, the other braced against the mantelpiece.

Rona opened her mouth, and words nearly staunched in her throat again. She caught Hailee's wide-eyed and desperate gaze from her peripherals. Rona pressed her lips together and swallowed hard.

"Did something happen to Z –" started Hailee.

One of Maxwell's brows arched. Hailee fell silent. Rona met her father's eyes again. Gray. Chilled and distant. Zoey had called them tombstone eyes once. Rona couldn't help but feel like the description was particularly accurate this morning.

Like a torrent, the story spilled from Rona's mouth. The club, the fight, Zoey storming out. Even the fact that Rona had used Maxwell's money for their cover charge and drinks – she wasn't sure why she told him, but she felt compelled to. As though her mind would leave no detail unsaid. She couldn't look him in the eyes – not quite. So she kept her gaze fixed on the unlit fireplace instead. Even in her peripherals, never once did Maxwell's gaze waver. Never once did his eyes flash or his expression change. And that was almost worse.

By the time she finished, Rona's gaze had fallen again to the floor, and the tears she swore she wouldn't cry had spilled down her cheeks. The only thing that tethered her to the living room was Hailee's hand on her shoulder.

"Sounds almost karmic, if you ask me," said Maxwell, the tiniest inflection of humor settling in his voice.

Rona looked up sharply, hot anger replacing her wild anxiety. "How can you say that? How can you possibly say that? That's my sister! Your daughter. Gone like –"

"You steal my money to go to a nightclub, get drunk, and do God knows what. You leave Hailee alone, which I've expressly told you in the past not to do." Maxwell studied his hand idly. "But I can't say that I haven't been expecting something like this."

"You – what?"

Rona looked from Maxwell to Hailee in shock, and her younger sister stared back, nonplussed. Why hadn't he imploded? Why were the windows not rattling in their frames with a Maxwell-level tirade? He was calm. Altogether too calm. A new kind of fear settled in the back of her throat. Anger, she'd expected. Calmness, though. She didn't know how to react.

"It's not unusual for family members of prominent figures to get taken and held for ransom. With all the crime documentaries you watch, you should know that, Rona," he said, his voice still infuriatingly calm.

"You're an accountant," said Rona.

Maxwell gingerly touched the scratch at his temple and glanced at his thumb as though checking for blood. "A *prominent* accountant. But, in any event, the case remains the same. Zoey is gone, and, if she's been taken by the people I suspect, calling the police will do infinitely more harm than good. They might even panic and kill her. How fast can the two of you pack?"

"P-Pack?" asked Hailee.

"Pack. A bag. Come on, girls, I didn't raise you to be stupid. You honestly think you're staying here after Zoey's been kidnapped?"

"I don't understand," said Rona.

Maxwell smiled coldly. "Then let me say it in a way you can understand. You two are going away. I've had one daughter taken. I'm not having the other two going the same way. Two friends of mine have agreed to take you for a while. They'll be here in about half an hour. Now, get your things together. If I'm going to get Zoey back, I don't want the two of you malingering around me."

"What?" asked Rona. Maxwell's gaze hardened. "No, I mean where. Where are we going? This is a lot to digest."

"Wales. I'll join you there later tonight. I have some calls to make." He checked his watch. "Twenty-five minutes. Better get moving."

Chapter 3

Gray light fell across Zoey's face. Morning. How was it already morning? The night felt as though it had lasted little more than three seconds. Her head ached and her mouth felt dry. She knew without opening her eyes that she was in for a nightmare of a hangover. She needed water, but she needed more sleep, too.

Behind closed lids, she groggily debated with herself. Water or sleep? Which did she want more? Which did she need more? Sleep. Right now, sleep definitely trumped water. She groaned and rolled over, trying to plunge back into unconsciousness. Water could wait. She shifted, struggling to bring her hands closer toward her chest. But they wouldn't budge.

That was when she realized her position.

Her numb, tingling hands were fixed above her head, wrists crossing over each other at an awkward angle. This was not a position she would ever *choose* to be in, let alone sleep in. Zoey's eyes flashed wide open, adrenaline putting her senses on high alert. Up. Wake up. She heaved a breath and lifted her head, then blinked, struggling to clear her blurred vision. Gray walls. Not yellow. Abstract paintings. Not the familiar pictures of famous ballet dancers she had on her own walls. White bedclothes. Not her cream-colored bedsheets. Unfamiliar. This room was not her own. This was not a place she'd ever been before.

Horror and fear rushed in cold, sending icy shivers down her spine. Throat tight, she swallowed and looked around. Hotel, she was sure. Everything from the generic setup of the room to the smell told her that. Wide window, mirror on one wall, a door in the corner of the room that Zoey could only assume led to a bathroom. And a second bed. A second, *unmade* bed beside her own. One that had been slept in. Someone had been in here with her while she slept. Could it have been Rona?

"R-Rona?" she called, her voice small and trembling.

Please let Rona have done this. Maybe playing a joke on her? Payback for being a belligerent idiot the night before?

But then the memories surged back. The nightclub. The man she'd spoken to outside. The scuffle. Then nothing. She'd been . . . She didn't even want to think it. *Kidnapped*?

Get up. Get away. She had to get out of here. Wherever *here* was. Get home. Where was Rona? Had they, whoever *they* were, taken her, too?

A frightened whimper escaped her, and Zoey tried to get her hands loose again. This time, she heard metal clang against metal. She struggled for a moment, then finally managed to sit upright, balanced on her knees and elbowed the white pillows out of the way. Her hands were bound together by handcuffs and a chain that disappeared beyond the head of the mattress. Another second whimper caught in her throat. Handcuffed. To this strange bed in this strange hotel where a stranger had slept next to her.

Acute terror sunk its sharp claws into her back and circled her spine, a feeling that was both hot and cold at the same time, and Zoey stifled a scream. She pulled at the handcuffs frantically, metal clashing against metal and pillows falling to the floor. Breathing shakily, she forced herself to be still. She needed a plan. But what plan? How could she possibly escape this? What escape was there? What kind of person was she up against? Who had done this? *Why?*

Sound. The hotel room door clicked and swung open. All thoughts of escape flew from Zoey's head. She turned, keeping her movements slow and subtle. Horror snatched at her, stealing her strength. All that was left were trembles. Standing in the hotel room hallway was the man who had spoken to her in the alley outside Club Morceau the night before. The so-called bouncer. Ed – a false name, no doubt.

"Ah. Perfect timing." He turned to stick his head into the bathroom. "She's up."

Zoey's eyes darted to the bathroom as a second man entered the bedroom. He was familiar. Zoey took a tiny, stilted breath. Outnumbered. Helpless. He was the one who had touched her on the dance floor. She remembered the feeling of his fingertips running over her neckline and down. He looked on edge now – no longer the approachable, vaguely handsome man she'd taken him for – his face drawn and his eyes flitting nervously around the room. He swallowed and stayed near the bathroom doorway, giving way to "Ed". She found herself watching their faces. That was what people did in these situations, wasn't it? Studied their kidnappers' faces?

There was something malicious and violent in "Ed's" expression that made him look infinitely more menacing than his partner. A strange sense of humor lurked around "Ed's" eyes and mouth, as though he derived a certain amount of pleasure in this. Zoey felt pinned where she sat, and a sick, acidic feeling rose in her throat. She wanted to vomit. Ill and nauseous, that was all she could feel.

"Welcome back to the land of the living, Zoey Blackmore," said Ed, settling on the corner of the bed next to Zoey's.

Zoey couldn't help breathing a silent gasp of relief when he maintained some semblance of distance. The further away from her that they both stayed, the better.

She swallowed, her throat feeling dry, and tried to keep her voice steady. "How do you know who I am?"

"You told me who you were last night. That was all we needed. We know all about you. We've been watching you for months, waiting for a moment like the one you presented last night."

"Who are you?" asked Zoey, hating and cursing herself for the way her voice trembled.

He smirked. "Our names aren't important."

Zoey glanced between them. No names – not any that she'd ever learn, at least. Her eyes lingered on the man who'd approached her in the club, and she mentally dubbed him Groper. She looked back "Ed" and took a quiet breath. Calling him by a real name seemed warped somehow, and she settled on Bouncer instead.

"What do you want?" Zoey asked, leaning away as Bouncer leaned forward.

Terror urged her to *do* something. To not simply sit. She wanted to run, to crash through the glass window and make a wild escape. But much as she *wanted* to do just that, the handcuffs stayed her like a stone.

Groper took a single step forward. "That –"

Bouncer spun, cutting him off with a sharp shake of his head, then turned back to Zoey. "You're coming with us. If I were you, I'd save your energy. You're not going anywhere, unless we say so."

Zoey felt her blood course even hotter at his words. The same ferocious energy that bade her to run. She resisted the urge to show her teeth. Flight, apparently, was not an option. Freezing had yielded nothing. Instinct gave only one more option. Defiance.

She narrowed her eyes, hands curling into fists. "What makes you think I'll come with you?"

Bouncer stood and inclined his head, towering over her. There was something in the movement that, in an uncanny way, reminded her of her father The fire in Zoey's blood quelled immediately, and she shrank down, wishing the mattress would swallow her.

From her peripherals, she saw Groper give Bouncer a wary glance. Zoey swallowed, cold sweat pooling under her shirt. She was sure that the temperature dropped as he settled on the edge of her bed, the space between them now close to nonexistent. There was cold calculation in his eyes. Groper looked away, gaze on the carpet.

Silence. Zoey didn't dare breathe. He was close enough for her to make out the first beginnings of gray hair around his temples and the stubble on his chin. Why these details stood out, why they were important, she didn't know. All she knew was that they mattered. In this moment, they mattered.

"You don't have a choice. If you don't cooperate with us, we'll torture you, and I can promise you, Zoey, we'll have fun doing it. Who knows, accidents happen during torture. We might kill you." He folded his hands, a slow smile spreading across his face. "And if the need arises that we have to dispose of you, what's to stop us from returning to Hereford and snatching up a replacement or two? You've got two sisters to spare, and we know where they live."

Zoey tried to hold in the trembles that wracked her body. A terrified chill hit her. Promises of torture. The threat of murder. Those she felt nearly numb to – as though she expected them. Those were only threats on *her* life. Not directed toward Rona or Hailee. But for these strangers to threaten her sisters' lives. That was a promise too far. It touched something in her that she didn't even know existed.

She wanted to rage, to storm, to lunge at Groper and Bouncer and . . . and do *something*. And she would have if the handcuffs bruising her wrists weren't firmly in place. She tried a different tack.

"You wouldn't. Please. You wouldn't."

"Oh, we would, believe me." Bouncer's smile deepened. There was no kindness in it. Only viciousness. "I trust we've reached an agreement, then? Your good behavior and your compliance ensures your sisters' safety. And your own."

Zoey paused. One heartbeat. Two. She wanted to evaluate. To reason through to a solution. But there wasn't time. She breathed in once, the movement intensely sharp.

"If I do as you say, you won't lay a hand on either of them?"

"Correct."

Deep breath again. Zoey nodded. She had to. What else could she do but dance to the tune that these two men played to her? If this was what it took to protect Rona and Hailee, she'd do it. She had to. She'd find a way back to them as soon as she could, but now – for just now – she would do what she had to do to keep them safe. She closed her eyes and tried unsuccessfully not to flinch away as Bouncer leaned toward her, his thumb ghosting her cheek. A whine rose in the back of Zoey's throat, and she forced herself to swallow it away.

"Good. I'm glad we got that out of the way," he said. "Now, let's put down some ground rules. You'll do exactly what we say, when we say. You'll listen to us and only us. You will not speak to anyone. You will not sit next to anyone except Groper or myself. You will not fight us. You will not try to escape from us. Obey us, and we'll look after you and reward you. Break these rules, and we will punish you, or we will dump you and take your sisters instead.

We've got a flight to catch this evening, and I want you on your best behavior." He turned to his partner. "Get her things."

Zoey nodded and trembled. Bouncer grinned at her, the expression overwhelming in its cruelty. Behind the cruelty of his eyes though, there was another emotion. Zoey lowered her eyes. Triumph. He and Groper had already won. Anything that she did to try and fight them would endanger her sisters. The reality of the saying 'caught between the devil and the deep, blue sea' struck her in full force. All the desperation and drive she had to fight against them drained out of her. There was nothing she could do except submit.

Movement. Zoey jumped, pain streaking up each arm as her handcuffs rattled angrily. A plastic bag rustled as it landed on the pillow beside her. Zoey froze. She stared at Bouncer instead. He nodded, his eyes flickering to the bag. Zoey leaned forward, hands clumsy as she pulled the bag open. A change of clothes – black jeans and a dark, forgettable shirt. A French passport. A packet of papers stapled together. Bouncer reached into the bag and withdrew the passport and notepaper. At the bottom, Zoey caught a glimpse of something sharp and metal. Dizziness hit her. Scissors.

"Read these. Memorize the information in the passport. Memorize the information on these papers. The flight leaves at half past six. I expect you to know everything verbatim by the time you arrive at the airport. I assume you've been taught French."

Zoey paused, not sure if it was a statement or a question. Bouncer raised an eyebrow, and she nodded. "In school, yes. I know some. I'm not fluent."

"You don't need to be. You and my partner will be posing as an engaged couple returning home to France to get married. He will do most of the talking. You just have to sit there looking doe-eyed. The less you say, the better."

Zoey nodded, taking in the documents as Bouncer placed them individually on the bed in front of her. She swallowed. It sounded as though she and Groper would be travelling alone. Maybe they were leaving Bouncer here. Maybe this could open a chance to form some sort of plan. Groper looked nervous, less confident. Maybe she could try to empathize with him. Or maybe she could shake him off and escape.

Airports were public areas. Crowded, too. If she could slip away from him, maybe she stood some sort of chance at getting home. Getting her sisters out of harm's way. Powerless she may be, but, Zoey swallowed, she couldn't allow herself to close her mind to any possible chance of escape or rescue. This situation was her reality now. She couldn't allow it to overwhelm her. She mustn't. If she did, she'd lose herself.

"Where will you be?" she asked, looking up at Bouncer.

"Oh, I'll be on top of you. I'm sitting behind you on the flight, and I'll be behind you until we get to our final destination. Quell any thoughts of escape that you might form, my dear. Until we're done with you, you won't even use the toilet on your own. Try to run, and I will put a bullet in your spine, then we'll turn Hereford upside down until we find your sisters. Do you understand me?"

Zoey swallowed. Her throat felt as though it was closing. As though a massive hand was curling around it and choking the air out of her lungs. "I understand."

"Good."

He reached into the bag, withdrawing the scissors. Zoey wanted to sit still. She wanted to stop the trembles that coursed over her skin and made the metal links at her wrists jangle.

Suddenly, Zoey felt her necklace fall free of her shirt collar, gold pointe slippers dangling on the fine chain and swaying in time to her nerves. Bouncer's sharp eyes tracked it immediately. He reached out, and Zoey yelped, trying to pull back, but was stopped by the handcuffs. Bouncer's hand wrapped around the pendant, and he yanked hard, the chain pulling sharply against Zoey's skin as the clasp broke.

"Ah. Your file said you wear this all the time," he said, playing the chain through his fingers. "My friend here told me he'd seen it on the dance floor."

Again, she wasn't sure if it was a question or a statement. "M-My sisters gave it to me. Please. It was for my birthday last year. I – I can't lose it. Please."

What exactly she was asking for, she didn't truly know. Desperately, she didn't want her necklace taken from her. It was a comfort – a reminder of her sisters. Bouncer smiled at her, the expression lingering around his mouth and showing far too many teeth.

Bouncer turned to his partner. "Get rid of this. We don't need anything that might identify her."

Zoey watched in desperate silence as Bouncer passed her necklace to Groper, the broken clasp catching the morning sun as Groper tossed it into the wastepaper basket behind him.

"Now. I want you to go in the bathroom and get changed. We'll be cutting your hair when you're done."

"My hair?" asked Zoey. The question came out like a whimper.

Bouncer leaned forward. In spite of the small smile on his lips, the movement felt like a threat. "Be thankful we're not shaving it."

Chapter 4

Twenty-five minutes was not a long time. Not nearly long enough to get a life together. What it was long enough for was for Rona to panic and throw clothes at random into a duffel bag. How long were they going for? Days? Weeks? Did she need more than one pair of shoes? Her passport? A pink, stuffed penguin she'd gotten as a Christmas present from Zoey six years ago? Zoey. Zoey who wasn't here. Zoey who –

Rona swallowed hard and clutched the penguin tight to her chest. Clothes. Clothes were what she needed for now. Anything else she needed could be bought whenever they got to – where were they going? Wales? It *was* Wales, wasn't it? Rona sighed heavily and sat down on her bed, fingers pressed against her eyes. Twelve hours ago, Zoey had been here. Safe. Twelve hours ago, they'd been getting ready to leave the house. But now . . . Rona shook her head and sniffled, trying to stifle the sob in her throat.

A light knock on her door startled her, and she lunged to her feet. "Hello?"

Maxwell never knocked. Maxwell just entered. Hailee was busy packing, too. So who was –?

A young man with curly brown hair and wire-rimmed glasses opened Rona's bedroom door halfway. "Hello. I was sent up to see if you needed any help."

Rona stood still and looked him up and down, the penguin clutched in her hands. Ankle-length boots, dark jeans, a white-collared shirt, and a small nervous smile. He was utterly forgettable.

"Who the hell are you?" she asked.

He laughed quietly and fidgeted in the doorway. "Ah. I'm Flynn. Flynn Edmunds. I'm Maxwell's . . . I'm his primary assistant and tech analyst. He sent me up to see if you needed any help packing."

"This is a first, having Maxwell send his intern to help me pack," said Rona.

"He called me this morning saying he'd had a family emergency. So, yeah, it's a new thought for me, too."

Rona stared at him. "Get out."

Flynn fiddled with his hands, not moving. "He said this is how you might –"

"Get. Out."

He reached for the door handle. "If you need anything –"

Rona launched the penguin at him. Flynn whipped out of the room just as the stuffed animal struck the door with a pitiful *squeak*. Rona wanted to scream, but she knew that if she did, she'd end up crying again. She stormed across the room and picked up the penguin. It was coming with her. Regardless of whether or not she needed it. Need. That word. She didn't need *things*. She *needed* her twin sister. But Zoey wasn't here. Zoey was gone.

Rona dropped the penguin into her bag. For the first time in years, she took note of the little golden dancing shoes the toy wore on its feet. She'd forgotten about them. A fresh wave of emotion caught in the back of her throat as she touched the little golden shoes, a visceral reminder of Zoey's necklace. Rona took a deep breath, zipped her bag closed, and pulled her door open, doing a cursory look behind her. Bed made, lights off, windows shut, chargers gone from walls. The gray day made her bedroom look odd – uninhabited. Like a guest room. Rona caught herself before her lower lip trembled, and she shook her shoulders to steel herself. She pulled the door shut and stepped out onto the landing. Four heads turned, and four sets of eyes landed on her. Rona froze. She wanted to scramble back into her room and lock herself away. Instead, she descended the stairs, bag in hand to face Maxwell, Flynn, and two others she didn't recognize. One man and one woman.

Rona set her bag down at the bottom of the stairs and took a breath. "Hello."

Maxwell nodded at her. "My daughter, Rona. Her twin sister, Zoey, is the reason you're here. Rona, this is Simon and Charity Hunstan. Former coworkers of mine. Flynn you've already met."

Rona nodded, the movement feeling stiff. Simon, tall and smiling. Blond and blue-eyed. He wore glasses similar to – no, identical to – Flynn's. He took a few steps toward her and stuck out a hand.

"Hello, Rona. Nice to finally meet you. Even though it's under some pretty unpleasant circumstances."

"Yeah," replied Rona simply. The single word seemed to cost effort.

Letting go of Simon's hand, Rona turned just in time to see Charity limping toward her. Mousy brown hair and brown eyes. A metal cane matched every other step. Rona tried to hide her curiosity. Charity couldn't be any older than forty? Maybe a muscle disorder? A recent surgery? Rona forced herself not to stare.

"Pleasure to meet you," said Charity.

Rona nearly flinched. There was something in Charity's voice. Something cold and calculating. Something she'd heard before. She couldn't help glancing at Maxwell.

"Flynn will be going to Wales with you, along with Simon and Charity," said Maxwell, not meeting Rona's eyes. He crossed the foyer to the bottom of the stairs. "Hailee! Time to go."

"I will?" asked Flynn.

Maxwell turned. Rona tensed, and from the corner of her eye, she saw Flynn stiffen, squaring his shoulders slightly and leaning back a fraction.

"Yes," replied Maxwell. "Don't worry. It's all been approved with upper management. Think of it as some paid time off."

"Right," nodded Flynn, eyes dropping to the carpet. "Thank you, sir."

"Nice to have you, Flynn," said Simon, his voice oddly jovial. "Looks like this is shaping up to be a bit of a party. Hope the farm can handle it."

Rona glanced at him again. That accent. Where was he from? America, possibly? But then how had he met Maxwell? She bit the inside of her cheek. That felt like a question for later. Once they were out of Maxwell's radius.

"I'm sure we'll be fine," replied Charity, cane clacking against the entrance tiles. "The Roost is big enough for guests."

"Hailee!" called Maxwell again, starting up the stairs.

Rona inhaled sharply, hand dropping to her phone to text Hailee. Just as she was unlocking the screen, Hailee's door opened, and she emerged. Not a moment too soon. Maxwell was already halfway up the stairs. Rona breathed again.

"Sorry," said Hailee. "I couldn't find a jacket."

A tiny smile flitted across Maxwell's face as he waited on the stairs for Hailee. Taking her suitcase from her, they walked down together. Rona smothered her confusion. An unprecedented act of generosity, coming from Maxwell. She glanced over at Flynn. Behind his glasses, he looked just as confused as she felt. But that confusion seemed undercut with something else. Fear, maybe? Rona wasn't sure. She slid her phone back into her pocket. Seemed she and Hailee weren't the only ones who preferred to give Maxwell a wide berth.

"Right," said Maxwell, picking up Rona's bag from the bottom of the stairs. "I'll see you all in Conwy later tonight. Shouldn't take you much more than about three hours to get there."

"Why aren't you coming now?" asked Hailee.

Maxwell offered a smile that looked more like a snarl as he handed Hailee's bag back to her. "I have some calls to make if I'm going to get Zoey back in one piece. Speaking of – Flynn?"

"Sir?"

"Anything?"

"Last tracked him in Norway, sir."

"Good. Once *he* gets wind of this, he'll be circling like a shark in bloody water."

Rona laughed in disbelief, unable to stop herself even as Maxwell turned to her.

"Something funny?" he asked.

Before she could stop herself, she spat out, "This is insane."

"Meaning?" asked Maxwell, his tone low.

Rona swallowed hard. "I'm just . . . I'm so worried about Zoey. Who are you tracking? What's this person got to do with Zoey? Please, can you just tell me and Hailee what's going on?"

Maxwell blinked once. "No."

Rona shook her head and jumped as Charity touched her shoulder with a small, frail-looking hand that was surprisingly strong.

"We'll get a room ready for you, Maxwell," she said.

Rona hesitated as Charity turned her toward the door. It wasn't a forcible movement, but it somehow *could* have been. Reaching down for her bag, Rona looked over her shoulder at Maxwell before walking to the door – or rather *was escorted* to the door. He raised one hand in a distracted kind of farewell, phone in his other hand.

Rona stepped out of the front door behind Simon and Flynn, followed quickly by Hailee and Charity. Over their shoulders, Maxwell had already turned his back. Rona took a shaky breath and swallowed hard. Desperately, she hoped he knew what he was doing. If he didn't . . . she didn't even want to think about what might happen.

~ ~ ~ ~ ~ ~

Gabrielle Lavaud. Her new, false name. Zoey swallowed hard as she exited the airport terminal holding Groper's hand, with Bouncer directly behind them. France. Charles de Gaulle Airport. Zoey's hair just barely brushed the tops of her shoulders. Evening. How was it already evening? The first early stars had already made an appearance in the sky. The day felt as though it had been swallowed, time passing in a blur. Travelling to Birmingham airport. Through security in England. Boarding the plane. Two hours of flight, before landing in France. Cut off from England by the English Channel. It all felt surreal – like it had happened to someone else. But it had happened to her. And she hadn't fought. Zoey swallowed and blinked up at the evening sky. The last rays of golden sunlight felt treacherous.

Zoey glanced sideways at Groper. He hadn't let go of her hand since they had come through the electronic passport scanners at the immigration check. She felt sick. Getting into France had been far easier than she'd anticipated. Border control asked only the most basic questions. No challenge to cross-examine "the happy couple". No answers that might have alerted an airport worker to her situation. No help was on the horizon. None, whatsoever. That was almost the worst part. She couldn't help herself, and no one else was coming to help.

Bouncer pulled his phone out of his pocket. "We have a car to drive ourselves to Gare de l'Est."

"How far away is it?" asked Groper.

Zoey looked at the ground, trying to seem as though she wasn't listening in to their conversation. Groper let go of her hand to shift the bags on his shoulder. Zoey fought the urge to bolt. She could run. She could scream. She tensed to act, but Rona's and Hailee's faces swam in front of her vision. She didn't dare. She swallowed and stayed where she was. The powerlessness made her feel sick.

"Being delivered," replied Bouncer. "Thought about taking the metro train to Gare de l'Est, but it would be too crowded."

Zoey heard the unspoken part of his sentence. *'Too many places for us to get separated and for her to escape.'* She took a breath and looked around the pick-up area of the airport. Charles de Gaulle Airport was in constant movement. Constant chaos. Cars shuffled. Shuttles sped up and down between terminals. People walked, ran, pushed, and shoved to get where they needed to go. Nothing was out of the ordinary because nothing was noticed. In this place of life convergence, people focused on their own affairs with a single-track mind. There was no way to single anyone out. To tell anyone that she needed help.

Zoey closed her eyes and wished to be anywhere but here. Hereford. The dance studio where she'd performed her last recital almost two years before. In the kitchen at home bickering with Rona or Hailee. Anywhere but here. She just wanted to be home.

Zoey glanced at Groper and Bouncer. They seemed on edge, talking between themselves. She paused. They looked distracted. This might be her only chance. Was it worth the risk? Could she escape them? How far could she push them before their patience snapped? Zoey paused. Fury tempered her desperation. These two men. They had snatched her from her sisters. Go. Go when they expected it the least. She had to try. However futile it might be. She'd find a security person, tell them everything, plead for them to take her back to England, for them to send police to Hereford to keep her sisters safe. She inhaled, getting ready to step back and bolt. She just needed to get away and lost in the crowd.

Zoey stifled a noise in her throat as Bouncer reached out and gripped her shoulder. She looked up, and he glanced down at her, a smile sliding across his face. A sinking pit of despair opened in her stomach, and the opportunity she could have seized slipped through her fingers. Groper took hold of her hand again.

Bouncer's phone pinged, and he pulled it from his pocket. "We need to meet them in the underground garage. Near the rental cars. Come on. We have a train to catch later tonight."

"Train?" asked Groper. "I thought we weren't taking trains?"

"Not the metro. Above-ground trains will be better. This one's a late train, too. Fewer people."

"And who's meeting us?" asked Groper. Zoey seethed in silence as he tugged on her hand. "Erik?"

Bouncer nodded wordlessly.

"Varek, too?"

"No. He's still up north with Marion getting things set up. It's just Erik today," replied Bouncer.

"Where are you taking me?" asked Zoey.

The words were out of her mouth before she could stop them. Groper and Bouncer paused. Bouncer smiled, but Groper still looked uncomfortable, glancing around nervously before looking at Bouncer for direction.

Bouncer inclined his head. "Why does it matter where you're going?"

Zoey's heart thudded. What was the plan for her? Why her? Of all people in the world, why *her*? She lowered her head and forced air into her tight lungs. Bouncer turned to reenter the airport. Zoey paused. Back inside. To what end? She couldn't motivate her feet to move. Tug. Zoey stumbled as Groper jerked hard at her hand. She took a breath and stumbled, walking half a pace behind him.

She caught movement in her peripherals, but she was too wrapped in her own thoughts to register it. She stumbled over someone's duffel bag, elbows cracking on the hard airport floor as her normally good balance failed, her hand ripping forcibly out of Groper's.

Free of contact. Zoey looked up. Bouncer had already wheeled around, eyes blazing. Groper froze, mouth slightly open. Was this her moment? Zoey started to push back up to her feet, every instinct preparing her to bolt, then there was a hand at her throbbing elbow.

"I'm so sorry about that. Are you alright?" asked a crisp, English voice at her side.

Zoey turned. A dark-haired, young man was helping her up. His eyes though, were what struck her. Cold, hard as steel. So blue they were almost colorless. Calculating. They didn't match the soft smile that he gave her. She opened her mouth to reply. This could be her salvation. This could be the start to the end of this nightmare.

"She's fine," said Groper, striding forward and taking hold of Zoey's hand again. "Are you alright, dear?"

Zoey released a bated breath. Too late. Another chance missed. The nightmare continued. She forced a smile, her eyes lingering on the stranger's. Help. Please.

"I'm fine," she nodded.

"Come on," said Groper, slipping his arm around her waist. Zoey had to fight not to recoil and shove him off. She looked over her shoulder as Groper pulled her away, expecting to see the dark-haired man setting his bag to rights. But he wasn't. He was watching them, his head tilted a fraction to one side as though studying something. Even his chilled eyes were pensive.

Chapter 5

The airport parking garage was full of dark shadows. Weak, fluorescent lights turned what little could be seen into a dull yellow. A working underbelly of the place. Every now and then, a car passed them, ascending and descending the floors of the concrete foundation. Zoey lowered her head and stayed just a step or two behind Groper, who had mercifully let go of her hand. She would have made a break for freedom, if it weren't for Bouncer sandwiching her in between the two of them. Even if she did try, Zoey had to wonder how far she could realistically get before she was stopped. Either by them or by the parking garage itself, a confusing mess of concrete. In spite of that, the desperation to bolt felt as though it was rising with each step she took, becoming a ringing pitch in her ears.

She tensed as they arrived at an empty floor of the parking garage. Only one car stood parked near the exit ramp.

"That's it," muttered Bouncer, half raising a hand toward the car.

"Where's Erik?" asked Groper.

Zoey glanced at him. His voice had an uneasy quiver in it. She turned to look at him fully. How old was he? He might even be the same age as her. Did he even realize what he was doing? Movement just over Groper's shoulder caught her attention. A tiny gasp left her mouth, and Zoey felt herself stop.

On silent feet, someone joined them. Had he been tailing them or had he just arrived? He stepped further into the light. Even in the yellow glow, his red hair was vibrant. Between that and the meanness in his eyes, Zoey knew she could recognize him again in an instant.

His jacket hung open, and Zoey could just see the grip of a handgun above the waistband of his jeans. She froze, her lungs no longer working and all breath stilling in her chest. This was it. She was going to be killed. She was certain of that. What a waste of effort. Kidnap a girl, steal her away to France, only to kill her in the basement of an airport parking garage. No. No. There had to be more to it than that. If her family was wealthy, this would have made more sense. But they weren't.

She should have run when she'd had the chance. She should have run in England. She should have run outside the terminal. She should have run as the stranger helped her up.

Holding back a sob, she thought of Hailee and Rona. She'd never see them again. She hadn't even been able to say goodbye.

Bouncer paused next to her, one hand gripping her shoulder. Groper stopped, too, skittish eyes fixed on the car nearby.

"She's got good senses," said the newcomer, stopping a short distance away and folding his arms. "You two never even knew I was here. Maybe we should *hire* her instead."

Groper and Bouncer spun. Zoey narrowed her eyes and glanced at the exit ramp of the carport. Could she make it there before Groper and Bouncer grabbed her again? Not a chance. It was too far away. Maybe against Groper and Bouncer, she had a chance to outrun them. But someone holding a handgun? No. There wasn't a hope.

Zoey steeled herself against whatever might happen in the next moments. Her hands trembled at her sides. She stiffened as the newcomer approached, closing the empty distance between them. She didn't like the look in his eyes. Calculating and remorseless. He smiled, the expression chiseled and cold.

"Zoey Blackmore," he muttered, cocking his head to one side. "Nice to finally get eyes on you."

Zoey clenched her jaw, every muscle tense. Instinct told her that the man's statement was not one she was expected to reply to. Were Groper and Bouncer going to give her over to this man? Was *that* her fate? Somehow that made her feel even more nauseated than she already was. Which was worse? This man who smiled without empathy? Or Groper and Bouncer, who had taken her away from home?

"Erik," said Bouncer, stepping forward and extending a hand.

Erik. So this was the Erik that Groper and Bouncer had mentioned earlier. Desperately, Zoey noted it. If she survived this, she'd remember that name.

Erik's eyes narrowed a fraction, darting down to Bouncer's extended hand, then back to his face. Bouncer glanced away and dropped his hand back to his side.

"Everything going as planned?" Erik asked.

"Just fine, so far. We're on schedule," replied Bouncer.

"As you should be. And it had better stay that way," said Erik, his sharp smile reinforcing the malice in his words.

"You mentioned you'd be meeting us."

"High profile assignment. The Czarina wanted verification that you'd accomplished your task. Unfortunately, I can't escort you to your next stop. Urgent business in Romania. I'm sure you understand."

Bouncer laughed, a trace of nervousness sneaking into the sound. "Well. You can see for yourself; we've got her in hand."

"Indeed," replied Erik, his hand going to his belt.

Zoey tensed, rocking back, blood thrumming through her veins. His fingers skated along the grip of his firearm, and Erik paused. Then he laughed quietly and reached further inside his coat, pulling a phone out of some internal pocket.

"Smile, Zoey," said Erik, raising the phone.

Zoey didn't. She ground her teeth together to keep from spitting on his shoes. Erik tilted his head, then shrugged, and tapped the phone screen once.

"The Czarina's going to love this," he said, one side of his mouth slanting upward as he tucked his phone back inside his jacket.

Bouncer cleared his throat. "Any sign of *him*?"

"No," scoffed Erik, dark eyes rolling. "He's not even in the country. Nothing to worry about."

Zoey fought not to wring her hands together, bite her nails, or scratch at her own skin. Resist the urge to do anything that might belie her fear. The Czarina? High profile assignment? This didn't make *sense*. What kind of world had she been pulled into?

Erik turned. Zoey stepped backwards as his dark, cruel eyes landed on her. She'd never seen anyone with eyes this cutting. He advanced a step, looking her up and down. Zoey's breath hitched. Two sets of hands stopped her before she could back away from him.

Erik laughed, waving Groper and Bouncer away. "Don't bother with that nonsense. She's not going anywhere. Are you, Zoey Blackmore?"

Zoey looked up at him, a cold stone of fear settling in her stomach. Her mouth ran dry, and she couldn't respond. Words stuck in her throat like barbs. She dropped her gaze to the concrete floor.

Erik laughed. "She's pretty enough. I see why she was the first on the docket. And her background makes her just that much more desirable. Well done, boys."

Zoey barely heard Groper and Bouncer's responses. The asphalt underfoot wavered in front of her vision. Nothing seemed real anymore. She could hardly breathe, a sweeping kind of fury coursing through her. An object. That's how they talked about her. Something inanimate. Merchandise.

"Look at me." Zoey fisted her hands at her sides, and she turned her head sharply away. She wouldn't look at him. She was a human being. Slow movement registered in her peripherals, and cold metal pressed gently to the soft skin under her jaw, slowly guiding her head back. In the corners of her vision, she could see Erik's hand on the grip of his handgun. He grinned brightly at her. Zoey blinked back at him and locked her jaw.

"Now really isn't the time for defiance, Zoey. You're not the only one at stake here. Rona and Hailee are still in play." He pulled the weapon away and took hold of her chin in an iron grip, leaning in. "And I can't resist a moving target."

Nausea chilled through Zoey's stomach, threatening to pull her to the ground. Her throat felt thick and her tongue heavy. Much as she wanted to sneer a reply, spit in his face, she couldn't. Erik's eyes met hers, and Zoey found herself pinned, powerless to move. Erik would kill her if he saw a need. He would kill Hailee and Rona. There was no question about that. Maybe for the sheer thrill. Erik smiled again and nodded seemingly to himself before letting go of Zoey's chin and looking back at Groper and Bouncer.

"Knows when to stay in her place. Marion will like that. Happy travels. Key fob is in the floorboard. Change transport method at Gare de l'Est. And, Zoey, I'll be seeing you soon," said Erik.

Another horrified tremble worked its way up Zoey's spine, and it felt as though her chest clenched as Erik turned away and vanished between two concrete pillars, without even an echoing footfall to reveal where he'd gone. She couldn't tell if his words were a promise, a threat, or some combination of both.

She swallowed hard and fought to keep her lower lip from trembling. Frozen. She felt rooted to the spot even as she was nudged toward the car. At least her sisters weren't here. At least they were safe. Her good behavior, her fight to restrain fear and emotion ensured that.

~ ~ ~ ~ ~

Conwy, Wales felt like a world away from Hereford. Over one hundred miles away, and Rona felt as though she was on a different planet. Signposts were in a different language, but she'd been able to spot the translated word "Conwy" printed on one a few miles ago. The countryside was now rolling and mountainous. Even the stone here was darker. They'd turned off the highway some time ago and had stuck to winding, country roads for the last hour. Every now and then, the hills would level out, and there would be glimpses of the ocean. Rona fiddled with her phone and glanced out of the black Range Rover's back window. Flynn followed them in an identical vehicle.

Rona glanced at Hailee as her phone vibrated.

Hailee: "*This feels like a prison transport.*"

Rona tapped a return message. *"Blacked out cars and everything. Maxwell's hiding something."*

Hailee: *"Imagine that. Our dad. Hiding something. Call the BBC. Groundbreaking news."*

"You could talk to us, you know?" said Charity, twisting around from the passenger seat. "Rather than sitting there texting each other. It's rude."

"Leave them, Char," said Simon quietly.

Rona opened her mouth to start an apology.

Hailee beat her to it. "Sorry. We didn't even know the two of you existed until about three hours ago after our oldest sister vanishes off the face of the planet. I think we have a right to be a little standoffish. Forgive us for not being chatty."

"Wonderful," sighed Charity, shaking her head. "We've got two little Maxwells in the backseat."

"I haven't even said anything!" said Rona.

Hailee leaned forward in her seat. "We're not little Maxwells, you –!"

"Ahh! Look at that!" said Simon, laughing uneasily. "We're home!"

Rona inhaled slowly, the sheer frustration of the situation overwhelming her. In the next instant, she reached for the door's handgrip as Simon veered off the road onto a gravel driveway shrouded by broadleaf trees. Flynn turned in behind them. Rona shook her head and turned to stare out of the window. A hot, molten kind of feeling settled in her chest.

They rounded a bend in the driveway, and the trees cleared, revealing an old, stone farmhouse. One chimney rose from the center of the house, and a high stone wall ran the perimeter of a traditional courtyard. A very large storage barn stood apart from the house outside the yard, and a more modern-looking annex was just visible behind the main house. Rona spotted a few sheep grazing in the fields beyond.

"Welcome to The Roost," said Simon, putting the car into park in the courtyard and getting out. "Shame it took us this long to get you here. Grab your stuff. The back of the car's unlocked."

Rona slid out of the car and stretched, sighing heavily. The heady smell of country air hit her like cold water, thick with the odor of farm animals. Simon darted to the back of the car, waving and gesturing to tell Flynn where to park.

"It was only two and a half hours," said Hailee. "Not exactly a long drive."

"I'm sorry?" asked Simon, pausing. "I meant the last few summers. We've sent a few open invitations for you to come and visit us on – what do Brits say for vacation? Holiday? I suppose Maxwell didn't mention that, did he?"

Rona rounded the car to the back and pulled out her and Hailee's duffel bags. "You've had the offer open for us to spend summers? Christ above. What *else* hasn't he told us?"

Hailee stood at her elbow and sighed quietly, one hand tracing her forehead.

Simon joined them and reached up to pull the back closed. "Well, there is a bit more. You . . . you guys don't know who we are, do you? Beyond us being Maxwell's former coworkers."

"No, we just get in the car with strange people. We really *are* that stupid," said Hailee, voice like a knife edge. "Our older sister, you know, Zoey? That's probably how she got kidnapped."

"Hey!" said Rona, elbowing Hailee hard. "That's *not* funny, Hailee. I'm sorry, Simon – it is Simon, right? It's been . . . a hard day."

"Yeah, it's Simon." He laughed quietly and shook his head. "And don't apologize. I should have asked differently. Look, I don't think there's an easy way to say this. Charity and I are your godparents."

Rona dropped her bag. "What?"

"Ah." Simon scratched the side of his nose. "I guess he didn't tell you then. That makes sense."

"Simon!" called Charity, clacking around the front of the car. "The front door, please. I need to set up a room for Maxwell and get Flynn organized. Can he use your office?"

"Coming!" Simon turned back to Rona and Hailee. "Look, we'll fill you in properly later. Come on."

Rona stared at him as he slammed the back of the Range Rover closed. She turned to Hailee whose mouth was still open.

"Pick your jaw up," she said, tapping Hailee's chin.

"What is going *on*?" asked Hailee, shaking herself.

"I –" Rona sighed and shook her head. "I don't know, Hails. I really don't know, and I wish I did."

Chapter 6

A small fire crackled and spat in The Roost's living room fireplace. Rona sat on one of the low couches, massaging her temple with one hand. She'd quickly unpacked her bag in the annex hours ago, then returned to the main farmhouse. Why? She wasn't exactly sure herself.

She clutched the pink penguin tightly with her other hand. She sighed hard and looked around the room, taking in the tartan patterns, complete with mismatched furniture and wool blankets draped over couches and overstuffed chairs. Paintings and photographs of the Welsh hills decorated the walls. It was a warm, cozy kind of place, sitting areas oriented around a coffee table near the fireplace to make the close atmosphere even more intimate. But Rona couldn't appreciate it. Not until her sister returned safely.

How had Zoey gone missing only twenty-four hours ago? It was nighttime again. How was it already nighttime? Rona stared out of the large bay window. Darkness leered back at her, like some waiting monster. Had Zoey felt that same dark danger last night?

Time had slid past in the twenty-four hours Zoey had been gone. Packing in the morning, unpacking here at The Roost. Dinner had... somewhere occurred. She couldn't even remember what she'd eaten. An entire day gone to waste.

Rona swallowed and rested her chin in her hand, turning to face the orange flames. She and Hailee had been set up in the modern annex behind the main house under the pretense of giving them space and privacy. She wasn't sure where Flynn had vanished to. Had he been at dinner? She wasn't sure. More importantly, had Zoey eaten since they'd had dinner yesterday? Who had her? Was she alright? Had the people who'd taken her hurt her? Again and again, she asked herself the same questions, the inner narrative creating white noise inside her head. Rona sniffled and breathed a tiny, fragile laugh. When had she started crying again? Would she ever stop?

"Tea? That's what Brits do when they're upset, right? Make tea?"

Rona looked up quickly and swiped her cheeks dry for what seemed like the hundredth time. Her skin was becoming raw to the touch. Simon stood in the living room threshold, a tea towel draped over one shoulder.

She laughed in spite of herself, more tears falling free of her eyes. "Yeah. Tea would be great."

"Hey," said Simon, pausing in the doorway as he turned to go. "She'll be okay."

"I wish I could say I believed you," replied Rona.

Simon opened his mouth to reply, then his gaze fell to the hardwood floor, and he nodded, walking down the narrow hallway.

Hailee hesitated in the living room doorway and stared in the direction Simon had gone before stepping into the room.

"I wondered where you were. I checked your room in the annex, and . . . I got worried when you weren't there," she said, sitting on the couch next to Rona. She glanced at the penguin. "Zoey gave you that a few years ago, didn't she?"

Rona nodded and passed it to Hailee. "Yeah. She gave it to me about six years ago."

Hailee took the plush animal and curled around it almost immediately, pulling it tight to her chest, thumbing one of the gold shoes on the creature's feet.

"Remember the necklace with dancing slippers on it that we gave Zoey for her birthday?"

"Yeah," replied Rona, turning and pulling a wool blanket off the back of the couch, draping it over both of them. "Pointe shoes. Every time I would look at them, they reminded me of how much Zoey loves dancing. I just hope . . ."

Silence lulled, and Rona looked back at the fire. She wanted to crawl out of her own skin.

"I don't want to be alone," said Hailee quietly. "I wanted to go to bed, but I didn't want to stay out in the annex in the dark. Not without you. It's quiet here. Too quiet."

"I know what you mean," replied Rona. She pulled her legs up onto the couch. "But I don't think I could sleep at the moment."

She caught movement in the doorway and immediately straightened, feet back on the floor. Simon reappeared, carrying three steaming mugs. Rona watched as confusion crossed his face, and he hesitated for a moment. He set all three mugs on the coffee table and leaned on the wall near the fireplace.

"You can have your feet on the seats if you want, Rona," he said. "We don't stress about that sort of thing here."

"Oh. Thanks." Rona leaned forward and picked up her mug but didn't put her feet back where they had been. "Any updates?"

Simon shook his head. "Nothing that I've heard yet, but Charity and Flynn have been holed up in my office all evening. They'll find something."

"I hope you're right," said Rona, adjusting the way she held the mug.

Beside her, Hailee leaned forward and picked up the second mug, took a slow sip, and gagged loudly. Rona turned to her, a horrified comment on the tip of her tongue, but Simon hissed in an embarrassed way through his teeth.

"It's horrible, isn't it?" he asked.

"Foul. What did you do to it?" asked Hailee.

Simon offered a small, embarrassed smile and looked at the fire. "I couldn't tell you if I tried. I haven't really mastered the whole tea-making thing, yet. It's why I drink coffee at all hours of the day and night."

Rona elbowed Hailee hard in the side, then turned to Simon. "I'm sure it's fine. Hailee's just dramatic."

"You'd be dramatic, too, if someone tried to poison you," muttered Hailee, setting her mug back on the table.

Rona glared at Hailee for a second, then took a sip of her own tea. She resisted the urge to cough as the taste hit her tongue. She'd had better tasting dishwater. All the same, she forced herself to swallow and tried to smile at Simon.

"Thank you. It's lovely," she said.

He laughed softly. "You don't have to drink it if you don't want to."

Rona grimaced at him and set her own mug back on the table.

"Anything from Maxwell?" asked Hailee.

Simon paused. "No. He hasn't said anything to me since he got here. Might have said something to Charity, though. I think he's been sleeping since he arrived."

"He hasn't said anything to me either," said Charity, materializing in the hallway at the base of the stairs. "But Flynn *has* found something if you'd care to have a look."

"Of course, we'd care to!" snapped Hailee, launching to her feet. "What kind of a question is that?"

Rona flinched, standing after Hailee. From the play of shadows across Charity's face, Rona could see the tightening of her lips and the hardness in her eyes. In her peripherals, she saw Simon stand upright, and she felt his gaze on her.

"We're tired. Sorry," said Rona. She glanced at the floor and back at Charity. "We'd love to see what you've found."

Charity hummed in the back of her throat. "Come with me."

Hailee followed Charity immediately, leaving the penguin behind on the couch. Rona paused, picked it up, and tucked it under her arm. Discarding it on the couch felt . . . cruel somehow.

"Rona?" said Simon, touching her elbow gently.

Rona jumped, sidestepping, her heart leaping into her throat. She recovered herself a moment later.

"Yes?"

"Answer me honestly," said Simon, his glasses glinting in the firelight. "Are you alright?"

"I'm fine. Just rattled. That's all," she said, forcing herself to meet his eyes.

"Okay," he said, taking a slow sip of what smelled like coffee.

"Honestly, I'm fine," said Rona, her voice hitching on the last syllable.

"I believe you," nodded Simon.

"No, you don't."

"Not for a second. You're a terrible liar. Listen, I know you don't know me, and I don't know you, but I *am* your godfather. I just . . . I want you to know that you can talk to me if you need to. Or want to. When I ask if you're okay, you don't have to lie. Okay?"

Rona opened her mouth to reply, but the words stuck in her throat, and her eyes prickled. There was a *look* on Simon's face. Something so open and genuine. She couldn't hold his gaze. She nodded sharply and turned on her heel, marching toward the stairs, glad somehow to leave Simon and the warm living room behind.

By the time she reached the top of the stairs, she felt clearer, her mind a little more centered. It was just the whole situation that had her so on edge. That was all it was. Looking both ways, she headed toward the only room on the second floor with a light on.

An office, decorated in warm colors. China plates hung on the walls, a large desk stood center, and worn, wood furniture lined the remaining space. Was everything in this house designed to be warm and welcoming? It was so unlike her own home. It made her uncomfortable.

Rona moved further into the room, pushing the door closed behind her. Flynn, Charity, and Hailee stood clustered around a large computer, its blue light throwing off eerie shadows. They glanced up at her. Flynn flashed a small smile, standing and leaving the desk chair open. One side of Rona's mouth twitched up as she tried to return his smile. It could have been the weakest smile she'd ever given.

"What did you find?" she asked, rounding the corner of the office desk.

"I've been tracking CCTV footage in and out of airports since we got here," said Flynn. "I spotted someone matching Zoey's description leaving from Birmingham International Airport this afternoon. Heading to France. Haven't really found where she is yet, but I think we're getting closer."

"Oh, thank God!" breathed Rona, collapsing into the office chair. "She doesn't have her passport. She can't leave the country."

"That's what I told them," Hailee muttered. "Maxwell keeps our passports under lock and key."

"Rona," said Flynn. He glanced at the floor and shook his head. "She's *in* France. I picked up footage of someone who looks like her at Charles de Gaulle Airport in Paris a few hours ago. I'm still working through footage, but we think she's left the country."

"You're wrong," said Rona, her eyes roving over the still images on the computer screen. Grainy CCTV footage. "It can't be her. I repeat, she doesn't have her *passport*."

Flynn swallowed audibly. "Then can you confirm for me?"

"I'll confirm that you're wrong," snarled Rona.

Flynn pressed his lips together hard and leaned over the desk, navigating through screens so quickly they turned into a blur. On Rona's other side, Charity shifted her weight, her cane clacking against the wood floor as she moved.

"I don't think you girls realize that a passport is not something that would stop Zoey from leaving the country," Charity said.

Rona spun, sharp words already barbing her tongue. Flynn rested a hand on her shoulder, and her response died in her mouth. She looked back at the screen and inhaled sharply, the air sticking in her lungs.

"This is from Charles de Gaulle Airport earlier this afternoon," said Flynn, his voice a thousand miles away. "We're still a few hours behind them, but we'll be able to keep tracking them through cameras."

This footage wasn't grainy. It was crystal clear. A young woman walked through an airport terminal, staring at the floor, flanked by two men. One of them held onto her hand. Rona leaned forward as someone in the terminal kicked their bag in front of the woman, the woman who Rona was convinced could not be Zoey. The woman fell to the floor, and the person who'd kicked the bag in the first place went to help her up. A brief exchange of silent words. Zoey – the woman – exited the frame, still flanked by the two men with her. Rona shook her head, unable to tear her eyes away. High cheekbones, sharp jawline, an easy gait. Hair so dark it was almost black – the hair –

"The hair's too short," said Rona, shaking her head again. "Zoey's hair is longer than mine. That girl's hair is just above her shoulders. It's not Zoey."

"Rona –" started Flynn.

"It's not *her*!" Rona stood and spun on him, the chair colliding with the office wall. "It's not her! It can't be her! She's coming home! She's not in France!"

Flynn took a few steps back, blinking at Rona owlishly. Rona fought the urge to hurl the computer off the desk. She felt and heard Charity and Hailee backing down behind her. They had all missed the point. That wasn't Zoey. It just wasn't.

The door creaked open again, and Rona vaguely noticed Flynn snapping straighter. She turned slowly. Maxwell Blackmore cradled a cup of tea in his hand and pushed the door shut behind him. Rona inhaled and stepped toward Flynn, surrendering her space behind the computer. "Don't be so irrational, Rona. If you can't identify her, I will," he said, voice the essence of calm as he approached the desk. "Play the clip again, Flynn."

Flynn cleared his throat and replayed the clip. Maxwell hummed softly, taking a slow sip of tea. He swapped a quiet greeting with Hailee and Charity, words in a tone that Rona could somehow hardly hear. He would agree with her. He'd say it wasn't Zoey. Just like she had. Because it *wasn't* Zoey. Zoey wasn't in France. Zoey was coming home. She couldn't be an entire country away. She just couldn't.

"That's Zoey," said Maxwell, setting his mug on the desk and tapping the keyboard to pause the footage. "You said this was at de Gaulle?"

Rona opened her mouth to deny it, but Maxwell glanced at her from the corners of his eyes, and her protests died in silence.

"Yes, sir," nodded Flynn.

"Well, at least we're on her trail and . . ." Maxwell's voice trailed off as he stared at the computer screen with an intensity Rona had never seen before. His mouth still hung partly open.

"Sir?" asked Flynn.

"You said there'd been no sign of him," snarled Maxwell, turning to Flynn.

"I – there hasn't," said Flynn. "We tracked him in Norway last."

"Then who do you call this?" asked Maxwell, his voice dangerously low as he zoomed in and enhanced the image on the screen.

Rona glanced at the frozen footage. The passenger who'd kicked their bag in front of Zoey. Flynn's mouth fell open, and he stared at the screen in what could only be described as fear. Rona couldn't help feeling utterly confused. The man on the screen stared back at them all through the recording, a small, amused smile on his face. There was an intensity in his eyes, a laser kind of focus, that made Rona wonder irrationally if he'd known the CCTV camera had been there and recording him the entire time.

"Scramble a team. Paris. I want us there in less than five hours," snapped Maxwell, turning on his heel and heading for the door.

"Max!" called Charity, limping after him. "You're exhausted. You've hardly slept since you got here. You shouldn't go."

"I'll sleep on the way," he said, wrenching the door open.

"Leaving already?" asked Simon, who'd been about to enter the room at the same exact time. He paused. "What's wrong?"

Maxwell laughed bitterly as he stepped around Simon. "They'll fill you in."

"Maxwell, what's going on?" called Simon, turning to start after him.

"Sarajevo!" shouted Maxwell, his footsteps loud on the stairs.

Simon swore. Flynn collapsed into the desk chair. Charity sighed sharply, shaking her head as she walked back across the office to the window. Hailee joined her there. Rona blinked and pinched the bridge of her nose. The pink penguin was still trapped under her arm, its glass eyes staring up at her all too brightly. She heard her father's car start and wheels crunch across the gravel. Rona took a deep breath and glanced at the man on the screen. He stood frozen in the frame, the tiny smile reaching all the way to his blue eyes.

She took another deep breath, trying to keep her voice as calm as possible. "Can someone please, for the love of Jesus, Mary, and Joseph, tell us what's going on?"

Chapter 7

Zoey rested her head against the train carriage's large, rectangle window. They had left Gare de l'Est, the train station in Paris, over an hour ago. The lights of the city had long since faded, leaving behind only darkness. Zoey glanced upward at the night sky. Pitch black. No stars. Not a guiding light to be seen. She blinked rapidly as the train picked up more speed. Where they were going beyond this, she didn't know. The thought of the unknown made the hairs on the back of her neck stand up and her blood run cold.

She hadn't eaten . . . since she and Rona had left home. Was it only last night? Or had it been longer? Time counted in hours had discontinued, settling into a fragmented rush of details to be remembered. She should be hungry. She should be *starving* by now. But she just wasn't. All she felt was sick. Sick and tired. She blinked hard and shook her head, trying to throw off her tiredness, but it clung to her like a cloak. Stay awake. Review what little she knew.

France. She was in France. Where she had to – at least for a short time – pretend to be French. Pretend to be Gabrielle Lavaud. England was behind her. The last look she'd had of England had been *Birmingham*. Would she ever see England again? How was this going to end? How could she possibly fight, plead, or scheme her way out of this?

Erik's words, '*See you soon*' from the parking garage rang in Zoey's head, sending a shiver down her spine. She resisted the urge to sob, clenching her jaw to bury the terror down. Erik. They'd mentioned someone called The Czarina and another someone called Marion. Something about a high-profile assignment. How could she get home? What kind of people was she up against? This was a strange and horrible world where nothing that she knew applied. Reality pressed against her. Her kidnapping had not been something random. Something that had happened by chance.

She swallowed, fighting trembles as she tried to focus on what lay beyond the window. She hoped Groper and Bouncer couldn't see her eyes. Rationally, she knew they must be able to. She could see their images clearly reflected in the glass. She closed her eyes tight, blocking them out. She had to think. Figure out some kind of escape. Maybe she could launch herself off the train? She resisted the urge to shake her head. She could launch herself off the train, sure. If she wanted to die. No. Now wasn't the right time. She'd have to wait for a better chance.

"Only an hour left on the train."

Zoey flinched and her eyes flew open as, beside her, Groper touched her forearm. They had taken an open table seat on the train. Zoey had found herself wedged in the corner, Groper next to her, and Bouncer had claimed a seat on the opposite side of the table. Trapped. Zoey almost curled her lip in disgust as Groper's hand slid down her arm and into her own hand. She opened her eyes and met his dark ones. She knew she should have flashed him a smile to keep up the act, but she didn't. She couldn't bring herself to. Besides, there were very few other people close enough to see them.

To anyone else on the train, his sweet touch would have been perhaps loving. But Zoey knew better. In him taking her hand, he was ensuring that there were hands on her. Physical contact. Something to cage her in and keep her where she was. Zoey looked back out of the window, hardly taking notice of Bouncer standing up and leaving the table. For right now, she was trapped here. Free hand trembling with nerves, Zoey pressed her fingers to the space at her neck where her gold necklace used to hang. Finding nothing, she fiddled with her shirt collar instead.

Evening crept its way in, crushing the sky to a bruised purple. This would be her second night missing from her sisters. Were they worried? Of course, they were. What a stupid thought. She'd be worried sick if Rona or Hailee had vanished. Were the police looking for her by now? Surely *someone* was looking for her. Rescue couldn't be far away. Right?

Zoey glanced at the digital display above the train carriage's door. She waited, and, after a moment, details of arrival slid in a ribbon across the screen. This train terminated at Nancy. A tiny fragment of French geography that she'd learned years ago in class rose in her mind. Nancy. A small town near the German border. In the Northeast French Region. Known for late Baroque and Art Nouveau landmarks. Not that any of that information helped her.

"Here."

Zoey raised her gaze as Bouncer returned and offered her a sandwich in a plastic container. She hesitated for a heartbeat, then began to reach for it. Bouncer jerked his hand away, pulling the sandwich out of her reach. Zoey stared at him, uncertain and balanced on a knife's edge.

"Behave," he said, finally setting the container on the table in front of her.

Zoey watched him sit down before she moved to open the container. She paused. Her stomach churned at the thought of eating. She didn't want to eat. She knew she needed it to survive, but the very thought of eating made her ill. The pit of nausea in her stomach was entirely too volatile. She pushed the sandwich away and turned, looking out of the window. Anything not to look at Groper or Bouncer.

She could still see their dim reflections in the dark glass. Groper leaned forward, fiddling with his phone. Bouncer drummed his fingers absently on the table. Each of them with an untouched sandwich in front of them. She didn't want to look at them. She wanted to curl up in a ball and hide. Every second took her further from home and closer to a doom that she was certain was looming. She swallowed and tucked a strand of her shortened hair behind her ear. There had to be something that she could do to get out of here. Something. Anything. But what?

"Do you need the restroom?" asked Bouncer.

Zoey stared at him, then mutely shook her head.

Bouncer nodded, pulling his own phone from his pocket. "Eat something, then have a rest. We have much further to go before we stop."

Zoey balked. The sentence was spoken simply, but she couldn't figure out whether it was a suggestion, a statement, or a command. It could have been any of them.

Before she could react, Bouncer suddenly stiffened, his gaze locked on the opposite end of the train carriage. Zoey resisted the urge to turn as she heard the carriage door behind her slide open. Voices. Loud, English-speaking voices, their sources finally passing into view. Taking a wary glance at Bouncer, Zoey watched the aisle as the group passed them. She swallowed and watched them, wondering if she could catch their attention at all. The first two members passed their table without much more than a glance. They looked near identical. Zoey wondered if they were twins. She ran her fingers over her mouth to keep from sobbing aloud. The similarities between these two strangers reminded her of Rona. Her own twin. What she wouldn't give to be back with her.

Then Zoey stiffened as the third person in the group, bespectacled and black haired, looked in her direction and paused for half a step. Behind his glasses, his eyes flashed concern. Zoey caught Bouncer's glare from her peripherals, his meaning clear. *Behave.* She gave the man a polite, reserved smile. The man seemed to relax and kept going, following the first two figures down the aisle.

"Go on," said a voice further back in the carriage. "You're not going to find the 'perfect place'. Just sit down at that table there."

The fourth member of the group came into view, and Zoey froze. A young man. Just about her age.

A tiny flame of hope took root in her chest, and Zoey couldn't help but stare at the four of them as they settled down at a table just beyond theirs. Was there a way to communicate with them? A shoe collided hard with her shin under the table, and Zoey bit back a hiss, lowering her gaze and turning her eyes back out the window. If Groper and Bouncer even thought that she was trying to form an escape, or make contact with the men near them ... she took a breath. She didn't know what would happen. Think of Rona and Hailee. She had to. But it was getting harder to justify her own quietness as a protection for them. She wanted to be home. She wanted to be back with them. She'd never be able to do that if she didn't try to get away from Groper and Bouncer.

Could potential rescue possibly be within speaking distance? She could scream. She could put up a fight. But what use would fighting be if she, and the others on the train, ended up dead?

Bouncer's words from that morning rang in her head *'Torture will come first'*. She took another breath, ignoring the way it shuddered in her chest as she inhaled. She clutched at her shirt under the table. It was the only comfort that she could afford herself. She bit the inside of her cheek and looked up as Bouncer picked up his phone again. From her peripherals, she caught sight of the young man. Intense, brown eyes caught her own, and Zoey found she couldn't look away.

The confines of her own private thoughts screamed, railing against the physical captivity around her as she watched him. Desperation threatened her, panic rising back to surface level. In her forced silence, she clutched to a thought, trying to broadcast it like a radio wave.

'Help me. Please, help me.'

Then the man blinked and broke the gaze between them. His eyes lifted to the carriage door, that had slid open again, and allowed an old man to enter.

The brief moment they'd shared in that gaze had felt somehow important. As if a secret message had passed between them. But she couldn't be sure. Perhaps it was just desperation making her imagine things.

Zoey looked away, resting her elbows on the table buying her head in the fold of her arms. Suddenly something like reassurance swept over her, and she shivered. Her mind immediately flew home to Hereford, to the sounds of Rona and Hailee bickering good-naturedly. To the kitchen smells of dishwasher fluid and hot tea brewing. To the gentle rays of sunlight that peeked through her pale curtains and painted her bedroom awash with the morning. In her mind, she could almost hear her sisters, their laughter and their almost-so-close voices like beacons.

Resolve pressed its way back into her chest. A sense of drive. She would make it home. Back to her family. Somehow. And she swore it wouldn't be in a coffin.

This was a public place. She sat back up. Groper and Bouncer wouldn't harm her here. She had some semblance of hope at the adjacent table. For now, she would bide her time. She fought down the nausea in her stomach and reached for the sandwich in the center of the table.

~ ~ ~ ~ ~

"Up."

Zoey was startled awake as Groper shook her shoulder hard. No longer moving. Yet the train felt active. She could hear the white noise of shuffling movement. She sat up and blinked hard, trying to get her bearings.

"We're getting off," said Bouncer.

Zoey swallowed and glanced over at the table where the other passengers had been. Gone. All four of them were gone. Despair rose in Zoey's chest. She couldn't help feeling betrayed. She resisted the urge to fiddle with her not-there necklace and started to stand up. They couldn't have known she needed help. Regardless of how long she locked eyes with the young man across the way, he wasn't telepathic, and neither was she. No help was coming. She was alone. And she would have to help herself.

Taking a breath, Zoey fell in line between Groper and Bouncer, letting Groper take the lead out of the train carriage and onto the platform. She couldn't help but notice that Bouncer stayed directly behind her. Zoey glanced over her shoulder and faltered as she met his eyes. A tiny smile crossed his face. He was *enjoying* this. And anger bit the back of her throat. Watching her panic internally as each powerless step she took carried her further from home.

"Get out of the way," snapped Groper.

Zoey looked up. An old man lingered on the platform just beyond the door.

"Excusez-moi!" he cried, sounding aghast.

Zoey's wanted to shoot the old man an apologetic glance, but Bouncer grabbed hold of her shirt before she had a chance. His other hand landed on Groper's shoulder. Zoey stumbled as he shoved them forward, a terrible fury in his forcefulness. A chill raced up Zoey's spine, but not before she met the old man's eyes. She froze. Those eyes. She had seen them earlier in the day, she was sure of it. How she knew it, she wasn't sure, but she knew she was certain of it. Blue. Icy. Calculating. They were not the eyes of an old man. They were the eyes of someone much younger.

Words. English words. English words in France. The worst possible ones she could have chosen. They spilled before Zoey could stop them.

"Help me. Please."

Tension. Silence. Zoey's heart plummeted. She could feel Bouncer staring at her. His hand turned into an iron tight grip on her shirt. She didn't dare move. The old man gave a wary glare and shuffled away, muttering something under his breath. Zoey's teeth chattered. The mistake had been made. She jumped as Bouncer shoved her forward again. Wild fear rose in Zoey's chest as Bouncer let go of Groper. She was his sole focus now. He took hold of her bicep and walked through the station. It was quiet. Most people were home by now. No one around to see her distress.

Blood rushed in Zoey's ears, her heartbeat pounding. Were its' beats numbered? How many of her kidnappers' buttons could she press before she became too much trouble to keep alive? She didn't even know what they wanted her for. Had she just made a fatal error?

Bouncer turned to Groper. "Get the car. We'll wait for you around the corner from the station."

Terror rose in Zoey's stomach as Groper retreated without a backward glance. Bouncer stood very still next to her, his fingers gripping her arm like talons. Zoey couldn't fight the shiver that traveled up her back as Bouncer leaned down. She tried to back away, but Bouncer held her fast.

"Do you remember what I told you?" he asked, his voice soft and smooth.

Zoey swallowed, her mouth suddenly going dry, and nodded.

"Good."

Nausea gripped the back of Zoey's throat, and she wanted to vomit. It had just been a mistake. But what good would arguing do? There was no winning here. Her legs shook as she fell into step with Bouncer. She should have thought better. But there was no thinking in the moment. Just instinct.

Swallowing hard, she realized with a sinking feeling she might have dashed any and all hope of escape. Her captors would tighten their hold on her now more than ever. Home felt as though it was slipping through her fingers like sand.

Two sets of headlights caught Zoey's attention. Groper was back – he had to be. Another shiver caught Zoey, and she had to fight to stay on her feet. The first of the two cars – a silver Mercedes – passed by her and Bouncer. Zoey would have prayed that the driver gave a backward look, but she knew they wouldn't. No one did. Zoey swallowed as the second car slowed.

"Going my way?" asked Groper, rolling down the passenger window.

"Very funny," replied Bouncer. He turned, and Zoey recoiled as his eyes settled on her. "You will sit in the back seat. You will not cause trouble. You will sit and do exactly as we tell you. Do you understand me?"

Zoey nodded mutely, too afraid to speak.

"I don't know if you do," replied Bouncer. He sounded pensive. "I feel as though we've had a conversation very similar to this one earlier today."

His hand came off Zoey's arm, and she thought of running. Before she could stop herself, she looked back at the doors to the train station, the lights shining brightly against the night. Help was in there. She could reach it.

Bouncer's hand flew toward her. *Whack!* Zoey yelped as her head cracked to the side. She saw stars. Dazed. Her cheek burned. Stinging. She clapped one hand to her lip, heated skin meeting her fingers. Slapped. Tears pricked at the corners of Zoey's eyes. Then she paused. She tasted metal in her mouth and pressed her fingertips to her lip. She felt something wet and warm. She looked at her fingertips. Red. He'd split her lip. Taking a sobbing breath, she tried to look up at Bouncer, but a hand caught her hair, slamming her stomach down into his rising knee. A cry, softer than she'd anticipated, left Zoey's mouth, and she crumpled to her knees, stunned and winded. The hand in her hair vanished, only to grab her tightly around the throat. Air stalled in her lungs.

"I asked you a question," snarled Bouncer, his voice still low and even. "I expect an answer. One that's loud and clear. Again, do you understand me?"

Zoey nodded, desperate. Bouncer's fingers tightened, and he tilted his head slightly, a tiny smile crossing his thin lips.

"Yes!" Zoey rasped, sobbing for air that didn't come. "Yes, I understand."

"Good. Try to talk to anyone again, and we'll see how vocal you are about a shattered kneecap. Get in."

Bouncer released her. Zoey inhaled with a shudder, air flowing painfully down her aching throat. Her chest and lungs didn't want to work properly. Shaking, she pushed back to her feet. What else could she do? Groper and Bouncer were both bigger than her, stronger than her. She didn't stand a chance.

"Sit in the middle," said Bouncer, leaning over her to yank out the seatbelt, wrapping it roughly around her. He lifted his eyes to glare at Groper. "Put the child lock on her door."

Zoey slid as far away from Bouncer as she could get, hardly paying Groper any attention as he got out of the car and walked around to the back doors. Her lip oozed blood and her head spun. She wanted as much distance between herself and Bouncer as possible. She resisted the urge to glance at the far door. It was already open. Did she have enough time to slip out of it? The only obstacle was Groper, crouched near the ground, fiddling with the child lock. Bouncer grabbed hold of her wrist, and Zoey stiffened, desperate to pull away from him.

"Don't even think about it," said Bouncer.

Groper paused where he stood at the back door, and his eyes widened, face drained of blood. "Is – is she bleeding?"

"Don't worry about it," replied Bouncer.

"They want her unharmed. You know that. Erik . . . You know what he'll do to us!?"

"She fell in a hotel room. That's all," snarled Bouncer. "Cuff the other wrist. I'm not having her try anything else."

Zoey couldn't keep herself from jolting away. Why did she need to be unharmed? Why did some unknown figure want *her*? This person calling themselves The Czarina? Or the Marion they'd mentioned? No questions left her mouth, and Zoey knew even if she asked, she'd get no answers. Groper leaned into the backseat from the opposite side. Desperation settled in Zoey's stomach as she watched Bouncer click one handcuff loop shut around her wrist. He attached the opposite end of the cuff to the backseat headrest. On her other side, Groper copied Bouncer, cuffing one of her wrists to the other backseat headrest.

Trapped. In every sense of the word. Zoey snapped a breath. Panic caught her. Don't panic. She mustn't panic. But how could she do anything but? She was well and truly trapped. Animal fear inside her screamed to struggle, to kick, to thrash, to run. But she couldn't. She was already pinned. She closed her eyes and restrained a whimper. Groper returned to the driver's seat, Bouncer to his right in the front passenger seat.

More than ever, Rona and Hailee's faces swam in front of her eyes. Home. She wanted to be home. To wake up and let all of this be a terrible nightmare.

But even as those thoughts crossed her mind, she remembered Bouncer's threat. Her sisters were the reason that she had not put up more of a fight. The promise of these men tracking down her family held her in place, cementing her where she sat. And until she found a solution or formed a solid plan, the nightmare would continue. Until they reached their destination. Zoey swallowed. But what then?

Chapter 8

Rona paced back and forth through The Roost's living room, her penguin watching her glassily. She put her hands in her pants pockets, pulled them out, chewed her cuticles, then slid them back into each pocket. Repeat.

Maxwell was hours gone, leaving tension and anxiety in his wake. She was bone-tired, but she knew she couldn't sleep. Out of exhaustion, Hailee had faced her fear of the night, the loneliness, and gone out alone to the annex hours ago.

Rona turned and stared at the penguin, almost angry with it now. But her anger died quickly, and she lowered her hands again to put them back into her pockets. Removing them once again, she saw dried blood on the side of her thumb and embedded under her nails on her right hand. When had she torn apart the skin on the side of her fingers? She bit her nails again, tasting iron in her mouth.

"Exhausting yourself won't help her, you know? Why don't you get some rest?"

Rona spun. Flynn stood at the bottom of the stairs, coffee cup in his hand. Rona lowered her hands. Flynn's brown eyes followed the movement.

"I don't think I can," said Rona, folding her hands together inside the front pocket of her sweatshirt.

Flynn smiled gently and crossed the room, sitting on the couch. "I know this isn't easy. But we'll find her. I promise. Your dad should be in France by now."

"Who did you see earlier?" asked Rona, collapsing onto the couch opposite Flynn. "On the computer footage, with Zoey?"

Waiting for his answer, Rona pulled one of the wool blankets off the back of the couch and draped it over her shoulders.

"Someone very dangerous," said Flynn quickly, turning to look into the fireplace's dying embers. "Your father has tried to keep him under surveillance for the last few years, but he has an uncanny ability to slip off the radar."

"And he's in the same city as Zoey?" asked Rona, needing to confirm what she'd seen. The words wanted to stick in her throat.

Flynn nodded, his eyes fixed on his coffee cup. Rona took a heavy breath, trying to calm her thundering heart. Zoey. Oh, Zoey. Rona pressed her palms to her eyes, struggling to fight back the prickle behind her eyelids. Change the subject. This was going to make her cry.

"Who exactly is Maxwell?" asked Rona, shifting to lie on her back. "He's always told us he's an accountant, but accountants don't have people put under surveillance."

Flynn sighed and rested his chin in his hand. "I'm not sure I'm the right person to tell you that, Rona. What I can tell you is that Maxwell's a pretty powerful person himself. He has military powers at his disposal, and he's got links to the Secret Service Agencies."

"*Why* though? Why does he need these kinds of connections?" asked Rona, rolling onto her side. "Who is he?"

Flynn hesitated then opened his mouth, a strange look in his brown eyes. Something nervous. Rona caught herself leaning forward. His eyes flitted away for half a second, and Rona fought the urge to sit up and wring the answer out of him.

Then Flynn's phone chimed.

"It's about Zoey," he said, after pulling it free from his pocket. "Another camera picked her up. Want to come and see where she is?"

Rona hurled her frustration aside. Zoey was more important. She nodded and pushed the blanket off onto the floor. Maybe, just maybe, Maxwell was closing in on her sister by now. Maybe Zoey would be home by the morning. A glimmer of hope flickered in Rona's chest, and she followed Flynn back up the stairs. It was impossible not to notice how quiet the house sounded at night. Floorboards creaked and groaned with every step.

Down the hall, Rona could hear Simon snoring. She assumed Charity was with him. Oh, sleep. At least the night would do the mercy of passing quickly for them. She followed Flynn into Simon's office and rounded the desk. The image of a train station lit the screen. Nancy, France. How had Zoey got so far away so quickly?

Rona leaned forward, eyes scanning the platform for any sign of Zoey. Any person who remotely resembled her sister. Then. There. In the crowd of disembarking passengers. Zoey. Rona's breath caught in her throat. Zoey accompanied this time by only one man gripping her upper arm and ushering her down the platform. Rona pressed a hand to her mouth. Zoey looked stricken. Afraid.

"Is that man there?" asked Rona, turning to Flynn. "The one from earlier?"

Flynn shook his head. "I don't see him. That doesn't mean much though."

"What do you mean?" asked Rona.

"He's clever, and he's got a knack for staying off cameras. And it's funny how easy it is to not look like yourself through a camera lens. I'm surprised really that they aren't taking more precautions with Zoey. Oh! Out of frame. Hang on."

Rona swallowed hard as Flynn flashed between camera lenses. "Is all this happening in real time now?"

"No, we're on two or three hours of delay," replied Flynn.

He finally settled on an angle from outside the station. Rona sank onto the desk, perching on the corner and wringing her fingers together as she watched Zoey and her captor march in silence toward a car. Every now and again, the camera would jump, images flashing warped or movements slightly fragmented. Then the man holding Zoey turned her sharply. Rona leaned forward, anxiety gathering in the pit of her stomach. Something bad was going to happen. Something bad was going to happen to Zoey. And there was nothing she could do to stop it.

Zoey's head snapped hard to one side. The image pixelated and distorted. A knee crashed up into Zoey's chest. The man seized Zoey's throat, dragging her up. Rona stifled a cry, hands pressed against her mouth. She saw Flynn moving to exit the screen and grabbed his wrist. It felt wrong to watch this, but it would feel worse to leave Zoey alone. But what could she do?

Nothing. There was nothing she could do. There was no way to help.

The image pixelated and cleared again. Zoey looked like she was sobbing or, perhaps, trying to catch her breath. Rona bit her knuckle. *Do something*, Rona urged her in silence, even though she knew the moment had passed long ago for her twin. And what could Zoey possibly have done? What act could she possibly perform to defend herself? Rona closed her eyes hard, but by the time she opened them, Zoey was out of the frame. The car's taillights vanished out of the camera's field of view.

"Rona," whispered Flynn. "I'm sorry. I shouldn't –"

"They're torturing her," said Rona softly. "How far away is Maxwell?"

"Leaving Paris, last I checked," replied Flynn. "He's driving, so he's a bit behind, but he'll catch them. You watch."

"Can you track the car that Zoey's in?" asked Rona.

Flynn nodded. "If you give me my hand back, I can. It'll take a little while, but I can do it."

Rona looked down. Her fingers still held Flynn's wrist in a vise grip. She pulled back, but his hand caught hers, and he squeezed her fingers comfortingly before letting her go.

"It'll be alright. Give your father a few hours, and he'll be on them."

Rona nodded, as she turned and walked out of the office.

Her head felt full. Too full. Her own thoughts and questions trailed into anxiety and speculation. She collapsed on the couch, tugging the tartan blanket back over herself. She wasn't sure how much faith she had in Maxwell catching them. Zoey and her kidnappers were still hours ahead of him, and there wasn't any telling how many of those hours Zoey had left.

~ ~ ~ ~ ~ ~

Night seemed endless. Zoey knew she should sleep. She knew her body was tired and her mind even more so, but she couldn't. Stress and nerves kept her awake, on edge. Sleep would not come. And Zoey didn't think she wanted it to. Being asleep would make her even more vulnerable.

She glanced out of the window. No lights shone. No sign of civilization. No indication of a town. Not the outline of any structure. There wasn't even another car on this stretch of road. Not a single star shone from above.

Gray eyes closed; Zoey restrained the scream that dammed her throat. Even drawing breath was hard. The world was crushing inward. Her very location – cuffed in the backseat of what she assumed was a rental car in France – served as a reminder of everywhere that she was not. She would rather be standing alone in some desolate field than here in this mobile prison.

The silence was deafening. Neither Groper nor Bouncer spoke. Even the navigation system, hidden from her view, was muted, with Groper only checking it periodically. Trying to keep her movements slow and subtle, she stared out into the dark, searching for a marker. A light. Something, anything to reveal where they were. Anything. Once she knew better where they were, where they were going, she might have a chance to plan an escape.

There had to be *something*. Then, in the dark, a single star appeared, as though sparked into life. Zoey stared at it, fixated. A thrill of adrenaline came alight in her blood. She had her mark. Just a tiny glimmer to guide her if she ran. A tiny voice inside her warned her to calm down. To think. Zoey tried to breathe. Her chest felt that it was clenched in a vise. Calm down. But she couldn't. Determination and terror reared into overdrive. Fight or flight. Or both at once. Fear tore through Zoey's chest. Away. She had to get *away*!

Now! While she had a focal point. Desperation unlike anything she had ever felt before mandated it. She suddenly understood why trapped foxes chewed their own legs off.

A sudden scream tore loose from her throat, and Zoey launched herself against the confines of the handcuffs, pulling with all her strength. Break free! Get away! Now!

"Get hold of her!" shouted Groper, swerving slightly on the road.

In the soft glow coming from the dashboard, Zoey caught sight of Bouncer turning to her from the front passenger seat. One hand reached behind his back, fumbling for something. What he was going to try and do to her, she didn't want to find out. Twisting like a cat, she kicked out wildly. One shoe connected hard with Bouncer's shoulder, knocking him hard into Groper. A deafening bang and an iron tang filled the car, and Groper choked out a stifled scream.

The car ripped sideways, Groper still gurgling in the driver's seat. Brakes shrieked. Headlights lit up the guardrail. Zoey's vision blurred. The world spun as the car swerved. Her seatbelt snapped tight, nearly crushing her chest. The handcuffs bit down sharp around her wrists. Glass shattered. The windshield blasted out. Metal screeched on metal as the car's hood crumpled. Airbags deployed. A second *bang* broke through the car's interior. Zoey screamed, the sound torn from her own throat with ease, as a line of searing pain and heat tore across her upper left thigh. Her head slammed sideways against one of the backseat headrests, and the world went white then dark, her ears ringing.

Stillness. Utter stillness. Zoey let out a long, low groan No movement at all. The car had stilled. How long had it been still? Seconds? Minutes? She didn't know. Zoey looked up, blinking to clear the foggy feeling in her head. Her thigh pulsed and throbbed. She couldn't feel her toes. In the dark, she looked down. She couldn't see anything, but her thighs felt sticky and wet. She smelled iron in the air. She gritted her teeth as pain thudded upward from her thigh to her heart which thundered at triple speed.

Bleeding. She had to be bleeding. Heavily, from the smell and feel of it. She looked at her wrists. Blood leaked down from where the metal handcuffs had bitten down around them.

Everywhere she looked, there was either broken glass or blood. The car's airbags had deployed. Blood spattered Groper's driver's side window. The windshield was shattered – an empty hole in the dark. Only one headlight beamed out, a tiny candle trying to illuminate an ocean of night.

She tried to distract herself. Help would come. They had just been in a car crash. Surely other people would travel on this road before long.

Zoey's eyes froze as she looked at Groper. Slumped forward, his neck twisted almost backwards, blood spilling over from his lips, his eyes open, yet seeing nothing. Dead.

Zoey's breathing quickened. Groper was dead. She was trapped in the middle of nowhere in a vehicle with a dead body. A dead body. A corpse. Horror and terror conjoined. Zoey screamed.

"Shut up!" snarled a voice from the front. Not Groper. Bouncer.

Zoey barely heard his command, barely saw him twist around in the front seat, barely registered him until he reached between the seats and gripped her thigh tight. One thumb pressed hard onto the wound. There was new reason to scream. Bouncer's grip tightened. Chest heaving and shock lancing through her, Zoey forced herself to quieten. That was the only thing that would stop him. Quieten. She had to.

Trembles still shaking her bones, Zoey looked up. Alive. She was still alive, even if Groper was not. She and Bouncer both were. His hand moved away from her thigh. Zoey thought she caught sight of something metal glinting under the low, artificial light. She looked down. Bouncer slumped over the center console, blood dripping from his nose and mouth. How his back hadn't been broken, Zoey didn't know. Still alive. Trapped in a car with one of the men who had kidnapped her. Zoey met his eyes as he looked up. A spike of fear tried to force its way into Zoey's chest, but there was no more room for it. Confusion crossed over Bouncer's face, as though he couldn't quite believe what had happened. He pushed up, one hand slipping on a puddle of blood on the center console.

"Are you hurt badly?" he asked.

Zoey stared at him. They were in the middle of nowhere, in a crashed car, complete with a dead body, and her kidnapper was asking if *she* was injured? Light fell across Bouncer's face from behind the car. Zoey turned in her seat to look over her shoulder. Headlights. Another car was coming toward them. And it was close. Hope. This was it. *This* was her chance to get away. Zoey moved to rattle one of the handcuffs, but Bouncer moved first, pushing backwards through the mess of airbags and broken glass to reach the blown-out windshield. A new fear broke in Zoey's chest as she watched Bouncer slither out of the gap and stand up on the road in front of the car. He was leaving her. Alone with Groper's dead body and the smell of blood. She should be happy. She should. One abductor dead. The other leaving with help on the horizon. But she didn't want to be left here. Not with a dead body.

Outside, Zoey heard Bouncer's footsteps crunch unevenly on the gravel and glass outside the car. He was injured, too. The back door swung open.

"Get out. When that car reaches us, you will say nothing. We do not need any help. I'm going to have some of my people take us the rest of the way, and others will stay and clean up this mess."

Zoey tensed. Even with the oncoming car, would she have any room or leeway to pass a message? She watched Bouncer as he reached up to the backseat headrests and undid the handcuffs, pocketing them. Instinct told her to lunge for the opposite door. Launch out and disappear into the night. But her leg gave another insistent throb, and defeat crashed in. She wouldn't make it far.

Groaning, Zoey unlatched her seatbelt and slid from the backseat, her injured leg clumsier than it should have been. She put weight on her injury and yelped as her knee buckled under her. Blood ran down her leg and she shuddered. With a groan, she leaned on Bouncer and looked up. The second car was still coming. It hadn't turned off. Still coming. This was it. She would do something. This time, she would. She would not allow this opportunity to slip away. It may be the last one she got. Next to her, Bouncer moved, pulling a phone from his pocket. He tapped the screen a few times then pressed the phone to his ear.

"Car crash on the A4. We're near Eckartswiller. My partner is dead. Target still in possession." A pause, then Bouncer spoke again. "Thank you."

Zoey saw her own shadow fall behind her, and she looked up. Headlights distorted her night vision. Gravel crunched as the car slowed, pulling onto the roadside. Darkness crushed in behind the new arrival. Overhead, the clouds cleared, thousands of stars finally exposed in the night sky. Zoey raised one hand to her eyes, just able to make out the Mercedes symbol on the front of the car before its driver flicked on the vehicle's high beams. Dazzled, Zoey heard the car's door slam.

Fear flooded through her veins. What if this was some of the help that Bouncer had called for? But how could anyone working with him have gotten here so fast? No. This was something different. What if this was something worse? What if this was Erik again?

Zoey squinted against blinding white headlights. She could just make out a shape. Someone tall. Slim. Footsteps sounded on the asphalt. Purposeful. Poignant. And stop.

A voice rang out from the silhouette. A man. "Fancy finding you out here, Ewan."

Bouncer inhaled sharply. "*You* ..." Zoey could hear the terror in his voice. His grip on her arm faltered. "How did you find us? I covered all of our tracks ..."

A quiet laugh. "I'm one of the best, Ewan."

Zoey glanced sideways at Bouncer – his real name was Ewan? His face shadowed over with fear, eyes riveted to the figure in the headlights. Then he hardened. Zoey's stomach clenched as Bouncer reached backward. Armed. He had to be. There was no way he wasn't. Would he really kill the man in the shadows?

A tiny *click* sounded in the night, and Bouncer hissed a low breath. "She is mine. I have a new team coming. She's property of The Czarina, and she will be delivered. Don't try and stop us."

The newcomer laughed quietly. "Is that a threat?"

Zoey took a shaky breath. Tension clung to the air like static now. Gravel crunched as the shadowed figure moved forward a step. Metal flashed in the bright headlights as Bouncer pulled something free from his waistband. Zoey stumbled hard as he shoved her away, screaming as her injured leg buckled without his support. She fell hard, colliding with the solid ground. Blood drenched her jeans. She felt it running free across her skin.

Zoey wanted to move, to crawl away, to get out of the way. But her body wouldn't move. Fear pinned her against the asphalt.

"A promise," said Bouncer. "My people are already on the way."

"What a shame," mused the man in the dark, his tone effortless and casual. "I came here to stop you. Zoey, look away for me, please."

Movement. Zoey whipped away, her cheek scraping against the glassy pavement. The shards glinted like starlight in the dark. Her name. This man had used her name. Her name which Bouncer hadn't uttered since the day he'd kidnapped her. How did he know her name?

Two gunshots cracked the night. A gaging sound jerked from someone's chest. Zoey couldn't be sure whose. Then a *thud* sounded near her, but she covered her head with her arms and refused to look. She didn't want to see. White flashed in front of her eyelids. Seconds of silence. Footsteps. Pause. A low, pained groan. Pause. A third shot. Zoey flinched at the sound and curled into a ball.

Silence dragged out as seconds passed. Zoey almost wanted to lift her head. But she didn't want to see a dead body lying near her, as she was certain one would be.

Footsteps, purposeful without being hurried. No unevenness. So . . .? The stranger?

A figure blocked the glow of the headlights. Zoey could see a silhouette through a gap in her arms. Not Bouncer. And Zoey knew. She *knew*. Her body shook. She would never see her family again. She wanted to scream, to cry, to beg. Yet she could do nothing. This was it. She was to die here. On a roadside in France, with the smell of asphalt and car fumes in her nose.

Even if Groper and Bouncer were alive, it would have been better than this. This man had already shot Bouncer, and she was next. She would die as Gabrielle Lavaud – far from home. No one would ever know what had happened to her. A *clunk* of metal settling on metal. Footsteps again. More quiet.

"Zoey? Zoey Blackmore?"

Gray eyes opened, blurred with tears. She raised her head, her tear tracks chilling in the night air. When had she started crying? She could see the details of the man now. He had come closer, and the lights of his car shone on his face. Blue eyes so piercing they seemed to see right into her. High, well-sculpted cheekbones. Memorize his face. This could be the last one she ever saw. A few strands of short, blond hair fell across his forehead. Zoey tensed and tried to scramble away as he dropped to a crouch nearby. She fought to rise to her feet, but her bleeding leg failed her. Her entire body shook. Escape wasn't a possibility. Neither was fighting. He was armed, and she wasn't. She was injured, and he wasn't. Empathize. Beg. That was all she had left.

"P – please," she said. It was the only word she could summon. She tried not to think of Bouncer lying dead behind her or Groper dead in the front seat. Two corpses. She'd be the third any moment now. She felt her throat close. A sob threatened to override her.

Try again. "Please, don't . . ."

She couldn't choke out those last words. *Please don't kill me.* To mention it seemed to incur it. Silence settled.

He raised his hands. Empty. "I'm not going to hurt you, Zoey."

Zoey's eyes went from one of his hands to the other. Her trembles eased a fraction. "What . . . who . . . ?"

"My name is Sascha Sarajevo, and you are Zoey Elaine Blackmore. I'm here to help you. Can you stand?"

Zoey studied him, silent. Stars glinted in the night sky behind him. Someone to help? But how? How had he known? What reason did she have to trust him? He could be just as bad as Groper and Bouncer – this Sascha Sarajevo. She stayed still.

"Zoey," said Sascha, showing his empty hands again. "I know you're scared. I know you have no reason to trust me, but I can't let you stay here. Other people, people like Ewan, may be on their way already. You're hurt. Please, let me get you out of here."

Words. They were on Zoey's tongue before she could even register them. "He called someone."

"Then we have even less time than I hoped. Zoey, can you get up for me?"

Zoey stared at him. Again. *Could* he be the lesser of two evils? Or was he a new monster to ruin her? She stiffened as he stood up, towering over her. Then he reached down. Zoey blinked. His hand. Open and unarmed. His other was in clear view. She sat up further, adjusting her position.

"Let me help you get home."

That word. Home. It stirred her into action. Zoey reached up and gripped his hand tight in her own. She tried not to pull away as Sascha's hand closed around hers in return. He stepped backward, and Zoey groaned as he pulled her to her feet. She hissed and faltered as she put weight on her injured leg. It began to buckle beneath her. Sascha stepped in before Zoey even realized he'd moved, one arm sweeping around her waist and holding her steady.

"Lean on me," said Sascha. "It'll help."

Zoey nodded and slung her arm over his shoulders, gritting her teeth as she hobbled to his car. She shoved down the bite of fear that threatened the back of her throat. This could be the decision that got her home, or it could be the decision that broke her. But it was a risk she was willing to take.

~ ~ ~ ~ ~ ~

Someone was shaking her shoulder. Rona's eyelids flickered, heavy as she forced them open. For a moment, she looked around, confused. She wasn't where she expected to be. She should be in her bedroom out in the annex.

"Rona."

She looked up. Flynn. She blinked a few times, clearing her head. She was still in the main house with Flynn. The curtains had been drawn, closing out the night. Most of the lamps had been turned off, the light dim and comforting. She must have fallen asleep on the couch.

Suddenly, she noticed the drawn, horrified expression on Flynn's face.

"What happened? What's wrong?" demanded Rona, pushing aside the blanket she'd fallen asleep with and sitting up.

Flynn pressed his lips together and swallowed. "I've just got off the phone with your dad. He's coming back."

"Zoey?" asked Rona, hope flickering in her chest.

Flynn shook his head. "Zoey's off the cameras. I don't know what happened. I caught their car on one camera, but not the next. She hasn't reappeared."

"Could they have turned off the road?" asked Rona. "Taken a route without CCTV?"

"No," sighed Flynn, sitting next to her. "Your father's at the place where Zoey vanished now. There was a car crash. He . . . there are two bodies there."

"No," said Rona, shaking her head. "Don't you dare say –"

"It's the men who kidnapped Zoey. She isn't there."

"Do you think she started walking?" asked Rona. "If I'd been kidnapped and my kidnappers were killed in a car crash, I'd try to get somewhere safe."

Flynn sighed and pressed a hand to his forehead. "Only one of them was killed in the crash. The other one was shot. There's been a changeover, and she's off the radar."

"Don't tell me that means what I think it means," whimpered Rona. Not now. This was too much. Following Zoey virtually had been her only source of hope. Her only way to know her sister was alive.

"I can't keep any eyes on her. She's gone."

The world folded in half as Rona leaned down, burying her face in her hands. This couldn't be true. This had to be a nightmare. She would wake up any moment now to Flynn shaking her shoulder to tell her Maxwell had found Zoey and was bringing her home. Her chest constricted. This was no nightmare. Rona sobbed, tears tracking hot down her cheeks. She wanted to be held. Told by someone who was older and wiser that everything would be alright – that there was a solution. That this could be fixed.

But how could this ever be fixed? Zoey was gone. Gone. The sound that left Rona's mouth wasn't human. An arm settled around her shoulders, holding her close. Rona wrapped her arms around herself, leaning sideways into Flynn. She barely knew him, but she appreciated his closeness all the same. His softly whispered apologies and words of senseless comfort felt like an island in a sea without resolution.

Chapter 9

Waldkirch, Germany. A hotel that Zoey hadn't caught the name of. The night had passed. Morning. She lowered the white towel she had used to dry her hair. Clean. It smelled faintly of bleach. She held it in front of her body and studied her face in the hotel mirror. Gaunt. She looked half dead. Her hair hung stringy, barely brushing her shoulders. Black shadows colored the areas beneath her eyes. Her cheekbones stood out rigid. The cut at the side of her lip had scabbed over.

Her blood ran cold even as she thought of Bouncer. Her last glimpse of him had been of his dead body on that deserted road. Zoey swallowed. She couldn't think about that. She mustn't. Bury it. Repress the memories until she was ready to deal with them.

One hand dropped to her left thigh. A white bandage, still slightly damp from the careful rinse she'd managed to take, along with thick gauze padding, was still wrapped tightly around her leg. Below that layer were butterfly bandages holding her skin together.

The wound was a grisly reminder of the night before. A rogue bullet from Bouncer's handgun had grazed the top of her left thigh during the crash. She had been lucky. It could have been worse.

She took a sharp breath and looked away from the mirror, turning instead to the small, bathroom window. Through the window, she could see the world beyond. Cows lowed in nearby hillside pastures. Tree-covered mountains framed the village. Green. Everything was so green. Bursting with life. Peace seemed to hover over the village.

Last night, she had been able to see only what the streetlights had illuminated, but for the first time in what felt like a lifetime, she knew vaguely where she was. The morning showed an old city, red-roofed and stone. There was something calming, perhaps almost haunting, about the village's peace. As though it wasn't real and could never be real. A stillness resonated over the air. Even the early morning bird calls seemed distant. Zoey took a breath and clung to the towel in her hands, still staring out the window. The fibers felt rough against her skin. That was real. A church spire towered above red roofs and cream stones. No structure stood higher than it. That was real.

Zoey breathed, setting down the towel on the countertop and her hands shifting to cling onto the porcelain sink. It felt cold beneath her hands. She was real, and she was alive. Sascha had appeared. Somehow. In something akin to divine intervention. The nightmare with Groper and Bouncer was over. A few blackbirds darted across the blue sky. More cows lowed against the morning.

Zoey lifted her head, avoiding her own eyes in the mirror. This was the place Sascha had decided to stop last night. Why here of all places, she didn't know. And she hadn't asked. Last night hadn't been the right time. She had just been plucked from the clutches of Groper and Bouncer, persuaded into Sascha's car, and whisked away.

After some time on the road – Zoey hadn't kept track of how long they'd driven for – Sascha had given her first aid for her leg on a darkened roadside, but after that, they had been on the move again.

Now though, they were in a weird state of static. Zoey had both too much and too little to say to him, that much she knew. The air was tense. Thick. Awkward. As though neither knew *what* to say to the other. She certainly didn't know what to say to him. She had more questions than answers, and no clue where to start.

Zoey swallowed and pulled her clothes back on. They were filthy. She had worn them since Saturday morning, travelled in them and bled heavily in them. She glanced at her black jeans. A large tear had split one of the legs. The white bandages showed through from underneath. She could smell blood thick on the fabric. It made her stomach churn. Look away. She had to. Zoey elevated her chin and darted a glance back at her reflection in the mirror. She straightened her shirt. She was a mess. She missed clean clothes, her own things ... but more than that, she missed her own people. Her Rona, her Hailee. Even Hereford, she missed. Home. But standing here missing them would get her nowhere.

Zoey took a steadying breath and pulled the bathroom door open. Sascha lay in the center of the bed closest to the door. Exactly where he'd been when Zoey had escaped into the bathroom. In the last hour, he hadn't moved an inch. His hands were still folded on his abdomen. His ankles were still crossed. Only the rise and fall of his chest showed that he was even alive. Zoey folded her arms and leaned on the bathroom's doorframe. She studied him. He was tall and well-built. Broad shoulders and long legs. There was a quiet sense of power to him. A keenness to him that made him seem angular somehow. His blond hair fell back away from his face, accentuating the sharpness of his profile. There was so much that she wanted, that she needed, to ask him about. But how could she articulate her questions? Where did she begin? Would Sascha even answer her questions? She folded her arms more tightly. Only one way to find out.

She cleared her throat. "Are you going to tell me what's going on?"

A pause. Zoey tilted her head, eyes darting toward the door. Was Sascha asleep? She shifted her weight. A few seconds more. No reaction. The hotel room door wasn't far away. Possibly thirty feet. She took a step toward it. A floorboard creaked underfoot.

"Are you sure you want to do that?"

Zoey swallowed and looked at Sascha. He hadn't moved. Even his eyes were still closed. She took a shuddering breath. There hadn't been aggression in his tone, not even a challenge ... but there didn't have to be. If these last days had taught her anything, it was that there didn't have to be anger or aggression in someone's tone for them to do something unspeakable. A shiver ran up her spine again as she thought of Erik's words to her at the airport.

"Are you a mind reader, or something?" she asked, fighting to keep her voice under control. A cold fist of fear settled in her chest – she wasn't sure if it had ever left.

One corner of his mouth twitched upward, eyes still closed. "I have a good understanding of people. I can generally predict the next course of someone's action."

"Well, I can't. So, I'll ask you again, are you going to tell me what's going on? Because I'm . . ." Zoey stopped herself.

She could feel her throat closing up with unshed tears. She mustn't cry. Not here. Not in front of him. She couldn't show him any weakness. Calm down.

She swallowed and took a quiet breath. "I'm a little confused."

Eyes flashed open. Blue. That same sharp blue that had held Zoey the first time she had met him. She met Sascha's gaze as steadily as she could. The piercing quality about it made her feel just as on edge as it had the night before.

"I would be surprised if you weren't," said Sascha.

He uncrossed his legs and sat halfway up, leaning on his elbows. It was hardly a threatening position, but Zoey still resisted the urge to retreat back into the bathroom.

"What do you want with me?" she asked.

"You needed help."

"I did."

"I helped."

"You did."

Sascha stood. Zoey lifted her chin and put her shoulders back. He was much taller, better muscled than she was. She had no doubt he could overpower her if he wanted, but this time, she had no plans of going down without a fight. She planted herself, settling as steadily on her feet as she could.

He raised his hands, showing open palms. "I'm not here to hurt you."

Zoey narrowed her eyes and set her jaw. Relaxing was not on her itinerary. "How can I know that? Why should I trust you?"

Sascha sighed quietly, and Zoey blinked, confused. His hands dropped back to his sides. Zoey eyed the space between them. Even if she hadn't been hurt, she knew he could close any space between them much more quickly than she could evade him. With her injury . . . one good stumble and she was done for. She stiffened as he tilted his head to one side.

"Zoey, if I were here to kill you, I would have done it last night." An icy kind of horror spread through Zoey's body, and she looked away sharply, making sure to keep him in her peripherals. *Would* he have killed her last night?

"Don't look away like that. It's true, and I don't plan on lying to you about what's happened to you. You want answers. I'll give them to you, regardless of whether or not you like what I say."

Zoey breathed and looked back up. "Then what do *you* want with me? What's going to happen now? Why am I here? Who *are* you? I mean, I only know your name. Nothing else."

Sascha held up a hand. Zoey flinched and eyed him warily, but breathed as he made a calming motion.

"I will answer every question that I can, but to have them rapid fired at me does not make that easy. I want nothing more with you than to help you. You are here because this – being with me – is the safest place for you at the moment. Our next step is to make the trip to a safe house in the town of Bayrischzell, Germany. From Bayrischzell, we will be able to negotiate getting you home –"

Zoey couldn't stop herself from gasping, relief rising through her chest, and clapped a hand against her mouth. This was his second mention of getting her home since she had met him.

She steadied herself, injured leg trembling. "I'm going home?"

Sascha blinked. "You are. But it will take time and careful planning, so please try not to get too excited at the moment. You may need multiple false passports. Those alone will require time – weeks or months – for me to get for you. Getting you home will not be immediate. As for my name, I told you last night. My name is Sascha Sarajevo."

"And that's your real name?" asked Zoey.

"It is the name that I use."

Zoey nodded. Perhaps a straight answer about his name for now was out of the question. A sick kind of doubt settled in her. He could just be leading her on. Creating a merry dance for her to follow, while he worked the same angle as Groper, Bouncer, and Erik. Was he any different?

She tightened her fingers, gripping her shirt sleeves. "So, the only thing you want with me is to get me home?"

"Yes. I have no ulterior motive, except that I want to know you have been reunited with your family. No one should have to go through what you've been through."

"How can I trust you?"

"You can't. You will have to take me at my word. Just as I will have to take you at yours."

Zoey looked away, taking a steadying breath. That wasn't much. But it was all she had. A mutual sense of wariness might be the best she could have hoped for.

She met Sascha's eyes again. "How did you know I was there? My situation? I don't understand."

Sascha shifted. "Primarily, I recognized the men with you. Secondly – and it may sound odd, but it comes with being a man in my position – I get a lot of my information from the dark web. Sources there, though fewer, have a tendency to be more . . . open, with information of all types shared freely amongst certain spheres, and will notify one of things that surface-level news will not. It operates as surface-level news does not. Your kidnapping was one of the things of which I was notified."

That cold shock of horror spread through Zoey's body again, and she rubbed at her collarbones. "People talked about me being kidnapped?"

"Yes."

"And . . . were you sent to come and help me?"

Zoey fought the urge to let her hopes rise. Please, let someone have sent Sascha. He'd mentioned he had a certain position in life. Undercover police? Secret service?

He shook his head once. "No. I did this of my own accord. At personal risk to myself. As soon as I heard that you had been kidnapped, I began keeping my eyes open for you, but it is simply due to luck that I was at de Gaulle Airport in Paris, at the same time as you."

"I – you were in Paris?" asked Zoey. "I don't remember seeing you."

"You wouldn't. I kicked my bag in front of you at the airport and tripped you. I had to be sure of who you were."

"But . . ." Zoey shook her head. "That man had brown hair."

"I never look like myself when I use public transport. I got off the train with you in Nancy as well. I was the old man."

Zoey rocked back on her heels and stared at him. "That was why your eyes looked familiar. I spoke to you."

"And that was what convinced me to follow you."

"Why?" Zoey cringed inwardly. The tremble in her voice was not well hidden.

"I want to help. There is no darker reason. I just want to help you. I know the things that happen to those subjected to crimes like these, and they aren't pretty. You deserve a better life than that."

"You said that my being with you was the safest place for me. Why are you so convinced I'm safe with you? Won't these dark net people know that you're here and what you've done?"

"Please sit down, Zoey," said Sascha, motioning to the bed closest to the window.

Zoey glanced where he had indicated. The bed she had slept in the night before. She paused, not sure if he had given an order or made a request.

"It's not a trick," he said. "That injury you've got can't be easy to bear, and I just think that it might be better if you were seated to hear this. If you would prefer to stand, though, that's fine as well."

Zoey released a quiet, shuddering breath as she made her way to the bed and sat down on it. Sascha sat down across from her, and Zoey pushed herself further back across the mattress, putting more space between them.

Sascha didn't comment on it. "Information is sacred unless made public or placed in a public arena, so, no, no one will know you are with me or I am with you. I am so convinced that you are safe because of my line of work. I'm a hitman. If the more elegant title makes it more palatable, I'm a hirable assassin."

Zoey sat still. Her heart jumped wildly in her chest. A murderer. She was sitting across from a murderer. The lesser of two evils? That was what she had thought last night, wasn't it? God above. How wrong had she been? What had she gotten herself into?

She fumbled a moment before finding her voice. "You're a killer? You kill people for money? That's what hitmen do, isn't it?"

"Yes, and I am willing to use the assets that I have to help you get back to your family. I have no intention of hurting you. Do you understand?"

"You kill people for money, but you're not going to kill me?"

He nodded. "That's right."

"You can't expect me to trust that." Zoey stiffened as he leaned forward and folded his hands together.

"This isn't about trust. I'm not asking you to *trust* me. I'm asking you to let me help you. I have no intention of hurting you or allowing harm to come to you. If I had either intention, I would never have let you see me in Paris. Would you be willing to accept my help, in spite of what I am?"

Zoey looked him up and down, pausing when she reached his eyes. There was an earnestness in them. He had saved her last night. He had taken her out of harm's way. He had shown no outright aggression to her. An alliance with him might not be a bad thing. But the kind of man he was . . .

Breathe. She glanced over her shoulder, out the window and then back at him. He might be her only chance.

She tried to offer a tiny, shaky smile, but the expression wouldn't come. "The hitman feature may take a while to process, but I just don't understand why you're willing to help *me*."

"Because I want to, Zoey. I want to help you. I have a reason, but I'm afraid I can't tell you what it is yet."

Zoey held eye contact with him. Sascha's blue eyes with her own gray ones. They looked oddly concerned. She took a deep breath. Dark web. Her own kidnapping – the orchestrated nature of which she couldn't quite bring herself to ask about yet. Sascha himself. Assassin. Hitman. Murderer. It was a lot to take in. And an assassin wanting to help her for . . . some reason that he had admitted he was hiding. An edge made its way into her chest, and she tightened her jaw. Why? *Why* exactly did he want to help? They didn't know each other. But he was also the only person who had been sympathetic to her over the last few days. He was offering help. Something that, if she was ever going to get home in one piece, she would desperately need. She folded her arms again.

"I want to know something."

"Please."

Zoey looked away, breaking the eye contact between them again. She gingerly stood up and limped to the bedroom window, looking out and taking in the red roofs and the church spires. Would this be the last town she saw? Would this be her last day of freedom? Did she even dare to ask the question lingering on her tongue? She took a breath. The physical distance between them made asking the question easier.

"Are you just going to . . . keep me? Hidden away in some dark room so that no one sees me?"

She flinched and snapped around to face Sascha as she saw him stand up in her peripheral vision. She swallowed, her heart racing. Her hands balled into fists at her sides. She was ready to run, to fight if she had to. Hitman or not, she would put up a fight against him. She was never going to go down without a fight again. Then she processed how he had moved. Out of her way to the door. He motioned to the cleared pathway across the hotel room.

"You are free to leave anytime you would like. I do not recommend it, as there will now be people looking for you and many of them have nefarious intent. Getting back to the United Kingdom without help will be more difficult, but if you want to leave, you are free to go. I will not stop you. I am not your captor, and I never will be. Just know that if you leave, I will not be able to help you anymore."

Zoey glanced at the door. "You wouldn't chase after me?"

"You are not a prisoner, Zoey. If you choose to leave, all that will happen is that I will deny that we ever met, and I would request the same from you. I would ask that you do not look for me, tell anyone that you met me, or tell any authorities that you had contact with me, as any of these courses of action may be to the detriment of us both."

Zoey looked between Sascha and the door. The door meant freedom. The door meant home. But the door also meant exposure to danger. She didn't speak any German, and her French had always been awful – really her worst subject in school. Getting back to England without any money would be impossible. How would she ever cross the English Channel? How would she even *get* to the Channel? Would someone – one of these people from the dark regions of the internet or even someone affiliated with Groper, Bouncer, and Erik – recognize her between here and there? If so, would they kidnap her again? Likely. She swallowed. Sascha. He was willing to help her. He had rescued her last night. Assassin, yes? But he had also saved her life – and if not her life, then her future. He had brought her here. Not safety, not exactly. *He* wasn't safe. But he was a barrier. Something to stand between her and . . . everyone else. Perhaps he really was the lesser of two evils. Zoey narrowed her eyes a fraction and folded her arms.

"How are we going to do this?"

Chapter 10

Sleep hadn't come for Rona. Not true sleep. Only moments of rest in between wakefulness. Time slipped away like fractals of color in a child's kaleidoscope.

Now, exhaustion clawed at her chest, threatening to drag her down if she so much as sat for a moment. She didn't sit. She paced the living room. She made tea. She let it grow cold and brewed it again.

She stood in the kitchen now, hand under the running water as she cleaned her tea mug for the thousandth time since Zoey had vanished from the cameras on the monitor upstairs. The blue mug's slick, ceramic handle felt like a flimsy grounding tool in a world of uncharted terrain.

Right now, Flynn lingered in the doorway like a helpless shadow. Rona almost ignored him, but it was nice to have *someone* with her. She didn't want to face Hailee – who'd almost certainly be up by now. She'd have to be told terrible news all over again. It had been hard enough to tell Hailee the first time that her oldest sister had been kidnapped. At least they'd had some idea of where she was. Now for her to have vanished completely . . . Rona swallowed hard, forcing down the tightness in her throat. Upstairs, the shower turned off, and water hissed in the pipes for a moment more. Rona tensed. Maxwell had returned very early that morning, his black Range Rover in the driveway a bitter reminder that he'd lost Zoey's trail.

"It's going to rain," said Rona, watching the world beyond the window.

The words that left her mouth in a voice that was not her own sounded disgustingly normal. They tasted like sawdust on her tongue. She could have laughed. Rain. What a natural occurrence in a world that had turned sideways and blurred the line of natural and unnatural. Normal was gone. Zoey was gone, and normal had been taken with her. Rona tightened her grip on the mug's handle.

"Rona," said Flynn in an agonizingly soft voice. "It's been days since you've slept properly. You need to rest. Staying awake won't magic Zoey back here."

Rona turned, the mug slipping from her fingers and shattering on the tile floor. She stared at it, feeling somehow as though she'd missed a step coming down the stairs. She *should* have reacted. She *should* have jumped at the sound. But she hadn't. There was only this strangling numbness inside her chest.

Rona swallowed and forced herself to speak. "Neither will going to sleep."

Flynn rubbed his forehead. "Look. At least go sit down and wait for your dad to come downstairs."

Rona stared at the broken pottery on the floor. "Why is this happening?"

Flynn stooped and started picking up the pieces. He sighed hard but didn't reply, as he stood to throw the pieces into the trash bin.

"I wish there was something I could do, Rona, I do," he said gently, brushing off his hands. "But right now, we need your dad."

Rona stared at him. "He hasn't been much use so far."

Flynn lowered his gaze to the floor. "I know."

Rona turned, looking back out the window. A single, brave blackbird hopped across the front lawn, scratching and seeking in the wet grass.

"Not that you want it, but in my defense, I thought I was up against something entirely different."

Rona turned, all sluggishness vanishing at the sound of her father's voice. He leaned in the doorway, black hair still wet. Flynn snapped straight, hands by his sides.

"I'm so –"

"You and I will talk later," said Maxwell, glaring at Flynn as he marched into the kitchen. "Is there tea? I'm tired."

Rona swallowed and took a few steps away from Maxwell as he approached the kitchen counter. "In the pot."

Maxwell pressed the back of his hand against the pottery. "Cold. Make it again."

"I am not a servant!" snapped Rona, her emotions filling the space just under her skin. She could have punched him. To come back here without Zoey, to come back after swearing he could help, it was too much. She stepped up to him, taking back the space she'd given him. Maxwell sighed and pulled down two more blue mugs from the cabinet.

"I said 'make it again', Rona. At the very least, brewing it will give Hailee time to get in here. I don't want to have to repeat myself." He turned to Flynn. "I need you to pull footage of the last few hours. Find out how long he's been on their heels. We don't have much information, but we have to work with what we have."

"Yes, sir," nodded Flynn, reaching behind Maxwell and turning the kettle on.

"When you've done that, I'll –"

Rona smacked one of the mugs off the counter. The second blue casualty of the morning. "Am I invisible?"

Maxwell turned and stared at her, his gray eyes – eyes so like Zoey's – pinned her like a specimen beneath a microscope. "You may as well be."

"You –" started Rona, searching for a fitting insult. But there was no insult she could hurl that would level her father down. Foul. Vile. Pathetic. Useless. But nothing powerful. Nothing that would leave an impact. "I, what?" asked Maxwell as the water began to boil. The side of his mouth pulled up into a smile. Something cruel and vicious. "Go on, Rona. I, what? What do you want to say?"

"I don't think Mum just vanished. I think she left you *on purpose*," hissed Rona, turning on her heel and storming from the kitchen.

A third mug sailed past her ear, stopping her in her tracks as it crashed and shattered on the kitchen's wooden doorframe. A hand seized her upper arm. Rona yelped as Maxwell spun her around and slammed her back hard against the wall. She couldn't move. Her father's eyes could have burned through her.

Lip curling, Maxwell tightened his grip on her arm. "Don't you dare, and I mean *dare*, talk about her. You don't know anything about that."

Rona gaped at him, and her lower lip trembled. She caught movement on the stairs, but she refused to let her eyes so much as flicker away from Maxwell.

"Come now, Maxwell," sighed Charity, long-suffering patience filling her voice. "Throwing things again? And in my home? I thought we'd gotten over this."

Rona didn't breathe as her father's eyes flitted away from her own for a moment. When they made eye contact again, one of his dark brows lifted incrementally. Rona breathed sharply and gave a tiny nod. The tension drained away from Maxwell's expression, and when he turned away, a bright smile had already lit his face.

"Charity. We made some tea. I hope you don't mind. I need you for a moment before we talk to everyone. I'm sorry about the mess. It'll get cleaned up," Maxwell said, meeting her on the bottom step.

In her peripherals, Rona saw Maxwell give her a dark look, and she stiffened. Aside from that, she couldn't move. Her eyes stayed fixed on the scattered pieces of ceramic mug at her feet. She barely registered Charity's three-beat gait as her and Maxwell passed by. The only things that were real were the doorframe pressing into her back and the ghost of Maxwell's grip on her arm. An arm settled around her shoulders, guiding her into the living room and sitting her down on a sofa. Rona moved without resistance. She'd forgotten, in a way. The reasons they never snapped at Maxwell surfaced again. They'd been washed away somehow, lost amongst all the fear of the last few days.

A few minutes later, a glass of water was pressed into her shaking hands. When had they started shaking? Someone's hand was on her shoulder, but Rona could only focus on the wood grain of the table in front of her. She lifted her hand, pinching away tears before they could fall from her eyes.

"What happened?"

Simon. Rona looked up at the sound of his voice. He stood just at the threshold of the living room, poised to move down the hall into the kitchen.

"Family argument," said Flynn from beside her.

Flynn. Rona turned to face him. And in his brown eyes, she saw pity. She dropped her gaze back to the floor, and something in her burned with shame.

"Blackmore family arguments are legendary," said Simon, walking into the living room instead of continuing down the hall to the kitchen. "Are you alright, Rona?"

Rona nodded mutely. Then she shook her head. Her arm burned now where her father – her own father – had grabbed her. She lifted a hand to her mouth and bit her knuckle, trying to steady herself. Flynn's hand slipped from her shoulder. Steady herself before Maxwell –

"Oh, stop it, Rona."

Rona forced herself to swallow and beat back her tears. Clear her eyes and neutralize her expression. She pressed her lips together hard and lifted her gaze to meet her father's as he leaned on the mantelpiece. Hailee slipped into the room like a shadow and sat in silence on Rona's other side.

"I didn't find Zoey," sighed Maxwell.

Rona could have strangled him. All the vitriol from moments ago was gone, replaced with a heaviness that sounded artificial.

"Where is she?" asked Hailee, her brown eyes wide.

Maxwell swallowed. "I don't know. She's vanished. I promise all of you, I will not stop looking for her, and I will be having Flynn stay here to try and work on finding her. For now, there's nothing I can do. I don't know where she is. I –"

Charity stumped forward a step and rested her hand on his forearm. The shadow of a smile swept through Maxwell's eyes. From her peripherals, Rona saw Simon twitch where he sat, a muscle moving somewhere in his jaw. There and gone before Rona was even sure she'd seen it.

"What is it, Maxwell?" Charity asked.

"I know *who* she's with, but that only concerns me all the more."

"Maxwell?" asked Hailee, her voice small. She cleared her throat, but when she spoke, her voice cracked. "Who?"

Maxwell lifted his chin. "His name is Sascha Sarajevo. He's a criminal for hire, and he is exceptional at what he does. Our only option is to wait until Sarajevo plays his hand and exposes where they are."

"Why don't you go after him now?" asked Hailee, a few tears escaping the corners of her eyes.

Maxwell levelled his gaze at her, and Rona saw his eyes harden. Be gentle. Please, for Hailee's sake, be gentle. But Rona knew better. Her father was brutal at the best of times, savage at the worst.

"I believe he will kill her if he feels like he's being tracked. Zoey would not be the youngest person he's killed. She'd be just another number to him. We can't pressure him until he shows his hand."

Rona wanted to launch to her feet, to shout, to storm, to scream. There was no need for him to have said that. But she didn't move, the ghost of his grip on her arm pulsing.

"What are we to do in the meantime?" asked Simon, reaching over and putting a hand on Hailee's shoulder as she turned away, lower lip trembling.

Maxwell's lip curled for a second, before he was able to wipe away the expression. "I will be diverting myself here for some time. I was hoping that just moving Rona and Hailee here would be safe enough for them, but now that Sarajevo is in the mix, I fear I may have been mistaken."

"Why?" asked Rona, her voice smaller and far more hesitant than she would have liked.

Maxwell tilted his head, and he glanced at Charity, who shrugged.

"They'll need to know sooner or later," she said.

He folded his arms, setting his mug of tea on the mantel. "I believe Zoey has been taken by a human trafficking agency as retribution for work I've been doing overseas. I can't afford to be so careless with the two of you."

Rona stared at Maxwell. She could feel how tense Flynn was beside her, his knuckles white where they rested as fists on his thighs. His expression wasn't entirely readable, but if Rona had to wager a guess, she'd have called him furious.

Chapter 11

Hereford was quiet and peaceful. A warm, summer sun streamed down through the branches overhead. Zoey breathed. Home. She was home. She stood stationary in the driveway, studying the house. Her sisters were in there. Home. Family. Relief welled up through Zoey's chest. She rocked forward on the balls of her feet, running up the driveway, loose stones scattering away underfoot. She grinned as she drew closer. Then the screaming began. Rona. Hailee. Screams. They rose to the sky even as Zoey ran. Desperation lashed its claws against her chest, and Zoey extended her stride. Running. Running for home. Running for her family. She had to reach them. Yet, even as she sprinted for them, the driveway grew longer. Each stride she took put her further and further away from them. Darkness began to crush in. Home dissolved into nothingness. Zoey screamed as the driveway crumbled beneath her feet. Darkness reached out for her, grabbing her in its hands and dragging her down.

~ ~ ~ ~ ~ ~

Blood pumping, a gasp strangling her throat, Zoey came awake. Nothing familiar. Foreign. Windows. Car. She was in a car. Unrestrained. No one gripped her shoulder or arm. No handcuffs held her wrists. Dense, dark pine forests outside. Mountains beyond. High, rugged mountains dashed with deep green and soft gray. Distant, jagged peaks clawed at the sky. Moving. She was moving. Being driven somewhere. She grappled for where she was. Where? Forests? Wide, green vales between mountains? Had she ever been anywhere that might look like this? Not in England. Nowhere she had seen in France. Where? Where had Groper and Bouncer moved her to now? But how could they have moved her when they were both dead?

"Zoey. Are you alright?"

Zoey flinched away and looked left. Sascha in the driver's seat. One hand gripping the steering wheel, the other reaching partway across the center console. She shied away, curling into a ball as she pressed hard against the passenger door, and hissed as her quick movement jarred her leg. Pain set her nerve endings on fire, and she covered her mouth to stifle the groan that threatened to escape. Sascha glanced at her, concern flashing once through his blue eyes, then returned his free hand to the steering wheel.

"I'm fine," she squeaked, her voice tight with pain. She took a few deep breaths, exhaling hard. "Where are we?"

"Arriving into Bayrischzell now. We only have about ten minutes left until we reach my safe house."

Zoey turned and looked out the window. She made a concentrated effort to force down her heart rate. The road was narrow and winding, with tree-covered mountains on either side. Afternoon clouds scudded low over the rocky peaks. In the distance, Zoey could see higher mountains, their summits bare and uncapped by trees. Some determined patches of snow clustered in shadowed gullies. The Alps. All she could feel was apprehension. In this foreign place with this foreign man. It wasn't a thought that put her at ease.

She glanced at Sascha from her peripherals and reviewed their conversation from that morning. Assassin. Murderer. The man who had known about her kidnapping. The man who had decided to pull her from Groper and Bouncer's grasps. Now the only person who was able to help her. And she had willingly come with him. Not that she'd had much choice. It was either this or have no chance of ever returning home.

One of Sascha's fingers twitched on the steering wheel, and he pointed ahead. "Bayrischzell. Ever been to Bavaria before?"

Zoey shook her head and looked through the windshield. Ahead of them, the mountain valley opened wide. Nestled in its flat bottom was a small town. A cluster of pale cream buildings with red roofs. A dark, church spire towered above all the other buildings. Against the sunlight, Zoey could see a few solar panels glinting on house roofs. The mountains beyond framed the town, making it seem sheltered. Zoey nearly smiled. It looked like a nice place. Homey. Sweet. *Safe.*

"How did you find this place?" asked Zoey.

"It's off the beaten path. Quiet. Perfect location for a safe house."

"I should have asked earlier, what *is* a safe house?"

"A place that people like me use when we have to lie low for a while. Think of it as a hideout. Good thing is, no one looking for you knows this house exists, and I'm pretty well-versed in covering my tracks. You should be safe here."

Zoey hesitated. "Did you know him – Ewan, I mean?"

"I knew *of* him. The circle I work in is small, and most of the people I know are unpleasant, but that's one of the casualties of my job."

"You've worked with them?"

"I've contracted with his employers in the past, but never had to work directly with him." Sascha shook his head. "Not my area of expertise. I'm an assassin, Zoey, not a trafficker."

"If it's any consolation, you're doing a very good job of kidnapping, as well." Zoey almost bit her tongue as the words left her mouth. It was meant to be some weak attempt at a joke, but what if Sascha thought she was accusing him of kidnapping her? Then Sascha coughed, and Zoey thought that one corner of his mouth lifted a fraction.

"I'm hardly kidnapping you, Zoey. If I am, it comes as a surprise to me."

"I know. I'm sorry."

Zoey met his eyes as he glanced away from the road, and she relaxed as she caught the shadow of a smile.

"You have nothing to apologize for. How's your leg feeling?"

As if on cue, a second stab of pain radiated outward from the wound, and she hissed through her teeth. "It hurts. A lot. I'll need something for it soon. And I ... I may need your help rewrapping it."

"I have some ibuprofen in my bag in the back. I'll get them as soon as we get to the house. They're not prescription painkillers, but a high dosage should take the edge off. Keep taking them for a few days. If you end up needing something stronger, let me know. I also have some narcotics I can give you, but only if you really need them."

Zoey swallowed hard, her throat working against her. "I'm hurting. A lot. I don't like the sight of blood, and I'm . . . I'm worried it's still bleeding."

Sascha paused and nodded. "If it's any comfort, any bleeding should have stopped, but I'll help you change the bandage if you want."

Zoey nodded, then turned her attention back out of the windshield as Sascha turned off the main road onto a narrower, gravel track. Trees closed around them, forming a deep, green tunnel with mostly pines and deciduous trees intermingled.

Beside her, she heard Sascha shift gears. She looked further into the forest. A few boulders were exposed through the leaf litter. Zoey narrowed her eyes. The ground was definitely sloping upward. She rested her head against the seat's headrest.

Her thoughts returned to her family. How long had it been since she'd been abducted? Two days? Three? Time had blurred. There had to be some way that she could contact her sisters. To let them know that she was alive. Rona. She must have been so confused and scared when she couldn't find her outside the club. Was she alright? Then a chill of fear snaked through Zoey's chest as the possibility of others like Groper and Bouncer going after her family. Were they safe? Were they being watched now?

"Here we are," said Sascha.

Zoey looked up, her mind jerking back to reality. Trees had been partially cleared from the area, leaving a fragment of the mountainside flat, bare, and grassy. Enough had been left though, that the space didn't feel exposed. If anything, it felt private. Secluded. Even Bayrischzell below was obscured by the trees. Ahead, was a small, two-story house built in the same style Zoey had seen in Waldkirch – cream walled and red roofed. She could see solar panels glinting on the rooftop here, too. A low, stone wall extended a short distance from one side of the house, and Zoey had a feeling it might be a patio border. A three-car garage stood separate from the house, forming a property barrier. A line of trees bordered the back of the house, an alpine meadow opening up beyond. She took a breath. This place. This was where she was to spend an indeterminable amount of time with Sascha. Would he hold to his promise? Would he help to get her home?

Sascha stopped the car, and Zoey heard the brake ratchet into place. She pushed her door open, standing gingerly, glad that her uninjured leg would be the first to step out. Her bad leg wobbled as she put weight on it, and she hissed as she turned to close the door. A cool breeze rustled the tops of the trees. Zoey inhaled. Clean, mountain air caught deep in her chest.

She paused as Sascha opened the back door and pulled a backpack and a large, black duffel bag from the backseat. She watched him as he locked the car and started toward the house. After the last few days, why should she trust him? Granted, she didn't have much of a choice, and at least he hadn't been cruel to her . . . yet.

Zoey took a slow breath and limped into step a few paces behind him. And suddenly, her heart ached. She recognized the way he walked, the stride and carriage were familiar to her. He walked like a dancer. Light on his feet. Ready to move if he needed to. There was a graceful elegance to his movements.

Zoey gently touched her leg and took note of her own uneven stride. There was no chance of her walking normally in the immediate future, let alone with anything remotely like grace. Tears prickled at the back of her eyes. Was her dancing something that had been stolen forever by one rogue bullet?

Don't think about it. She mustn't.

Sascha paused at the front door, and Zoey quickened her pace. She didn't want him to feel as though he needed to wait for her. Then she realized he was entering a code into the door's security panel.

"Just in case you're ever outside and need to get back in, the code to this house is 74-13-91," said Sascha, punching the digits into a number keypad.

Zoey nodded. "No one else knows the code?"

"Just you and me."

"And no one else knows it's here?"

"Just you, me, and the man who sold it to me."

"Do you live here?" she asked.

Sascha paused and gave her a piercing look. Then he blinked and the expression was gone. "Only sometimes."

Zoey nodded once. After the sharpness in that look he'd given her, she didn't plan to press for more information. She stepped inside the house behind Sascha and looked around as he turned the lights on. This was where she would be living for God only knew how long. Familiarize herself with it. Especially the exits. Just in case. The interior was open plan, the kitchen, living room, and dining room being all one space. The living room had a small fireplace and was bordered from the rest of the house with couches and chairs blanketed in dust covers. The kitchen had a small bar and an island, making it seem larger than it really was. Two closed doors led off from the main floor, and, near the furthest of the closed doors was a set of stairs that ran up to the second floor. Glass doors at the back of the house opened onto a patio, and Zoey could see the outline of distant mountains through a gap in the trees beyond. She tensed and looked over her shoulder as Sascha shut the door behind them. The air smelled stale, as though no one had been here for some time.

"There's a master bedroom on the ground floor, and a guest bedroom upstairs, with its own bathroom. Do you want to be upstairs or down?" asked Sascha.

"It's up to you," said Zoey. She rested her back on the kitchen bar, taking a bit of weight off her injured leg. It throbbed painfully from her injury, while her other leg felt strained after working harder than normal.

"I'd recommend that you take the master bedroom as it's on the ground floor, and, with your leg, going up and down stairs will be no easy task. Though you may feel a bit safer on the second floor. The choice is yours, Zoey."

Zoey folded her arms and watched him, her eyes locking on his. She didn't know what she was looking for. Ulterior motive, perhaps? Sascha held still, and Zoey couldn't help wondering if he was intentionally keeping his gaze steady and soft for her benefit. She weighed his words. Yes, stairs would be difficult, but it would give her a bit more space between them. Was that what she needed right now? It felt like it. She didn't know.

"Second floor, please," said Zoey.

"Alright," nodded Sascha. "I'll drop some things in the master bedroom then we'll get you settled."

Zoey nodded and relaxed a fraction as Sascha picked up his duffel bag from the floor. Her family. She needed to get in touch with them. Somehow. She had to let them know that she was alive. She *had* to.

"This place. Is it safe?" she asked, forcing her words not to shake.

"Perfectly. Or else I wouldn't have brought you here. I'll be going down into the town shortly. What do you need? Clothes, toiletries, anything else?" he asked, straightening with his bag in his hand.

Zoey stopped dead, her thought pattern derailing, as she stared at Sascha. She remembered Bouncer's gesture on the train. He had offered her food then, trying to ensure good behavior. Was that Sascha's game here? What was he doing this for? No person did *this* out of the goodness of their heart. Did anyone ever do anything for sheer goodness? He shifted his weight, turning back to her, and Zoey stood rigid. She couldn't move.

"Zoey?"

She stared at him, not wanting to reply. Just how much was he trying to trick her? What would she owe him at the end of this? She stayed silent and tensed, feeling the pause drag out between them.

"Why?" she asked.

Blunt. The question itself felt as though it barely made sense. But what else could she say? Sascha stood still, and Zoey wondered if he was trying not to make sudden movements.

"I'm asking if you need anything so that you can be comfortable."

"I've asked before, I know, but what do you want from me?" she asked, her voice sharper than she had intended.

Sascha didn't miss a beat. "My answer is the same. Nothing. This isn't an exchange, Zoey. I'm offering to get clothes for you so that you can be comfortable. That's all."

Zoey raised her chin a fraction, not sure how to respond. She tightened the fold of her arms as Sascha dropped his bag and lifted both his hands. Seconds passed as Zoey watched Sascha. He didn't move, his open palms raised to shoulder height in something like a surrender. A shuddering breath caught Zoey's throat as she exhaled.

"Okay."

"You'll be alright here for a few minutes?" he asked.

Zoey nodded. "Yes."

"Alright. Make yourself at home. I'm going to put my things in the bedroom, and then I'll be off."

Zoey didn't respond. She watched as he picked up his bag again and vanished through one of the doors off the living room. She held her position. With a quiet *thud*, the door closed behind Sascha. Zoey stood still. Her feet felt locked in position. She wanted to move, to go to the door, to test if Sascha had somehow locked it. Yet she stayed where she was. Her lower lip trembled. What had she done? What kind of a choice had she made? Her chest felt tight. Weak. As though some resolve was breaking. She'd spent the last few days trying not to cry. Trying not to break apart. Trying not to show any weakness to people she knew would exploit it. But now? She didn't know if holding strength and resolve was helping her or weighing her down.

Slowly, feet moving of their own accord, Zoey moved across the small open space of the kitchen, back to the front door. She pushed the handle down, and the door swung inward. Unlocked. Zoey breathed, a gust of chilled, mountain air filling her lungs. Sascha was telling the truth.

Afternoon sunlight flickered through the trees, turning the leaves and needles golden. Zoey didn't know how long she stood in the threshold of the door, watching the world beyond. It couldn't have been long. Not a prisoner. Sascha wasn't trying to cage her here. She rocked back on her heels. The only thing that kept her here was that she had accepted Sascha's help. The tension in her chest eased, and she took a deep breath. A floorboard creaked some distance behind her, and Zoey spun around sharply. Her leg flared up painfully in response, and she winced. Sascha emerged from the master bedroom, a stack of clothes balanced on one arm, a pill bottle in his other hand.

"You're welcome to my wardrobe until we get some clothes for you. I don't know how much of what I wear will fit you, but something is better than nothing. I'll try and get you some new clothes this evening," said Sascha, setting down the clothes and the pill bottle down on the kitchen bar. "Start taking these. It's just ibuprofen, but it'll help."

"Thank you," said Zoey, stepping back from the door and moving to close it.

"Leave it open. It'll do the house good to get some fresh air in it," said Sascha. Zoey followed his gaze as he darted a glance at the fridge. "There's no food here yet, so while I'm out, I'll pick something up, if that's okay with you?"

Zoey hesitated, not sure if he was asking a question or telling her what he was doing. Silence stretched out between them again. Sascha tilted his head a fraction. A question then.

"Whatever you think is best," she said, walking painfully back through the living room to the kitchen.

"Okay. I'll be off in a moment then."

Zoey paused. Her leg trembled underneath her, and she folded her arms, groaning low in her throat as she shifted her weight to lean on the countertop. The hard edges of Sascha's face softened. His expression was unreadable. Zoey wasn't sure, but she thought she detected some traces of sympathy in his gaze. She couldn't help bristling. The last thing she wanted was pity.

"I won't be long." He pulled a black cell phone from his pocket and held it out. "My other phone's number is in here if you need anything while I'm out."

Zoey blinked at him. Why was he doing this? Just who was he? Those blue eyes shone with a weight all of their own unlike anything she had ever seen before. She didn't take the phone.

"What's to stop me from calling the police?" she asked.

Sascha tilted his head. "Police number's 110. But I have to caution you, Zoey, I don't take too kindly to police. We have a tendency to be diametrically opposed. Besides, do you want police, or do you want a professional? Because I can guarantee you that only one of us can get you out of this."

Zoey swallowed and lowered her gaze to the counter. "Point taken."

"Just stay off the stairs until I get back. I'd rather that I were with you the first time you try going up them." Sascha paused, then set the phone down on the kitchen counter. "There's no password to it. Text me if you need anything."

"Okay."

Awkward. Zoey glanced at the phone, then looked back at Sascha. He gave her a stiff nod and walked out of the front door, leaving it open behind him. Zoey took a breath. She was alone. Completely alone. She didn't know if she was reassured or disconcerted that Sascha hadn't locked or even closed the door. Outside, she heard the car engine start. She turned to look at the phone on the countertop. Slowly, she reached for it and picked it up, weighing it in her hand. It wasn't any Apple or Android product that she recognized. There was no distinguishable mark on it. No brand. No nothing. She tapped the screen twice. *Swipe to unlock.* Zoey dragged one finger upward and unlocked the phone. Black background. There were only six preinstalled apps on the phone. Texting, calling, contacts, calendar, photos and the camera. Zoey tapped the contacts app. Only one contact. S-1. Zoey gave the door a quick glance. That had to be the number to Sascha's other phone. She didn't press it. She moved to the photo app. One photo. A black screen. Zoey figured that was the frame being used for the background. She switched to the texting app. Not a single message had been delivered or sent. She put the phone down. There was nothing. Nothing good. Nothing bad. Nothing she could use to draw any conclusion about Sascha or who he might really be.

Zoey turned, fixing her gaze on the clothes Sascha had left on the bar. Maybe she would feel better once she changed into something clean. But they were Sascha's clothes. She shook her head, turning away from the kitchen and walking to the darkening living room area. She folded her arms. This house. No pictures on the walls. Nothing descript. No character. It was lifeless.

She moved further and opened the back door, stepping out onto the patio. A low, stone wall ran around the perimeter. She breathed and sat down on it. The warmth of the sun still radiated from the stones. Not a single songbird chirped, and the pines were eerily silent. Watching them sway in a gentle breeze, Zoey quickly saw why. An eagle perched on a low branch, its feathers dark against the green pines. Great talons gripped the bough, and, with piercing, yellow eyes, it regarded her over a sharply curving beak. Zoey stared back. Transfixed. She'd never seen a bird quite as big or as dangerous-looking as this. Then, the eagle opened its wings, and, feathers whistling against the air, took off. Zoey watched it disappear over the trees.

She drew her uninjured leg up to her chest and wrapped her arms around her knee. She knew that somewhere beyond those trees, the town of Bayrischzell *existed*. A world away, really. Did the people know that there was an assassin walking among them?

Zoey shook her head, her thoughts turning back to her sisters. She had to contact them. She *had* to. But how?

She looked down at the phone Sascha had left her. It was useless to use it to try calling Hailee or Rona. She'd never memorized their numbers. She could still feel her own phone slipping through her fingers that night at Morceau. How stupid she'd been. Zoey ran a hand through her hair. She felt like a rat caught in a maze. Just when there was a glimmer of hope of finding the way out, she'd round a corner only to find another dead end. She was caught by her own consent, by a man she knew little about, other than he was an assassin. And that was enough.

Chapter 12

The quiet was the most unnerving thing. Zoey sat a few seats away from Sascha at the kitchen bar. She'd taken the pain medicine and changed into the clothes he'd left on the counter for her, just before he'd returned with a bag of clothes in her size, toiletries, and two boxes of take out. The fridge had been stocked with various groceries, three small boxes – black tea, herbal tea, and decaffeinated coffee – took up one small corner of the kitchen counter.

Zoey glanced over at Sascha as he ate, then looked down at her own meal, untouched. She bit back a frustrated sigh. Hunger gnawed at her stomach, but each time she looked down at the food, her appetite died. It was as though she was trying to force down a pile of ashes.

She stole another look at Sascha and froze. Those blue eyes were on her. Weighty, intense, piercing. Zoey blinked at him, opening her mouth and grappling for an explanation. She couldn't help feeling reminded of the eagle's sharp, yellow stare from earlier. No words came, and she closed her mouth.

Sascha put down his fork and turned fully toward her. "It's not poisoned, you know. You *can* eat it."

In spite of everything, a flash of humor sparked in Zoey's chest, and she felt one side of her mouth pull upward. "Were you thinking of poisoning my food?"

Sascha's eyes flashed warm for a second, the expression gone in the next instant. "Poison is a woman's weapon. Not really my style."

His style. The amusement in Zoey's chest died. In the moment of casual conversation, she had almost forgotten what he was. She sighed and adjusted her position to face him.

"I'm not . . . not very hungry. I'm sorry."

He shrugged. "You don't need to apologize for not feeling hungry. After everything that's happened, I can't say I'm surprised. But you need to eat something."

"Later?" she asked, tugging the shirt she was wearing back into place. She hadn't changed into her new clothes yet, and Sascha's were far too big on her.

Internally, Zoey started. Why had she asked? *Why* had the word come out like she was asking for permission? She answered herself in the next instant. Fear. Fear of him. Fear of not knowing what his reaction might be.

"Whenever you like," shrugged Sascha. "I'm not going to force you to do anything. But I advise eating something so that you can take some more ibuprofen for your leg. Over an extended period of time, the dosage you'll need is higher than most would recommend, and it isn't one you'll want to take on an empty stomach."

Zoey nodded and turned to look at the bottle of pills on the counter. Eat something. She needed to. Her body would probably thank her later. She eyed the food again. Some form of meat in a dark sauce, dumplings, and some sort of cabbage salad. She picked up her fork and took a hesitant stab at one of the dumplings. Potato. She chewed it, taking longer than she thought she ever had with food before. Swallowing was like trying to force down a brick. It wasn't that it tasted wrong. It was the act of eating. Living. Existing. Facing the reality of what had happened. Zoey shook her head and put her fork down.

She swallowed and pushed the container of food away. "What do I owe you?"

Sascha blinked. "Pardon?"

"For everything you're doing and have already done. What do I owe you?"

A pause and a head tilt. "You don't. Like I said earlier today, I'm doing this because I want to help you. No other reason."

Zoey nodded. She didn't want to make him repeat anything he'd already said – her father hated repeating himself, and she wasn't sure if Sascha was of the same mind. She didn't want to push any buttons. She changed the subject.

"How old are you?" Zoey swallowed as Sascha paused, and she caught a flash of suspicion in his eyes. It lingered long enough to be a possible warning. "I – I don't want to pry. I was just thinking . . . if we're going to be together for a while, we might as well get to know each other. I'm sorry. I shouldn't have asked."

She looked away and took a breath. The man was an assassin. He lived in secrecy. Of course, he would be wary of giving away information about himself. She fixed her gaze on the faux marble of the bar top. She could feel those blue eyes on her. She understood why any songbirds nearby had been silent earlier.

"Twice," he said.

Zoey looked back up at him. "Pardon?"

Sascha rested his elbows on the bar, the glacial coldness in his eyes thawing. "That's twice you've apologized to me in the last ten minutes."

"Sor –" Zoey bit off the rest of the word.

Sascha made a strange noise in the back of his throat, adjusting the way he sat. Zoey looked at him fully. He was facing her, body language more open. A strand of background trivia that she had learned years ago surfaced in her mind. Her eyes flicked down. One of Sascha's feet pointed in her direction. Zoey hesitated. He was paying attention to her. She didn't know if that was a comforting thought or not.

"Twenty-six."

She looked back up, meeting his gaze. "What?"

"You asked how old I am. I'm twenty-six." Sascha quirked a tiny smile, one corner of his mouth turning upward. "You'll have to forgive my hesitation. I'm not very used to answering questions about myself."

Zoey nodded. She wasn't sure whether to return his smile or not. "I'm twenty."

"I know."

Zoey turned to him, his sentence derailing her. "You know? What do you mean?"

Sascha thumbed his lower lip, then rested a hand on the countertop and pushed away his own box of food. "Let's rewrap your leg. I'll explain as we do."

Zoey hesitated. She was still trying not to think of what lay under the gauze wrappings. Butterfly bandages. Torn muscle and skin. A long, deep gash running diagonal from her knee to the far side of her upper thigh. Lucky. She'd been incredibly lucky. All the luck in the world though, didn't make her feel any better about what she would see when the wrappings around her injury were taken away.

She followed Sascha from the kitchen to the living room where he pulled the dust cover off the couch. Kneeling on the floor, he slid a large, deep drawer out of the coffee table. A first aid kit. Maybe kit wasn't the right term. More of a first aid crate than a kit. On the top layer, she could see rolls of bandage and gauze, tubes of ointment, compresses, disinfectant, alcohol wipes, medical tape, two different kinds of scissors, and a sewing kit. Zoey sat down on the couch nearest him and pulled up her trouser leg, which had already been rolled up several times, exposing the bandages. As she watched him crouch down on the floor and sift through for the items he needed, she wondered if he had ever stumbled into this silent, blank place, injured and in need of help. It wasn't a nice idea, but, somehow, it made him seem more human.

Catching sight of Sascha rocking back on his heels, Zoey snapped out of her morbid thoughts. He'd picked up the bandage scissors. She pressed a hand to her hair and stared at him. Sascha tilted his head and put the scissors down on the coffee table.

"I thought so," he said quietly.

"What?" asked Zoey.

"They cut your hair, didn't they?"

"How did you know?"

"It's one of the easiest ways to change a person's looks," he said, unrolling a section of bandage. "I can't easily rewrap your injury without the scissors though. Are you alright with me using them?"

"Only the bandages?" asked Zoey, cringing as her voice hitched in an unexpected tremble.

"Only the bandages," replied Sascha.

"You won't . . .?" Zoey let her question trail off, not entirely sure what she wanted to say herself.

"I've got very steady hands."

"Okay," nodded Zoey, exhaling a heavy breath. She couldn't help tracking Sascha's movements as he picked the scissors back up.

He paused. "You look worried."

Zoey laughed nervously, trying to cover the insistent trembles in her voice. "I hate the sight of blood."

Sascha nodded. "I understand. Like I said earlier, you shouldn't be bleeding anymore. This wound, by some miracle, was superficial. Tore off skin and some muscle, but nothing more. If you *are* still bleeding, I'll take you to the nearest hospital. I've had injuries like this before myself, Zoey. They don't bleed for long."

Zoey swallowed hard and nodded, fighting to keep the corners of her mouth from trembling. Regardless of what Sascha said, she couldn't fight off the iron talons of fear that threatened to seize her chest. The coolness of Sascha's hand took her by surprise when he rested his palm on her knee, and a quiet yelp escaped Zoey's lips. He took his hand away before the sound had been fully made.

"I'm sorry," said Zoey, covering her mouth and looking away. "I'm sorry."

"You don't need to apologize. If it makes it easier for you, you can hold onto my shoulder. I'll tell you everything I'm doing before I do it."

Zoey nodded but kept her hands where they were. She stiffened, fighting to stay silent, as Sascha rested one hand against her knee again and set the scissors to the bandages. The sound of the metal blades slicing through white wrappings rang like an alarm bell. She drew a short, sharp breath.

"I'm just cutting away the old bandages now. As for knowing your age, it was available online. The same place where your kidnap was discussed."

Zoey heaved a breath through her nose. How he knew all about her – she'd almost forgotten. A grim subject, but she was glad of the distraction all the same. "On this dark web place that you mentioned?"

"Yes. Bandage is about to come off. I'm going to clean the area with alcohol and antibiotic ointment now."

Cold swept through Zoey's entire body, and she locked her gaze on the far wall. Her breath hitched as she felt the dressings fall away. Rubbing alcohol contacted the area, and Zoey groaned low in her throat at the sting. Without thinking about it, one hand shot out, snatching Sascha's shirt in a hard grip. A few tears gathered in the corners of her eyes. Her heart thundered in her chest. She didn't know where to look – anywhere but at Sascha.

"The ointment's done. Now it's just rewrapping, and you'll be finished."

Zoey glanced down in spite of herself. Brown, congealed blood had gathered at the top of her leg. A livid line carved a wide, diagonal cut across her skin. Butterfly bandages barely pinned the separated skin together. Dark blue and purple bruises patterned her thigh. Zoey's vision swam. Her sense of balance faded to nothing, and she swayed where she sat. Nausea gripped her.

Sascha spoke again, his tone light, almost jovial, and he rocked back on his heels. "You were very lucky, you know."

"Do I want to know how?" she asked, the room still spinning.

"If Ewan's gun had misfired to the left or right, he'd have caught you in a much worse place. You'd have ended up either dead or with a shattered kneecap. You're lucky that this injury is as superficial as it is. Miraculously lucky."

Sudden panic rose in Zoey's chest. The brutal reality that she was lucky to still be able to walk struck her in a different way. Fear charged her emotions, and her mind flew to her sisters. If her online information was available, it might lead other people to her sisters. She had to get back to them. Desperation reared its head, and Zoey nearly tore away from Sascha's gentle hands. Everything urged her to scramble to the door, to race back to England regardless of the obstacles. Her leg gave an insistent pang, and reality crashed down on her shoulders. She'd never make it without Sascha's help.

"How *much* do you know about me?" she snapped, the words harsher than she had intended them to be. If Sascha noticed, he gave no indication of it.

He didn't look at her, instead, he wrapped bandages as he spoke. "Zoey Elaine Blackmore, born in Hereford County Hospital on the twenty-seventh of May. Identical but older twin to Rona Belle Blackmore, and oldest sister to Hailee Felicity Blackmore. You stand at 5'6" or 1.65 meters, depending on the country you are measured in. You weigh 124 pounds, 56.2 kilograms, or 8.8 stone, again, dependent on the country. You are listed as having brown hair and gray eyes, have no known allergies to medication, and no current prescriptions. Your phone number, NHS number, and NIN number are also available among the rest of your information. You are a resident of the town of Hereford, though your exact address has been carefully covered.

"You are the oldest daughter of Maxwell and Jodi Blackmore. Your mother vanished when you were younger. You are twenty years old, and you and Rona have finished school. You were accepted to the Royal Conservatoire of Scotland in Glasgow for their dance program, however, you have not yet stated that you will be attending. This is your second application and second acceptance. Your father was recently sent out of country to Spain, shortly after which time, this information became available. Am I wrong?"

If she was breathing, Zoey wasn't aware of it. Her mouth was open, yet she found herself powerless to close it. Clinical. A cold assessment of who she was. And everything was exactly right. Down to the details.

"How –?" Zoey took a heaving breath and swallowed as her voice shuddered. Her fingers tightened on Sascha's shirt. He looked up, eyes guarded. Zoey plunged on, words scrambling. "Why do people need that information about me? Why are they looking for me? For us? For me and my sisters?"

Sascha hesitated, blue eyes narrowing a fraction. "I'll tell you, but not tonight. I think you've been battered enough for a few days, don't you?"

Zoey bristled. "Tell me."

"You're not ready to hear it," said Sascha as he snipped off a piece of medical tape. "I promise, Zoey, I will tell you. But you need some time to process everything that's *happened*."

Anger mounted higher in Zoey's chest, and she felt herself gear up for an argument. She wanted to know *why*. Why this had happened. Why everything had been so organized.

Why and how so many people knew about her and, supposedly, her family. Why men like Groper, Bouncer, and Erik were involved. Then she caught the concern in Sascha's eyes and sighed. Maybe it was best to let it go for tonight. Let her mind rest.

"My sisters . . . is their information out like this as well?"

Sascha's eyes flashed away. "Yes."

"I need to call them," said Zoey, panic rising again and shoving resignation out of the way. Her heart thundered in her chest, beating even faster if that were possible, and she pulled the phone Sascha had given her from her pocket. "I need to warn them that there are people looking for them. That there are people who . . ."

Zoey slowed, catching sight of Sascha's gaze again. There was a request for quiet there. She took a breath, holding the phone in her hand. Almost offering it to him in a silent plea for him to do something.

"I understand your sentiment. I know why you want to talk to them, but don't you think that this is exactly what someone who is seeking you out wants you to do? Call your family? Try to warn them about what might happen?"

"But they're my *family*. They need to know that I'm alive . . . that what happened to me might happen to them."

"Zoey." Sascha's voice was only a fraction sharper this time, but Zoey flinched at it all the same. "You have to disappear. I'm helping you do that. I know how to disappear. When we've thrown the people who've been after you off your scent, we'll contact your family, but not before. Right now, it's not a good idea."

"But . . ." Zoey looked away, taking a deep breath and hearing the way it shuddered in her chest.

He rested a hand on the phone, his fingers only hairs' breadths away from her own. Gently, he pressed her hands down into her lap. "We'll contact them soon, I promise. We'll find a way to get in touch with them, but for now, you need to vanish. You need to give your pursuers no indication of where you are."

Zoey swallowed. "And who are my pursuers? Exactly who are they?"

Sascha's fastened the bandages down with a final strip of medical tape. ". . . I'll tell you. Soon, but not tonight, Zoey. For tonight, try to relax. Try to rest. I know that's difficult, but, like I said, you need to process what's gone on. Your body needs to rest, regardless of how much your mind may disagree."

Closing her eyes, Zoey took a deep breath. How much did Sascha know, and how much was he hiding from her? She lowered her head, looking at the floor. Had she been right to trust him at all? A killer. A murderer. She swallowed and looked back up, doing her best to wipe all expression from her face. Sascha's eyes were still on her, and she studied him, making eye contact. She wondered if there was tension between them, or if she was imagining it. There was a feeling like impending thunder in the room. Those blue eyes flitted away, then returned, the expression in them softer.

"I'm sorry, Zoey," he said. "I'll tell you everything I know soon, but right now the time isn't right."

Zoey blinked at him, then shook her head. "I'm going to bed. It's upstairs, right?"

"It is. Bedsheets and blankets are already on the bed. Do you mind if I follow you up the stairs? Your leg may be . . . unpredictable."

"Do what you want." Tiredness and resignation crashed over Zoey, and she shook her head, her shoulders falling forward. "I don't care."

She pulled away from him and stood up, her leg trembling as it took her weight. She didn't pause to see if Sascha stood up or not. She walked across the living room, heading for the stairs, and found herself taking distinct notice of the unevenness in her gait. Injured, staying with a killer, unable to contact her family. Only days ago, she'd been standing in line to go out clubbing with her sister, stressing over the fact that they'd used their father's card to cover their club entry fee. How inconsequential that seemed now. How was she supposed to get home? Just how much should she trust Sascha? Had she already trusted him too much? What about Rona and Hailee? Were they safe? Were they alright? Her thoughts were interrupted as she reached the stairs, which suddenly looked like a mountain to her. Her leg was already trembling just from crossing the small living room.

"There aren't many of them."

Zoey steeled herself, determination gathering in her chest as she raised her injured leg. A low groan immediately escaped her lips, and she doubled over in pain as soon as her leg took her weight. She snapped a hand out, fumbling to grab the handrail. She squeezed her eyes shut, hissing a breath in through her teeth.

"Are you alright?" asked Sascha.

"I'm fine." Zoey gripped the railing so hard she was sure her knuckles turned white. "Just . . . taking my time."

Her eyes snapped open as Sascha's hand gently touched her elbow. She turned to him, heart hammering in her chest. He leaned down a fraction, eyes full of concern. Zoey swallowed hard and forced herself upright. Her balance was off in a way that it had never been before. Unstable and unpredictable. She looked up the rest of the stairs. The rest of the mountain she had yet to climb.

The trembling words were out of her mouth before she'd realized she was speaking. "I feel like I'm going to fall."

"I won't let you. I'm right behind you."

Zoey nodded once, the movement rigid. She sniffled and started again.

Chapter 13

Mid-morning sunlight turned Zoey's room gentle yellow. She lay on her back on top of the blankets. She'd been so exhausted the night before that she hadn't bothered to so much as pull them down. Nine in the morning, according to the alarm clock next to her bed. She'd woken up twenty minutes ago, but hadn't braved going downstairs yet. After what little Sascha had told her the night before, she wasn't sure she could face it. She wasn't even sure she was ready to hear what else he had to say. Leaving this room, acknowledging what was beyond. That would make all of this real. She didn't want it to be real.

A few faint shadows cast by the pine trees outside danced across the wall, and Zoey found her eyes tracing their movements. Was this how existence with Sascha was going to be? Watching him? Waiting for the other shoe to drop? She pressed her palms hard against her eyes, taking a heavy breath as static danced behind her closed eyelids. She felt powerless. Not as powerless as she had felt with Groper and Bouncer, but powerless still.

There was a dull *thud* from downstairs, and Zoey sprung upright in bed. She hissed and groaned low in her throat as her sudden movement sent a jolt of pain through her thigh, the injury ensuring that it was unforgettable. Gritting her teeth, she looked at the door. The noises in this house were unfamiliar.

She swallowed hard and stood, her leg trembling beneath her. She needed to take some more medicine to take the edge off the pain. She couldn't remember where Sascha had put it the night before. Maybe he'd left it on the kitchen counter, along with her bag of new clothes. It was worth a look.

Setting off at a determined hobble, she crossed to the bedroom door. Hand hovering above the door handle, she hesitated. Would it be locked? Would Sascha want to keep her contained? She pushed on the handle and released a breath as it depressed. Feeling a touch more at ease, she emerged onto the upstairs landing.

Last night, when she'd come upstairs, she'd been too tired to take a proper look around. Now, as she wandered out of her room, she saw that the upstairs loft had a television that stood on a low table, bordered by a narrow bookshelf. Looking over the balcony she had a view of the kitchen, dining room, and larger living room below.

Turning around, Zoey inclined her head and approached the bookshelf. Dictionaries and phrase books for various languages took up one of the top shelves. Those might be helpful. She looked lower and her heart sank. German. Everything was in German. Zoey sighed. Why had she expected anything else? They *were* in Germany. She turned away from the shelf and limped toward the stairs.

The house was quiet – not the empty, echoing quietness of last night, but rather a more comfortable kind of quiet. It felt more lived in, somehow.

At the top of the steps, she almost hesitated but narrowed her eyes instead, determination rising in her chest. She didn't need a babysitter. Gripping the railing, she stepped off, keeping her movements careful. She arrived at the bottom of the stairs unscathed, and a rush of triumph swept through her chest. She smiled to herself in spite of the pain pounding in her leg now.

She looked toward the kitchen, searching for the medicine bottle. She breathed a sigh of relief, spotting it and her bag of new clothes immediately. Both still in the place they had been last night. A bottle of water stood beside the pill bottle, and Zoey felt her chest warm with gratitude. She crossed to the kitchen, and as she cracked open the bottle of water, she saw a handwritten note had been beneath it.

Take two.

-S

Zoey glanced around. Sascha. She hadn't seen him or heard any sign that he was here this morning. She darted a glance out of the kitchen's front-facing window. No car. All she could hear was the low hum of the refrigerator, interrupted by the occasional *thud*, which, now that she was closer, sounded like nothing more nefarious than the house settling. She was alone. Zoey opened the pill bottle and swallowed two, sipping water to wash them down.

Turning, Zoey limped across to the patio doors at the edge of the living room and folded her arms, looking outside to the mountains beyond. Wild and impressive. The Alps.

The mountains in front of her were so very different from the English Pennines. She remembered visiting the Pennines as a young child. She also had vague memories of her mother being there. The bare-headed Pennines with their rounded summits and dark stone couldn't have been more different to the Alps with their jagged, tooth-like peaks and sharp timberlines. A huge bird suddenly took flight from one of the pines outside and wheeled in the open sky beyond the window.

Zoey cocked her head to track the bird's flight. The eagle again? It was certainly big enough. What wouldn't she give to turn into a bird and fly back to her family. To leap ahead of all the careful planning Sascha had promised and simply appear back with her sisters.

She looked toward the front door. Exactly *what* was Sascha planning? Could he really help her? She thumbed the place where her necklace used to be, knowing full well that it wouldn't be there. Finding nothing, she bit a fingernail instead. He wasn't keeping her here. She could leave any time she wanted. But would that be her best option? Sascha still seemed like he would be her best shot at getting home. They needed to talk. This was her second day with him, and she didn't want to be in Germany for months on end. She wanted, she *needed*, to get back to her family.

The sound of a car locking outside startled Zoey out of her thoughts. She turned away from the patio door with her arms folded across her chest as the front door swung open. Sascha paused in the threshold, and Zoey found herself pausing as well.

He pushed the door closed behind himself. "Hello, Zoey." "Hello," she replied. She wanted to say more but was at a loss for exactly what *to* say.

"You got down the stairs alright, I see. Feel up to a walk, too?"

Suspicion reared in Zoey's chest. She inclined her head. "Why?"

"I told you last night that you needed rest. You've had some rest, and now we've got some things we need to talk about," said Sascha. "You've been cooped up. I assumed you'd like to have a look around outside while we talked."

She hesitated. "What about my leg?"

Sascha's eyes flicked down then back to her face. "It's been healing for over twenty-four hours. You should be alright to stretch it out a bit. It'll help rebuild some muscle as well."

Zoey hesitated again, then crossed the open space and fell into uneven step beside Sascha. With each stride, her leg throbbed, determined not to let her forget her injury. Zoey inhaled as she followed Sascha out the front door. The air here smelled sweet and clear. Maybe Sascha was right, maybe fresh air would do her some good. It might at least be a distraction.

"There's a hiking path along there," said Sascha, nodding through the thin line of trees that sheltered the back side of the house.

"Are you sure it's safe?" asked Zoey, hesitating.

"Yes. Over the years, I've taken quite extensive measures to ensure no one else knows this house is here. Like I said last night. Just you, me, and the man who sold it to me. I've also got some technology set up in the woods around us for some extra security."

"Okay," said Zoey, taking a deep breath. She let Sascha take the lead, content to follow behind him.

Sun-silvered clouds hovered in the sky overhead. Deep, forest greens and rich, grass greens that seemed almost too bright and full of life to be real. Delicate wildflowers swayed as the gentlest of breezes swept down from the mountains around them. Jagged, dark mountains reared to the sky on the far side of the valley below, a blue haze settling on their peaks. Rocky boulders jutted out at random intervals through the ground, no rhyme or reason to their patterns.

"The path leads toward Bayrischzell. If you followed it, you'd reach the town in a few hours."

"I somehow doubt I'm up for that long of a walk," grimaced Zoey.

"No. Not today. It's just a nice place for either a long or a short walk. We have lots of things we need to talk about, and I think better when I'm moving. You need to stretch your legs. This kills several birds with one stone," replied Sascha.

He glanced at the tree line, opened his mouth, seemed to stop himself, and closed his mouth again. Zoey waited with bated breath as Sascha walked onward in silence.

Zoey gritted her teeth against a wave of pain as she lengthened her stride to catch him. She couldn't wait anymore. "So . . .?"

"I apologize," he said. "It's difficult to know exactly where to start."

Zoey laughed bitterly, avoiding a rut in the path. "Maybe at the beginning."

"It's not always easy to disentangle where the beginning is," said Sascha. He fell silent, and Zoey felt as though she was balanced on a knife's edge. Soon, in Sascha's next few words, she would know exactly *why* everything had happened.

Sascha cleared his throat and stopped, a strange expression on his face. "They're called OMNI."

Confusion settled on Zoey's shoulders, followed by a touch of anger. Why now, of all times, was he being cryptic. "What? Who's OMNI?"

"The people who are pursuing you. The reason you were taken from your family." Sascha stopped, and Zoey took a steadying breath as he turned to her. "OMNI is the company who organized everything behind your kidnapping. They're a worldwide human trafficking organization specializing in high-profile targets."

Zoey blinked, then she laughed, taking a few steps to catch up to Sascha as he started walking again. "Human traff –? I can't even say it. Me? Trafficked? Is this a joke?"

"No," he replied, a cool, almost annoyed edge in his voice.

"Okay." Zoey stopped short, that touch of anger settling more firmly inside her. It wasn't her fault that this didn't make sense. "There's nothing high-profile about me."

Sascha gave a bark of laughter, loud in its derision, as it seemed to echo off the mountains, ringing back hollow. "Beg pardon?"

"There's nothing high-profile about me. I'm just an ordinary girl from Hereford," said Zoey, her voice sounding stronger than she felt. "I'm as normal as they come."

"Nothing high-profile . . ." Sascha's face darkened. "He hasn't told you, has he?"

Another flare of temper caught in Zoey's chest. They were talking in circles. This was getting them nowhere. "*Who* hasn't told me *what*?"

Sascha shifted his weight. "Your father. Maxwell hasn't told you what he is, has he?"

"He's an accountant. If that's considered high-profile, then that's news to me," said Zoey, stopping. Her leg throbbed and trembled under her.

"Accountant . . ." Sascha shook his head pinched the bridge of his nose. "If your father is an accountant, I'm a priest. Your father is a senior member of the British Special Air Service. The SAS."

Zoey took a step back, shaking her head. "No. That's wrong. You're wrong. No, he's an accountant. He . . . he isn't what you're saying he is. He can't be."

"Has he ever left on short notice for a long time? Has he ever told you where he's actually going? Has he ever told you about a tough day at the office or about any of his clients? Has he ever come back with mysterious injuries or come home looking like he's in pain? Has he ever shared anything with you about what he does?"

Zoey stood still, hands at her sides, Sascha's words crashing into her like hammer blows. Long absences on short notice, check. Vagrancies, double check. Mysterious injuries, Zoey's mind flew to the deep bruise she'd caught under one of his eyes after one of his many trips "to London". Seeming as though he was in pain? It had happened before. Many times. Never sharing anything? Zoey resisted the urge to laugh. Maxwell practically specialized in secrets. But it couldn't be true. This was absurd. Sascha had to have his wires crossed somewhere. Her father? An SAS operative? But . . . it made sense. The answers stacked up, one on top of another.

She locked her jaw and folded her arms. "Tell me what you know."

Sascha blinked once, his expression impassive. "Your father runs a shadow organization within the SAS. Its sole purpose is destroying OMNI. Your father got back from Spain recently, didn't he?"

Zoey nodded, words rising like bile on the back of her tongue. "He did."

Sascha looked out over the mountains. "He shut down one of OMNI's trafficking cells in Spain. Your information and both of your sisters' information became available only a few days later. It's likely that OMNI lashed out as retribution. For them to be able to market the children of someone like Maxwell Blackmore would be a feather in their caps. It's difficult to get a more attractive target than the child of an SAS member. Snatched from under the nose of a member of one of the most renowned service agencies in the world. It's a challenge for them and an irresistible prize for some of their patrons."

Sascha stood still, and Zoey took a step closer. She saw a muscle in his jaw twitch.

"What are you not saying?" she asked. She stood firm as Sascha turned to face her, his eyes more piercing than she had ever seen them.

He drew a sharp breath. "Two weeks ago, you were bought by one of the leaders of OMNI. Five hundred-thousand British pounds were paid for you. That was when Ewan and his companion were sent to collect you. The plan was to take you to a secure location for evaluation and pass you off to your . . . owner. When I saw you at Charles de Gaulle, I knew I had to help you."

"Bought . . . ?" The single syllable rolled off Zoey's tongue on its own. Her words seemed to have taken on a life of their own. "Why? What for?"

Sascha gave her a long look, his lips pressed hard together and a furrow between his brows, then he raised his gaze to look back out over the mountains. Silence fell, broken by the sound of the breeze through distant pine trees and the shriek of an eagle. Queen Anne's Lace bowed in the gentle wind.

"Rescuing you was the right thing to do."

It was his non-answer that finally tipped the balance. The tiny shards of anger that had buried themselves in her chest ignited, burning hot through her veins. All this circular talking. All these secrets and lies she'd been fed all her life. Only to culminate with this – trafficked, *bought*, because of her father's secret double existence. Her temper shattered.

Zoey took a step toward Sascha, and when she spoke, her words tasted like arsenic on her tongue. "Why do you even care? It's not like right and wrong matter to you."

Sascha blinked once, then spoke, his tone even and measured. "Forgive me for choosing to be kind, for once. I was under the impression you needed help."

"I don't want to be your charity case!" she shouted, angry tears welling up at the corners of her eyes. "I am not something for you to keep! To use to make yourself feel better about killing people. You're a *murderer*."

"Yes. I am." Sascha looked her up and down once, then turned on his heel, calling back over his shoulder. "I'll remind you, Zoey, you're hardly being *kept*. You can leave any time you like."

Zoey froze, watching him walk back through the meadow toward the safe house. Any fury, any temper that had burned in her chest, fizzled and died immediately. She couldn't breathe. She'd never get back to England without him. She *needed* him. She took half a running step after him. She'd beg him. Beg for his forgiveness. Say she was sorry. Her left foot hit the ground, and she buckled to one knee, her injury unable to take her own weight. She groaned and pressed one hand hard against her leg, looking up toward the safe house through tear-blurred eyes. Sascha had vanished from sight. What had she done?

Chapter 14

Night had long since fallen. Stars glittered outside the window. Zoey stood in her bedroom in the safe house, her newly-bought clothing folded neatly on the bed. By the time she'd reached the safe house, the car was gone and Sascha with it. The tiny alarm clock at Zoey's bedside displayed the time. 10:58PM. Sascha had been gone for over twelve hours. She swallowed, sitting down heavily on the bed. Was he coming back? She'd risked a look in the master bedroom, and his bag was on the end of the bed. But he owned this place. He could come and go at his own leisure, for days, maybe weeks, at a time if he chose. Zoey pressed the heels of her hands to her eyes, cursing herself. She took a shaky breath, lowered her hands to her lap, and glanced at the phone Sascha had given her. It lay dormant on the wooden nightstand. She could call him. She could text him. But . . . she swallowed. Would he even answer?

God. What had she been thinking? Letting her temper get the best of her like that? She'd driven away not only the person who could help her, but also the person who'd *saved her life*. Zoey drew a low breath and swore quietly. She'd screwed herself. Completely and utterly. How stupid did she have to be? She swore again, the word leaving her mouth in an angry hiss. She glanced at the phone again, then reached for it and used her thumb to unlock it. She tapped Sascha's contact once and started typing a message to him.

I'm sorry.
Her thumb hovered over the "Send" button, then she deleted the message.
I'm so sorry. I shouldn't have said that to you.
Delete.
That was horrible of me, and I'm so sorry. Forgive me?
Delete. She pressed the phone against her mouth and shook her head. She couldn't take back what she'd said to him. No text would ever make it go away. She swallowed. Wasn't

it worth it to try, though? She looked at the screen again. The words wouldn't come. But they had to. She took a breath and started typing.

I'm so sorry. You didn't deserve that. Is there anything I can do to make it up to you?

Before she could overthink enough to delete it for a fourth time, she tapped "Send".

The response was immediate. Too immediate. A tiny exclamation point hovered against the texting screen's black background.

"Message undeliverable".

Zoey's blood ran cold. He was gone. Completely gone. Once again, she was on her own. Even sitting, her knees felt weak. Breathing a little faster, she glanced at the clothes beside her. She didn't even have a backpack for them. She'd have to leave here with only the clothes she wore. She swallowed, her mouth dry. She didn't speak the language. She had no money. No documentation. Nothing.

In a trance, she stood and left her bedroom, still gripping the phone tightly. Carefully, she descended the stairs, crossed the living room, and stepped out through the patio door into the night. It was cold. Cooler than Zoey had imagined it would be for the middle of June. She tilted her head back, scanning the stars overhead. Their indecipherable patterns glimmered down impassively from above.

Even though she hadn't even closed the door to the safe house, she already felt lost. Could she even make it to the town on her injured leg? She lifted the phone again. Maybe she could call the police? Sascha had asked her not to the night before, but he wasn't here anymore. She'd driven him off. A wave of guilt crashed over her. She'd been awful to him. Truly awful.

As she deliberated, a sound caught her attention. Wheels on gravel. Thoughts of police forgotten, Zoey turned. Twin beams of artificial light travelled up the drive. She froze. She'd never get away from the house before the car reached it. Heart thundering, she bolted back inside, slamming and locking the glass door behind her. Erik. Surely, it was Erik. Or someone like him.

She hesitated at the bottom of the stairs. She'd be halfway up by the time the car arrived. Where else could she possibly hide? She turned, ignoring the way her leg burned against the movement. Sascha's bedroom. It was the only other room on this floor. She hobbled across the living room, wrenching the door open and locking it behind her. She clapped a hand over her mouth to cover her labored breathing and listened. Her heart sunk as she heard the front door open. But where could she possibly hide?

In any other situation, it would be ridiculous. But she was desperate. Heart jumping in her chest, she flattened herself onto the floor and wriggled under the bed. One hand still covering her mouth, she stayed very still and listened. Slow, careful footsteps rang on the wood floor. They paused, continued, paused again. They faded out of hearing, and Zoey would have thought they were gone had it not been for the occasional creak of a floorboard upstairs. Then they reappeared, pausing and continuing in an unpredictable rhythm. One that drew gradually closer. Zoey could have sworn her thundering heart would beat through her chest into the floor. From her spot under the bed, she could see a shadow on the far side of the bedroom door.

The doorknob jiggled.

Another eternal pause. The lights beyond the door turned off.

Zoey wanted to bolt. To smash open Sascha's bedroom window and vanish into the night. Her thigh pulsed insistently, reminding her of every reason that she couldn't. Of every reason that had driven her to take refuge beneath the bed.

The door smashed open, crashing into the wall with a devastating bang. Zoey could have sworn she heard plaster crack. She wanted to shut her eyes. But she felt transfixed. Her heart, which had beat so desperately just moments ago, felt as though it had stopped completely. Through the tiny gap between the bed and the floor, she spotted a red laser dot on the floor. Light that did not come from the ceiling strobed in the bathroom. There only for a second, then gone.

Zoey restrained the urge to wail. Why had she cornered herself here? A knee settled on the floor at the edge of the bed. She coiled herself to move. It would be agonizing to try and scramble to her feet, but it might be her only chance. Light flashed into her eyes, utterly dazzling. She moved, rolling out from under the far side of the bed and launching to her feet. Black spots danced in front of her eyes, her night vision utterly disrupted, and her hip collided with the end of the bed. She yelped, staggering, and her injured side buckled.

One hand caught her around the middle, the other steadying her at the shoulder and keeping her upright. Someone spoke softly to her, wrapping their arms around her, but their words didn't register. Zoey thrashed in the hold, flailing, clawing, and snapping at thin air. To get *away*. Panic coursed through her, and she twisted, burying her teeth in a shirt sleeve and latching onto the skin below.

Above her, her holder hissed a sharp inhale through their teeth and fell silent. Zoey stilled, heaving breaths in through her nose.

Her holder spoke quietly again. "It's alright. It's alright. You're fine. You're safe."

Zoey sobbed a breath and pulled away, dropping her bite. Sascha's voice. She folded in his arms, gripping his shirt and squeezing her eyes shut. Tears rose behind her closed eyelids. Dimly, she registered a lamp turning on and Sascha maneuvering her a few steps backward to perch on the edge of his bed. It hardly mattered. She wasn't going to be killed. She wasn't going to be kidnapped again. Sascha had come back. In spite of what she'd said to him, he'd come back.

"I'm sorry. I'm sorry. I'm so sorry," she sobbed, burying her face against his arm. She couldn't quite force herself to let go. "I should never have said that to you. I'm so sorry." How she made herself heard or intelligible between gasps, she wasn't sure. "I tried to text you. Say I was sorry. It didn't go through, and I thought – I thought..."

Above her, she heard Sascha sigh quietly, and one of his hands moved to cradle the back of her head, gently pressing her to his chest.

"I've been driving through the mountains all day. I had the phone off," he said again, his voice quieter this time.

Zoey took a shaking breath and leaned back, tipping her head up. "I'm so sorry."

One side of his mouth lifted in a close-lipped smile. "I can't say I was flattered by what you said. I needed to clear my head, but I'm not going anywhere."

"You said I could leave anytime I wanted," sniffled Zoey. "I thought you wanted me gone."

In the yellow lamplight, realization flitted across Sascha's face. There and gone before it could really even count as an expression. "Ah. I... what I meant was that I wasn't trying to *keep* you here. You're free to leave if you want. You're not a conscience-clearing prize. I suppose my timing could have been slightly better. When I saw you weren't upstairs, I thought the place had been broken into."

Zoey sobbed a tiny, jittery laugh, her head falling forward. She wiped her eyes. "You nearly shot me."

"Yes, I did," replied Sascha, echoing her tiny laugh. "Not exactly what I set out to do when I rescued you. Are you alright?"

"Rattled," nodded Zoey. She swallowed hard and exhaled. "Other than that, I think I'm okay."

"I don't believe you," said Sascha.

Zoey tried to take a deep breath, but a sob stopped her halfway through, and she shook her head. "Terrified."

Sascha gave her a long look, then stepped back, his arms falling away. "Let me make you a cup of tea. That'll help, won't it?"

Zoey stared at him, her chest tight with a rush of gratitude so overwhelming it nearly made her cry again. She couldn't reply. Mutely, she nodded.

Once again, that half smile lifted one side of Sascha's lips. "Join me whenever you're ready."

Sascha stepped away, and his footsteps receded. Zoey took a low, shuddering breath and rested a hand on Sascha's black duvet to try and ground herself. How ridiculous this all seemed now. Sascha hadn't abandoned her – he never had. Never even intended to. Not even after she'd insulted him. Could anyone really have blamed her for thinking that he had, though? And in her panic over him returning, she'd bitten him. She swallowed and stayed still for several more minutes, listening to the kettle boil in the kitchen beyond. As it clicked off, she forced herself to stand, her leg still trembling beneath her, as though slower to recover from the shock than the rest of her body.

Limping into the kitchen, she paused on the far side of the bar. Sascha stood in the kitchen, his shirt sleeve rolled up to his elbow. Red indents stood out on his skin, the bite mark livid. Zoey glanced at the first aid kit in the lounge. Its lid was open, a few bandages spilling haphazardly onto the coffee table. Complete humiliation settled in her stomach as Zoey looked back at Sascha. He swiped the area a few times with an alcohol wipe, then looked up at her.

Impossibly, he smiled, tossing the alcohol wipe into the trash bin. "That's quite a bite you've got. Nearly broke the skin through my shirt."

"Are you alright?" Zoey asked.

"I'll live," said Sascha.

Zoey paused as Sascha slid a rust-colored mug across to her. A teabag floated on the surface, milk swirling around it. Zoey stared into it for a few minutes, not sure what to say now or even if she *should* say anything. She glanced up at Sascha, his hands wrapped around a second deep orange mug. A teabag floated on the surface of his cup, too, but the liquid inside looked bright blue.

"What is that?" she asked, not sure where else to start.

"Butterfly pea flower tea. I never drink caffeine if I can avoid it," replied Sascha.

"Ah," replied Zoey. The kitchen deadened, as though the house, too, was reeling. She swallowed. "Can I ask where you went?"

"Switched out the car," said Sascha, tipping his head toward the driveway. "I had another one stashed in Switzerland."

"Ah," said Zoey again. She looked down at the bar and rubbed at an imaginary piece of grime. "I thought you were Erik. Thought he'd somehow found me."

Sascha paused, the mug halfway to his lips. "Erik? Erik Ardennes?"

Zoey nodded, glad of the distraction. "He was in Paris. At the airport."

Sascha hummed quietly. "That makes sense. I know he's contracted with OMNI at the moment. I suppose they'd want to confirm you'd actually been brought in."

"Are . . . do you still want to help me?" asked Zoey. She couldn't look at Sascha.

"Zoey, look at me."

Slowly, she lifted her eyes to him, much as she didn't want to.

He leaned forward, resting his elbows on the bar. "You got under my skin earlier, I'll admit to that. But nothing's changed. I told you I'd help you, and I will. If we could though, I'd prefer that you ditched the 'murderer' moniker."

"I think I can do that," replied Zoey with a grimace. Then she tightened her fingers around her mug. "This isn't normal, is it?"

"As far as human trafficking goes, no. Nothing about your situation is normal. OMNI only handles high-profile targets."

Zoey looked up. "Do . . . do you think they'll go after my sisters?"

"Eventually, they will," nodded Sascha. "But not right now. OMNI didn't wager on an assassin deciding that he wanted to involve himself. They know someone else got involved, but they don't know that it's me. Not yet. That's enough to stall them for a little while. They can't risk another kidnap, and they know your father will be aware of what's going on now. Our concern is getting you home. And doing it safely. On the drive, I did have some thoughts about getting you home."

Zoey gaped at him, thoughts stumbling to a halt. "Already?"

"They're just ideas at this point, Zoey. The trickiest part is going to be getting you back into England. We're going to have to jump through a lot of hoops."

"What about the British Embassy? Can't they help?"

"We can't use them safely. Going to the embassies or trying to get emergency travel documents, even under a false name, is the kind of thing they're expecting you do to. It'll reveal exactly where you are. The moment the name Zoey Blackmore comes up, they'll be down on you."

"So . . . what do we do?" asked Zoey.

"At the moment? We wait. For you to jump at a chance to get home is what they'll be expecting. You've been out of their hold just about forty-eight hours now. They'll be searching for any woman even roughly matching your description to be trying to cross the channel, get emergency travel documents, or find a way to get a false passport. Be patient. We're going to have to run the long game against OMNI. But there are other things we can work on in the meantime."

"Like what?" she asked.

"You need to heal. I suggest that we lie low until the end of next week. I'm hoping OMNI will not be looking for you so intensely by then. That'll give you a chance for some recovery."

"So, what do we do while we wait for my leg to heal up?" asked Zoey.

Sascha stared at her for a long moment, and Zoey squirmed, uncomfortable under his piercing gaze. He lifted his mug of impossibly blue tea and held it in front of his mouth.

"I meant more than just your leg, Zoey. You've been through a traumatic event. And another unintentional one tonight. You need rest. Let me worry about getting the passport. You focus on trying to feel safe again."

Chapter 15

Almost a week. Rona rested her hands on her hips. Almost a week since Zoey had vanished into thin air. Five days since her kidnappers had been found dead. Rona paused and adjusted her yellow bedspread, smoothing away an imaginary wrinkle.

And in those days, what had she done? She shook her head and let her hand drop to her side. The only productive thing she could think of to do – establish her and Hailee's bedrooms in the annex behind The Roost's main farmhouse.

It seemed as though they were here for the long haul. She supposed that was reason enough to be grateful for small mercies. Each room in the annex was set up as a suite with its own bathroom and large studio bedroom. If nothing else, they had space to themselves.

Maxwell had left a few days earlier, making no promises or statements about when he'd be back. He hadn't mentioned anything about going back to Hereford, and Rona hadn't had the courage to ask him. Listless, she lifted her head, making eye contact with the pink penguin, that leaned against the pillows in the center of her bed. Rona swallowed and scanned the landscape pictures on the pale walls. Wales. All nature pictures of Wales. Just another reminder that they were far from home.

Walking to the window, Rona watched one of The Roost's chickens as it clucked and pecked its way around the courtyard. She sighed and ran her hand over her forehead. It was a bright day. Agonizingly so. Not that the sun was much of a welcome sight. She was still worn out from not getting any sleep earlier in the week. Even with the sleep she did get over the last few days, she still had a lingering headache. And Flynn had been right. Avoiding sleep hadn't brought Zoey back.

"Knock, knock," said Hailee, rapping on the door of Rona's bedroom and stepping inside.

"Hey," said Rona, turning and flashing the saddest excuse for a smile.

"It's very yellow," said Hailee. "I thought you hated the color."

"I do," replied Rona. "It was all I could find in the airing cupboard."

"I'll swap with you. I got a lavender bedspread."

Rona laughed softly, but the expression fell away as quickly as it appeared. She had nothing to say. She wanted to talk. But she didn't know what to say anymore. Not to anyone. Zoey. Stolen away to Europe by a murderer. What hope did she have? Was she still . . . was she still alive?

As though sensing her dour thoughts, Hailee nudged her hard. "Don't look so miserable. I already offered to swap. You don't have to keep yellow sheets forever."

One side of Rona's mouth quirked upward. "Thanks, Hails."

"Hello, hello."

Rona turned, caught somewhere between wariness and a surprise sense of happiness. "Hello, Flynn."

"A little room full of sunshine," he said, stepping inside and looking around. "I like it."

Rona folded her arms. "I hate it."

Flynn faltered for a second, pursed his lips, and nodded. "Quite right, too. It's awful."

A soft rush of laughter cracked Rona's dark mood, and she finally smiled. "What are you doing here?"

"Maxwell told me I needed to stay here twenty-four seven until I'm able to locate your sister on the computer footage. I'm surprised he hasn't chained me to a computer, really. I suppose you're both stuck with me until I find something."

"I meant in my bedroom."

"Oh." He adjusted his glasses. "I'm lonely."

"Sounds like a 'you' problem," said Hailee, leaning against the wall.

"Hailee!" said Rona, not quite able to wipe the small smile from her face. "Sorry, Flynn. I don't think we're very good company, particularly not right now."

"But you're company nonetheless." He returned her smile. "Really, the two of you are the best Blackmore company I've ever had."

Rona exchanged a glance with Hailee and laughed. "That's not exactly a huge compliment, Flynn."

"Touché. How about a walk?" asked Flynn. "We're right on the edge of the Pensychnant Conservation Center. It's a big national park. We could at least look at some of the scenery."

Hailee laughed derisively, but Rona heard a note of genuine humor under her younger sister's harsh tone.

"Walking?" asked Rona. "What do you take us for?"

Flynn grinned and shrugged. "Worth a try."

"Shouldn't you be hanging around Simon and Charity? I mean, you're coworkers, aren't you? Or looking for that mass murderer who has Zoey?" asked Hailee, studying her nails.

"I've got a program sweeping for Zoey. It'll send me an alert on my phone if it picks up her location." Flynn looked away. "Although, I don't think we'll see Sarajevo on the cameras again for some time. I don't think we'd have seen him in the first place if he hadn't wanted to be seen."

Rona's good mood fell away, and outside a cloud crossed in front of the sun. Zoey. All alone with someone like *that*. How much time did she have left?

"How about that walk, Flynn?" said Hailee. Rona felt a rush of gratitude for her younger sister. "I think fresh air would do us a world of good."

~ ~ ~ ~ ~

The meadow behind the safe house was a place that Zoey found herself often. Almost a week had passed since the first time she'd been out here with Sascha. Zoey pinched the bridge of her nose and adjusted the way she sat on one of the exposed boulders. That had been such a disaster. It had taken almost five days for the bitemark on Sascha's forearm to fade away. She opened her eyes and sighed heavily, that familiar tendril of humiliation curling through her stomach.

She looked across the meadow in the direction of the house. Squinting, she could just see the outline of the new car – a black Mercedes – in the driveway through the trees. Sascha was here today. She swallowed hard.

A part of her wished he was off on one of his trips away from the house. It was always so much easier to think when he wasn't here. At least when he wasn't here, she didn't have the embarrassing reminder of hiding under his bed like a scared child, terrified he'd vanished. The memories of biting him and crying in his arms didn't launch to the forefront of her mind when he wasn't here.

A bigger part of her was glad he was here, her sense of shame aside. Beyond their conversation at the kitchen bar, she'd barely been able to look at Sascha, much less talk to him. When they'd spoken, the conversation had been awkward. Too formal and stilted. The truth was, she was lonely. Bitterly, bitterly lonely. Her sisters had made it their business to always be in hers. Now, there was only Sascha, who seemed perfectly content with a distant existence.

Sound overhead caught her attention, and Zoey tensed, ducking on reflex. A rustling branch and a whistle of heavy wings later, and the eagle soared out of the trees, only feet above her. Was it the same one she'd been seeing over the last few days? For a moment, Zoey watched it. It tilted its wings, skimming low over the grass, then banked and turned upward, rising over the safe house and into the open sky.

Zoey lowered her gaze and paused as she caught sight of Sascha between the house and the garage. He was too far away to make out any details, but he was walking with a sense of purpose. Zoey flushed immediately and looked down. She couldn't help feeling torn. She wanted to stay out here – away from Sascha and pretend she'd never sobbed against his chest. But another part of her screamed for company. For companionship. She swallowed, her two desires warring with each other. Then she looked toward the safe house again. Staying forcibly lonely like this was senseless.

Taking a deep breath, Zoey stood and crossed the space between herself and the edge of the meadow. She could swallow her embarrassment. She'd have to if she was going to be staying with him for an indeterminable amount of time.

She rounded the corner into the open door of the garage. She'd wondered but never asked why he didn't park the car in here. She leaned against the doorframe. The answer to her unasked question made sense now.

A balance beam and pommel horse took up a fair amount of floor space, flanked on the far side by a weightlifting rack and pull-up bars. In one corner, a punching bag hung from the ceiling. The place was a basic gym. Zoey raised her gaze. Sascha was halfway back to the door, a rolled-up mat in one hand. His other hand lowered slowly back to his side, empty.

Sascha's shoulders relaxed, and he gave her a small smile. "Hello, Zoey."

"Hey." Zoey hesitated just outside the garage, trying to return his smile, but only managing a grimace. She nodded at the mat in his hands. "What are you doing?"

"It's a nice day. I thought I'd go out on the patio and meditate for a bit. Want to join in?"

Zoey laughed. She hadn't meant to. The sound slipped out of its own accord. "You meditate?"

Sascha grinned, and the expression seemed to light up his face, accentuating his sharp features. "You say that like it's a bad thing. Grab a mat. There should be a few extras on the far end of the workbench."

"It's not a bad thing," said Zoey, moving into the garage and ducking down to pick up one of the exercise mats and banging it on the floor to dislodge any spiders that may have taken refuge in it. "It's just a surprise, I mean, same as your butterfly tea. Not something most people expect assassins would do, you know? Never really think about what they do in their downtime."

"Well, if I had no downtime, I'd certainly get a lot done, but it'd get boring after a while. Then again, I suppose hobbies aren't the first thing people think of when they think of someone like me," said Sascha.

"That doesn't seem to bother you," replied Zoey, slipping into step beside him.

"I don't really concern myself with other people. I don't normally give them time to form an opinion of me."

Zoey gave a dry laugh, trying not to think of the implications behind his words. An assassin Sascha might be, but he hadn't shown her any aggression, outward or implied. He'd been nothing but kind. Gentle, even. She followed him back to the patio, on the mountain-facing side of the house, rolled out her own mat on the tiles, and sat down. Overhead, the sun was bright and warm. The only shadows cast on the patio were made by the garden table and chairs a short distance away.

"Have a good morning?" asked Sascha, settling down beside her. "Get up to much?"

A stab at conversation. In all their meager conversations, he hadn't brought up the incident from the other day. Zoey felt herself smile, and she wondered for the first time if she wasn't the only one feeling awkward and wanting some company.

"Saw an eagle. At least, I think it was an eagle," she replied, trying to fold her legs into a comfortable position. "It was definitely big."

"Oh? Baldr and Morana must still be here. Good. I'll have to keep my eyes open for them."

Zoey raised an eyebrow, totally derailed. "Baldr and Morana?"

Sascha paused, then he offered a small but warm smile. "They're golden eagles. They've lived in the trees around this place since I bought it. I think they're a mated pair. Did you know eagles mate for life?"

"You named them," said Zoey, unsure herself whether she'd meant what she'd said as a question or not. She decided to press him a bit. "Why?"

"Why not? Powerful birds. They deserve powerful names," said Sascha, tipping his head back and scanning the sky.

"You . . ." started Zoey. She cleared her throat and started again. "You like eagles?"

Sascha froze for a split second, then smiled in a way that seemed ever so slightly melancholy. "Yeah. Probably a favorite animal if I had to choose one."

Zoey stared at him for a long moment, and, in spite of sitting on the ground, she felt caught off balance somehow and didn't know how to respond. She cleared her throat and changed the subject. "So why meditation?"

"Lots of reasons. It gives me an opportunity to measure my pulse and heart rate. Raises my awareness. Helps me cope with boredom when I have to be in one place for a long time. Helps me relax."

"I suppose I see where you're coming from," replied Zoey, adjusting the way she sat. She swallowed and hoped Sascha wouldn't be offended by what she was about to say. "I've been struggling with boredom myself lately."

"You're bored?" asked Sascha.

Zoey opened her mouth, breathing in to reply, then her shoulders fell forward. "No. I don't know why I said that. I'm lonely. I'm used to having two pretty loud people around me and having a lot going on. This is, well, it's almost eerie."

She leaned forward, plucking at a few strands of grass growing at the base of the stone wall. She nodded and turned to him, freezing under his gaze. She swallowed and an unexpected tremble ran up her back. There was something terribly piercing in his eyes that made her feel raw and vulnerable. As though his sharp eyes saw more than he let on. Then he blinked, and the expression was gone.

"You should have told me," Sascha replied. "There's not much I can do about being your only company, but I can try and be around more. If you'll have me."

"If I'll . . ." Zoey blinked at him. "I'd appreciate the company. But I don't want to intrude or make you feel awkward. Like you were nannying me or something."

"Luckily for you, I discarded my sense of shame years ago. And please, intrude as much as you like." Sascha's gaze turned back to the mountains. "It might help us get to know each other a bit better if you did."

"You already know everything about me, though," said Zoey.

Sascha scoffed and looked back at her. "No, I don't. I know your information. I know facts. I don't know *you*. In the future, there may come times where we have to trust each other. It would be easier if we knew each other on a personal level."

Zoey met Sascha's eyes again. There was a softening to the edge in them now. A smile pulled at her lips. She wasn't sure, but it sounded as though Sascha was trying to open up to her, as if he was becoming comfortable around her. Something in that resonated with her, and suddenly, she didn't feel quite so vulnerable.

She swallowed, embarrassment flushing her face. "Are we . . . are we good? After the other night?"

He paused, head tilted. "Zoey."

"Yeah?"

"Relax, alright? I might be an assassin, and I know that sets you on edge. But I'm not here to hurt you, and I promise you, I will not bring that night up. You *are* safe with me. Please, believe me when I say this."

Zoey watched him close his eyes, the rigid line of his shoulders softening as he took a deep breath. Had her embarrassment, her uncertainty around him been that obvious? She looked away and settled her line of sight on the mountains as well. She wanted to believe him. A warmth spread through her. One that had nothing to do with the sun overhead. It washed over her like warm bathwater and came to rest somewhere in her chest. She inhaled, breathing in the cool, alpine air, and some tension rolled out of her shoulders. For the first time since before she had gone to the Morceau Nightclub with Rona, she felt . . . safe. A smile touched Zoey's lips and she breathed. Maybe a tiny part of her *did* believe him.

In that moment, she resolved herself to try and get a better measure of him – to try and get to know him. It would be nicer to understand him rather than to simply coexist with him like she had been doing. For all that he was, maybe there was a friend to be made in him, rather than just an ally.

With Sascha's eyes closed, it was easy for Zoey to study him. His sharp features softened under the afternoon sun. His breathing sounded relaxed and slow. It was hard to imagine that he was anything other than this, a quiet man relaxing on an equally quiet hillside.

Stillness fell. Zoey tilted her head back, content to drink in the moment. It wasn't silence though, not really. Wind shifted the leaves and pine needles in the trees. In the apparent absence of Baldr and Morana, songbirds chirped, and undergrowth shuffled with the movements of small animals. This was peace.

~ ~ ~ ~ ~

Zoey reached out to catch the door as she followed Sascha back into the safe house. It wasn't until her hand came in contact with Sascha's that she realized he'd been holding the door open for her. The warmth of the touch, combined with his kindness, spread upward, expanding in her chest.

"Thanks," she said, feeling self-conscious.

Sascha nodded. "Hungry?"

Zoey balked. Food wasn't something she'd given much thought to lately, and her appetite had only just started to make a reappearance.

"I'm not sure," she replied, internally groaning at the wavering quality in her own voice.

"I can make something," said Sascha. "Want to help?"

Zoey paused, having already taken a few unsteady steps toward the stairs. It was rather ungrateful for her to expect him to make food for her and not help. No. It wasn't. It was *totally* ungrateful. Besides, she'd just made the resolution to get to know him better.

"Yeah, I'll help," said Zoey, shuffling to the kitchen.

Sascha paused where he stood at the sink, washing his hands. A tiny smile flitted across his face.

"Great."

"What are you thinking of having?" Zoey asked, resting against the kitchen bar across from him.

"Salad? Quick and easy."

"Sounds good," nodded Zoey.

She looked up as metal rattled against metal, and her heart skipped a beat as Sascha pulled a long knife from one of the kitchen drawers. She took half a step backwards. Sascha paused, then tossed the knife into the air and caught it by the blade, offering it to her handle first.

"There's a head of lettuce in the fridge."

Zoey reached for the knife, aware of how skittish her movements must look, but she offered Sascha a shaky smile as she took it.

Chapter 16

Breathing deeply, Rona couldn't help but appreciate the cool, salt tang in the air. Over the last few – how long had it been now? Days? A week? Over the last however long, she'd found herself and Hailee spending more time with Flynn and Simon. They were better company than Charity, who was infinitely less sociable and holed herself up in her office for hours most days.

In one direction, gentle waves rolled in to the sand and stone covered beach, curling down as they receded. Walks on Conwy Bay's rocky shoreline had become a part of daily life. The beach wasn't far from The Roost – within walking distance. Rona couldn't say that she disliked it. Walking was something to help occupy her mind, and that was something for which she was grateful. She turned, looking down the shore for Hailee, Simon, and Flynn. A smile settled on her lips as she spotted them. She watched Simon point to a cluster of wheeling seagulls overhead, as he offered a bag of crackers, she assumed, to Hailee. One by one, they tossed them into the air. Even from her distance, Rona could see the bright grin on Hailee's face.

Her own smile faded a moment later. Would it have killed Maxwell to do this with them? Flynn split off from Simon and Hailee and approached her. Rona nodded at him as he neared. She still wasn't sure how to take him. She didn't trust him – he worked for her father. How could she possibly trust him? But she liked him. Perhaps appreciated him would have been the better term. In any event, she enjoyed his company. Enjoyed it in the same way she enjoyed Simon's. She couldn't help feeling a little sorry for him, though. He had to feel as cast adrift as she and Hailee did. After all, he'd been ordered to stay here, too, until Maxwell said he could leave. It was just as unfair to him as it was to them.

"What?" asked Rona when Flynn was within hearing distance. "Not enjoying the seagull and cracker party?"

"No, I'm just not keen on seagull shi –"

The sound of Hailee squealing further down the beach cut off the rest of Flynn's sentence. Rona laughed, watching her sister and Simon scramble away from the circling birds. Hailee rid herself of the remaining crackers, hurling them onto the sand. The gulls immediately descended.

"Case in point," said Flynn, laughing and adjusting his glasses.

"Why do you think I'm all the way over here," grinned Rona. "Any updates?"

"In the last half hour?" Flynn gave her a sympathetic smile. "No, I'm afraid not."

"I just wish I could be over there," said Rona, turning to look at the sea. "Even just to pretend I was doing something. Has Maxwell sent anyone at all to look for her?"

Flynn shook his head. "Not yet. He's waiting for her to come back onto the radar again. There's no sense in plopping someone down in France. It'd be like looking for a needle in a haystack. Truth is, she could be anywhere in Europe by now. Or out of it."

Rona sighed, the beach afternoon losing its color. "That's true. What's the situation with the Sarajevo guy? I understand that he's some assassin. Thing is, I've never seen Maxwell react like that."

Flynn adjusted his glasses again and swallowed. "Sarajevo's dangerous. He's not just 'some assassin'. The guy's a professional. Maxwell's tried to have him brought into custody several times, but he's got a knack for slipping through everyone's fingers. But the actual connection between Maxwell and Sarajevo, I honestly don't understand it. I agree with you. Maxwell looked worried. I wish I had a better answer for you."

"I bet Charity knows more," mused Rona, more to herself than to Flynn.

"You're probably right on that count. They've known each other a long time."

"Are her and Maxwell . . . you know? I saw the way she looked at him the other day, and all that touching? It's weird."

Flynn laughed. "I don't ask."

"You should," grinned Rona. "I'd like to know."

"I would, but I'd actually like to keep my job."

"She's married to Simon, right?" asked Rona.

"In theory. That might be a sham marriage though. They both used to work for him. Who knows?"

Rona shuddered. "Gross."

"You were the one who put it into the world," said Flynn.

"Yeah, I wish I hadn't now."

Rona took another deep breath of sea air and turned back to watch the waves roll in. A few strands of her hair lifted in the breeze.

"You know you're facing toward the Hebrides, not France, right?" said Flynn.

"You know you're interrupting my wistful and thoughtful moment, right?" Rona shot back, turning with an amused scowl.

Flynn laughed, and Rona looked back at the sea, an odd, unnamable warmth settling in her chest.

~ ~ ~ ~ ~

It had gotten easier. Zoey had to admit that much to herself. The first few days she had to force herself to leave her bedroom, humiliation and anxiety still clawing at her. When all she'd really wanted to do was hide and be alone. Part of her still did. Part of her, though, a bigger part, was glad of Sascha's company. He was quiet and unobtrusive. As respectful of her space as she tried to be of his. The more she was around him, the easier his company became.

Now, she passed him some of the dirty silverware from dinner.

"I can help if you want," she said. "I might still be limping, but I've got two hands."

Sascha offered a tiny smile. If he was surprised by her asking, he didn't show it. "That would be great. I'll wash, you dry?"

"Sure," nodded Zoey, taking a clean fork from him.

It was painfully domestic, but there was something in the act of washing, drying, and putting away silverware and plates that was familiar. Habitual. Zoey breathed and felt some tension roll out of her shoulders. She'd done this countless times with Hailee and Rona. She paused in front of the kitchen window and gingerly rubbed her thigh, the dishtowel still in her hands. Her leg protested at movement, but that was gradually easing.

Outside, rainclouds had rolled in, darkening the evening sky. Bright white lightning flashed across the sky, and Zoey grinned. She stared out of the window, transfixed. Thunder rumbled, low and menacing, a few seconds after the lightning. Silverware clattered in the metal sink, and Sascha swore quietly.

Zoey turned. "You okay?"

"Yeah," replied Sascha, running his thumb under cold water. "Just cut myself with a knife."

"This from the man who tosses knives and catches them by the blade. It's like this was inevitable," said Zoey, keeping her tone light and teasing. She sobered a second later. "Seriously, do you need anything for it?"

"That's kind of you, but, no," laughed Sascha, turning off the water, drying his hands, and pressing a paper towel to his thumb. "I think I'll live. Weather's turned nasty."

If she hadn't spent the last few days listening to only Sascha's voice, she'd have missed what she heard in it. His tone shifted ever so slightly, inflected by something Zoey only knew as wariness.

"Looks like it. I've always liked storms, though," said Zoey, turning back to the window and grinning as lightning split the sky white again.

Sascha hummed and stood just behind her shoulder. "Well, that puts an end to our evening walk, I suppose."

"I think you might be right," replied Zoey as another flash of lightning tore across the sky.

Sascha inhaled sharply and took a step back from the window, his shoulders square and tense. There it was again. That wariness. Evident in the way he moved. Zoey tilted her head and pressed her lips together. Sascha hadn't reacted poorly to any question she'd thrown in his direction yet. She took the plunge.

"You're afraid of storms, aren't you?"

Sascha paused and tilted his head a fraction. An expression flashed through his eyes. Something that was almost, *almost*, offended. But not quite. Another rumble of thunder broke the quiet.

"I wouldn't say afraid necessarily, but I would hardly say I'm fond of this kind of weather," he replied.

Zoey gave him a small smile. She tried to keep any pity out of it. She didn't want him to feel as though she was patronizing him. She couldn't help but appreciate his vulnerability. Her leg gave an insistent throb, the hurt muscles protesting use. She walked across the kitchen to the bar; her steps more even than they had been just a few days prior. She leaned on the bar and propped her leg on one of the chairs, breathing heavily and taking pressure off the muscles.

"Any reason why?" she asked.

Sascha paused and glanced at the window. "The sound can sometimes be overwhelming. Lightning too, but I've never found that as troubling as thunder."

Zoey followed his gaze. She'd never really considered Sascha being afraid of anything. He was an assassin. He killed people. He wasn't the kind of person who had fears. Sometimes it was easy to forget that Sascha was human, too. She shifted her weight, and another growl of thunder followed a lightning flash. Sascha went still, narrowed eyes glaring out the window, a small furrow between his brows.

"Want to watch a film?" Zoey asked. "It'll be fun."

Sascha turned and stared at her, and another rumble of thunder snarled through the air outside. A small smile pulled at the corners of his mouth.

"I think that's a good idea."

"Great!" said Zoey. "But you'll have to pick it. I can't read any of the titles."

Sascha smiled fully and shook his head. Some of the tension eased out of his shoulders, and Zoey couldn't help but feel a rush of success.

Zoey flashed a quick smile at him and crossed to the stairs, hissing slightly as her leg panged. She tried to ignore Sascha shadowing her in silence. His habitual quiet still unsettled her a bit. Rona and Hailee were notoriously loud. Sascha, the polar opposite. At the top of the stairs, she walked to the couch and sat down on the arm.

"Any preferences?" asked Sascha, kneeling at the television stand.

"Nothing with clowns," said Zoey.

"Clowns?" asked Sascha, pausing and looking over his shoulder.

"Hey, you don't like storms, I don't like clowns. I don't make the rules."

"So not this?" he asked, holding up a DVD case with a snaggle-toothed clown holding a hatchet on the front cover.

Zoey grabbed a throw pillow and launched it at him, realizing after it had left her hand what she'd done. Her blood went cold. She'd just thrown something at Sascha. Thrown it at him like he'd been Rona or Hailee. Like he wasn't an assassin. Like she wasn't at his mercy. Like he couldn't kill at a moment's notice.

He caught the pillow midair and dropped it to the floor with a low laugh. He turned back to her with a smile. Zoey couldn't quite breathe, and she saw his smile falter. Maybe totally relaxing around him would be a little tougher than she thought. She looked down at her hands. From his position near the television stand, Sascha cleared his throat, and Zoey looked back up at him, forcing herself manually to breathe.

"You can put your blood back in your face, Zoey." He hesitated then firmed his jaw. "I was an older brother once."

Zoey opened her mouth to reply but couldn't quite form words. She swallowed and tried again. "I'm sor–"

The pillow sailed back across the small room and hit her squarely in the chest, and Zoey rolled onto the couch seat, laughing in relief. Immense relief. She clutched the pillow to her chest as she sat up, using it to quiet the tremors in her hands. Not angry. Sascha wasn't angry. He'd laughed.

"How about this?" asked Sascha, pulling another DVD from one of the shelves beside the television.

Zoey smiled a little shakily, recognizing the cover even if she couldn't read the title. A ballet horror film.

"Absolutely," she said, her heart rate slowing back down. "What's a film like that doing here?"

"Just because I'm a criminal doesn't mean I don't like watching the occasional film," said Sascha, turning the television on and raising the volume. "I'm human, too."

"Sure, you are," replied Zoey, laughing nervously as she propped one foot up on the table.

Sascha sat down on the far side of the couch, and the film's opening titles started across the screen. Outside, the thunder rumbled again, more muted now, the sounds getting lost in the on-screen music. Zoey looked at him, a question still at the front of her mind.

"Older brother?" she asked.

Sascha smiled, the expression tinged with a hint of bitterness. "I was the middle child, actually. Two sisters. One older, one younger."

"Do you talk much to them?"

"I'd need a Ouija board."

Zoey groaned aloud and buried her face in her hands. Foot meet mouth. "Sascha, I'm so sorry. I don't know what's wrong with me. I –"

She looked up as his hand settled on her shoulder, and he squeezed gently.

"Relax." His hand slid off her shoulder and he sat upright again. "I *have* got a sense of humor. You don't need to walk on eggshells. Not with me. Okay?"

Zoey swallowed and took a slow breath. "Okay."

"I never asked," said Sascha, propping both feet on the coffee table and crossing his ankles. "Why didn't you accept the offer from the Royal Conservatoire of Scotland? You still dance, don't you?"

Zoey laughed without humor and sighed with a heaviness she hadn't expected. "I still do. Or did until . . . this."

"Your leg."

Zoey nodded. "I don't know if I'll ever have the same range of motion ever again. Or if the muscles will ever recover properly."

"They will."

"You sound very confident," said Zoey, turning to face Sascha.

Sascha smiled, propping his chin in one hand. "I've been shot before, Zoey. A lot of it is a matter of reconditioning the muscles. It's not going to be quick, but you'll get there eventually."

"I hope you're right," sighed Zoey.

"You didn't answer."

"Hm? Oh, about the Royal Conservatoire?"

Sascha nodded, and Zoey sighed again, the sound heavier this time. She felt it down in her chest.

"It wasn't the right time." Zoey laughed in spite of herself as Sascha raised one eyebrow. "What?"

"That's a flimsy excuse if I ever heard one. What really stopped you?"

Zoey looked back at the television, watching the film but taking in none of it. "Maxwell. My dad. He wanted me to live at home until Hailee was old enough to look after herself. It was . . . it was the worst argument we'd ever had. He vanished for weeks. Threatened to cut all of us off financially. I worked at a shop in Hereford, but there was no way I could support us all on my own. I told Rona she should go to university without me, but she wouldn't. So, we both stayed. It's really not a big issue. It's just a couple of gap years."

"What do *you* want to do?"

Zoey blinked at him, opening her mouth and closing it again. She couldn't remember the last time someone had asked her what she wanted.

"I want to go. I want to go to university, to Scotland, more than I can say. Anything to get away from Hereford. Not my sisters, just that house. But I don't know how many more times I can apply before they deny me or before I get too old for their program."

"Why don't you just go? Hang the consequences."

Zoey laughed. "I can't abandon Hailee like that, and knowing Maxwell, he'd come after me and drag me back anyway."

"Kicking and screaming, I'd hope."

"Of course. I've got some experience with being kidnapped now. I think I've learned a bit from it." Zoey paused as Sascha chuckled softly, then she sighed, her own humor fading. "Hailee's only fourteen. She can't support herself at all. At least not for the next few years. And I . . . I won't leave her like that. Maxwell made sure I knew exactly how vulnerable Hailee would be without me or Rona. I would never have left her or Rona if, you know, *this* hadn't happened."

"That's impressively manipulative of your father."

"Yeah. He's good at that," said Zoey, leaning back against the couch cushions.

She glanced at Sascha from her peripherals. He looked focused on the film now, but she caught a pensive kind of look lingering around his eyes. She couldn't help but wonder if he knew her father. He'd said that his circle within Europe was small, and if Maxwell was what Sascha claimed, it was possible that they'd brushed shoulders at some point. Zoey thumbed the place where her necklace used to be. She wasn't entirely sure if she wanted to know.

A small smile crossed her lips, and she relaxed, tension rolling out of her shoulders as she moved her leg from the table and onto the couch cushion.

Sascha had asked her what *she* wanted. A warmth settled between her ribs. Sascha, in spite of being an assassin, was, and there was no other word for it, nice. He was good company and good conversation. Funny, even. Not a threat to her, she reminded herself. The last of the tension eased out of her shoulders for what felt like the first time in weeks. She, and she couldn't believe she was thinking this, enjoyed being around him. His eyes caught hers, and he returned her tiny smile. Zoey looked back at the television, attention finally settling on the film. The warm sensation in her chest only intensified.

Chapter 17

Blackness pressed in. Suffocating and monstrous in its totality. Only two flickering candles broke the darkness. Zoey lifted her head from the asphalt, glass shards dug into her cheek, sticky with blood. Not candles, she realized, staring at the lights, but headlights. Headlights shining from a sky full of distant stars. She inhaled. Choking car fumes seized her senses. France. She was back in France. Had she ever left? Zoey groped around in the darkness, stumbling as she stood up. She was injured. She knew that much. But her injuries mattered little to her. The headlights ahead of her grew brighter, illuminating the stretch of road where she stood. The very lights themselves seemed to be ringed with blue. Behind her, she could still hear the ruin of the car she had ridden in with Groper and Bouncer hissing as gasses and fluids escaped it.

The headlights brightened again, and Zoey saw three silhouettes walking through the beams of light. Even in shadow, she knew them. All of them. First came Sascha, his poignant, elegant stride unmistakable. Matching him step for step, energetic and determined... Zoey yelped and ran forward in her dream, all thoughts of injury fleeing her mind. Beside Sascha was Rona. Coming for her. Sascha was bringing Rona to her. Zoey ran toward them, but they grew no closer. The expanse between them yawned wide, unnatural night flooding the road. From behind, one shot rang through the night like lightning splitting an ancient tree. Zoey slid to a halt. Sascha crumpled like a marionette whose strings had been cut. She spun to face the ruined car. Bouncer lay on the ground next to the vehicle now, eyes wide and staring sightlessly into the blackness overhead. Little more than a shadow himself, Erik stood on the fringe of the headlights, a handgun balanced in his hand.

A slow smile crept across his face, and he raised the weapon a second time. "I aim my best at runners."

Paralyzed. Powerless. Zoey willed herself to move. Erik aimed a second time. Zoey couldn't shift. Her body was no longer her own. Erik's finger snapped the trigger back. Zoey felt a rush of air as the bullet passed just next to her head. A miss? No. Horror unlike *anything Zoey had ever known before bled through her chest a fraction later, as Rona let out a strangled groan and choked on the beginnings of a scream.*

~ ~ ~ ~ ~ ~

Zoey sat bolt upright in bed, the sound of her own scream forcing her awake. Unreality and reality were the same. She could still feel the sticky asphalt beneath her. She fought to get her bearings. Everything shook. Her hands, her legs, every single breath she took in came out shaky. She could still smell the car fumes. She clutched her blankets tight in one hand. The other, clung to her drenched shirt's fabric, scrabbling blindly for her necklace. Her pillow was wet. Her sheets were soaked with sweat.

The dream was gone. But it didn't feel gone. It still lingered, wrapping itself around the corners of her mind. Its presence felt as dark as the night outside. She glanced at the clock. Four in the morning. The witching hour had passed.

In the back of her mind, she could still hear the gargling notes of Rona's cry. Zoey balled one hand into a fist and bit down hard on her knuckle, stifling a second scream. Calm down. She had to calm down. But there was no calming in this. She was a captive of her own emotions, as much as she had been a captive of Groper and Bouncer. Powerless. Stripped of her autonomy. Stripped of herself.

Someone knocked on her door. It sounded like the shattering of a mirror, though a mirror she was relieved to have shattered. To have it broken brought her back to reality, tethering her to the ground. She was in Germany. She heaved a breath. But her dream still hovered, like a vengeful ghost.

"Zoey?"

Sascha's voice. Zoey bit down harder on her knuckle, seeing him fall in the surreal dream world again. Tears pricked her eyes again. She mustn't cry. To cry was a sign of weakness – Maxwell had always told her and her siblings that. Surely, Sascha, being the kind of man he was, would think the same. She heaved a shuddering breath, fighting to choke down fearful tears. Her throat closed, desperate for her to release her fear. Panic and control fought each other. Zoey's stomach turned.

"Zoey, are you alright?" asked Sascha. He was louder this time.

"I'm fine!" snapped Zoey, her voice cracking. She knew that there was no way Sascha had missed the tremor in those two words.

A pause.

"I'm coming in," said Sascha, his voice slightly muffled by the door.

Zoey opened her mouth to protest, but the door swung open before she could speak. Sascha stopped in the threshold, already fully dressed in spite of the small hours of the morning. Zoey felt his eyes scan her face. She sighed and looked away, covering as much of her face as she could with one hand. A flash of embarrassment heated her chest. Her dream wasn't real, yet it had reduced her to tears.

"Hey, steady," said Sascha. His voice was soft. Zoey heard him cross the room with those quick, elegant strides of his, and from her peripherals, she saw him perch on the edge of her bed. He spoke again, his voice low and comforting. "What's going on?"

Zoey shook her head. She couldn't look at him, shame sweeping over her. She couldn't tell him that this had happened because of a dream. He would laugh at her – Maxwell always laughed at nightmares. To fear a dream was ridiculous. But it didn't *feel* ridiculous. It felt real, painfully so. She sniffled and swiped tears away from her eyes as they threatened them.

"Two minutes," said Sascha. "You'll be alright for two minutes?"

A stiff nod answered Sascha without Zoey giving it permission. She looked up as he stood and left her bedroom. He was giving her time to pull herself together, she knew it. He couldn't want to be bothered with tears. He would want to talk to her when she was coherent. That must be what he was thinking. Gather up her shattered emotions and present an unruffled person? It seemed impossible. A sob choked up her throat. It *was* impossible. A hug. That was what she wanted. A hug from Rona, from Hailee. From both of them. Something solid to hold onto in this shaking ground. She wanted to wake up in Hereford. To forget that this world existed. To forget that this had ever happened. If she had convinced Rona not to go out that night. If she had stayed with Rona and not gone out onto the patio. If she had run from Groper and Bouncer at the hotel, at the airport, on the train, anywhere, this might not have happened. If she had been braver. If she had been stronger. If she'd fought. This felt like her fault. Was it? She breathed in, her breath hitching in her throat as she tried to steady herself.

The door swung inward again. Sascha. Had two minutes passed so quickly? Zoey forced herself straighter, composing her expression into something she hoped was neutral. She stared straight ahead, staring without seeing. She jumped as Sascha moved in her peripherals. He held two of the rust orange mugs from the kitchen. The colors seemed too warm, too cozy, too opposite to how she felt.

He set one mug down on her bedside table and sat down on the edge of her bed again, offering her the second cup. "Here. I feel like you could use this."

Zoey reached out and wrapped her hands around the mug. Hot. It was hot. It jarred her to reality. Her lower lip trembled as she caught the smell. Tea. Sascha had brought her a cup of tea. A memory flickered in the back of Zoey's mind. She had been very sick. Rona had brought her cups of tea and medicine. A sob escaped Zoey's throat, and a teardrop fell into her teacup.

"What's wrong?" asked Sascha, reaching across for his own mug. Once again, the drink was bright blue. His bright eyes were concerned, a small furrow appearing between his brows.

Zoey shook her head and looked out of the dark window. There was nothing to see. "You wouldn't understand."

One eyebrow lifted a fraction. "You saw me the other night, Zoey. Afraid of storms. Try me."

"Just a nightmare," she said. Her stomach turned in embarrassment and she tightened her fingers around the cup. "I'm fine. It's gone now."

"You say so, but it's lingering. There, in that place behind your eyes. I can see it."

"I shouldn't be having them. I should – I shouldn't be afraid anymore," said Zoey, addressing her tea. She hiccupped, breath caught between an inhale and a sob.

"Zoey." She looked up as one of Sascha's hands landed on her wrist. His grip was gentle, and his thumb traced tiny, mindless patterns on her skin. She met his eyes and found that she wasn't struck with the urge to pull away. Sascha was here. He was real. She turned her hand to hold onto him.

"Breathe. Having a nightmare, having fear, doesn't make you irrational or a coward. We all have nightmares," he said quietly.

"Surely, not you?" asked Zoey, laughing and grimacing through tears.

He squeezed her wrist gently. "Even me. Nightmares have nothing to do with being brave. For nightmares to manifest after what you've been through is normal, and you have been through something *awful*. Anyone would have them."

She took a hitching breath and resisted the urge to look away from him. "It was so real. Even when I woke up, I thought . . . I thought I was still in France."

Sascha tilted his head, and Zoey found herself compelled to continue. Now that the words had begun, they refused to stop.

"I can't forget it. That road. I was there again. I saw Rona. He shot Rona – I can't forget his face. Erik's. There was nothing I could do to stop him. I couldn't *do* anything. I felt *so* powerless. I still feel it. I still *am*. And now they're out there, and they're after my sisters, and there's nothing I can do to stop them. Even if I were home, I still wouldn't be able to do anything. I'd still be this – this – this . . . miserable, helpless, powerless . . ."

A soft, humorless smile crossed Sascha's face. It was the kind of smile that made Zoey's insides burn with shame. She didn't want his pity. She didn't *need* his pity. A disgraced tear fought free of her eye and began to race down the side of her face. Sascha's hand left her wrist, and he gently wiped her cheek dry with the pad of one thumb. Zoey closed her eyes and leaned into his touch. Anything to feel grounded again. In spite of it, her blood boiled. She hadn't known humiliation could flare this hot. She barely knew Sascha. He was a killer. This kind of weakness must be so foreign to him. She waited for him to offer worthless sympathy, waited for the backhanded comments about emotion and irrationality. They were the stock replies Maxwell used when he was confronted with this sort of thing. Sascha, surely, would be the same.

"Are you finished berating yourself for being human?" he asked, his hand coming to rest back on her wrist.

That wasn't the response she had expected. She scrambled to reply. "What?"

"What you've been through is trauma. For you to feel afraid, for you to have nightmares, for you to relive it, that is expected. You don't deserve the punishment you're giving yourself. What you're feeling is justified."

Zoey's lower lip trembled and she tightened her grip around her mug. "I felt so weak. I still do."

His thumb rubbed soothing patterns on her wrist, tracing the bottom of her palm. "Of course, you do. That's the entire point of what they did. It's the first step in breaking a person down. They took your independence and your strength from you, put you in a position where they were able to manipulate you and force you to surrender to whatever they wanted. What else were you expected to do? Resist? They'd have shot you. Or drugged you. Forced you to submit by some means or another. The result would have been the same. You would have found yourself the property of someone who had paid blood money for you, or you'd be dead. In either case, you would have lost whatever fight you put up. Powerless is what they made you. It's only natural that the feeling lingers, but it'll go. With time. You will not always feel the way you do tonight."

There was something in his voice – something in the quietness of Sascha's tone – that made Zoey feel calmer. This wasn't sympathy. Not exactly. It was reassurance. Zoey met his eyes, her own gaze flickering between them, searching for . . . she wasn't sure exactly what. Sascha's expression was steady, the look of a person who was familiar with what she was feeling.

Zoey took a steadying breath, her gaze falling to the blanket. She took a sip of tea, and the taste made her feel a little closer to home. Sascha didn't make a terrible cup of tea. It wasn't like Rona or Hailee made, but it wasn't bad.

The words fell from her mouth before she could stop them. "I feel like I should have done something. I should have made myself less vulnerable –"

Sascha's hand tensed on her wrist, the movement so quick it seemed as though it had been involuntary. "Stop. Stop that. You are not responsible for the evils of others. Don't you dare think that you deserved what happened to you."

Zoey tensed as Sascha let go of her and stood up, walking across the room to the window. It was getting lighter outside, the first fringes of a gray dawn ushering out the night. She threw back the covers and stood beside him, risking a glance at his face. Had she upset him? She didn't think so, but she wasn't entirely sure. There was a sharp look in his eyes, just as there had been the first morning she had been with him. Zoey took a breath and turned to him, opening her mouth to apologize, but Sascha turned to look at her before she could say anything.

"This is *not* your fault, Zoey. You were targeted because of who your father is and what he's done to antagonize OMNI. That's all. There was nothing *you* could have done to make yourself less susceptible. Maxwell painted a target on you and your sisters' backs and allowed a firing line that you never even knew existed to aim at you." He raised his mug to his lips and breathed in, but didn't drink it. His jaw clenched a moment, then a tiny smile, one that didn't reflect in his eyes, crossed his face. "You'll have to forgive the analogy. I don't know how else to phrase it."

A brittle laugh left Zoey's mouth. "The way you phrased it makes sense. That's how it feels." She took a sharp breath. "I don't ever want to feel like this again, Sascha. I wish I knew how to . . . how to do something to protect myself."

Sascha looked over. His eyes had kept their sharp look. "Why?"

Zoey shook her head and took a sip of tea. "It's stupid, but I feel like if I knew how to fight, or something like that, at least I could have defended myself if I'd had to. *Done something.*"

The beginnings of anger flared in Zoey's chest as Sascha gave a low laugh. The tiny smile on his lips reached his eyes now.

"What?" she snapped. The word felt altogether too harsh in her mouth.

"I know the feeling, but you don't want to learn how to fight, Zoey," said Sascha, raising his mug and taking a long drink of tea.

Her eyes narrowed as she looked out at the breaking dawn. Night was yielding to dawn in soft shades of gray, violet, orange, while the rising sun was still barely hidden behind the mountain peaks. Only the last few stars lingered in the sky. Zoey scoffed. Who did Sascha think he was to tell her what she did and didn't want? How was it okay for him to defend himself in the dangerous life he led, and not okay for her to simply survive an ordinary life? She took another sip of tea, but it tasted bitter on her tongue this time. She locked her gaze on the last of the night's stars, instead. Distant. Cold.

Sascha lowered his mug. "There's a big difference between fighting and winning. You don't want to learn how to fight. You want to learn how to win. I can teach you how to win."

A small, unexpected smile pulled at Zoey's mouth, the angry fire in her chest dying. "Would you?"

"If you want me to."

Zoey dropped one hand to her leg. It was steadier this morning, the injury becoming easier to bear. She felt steadier herself. "I do."

An odd smile curved across Sascha's lips, and he turned to look at her. Zoey lifted her gaze and met his eyes. She crossed one arm over her chest, adjusting her grip on her mug with her free hand. She had a feeling he was studying her. Good. A flare of resolve lit in her chest. Zoey didn't know why, but for the first time, it felt as though they were standing on the same ground. Sascha's blue eyes looked masked, not a trace of emotion escaping them.

He nodded. "Then I will."

Chapter 18

A rose-colored dawn yielded to a bright, clear morning. Zoey pulled a clean shirt over her head and paused near her bedroom window. Sascha had, quietly, stayed with her until the sun had risen fully. Only when it had broken over the mountains did he finally leave. Zoey couldn't help feeling grateful to him. There was something comforting in his silence. He had been there if she wanted to talk without being overbearing or pushy. Zoey paused and watched the morning, the mountains painted green and gold in the early sun. The sky itself was the softest shade of blue-gray, feebly clinging to the edges of night. Faint wisps of mist rose from the mountainside pines. There was something clean and bright about the sunrise itself. The night's stars were long gone, taking their distant light with them.

A small smile pulled at Zoey's lips, then she turned, a faint smell of toast wafting up from downstairs. Sascha had cooked most of their meals in the time she'd been with him, and he was a good cook. Better than Zoey was, but she typically tried to avoid cooking at home. Rona was the whiz in the kitchen. Zoey smiled slightly as she made her way down the stairs. The tainted glass she'd seen Sascha through for the first week they'd started this coexistence felt clearer. There was something . . . easy about this. A nameless kind of ease. A predictability. Something she liked. She rested a hand against her leg as she neared the bottom of the stairwell.

Zoey rounded the wall at the bottom of the stairs, and she leaned on the back of one of the living room couches. Sascha stood in the kitchen, a piece of toast balanced in one hand, his phone in the other. A steaming mug stood on the countertop beside him. There was a look of focus on his face, a small furrow between his brows. Zoey's smile deepened as she remembered Rona striking a similar pose one morning a few months ago. Sascha looked up, a smile flashing through his eyes.

"Good morning," he said. "Toast is on the counter. Tea is in the pot, coffee in the press. I'm afraid the coffee's decaf but take whichever you'd prefer."

"Do you have something against caffeine?" asked Zoey, crossing into the kitchen.

"Makes my hands shake," said Sascha with a quiet chuckle. "Can't have shaky hands in my line of work. Someone might get hurt."

Zoey laughed softly, without meaning to, and an unexpected rush of warmth settled in her chest. Affection? Couldn't be. Mustn't be. She shook her head and dropped a hand to her thigh. Her gait felt more even this morning. Almost normal. How long would it be now until the bandages could be removed permanently?

Zoey poured a cup of tea and picked up a piece of toast before turning back to Sascha. He was buried in his phone again, that focused look back on his face. What was it that he was musing over? Zoey raised her mug. She'd seen that look of focus on her father's face and her siblings' faces before. Pensive. Thoughtful.

"Take a picture. It'll last longer," Sascha said, not looking up from his phone.

Zoey beat back the flush that threatened her cheeks. Caught in the act. "Sorry. I was just . . . I was just wondering what had got your attention."

"Ask. You don't need to study me in silence," he chuckled, pocketing his phone. Then he smirked. "Though I do appreciate the flattery."

Zoey opened her mouth, the blush catching her cheeks, and grappled for a response. "You looked concerned about something. A penny for your thoughts?"

"A contact point wants to meet me tonight in Innsbruck. In Austria."

"Oh?" asked Zoey, taking a bite of toast. "What about?"

"Your passport," replied Sascha. His eyes danced in what Zoey thought was amusement. "I might live fast and drive fast, but you didn't think I'd been driving around Germany, Austria, and Switzerland for *fun*, did you?"

"I didn't know what to think. I honestly didn't know you'd been going so far afield," replied Zoey.

She took a sip of tea. How close was her passport to being ready? She lifted her eyes from the tea in her mug, a rush of gratitude flushing somewhere deep in her chest. That warmth came again, taking rest beside the gratitude in her chest and settling just behind her ribs. She swallowed, trying to clear it, but it refused to budge.

Sascha cleared his throat. "I'm tempted to recreate the Gabrielle Lavaud passport that OMNI forged for you, but I think that would be a bit on the nose. What do you think of the name Janine Genet?"

"I – I don't know. Does it have to be French?"

He paused. "No. I just thought it would be a way to spite OMNI."

"Very funny. Maybe something English? It might make more sense?"

"Heather Hunt?"

"Sounds perfect." Zoey paused and laughed. "That was quick." "Creating false identities is hard, but making up aliases is a pastime. I suppose I'm just used to it." Sascha nodded and picked up his mug. "Do you want to come to Innsbruck with me?"

"What?" asked Zoey, lowering her mug. "Me? Come with you?"

"Why not? You've been cooped up here, and if I were you, I'd be itching to go somewhere and do something. I can drop you off near the university, if you like. You'd blend in. You've got my phone number. I can do what I need to, and we could meet up later in the evening."

"But . . . this OMNI group is after me. Wouldn't they recognize me?"

"It's a possibility, but come on, Zoey, I wouldn't bring you with me undefended. That would just be irresponsible. I'd give you a handgun."

"You what?!" yelped Zoey, her mouth falling open. She floundered for a reply. "A *gun*? I – no, I couldn't. Absolutely not. I've never even touched one."

Sascha's grip on his mug wavered. His lips pressed into a fine line. "Pardon?"

"I can't fire a gun. Much less fire one *at* anyone –" Zoey lowered one hand toward her leg, and a strange burst of panic flared in her chest.

"No, no, no, no, no. That wasn't what I meant, Zoey." Sascha set his cup down. "You've never *touched* one?"

"*No*. Why would I need to?"

Sascha paused, and Zoey shifted under the weight of his stare. He blinked and shook his head. "Christ."

"Why is that so hard to believe?"

Sascha ran a hand through his short hair. "I'm just shocked that your father sent you out so undefended. Let you *live* without much defense. It's almost like he wanted you caught. It's shameful. Not a surprise. But shameful all the same."

Zoey scoffed. Then she frowned at him. Sascha? Annoyed about something her father had done? Why? They didn't know each other. Did they? If they did, her father had never mentioned Sascha – not that he mentioned much at all – and Sascha had only mentioned Maxwell in passing. She wanted to ask what he meant; her curiosity piqued. But she didn't.

"You don't know the half of it," she said, folding her arms across her chest.

Sascha glanced down at his mug and a pensive, dark expression flashed across his face, there and gone quickly, but Zoey was certain it had been there. Anger. Somehow, though, she felt that it wasn't an anger that was directed at her. Sascha looked up, a small smile pulling at the side of his mouth. Any anger that had been there moments before was gone now. She adjusted the way she stood, raising her mug.

"I think I know what we're getting up to today," he said, crossing to the sink and rinsing out his mug.

"Oh yeah?"

Zoey took a deep breath through her nose as she watched him. She had a feeling she already knew what Sascha was going to say. Her heart beat a little harder in her chest, though, again, it wasn't fear. She swallowed. Excitement, maybe? Possibly something closer to apprehension.

He turned. "I'm going to teach you how to shoot. You did say just a few hours ago that you wanted to learn how to protect yourself, and I won't be able to be around you all the time. If you ever need to know how to handle a weapon, you'll be able to. Thoughts?"

Zoey took a breath. This was an opportunity. One to be around Sascha and spend some productive time with him. In a way, it had been exactly what she wanted – a chance to get to know him better. And it was something she'd wanted to do ever since being kidnapped. Protect herself.

"I think I'd like to. No, I *know* I'd like to."

Sascha smiled. "Great. I'll see you outside in fifteen minutes."

~ ~ ~ ~ ~ ~

Standing on the patio at the back of the house, Zoey rubbed the blank space between her collarbones, fingers starting to become used to the absence of her necklace. She lifted her eyes from the stone patio and watched Sascha coming back toward her. On the garden table between them, lay two black, plastic boxes, their shell-like cases glinting under the midmorning sun. The chairs had been pulled away and gathered along the patio walls. Beyond Sascha, mounted to a tree was a large, wooden box backed with some form of metal. A paper hung in the center of the box. Zoey narrowed her eyes a fraction, crossing her arms nervously. It felt as though the big, black target on the paper was staring at her.

"What are you thinking?" asked Sascha, standing at the table. He'd changed from a tee-shirt, sweatpants, and socks to a long-sleeved shirt, black trousers, and boots. There was something jarring in it. Zoey tightened her grip on her upper arms. Dangerous. He looked dangerous. She took a breath. Two sides of him.

"I'm just curious how you're going to approach this," said Zoey. "The closest I've been to any firearms was . . . well, recently."

"We'll go slowly. Come closer," said Sascha, opening the snaps on the first of the black boxes.

Zoey paced closer toward the table, still not unfolding her arms. Her mouth ran dry as she leaned over the table. Black and lethal, a handgun rested in a foam bed. Zoey sucked in a sharp breath, the memory of a deserted roadside and loud gunshots cracking the night raced across her mind. A wave of phantom pain seized her leg. Her eyes flickered to Sascha. Was this the same gun he'd used to kill Bouncer that night?

"It won't bite," said Sascha. "It's not loaded."

But the one he'd used to kill Bouncer that night in France had been.

Swallowing, Zoey stood upright. Maybe this had been a bad idea. Again, white hot memory of that night charged up from her thigh. She could hear the low groan from Bouncer's throat as he hit the pavement. She snapped her head away, the movement sharper than she had wanted it to be. Gooseflesh broke on her arms in spite of the mild morning.

Sascha rested his hands on the table. "Talk to me. What are you thinking?"

Zoey shook her head and exhaled hard, a kind of anger flaring in her chest. "I keep seeing that night. It's like it's – I don't know – burned into my memory."

"That's perfectly normal, Zoey. Like I told you earlier. It's *normal*."

She pressed her lips together and nodded. Did this kind of thing really take so long to get over? Zoey pinched the bridge of her nose. "I just wish I could think normally again. Respond to things like I used to."

A cool breeze stirred the tops of the trees, and Zoey rubbed the gooseflesh away from her arms. She took the opportunity to look past Sascha and toward the valley beyond, trying to focus instead on the strength of the colors at play on the far mountainsides, to look anywhere but at Sascha. Those blue eyes of his were piercing again. Seeing through her, analyzing her. Zoey bit the inside of her cheek and swallowed.

Sascha stepped back from the table. "Maybe we shouldn't do this today." "*No*," said Zoey. It felt like a personal challenge now. Fear versus rationality. "I want to. We came out here so you could show me how to shoot. I still want to do that."

Sascha stayed silent. The pause between them dragged out longer than was comfortable. Zoey shifted her weight and folded her arms tighter across her chest, adjusting so that she stood squarely to face Sascha. He'd offered an escape. She wondered if he was waiting for her to buckle and go back on her decision. Gray eyes met blue, and Zoey refused to let her gaze waver. Sascha gave a miniscule nod.

"Only if you're sure."

"I am," replied Zoey. She hoped she was surer than she sounded.

"Alright," said Sascha, a smile breaking across his face.

The tension in the air vanished, and Zoey let her shoulders drop. Sascha reached into the case and withdrew the handgun. Again, Zoey was struck by how lethal it looked. She resisted the urge to fiddle with a nonexistent necklace.

"What is it?" she asked.

"It's a gun, Zoey, come on. I know you said you were new to this, but I didn't think you were *that* new."

Zoey laughed, the sound surprising her. She shook her head, unable to wipe the smile from her face. "You know what I meant."

"It's a Heckler and Koch SFP9SK. I had it made in Germany earlier this year. Small, quite light, holds ten rounds. I'd use it more, but it's a bit too small for my hands."

"You mean, you weren't using this . . ." Zoey let her sentence trail off. She had a feeling Sascha would know what she meant.

"No. I have a lot of weapons, Zoey. This is one of my spares. I haven't used this one since the day I bought it – practice shots aside."

It felt as though a band had been released from around Zoey's chest. This gun had never been used to kill anyone. There was something about that that felt like relief – shameful relief, but relief nonetheless. She rounded the table and stood next to Sascha.

"Muzzle. The business end," he said, setting the handgun down and pointing. "Front sight. Helps you know where your round is going to go. Barrel. Rounds travel along here. Rear sight. Aligns on your front sight to form a clear idea of where your shot will go. Trigger. Controls the release of rounds. Grip. Rounds discharge from inside here. This is also where you hold the weapon from. You're left-handed, aren't you?"

Zoey lifted her eyes from the gun on the table and laughed quietly. Perhaps bitterly. "How did you know that? Is that information in my file, too?"

"No," shrugged Sascha. "I'm just observant. Do you know your dominant eye?"

"I – no." "Okay. Make a triangle with your fingers, stare at the target in the box."

"Now what?" asked Zoey.

She couldn't help but feel awkward. She wondered if Sascha was above making a fool of her for his own amusement. Having sisters had made her hyperaware to being the subject of nonsense pranks.

"Slowly bring your hands toward your face, making that triangle smaller as you do. Don't think about it. Just let your hands fall naturally."

Zoey hesitated, then did as he asked. Why was it that whenever people said not to think of something, it always became monumentally harder? She blinked, the gap in her hands coming to rest in front of her right eye.

"Interesting. Do you wear glasses?" asked Sascha. "You can drop your hands now if you like."

Zoey turned back to him, dropping her arms to her sides. "Contacts normally."

One brow rose. "You what?"

"I normally wear contact lenses. I'm a little nearsighted."

"Are you telling me that you've been wandering around for the last week and a half without being able to see?"

"It's not that big of a deal. I'm not blind."

"Clearly not," replied Sascha, rubbing the back of his neck. He hummed and shook his head. "In terms of shooting, you're cross-dominant. Left-hand dominance and right-eye dominance."

"Is that a bad thing?"

"No, it's just a bit unusual. Dominancy normally tends to be on one side. Good thing is, I don't have to teach you like a leftie."

"Something wrong with left-handed people?" asked Zoey, a grin trying to cross her face. She fought it down, not sure if Sascha was being serious or not.

A small smile pulled at Sascha's mouth. "Everything is opposite. Your hand positions are all reversed for shooting. You write upside-down. You're just backward."

"That's not funny," said Zoey. "Being left-handed is a pain. I've still got to have Rona use a can-opener for me."

Sascha paused and a tiny grin pulled at each side of his mouth. "Now, that *is* funny."

"No, it isn't." Zoey shook her head but couldn't push down the laugh that rose in her chest. She gave up, laughing and grinning back at Sascha. "It's annoying."

"Well, if we come across any cans that need opening, I solemnly swear that I will open them for you."

"Oh, shut up. That is not funny!" yelped Zoey, still laughing.

She froze a heartbeat later as she realized what she'd said. There was a handgun on the table. A hitman in front of her. And she had just told him to shut up. She really, *really* – this wasn't Rona she was dealing with –

Sascha threw his head back and laughed, eyes closing. He shook his head but seemed unable to wipe the smile from his face. Zoey breathed a laugh, a smile returning to her face, and she remembered his good humor from a few nights previous. No more eggshells, she reminded herself. She relaxed, and that warmth pulsed in her chest. She met Sascha's eyes when he opened them and couldn't help feeling sheepish.

"That must be the first time in close to five years anyone has told me to shut up. Brilliant." Sascha chuckled again, the smile staying on his face. "Come on. Let's hope you do better with a handgun than you do with a can opener."

Chapter 19

Sascha pressed something into the palm of her hand. Looking down, Zoey saw a pair of earplugs. She swallowed, heart starting to pound again. This was happening. Beside her, Sascha tilted his head, as though considering something. He picked up the handgun from the table, then turned toward the target box. Zoey draped the earplugs around her neck.

"Come here. Stand in front of me."

Zoey hesitated. She eyed the weapon in his right hand, and a breathy laugh left her chest. "Okay."

"We'll just get you used to the position for now. I'm going to step up behind you and let you mimic what I'm doing. That alright?"

"Yeah," nodded Zoey. She stiffened as Sascha's chest bumped her back.

"Feet a little over shoulder-width apart. My feet should bracket yours."

A small rush of nerves ran up Zoey's back as she inched her feet further apart. She stopped dead as her shoes contacted Sascha's.

"Lean forward and put a bit of bend in your knees."

Zoey swallowed, doing as he asked. Was this supposed to feel awkward? "Better?"

"Better," said Sascha, bringing the handgun up in front of them.

Zoey leaned back a fraction, the top of her head just brushing Sascha's chin. Black weapon in front of her. The tiny gap in the rear sight Sascha had pointed out earlier gave way to the single rise of the front sight. How exactly was she supposed to use these pieces of metal to hit a target? She'd always thought it was just point a gun in the general direction of something and the bullet would find its mark. That was how films always made it look.

"Right hand underneath mine, Zoey," said Sascha. "You're left-handed, but your right index finger will be your trigger finger. Sounds opposite, I know."

The rumble of his voice vibrating against her back pulled Zoey back to the task, and the hair on the back of her neck stood up. She reached up, sliding her hand under Sascha's.

The handgun's plastic grip felt rough under her palm. Sascha's hand closed over hers, and Zoey took a heavy breath. She could feel the callouses on his palm against her knuckles. Had she always been this hyperaware of touch?

"Left hand now. You'll want to just press your left hand's fingers just in front of your right. Don't lace your fingers together and don't cross your thumbs. Extend your arms all the way, but don't lock your elbows out. Hold them nearly locked. Steady but not stiff."

"How do you remember all this?" asked Zoey, laughing nervously, trying to diffuse the tension.

Was there tension? Really? Or was it just her imagination? She bit the inside of her cheek. She had no reason to be nervous around Sascha. At least that was what she had to tell herself.

"Practice and muscle memory," shrugged Sascha.

She stiffened again as she felt Sascha's chest vibrate against her back as he spoke. A third chill ran up Zoey's back, and she could have sworn that in her peripherals, she saw the tiniest flash in his eyes, the tiniest upward tilt to his mouth. He laughed softly, and Zoey took a breath to stifle the shiver that threatened to run up her spine again. She took a deep breath, trying to calm her heart.

"There are five basic principles to firing, Zoey. Breathe, relax, aim, stop, and squeeze. Just try to work on breathing and relaxing for now."

"Yeah. Easy," Zoey replied a little sarcastically. Yet in spite of her nerves, a smile crossed her face. "This is very new for me."

"I know. Go ahead and rest your finger on the trigger. It's not loaded. You can't do any damage."

"Do you think I'd do damage?" asked Zoey, resting her finger against the smooth trigger.

"That *is* the intended purpose," replied Sascha.

There was a finality in his words that unnerved Zoey. Again, she wondered how many people this gun had fired through. She looked downrange, at the black, staring-eye of the target. This wasn't shooting at a person. It was just shooting at a printed spot of black ink. There was no danger here. So why did she already feel unnerved?

"Want to try firing?" asked Sascha.

Zoey took a deep breath and nodded.

"Alright. I'll just let our resident eagles know we're here so that we don't hit them by accident."

Sascha stepped away, and Zoey heaved a shuddering breath. Why had her lungs felt so constricted? She didn't know if it was the prospect of firing her first gun or Sascha being so close to her that was making her feel so antsy. Probably both. She rubbed her hands together, trying to dispel some of her nerves. She glanced toward the patio table and pressed her lips together hard, trying not to grit her teeth as she heard a quick rack of metallic sound.

"Earplugs in!" Sascha called.

Zoey clapped her hands over her ears, unable to cram her earplugs in in time. Sascha fired once into the ground. A single songbird flitted off a branch in the trees. Zoey lowered her hands, her ears ringing in spite of her having scrambled to cover them. There was a second clatter of well-oiled metal against well-oiled metal.

"I'll load for you this time. We'll put one round in and see how you do."

Sascha turned back. Zoey frowned, her eyes darting to Sascha and back to the handgun. Its barrel had grown close to six inches longer.

"What?" asked Sascha.

"That is?" replied Zoey, pointing at the gun.

"A silencer. It helps dispel some of the noise. Makes the noise itself less traceable. Probably not a good idea to let people know we're up here shooting," said Sascha. He tapped one of his ears. "Even though we're using one, I'd prefer it if you used the earplugs. They're still loud if you're not used to them."

Zoey nodded and turned back to the target, pressing the earplugs into place. She shifted her weight, returning to the stance Sascha had shown her. Her breath hitched in her throat as she felt him press against her back again.

"Can you hear me?"

Shaking her head, Zoey looked up at him. "Kind of. Your voice is really dull."

"That's how it should sound. Finger off the trigger until you're ready to fire. When you fire, keep your focus on that front sight, not on the target, and be ready for the recoil. Do you want me behind you?"

Zoey hesitated – did she really want Sascha so close to her again? She swallowed and nodded again.

"Then I'll stay."

The handgun came up again, and Sascha arced his right hand away from the grip. Zoey bit the inside of her cheek and slipped her hands underneath his again.

"Both eyes open throughout the shot. Use your dominant eye to focus on the front sight. Breathe. Deep breath in."

Zoey felt her shoulders rise as she drew a breath. She tried desperately to dispel her nerves. Her hands shook.

"*Relax*. Let everything else just fade away."

Zoey took another heavy breath, fighting to relax. How was she supposed to relax when her entire body was tense? When she felt his breath on the side of her neck with every word he spoke?

"Now aim. Eyes on the front sight."

Focus on the front sight? That made no sense. Why wouldn't she want to focus on where her shot was going? She shifted her focal point to the black circle on the target.

"Stop and hold your breath. Whenever you're ready, slowly squeeze the trigger."

Slowly? How could she go any slower? Her shoulders and arms were already shaking. Zoey let her right index finger fall to the trigger, squeezing slowly. Behind her, Sascha exhaled softly, his breath ghosting the shell of her ear. Had Sascha's hands not been covering hers, Zoey had a feeling she would have dropped the gun. Her finger snapped down sharp on the trigger, recoil snapping hard through her elbows. The round buried itself in the mountainside.

"Zoey?" he laughed quietly. "What was that? I said squeeze, not flinch."

She turned to explain. To say that she'd jumped. But when she did, Sascha had already leaned down marginally. His face was just inches away from her own, and all her words lodged tight in her throat. She saw details of him she'd never noticed before. The tiny dusting of faded freckles on his cheeks. The tiny scar that nicked through his left eyebrow. The slant of his smile. An irrational urge to kiss him flared in her chest.

Heat rushed to Zoey's cheeks, and she pulled away from him before she did anything stupid. Her skin had to be scarlet. She looked at the ground instead of at Sascha and held the handgun out to him by the grip. He pulled it gently away from her and lowered it to his side. Zoey took a deep breath and exhaled hard, finally able to look him in the face again.

Sascha raised a brow. "What was that all about?"

"What?" she asked, taking her earplugs out.

Please, don't let him ask her to explain why she'd pulled away so harshly. What she'd been thinking . . . wanting . . . only moments before. Because she couldn't explain it. Sascha was a *companion*. Nothing more. She swallowed. It had just been the closeness between them. That was all. That was it. "I don't know if I've ever seen anyone rip a trigger quite like that," replied Sascha.

"You try not flinching when there's someone breathing down your neck like it's their job," she said, taking another breath and shaking out her shoulders.

Realization flashed across Sascha's face, and he looked away. He lifted one hand to cover his mouth, but Zoey could see the pinched expression around his eyes. She sighed and rested her hands on her hips. Her cheeks burned with embarrassment.

"Go on. Laugh. I know you want to."

Sascha's hand fell away, grinning hard. "To your defense, even with my interference, you hit the tree."

"Really?" asked Zoey, whipping around to look. A surprised smile settled on her face.

"Yes, not the right tree. But you hit one of them."

"Maybe I'm not cut out for this," sighed Zoey, her shoulders falling forward.

"Nonsense. You just need to get used to shooting and to get into practice. We'll load up half a magazine for you and see how you do. Five shots total."

Zoey tilted her head and smiled as Sascha turned back to the garden table. He'd laughed, but he hadn't made fun of her. In spite of laughing, he'd been kind. Absentmindedly, Zoey lifted a hand to her mouth and traced her lower lip. How, in his profession, had he not lost that kindness?

"Here," said Sascha, offering her the handgun's grip.

"What?" asked Zoey, not taking it.

"Try again. See how you do flying solo. I won't be holding your hand every shot you put downrange. It seems that my being so close may be more of a hindrance than anything else. I'll be right here if you need help."

Zoey paused. "On my own? I mean, you trust me with this?"

Sascha raised an eyebrow. "Well, you're not planning to shoot *me*, are you?"

The gun lifted a fraction higher, and Zoey could have sworn she saw the tiniest hint of a challenge in Sascha's eyes. She stepped forward and wrapped her hand around its grip, her fingers brushing Sascha's.

He tapped one of his ears. "Earplugs back in. I'll be behind you. Be ready for the recoil, relax, and keep those eyes open."

Zoey put her earplugs back in, set her jaw, and turned back to the target. She both felt and saw Sascha come to stand at her left shoulder. She inhaled deeply and lifted the handgun. Relax. Exhale. Her shoulders dropped. Aim. Zoey grit her teeth, forcing herself to focus on the white dot on the back of the front sight. Stop. She wished her hands would stop trembling. Her finger dropped to the trigger. Now, squeeze. She could hear her heart beating, thundering in her chest. How much more would she have to squeeze? How much more pressure? Pressure. What would the pressure of his lips feel like on hers? She snapped her finger down, fighting to clear the thoughts from her head.

Bang!

A jump seized Zoey as the round fired. The gun snapped up out of position, recoil shuddering up Zoey's arms. She held still, staring at the target. Staring without comprehension. France flashed in front of her eyes. She was in the car again, pain searing across her thigh –

"Don't worry about where it went," said Sascha, his voice muffled. "If it doesn't hit the target, it'll hit the mountainside."

Not France. Zoey breathed. This wasn't France. She blinked fast, clearing fingers of darkness from her vision. Ground herself in the present. She *had* to.

"Fire again. Get rid of the next four rounds."

Her eyes darted to Sascha. Once had been jarring enough. Could she do it again? Would that desolate roadside appear again? She wanted to lower the gun and give her arms a break. They were shaking hard now. They ached. That had to be why they were shaking so badly. Not because that night had come again on this sunny morning. Zoey set her jaw. Four more rounds. That was all. She couldn't be further from that place than she was now. She breathed out and tried to clear France from her mind. She looked back down the barrel, focusing again on the white dot on the back of the front sight.

Fire. Groper's head hung awkward; his neck broken. Don't think about it.

Fire. Erik's grin as he made a promise to see her again. Tune it out.

Fire. Impact as the back of Bouncer's hand slapped her cheek. Stop thinking.

Fire. The crushing hopelessness as they drove across the French countryside. Stop. Stop. Stop. Stop. Stop thinking.

Click. Empty. Zoey's hands trembled around the grip of the handgun. She felt nauseated. She lowered the gun to her side, her hands still shaking.

"Let me take this," said Sascha, his voice just audible over the earplugs.

Movement. Zoey stiffened as Sascha reached toward her, forcing herself not to jump. She barely felt him pull the gun from her hand. She looked away. Her fingers were numb. She rubbed her arms, trying to steady her trembles. She felt ill. There was a low *thud*, and

Zoey thought she heard Sascha set the gun down on the table. Precious seconds to pull herself back together.

"You alright?" asked Sascha. "You look rattled. And not by me this time."

Zoey hesitated for half a heartbeat. Snap decision. Sascha had already put up with her nightmare earlier, and he'd put up with her nerves for days now. His patience had to be wearing thin. Her own certainly was. She was angry with herself for feeling this way, thinking this way – vulnerable, a wreck of uncontrolled emotions. She blinked. One white lie couldn't hurt, could it?

"I'm fine," she replied, hands on her hips as she took a deep breath.

She couldn't stop the motion. It had started before she realized it. Her hand reached up for the place her necklace had once rested, fingers closing on empty air once again. She played with the cotton collar of her shirt instead. Sascha's eyes followed her hand. She grinned at him, knowing how falsely bright it must look.

Silence. Zoey felt her smile fade, and she swallowed. Did the silence just sound more deafening because she felt guilty, or had the air really turned tense? It fell into a lull, and seconds felt longer than they should have. Time slowed. Zoey turned to him, trying to keep emotion off her face. Sascha blinked at her, his expression unreadable. Neutral.

"Let's see if you did the trees any more damage, shall we?" said Sascha, stepping past her.

Zoey pressed her lips hard together and fell into step behind him, eyes on the ground. Hot guilt settled in her stomach. Sascha had helped her so much, been so patient, and she'd lied to him. But only to keep him from having to put up with any more of her scattered emotions. She couldn't project them on him. She swallowed hard. Don't think about how she was feeling. Block it out. Move on. Think about something else. Like how close he'd – Zoey shook her head, trying to force that thought from her mind, too.

"You hit the target sheet here," said Sascha. "Watch your trigger control. It looks like you're pulling before you're really ready to fire."

Zoey raised her gaze from the ground to see Sascha pointing to a black hole in the bottom corner of the paper.

She forced a smile. "Maybe you should just give me a whistle to call for help."

"No, stop doubting yourself. You just need practice." Sascha traced a deep wound in the tree's trunk. "A lot of practice."

"It's so new. It's hard not to doubt myself," said Zoey, the smile feeling a little less forced now. "Like I said. A whistle might be better than me wasting your time."

Again, she couldn't help feeling intensely grateful to Sascha for striking easy conversation. Think about something else. This was a perfect distraction from her thoughts. Her shoulders dropped a fraction, and the guilty weight in her stomach started to pull back. She breathed, the coil of nerves around her loosening its hold.

"This isn't a waste of my time. If it helps you, it'll be worth it," he replied, a small smile flashing across his face. "And it's not hard. It's new. Everyone starts somewhere."

"Are you telling me you weren't much better than me when you first started?"

"Actually, I have a talent for this. I was nothing short of a prodigy when I started."

Zoey blinked. "Of course, you were. Why wouldn't you have been?"

Sascha turned back and smirked. "I'm just perfect by nature."

"Some people would call that cocky, you know."

"I call it confident."

"Does it echo? Having a head that big and nothing in it?" asked Zoey, feeling her smile relax and become genuine.

"Listen to you," laughed Sascha. "Rude. I'm wounded."

A few beats of laughter left Zoey's mouth, and she found herself smiling at Sascha. She adjusted the way she was standing, and her expression faltered. Sascha hadn't mentioned anything else about her going with him to Innsbruck tonight. Was that still on the table?

Zoey cleared her throat. "So, tonight? Yes or no?"

Sascha's smile morphed into a grimace, and he hissed through his teeth. "If we needed you to hit the broad side of a building with a considerable amount of luck, I'd say yes. But I would need you to be able to defend yourself with confidence if you had to. Not this time. I'm sorry, Zoey. I hate to extend offers and rip them away at the last moment, but this is a matter of your safety and mine."

"Can't say I didn't expect that's what you'd say," replied Zoey.

Her eyes darted to the deep gouges in the tree's trunk. Sap and resin began to gather around the wounds. She sighed, unable to keep herself from feeling disappointed. Sunlight glinted off the safe house's glass doors to the patio. It would have been nice to get away from these four walls, at least for a little while.

"How does this sound," said Sascha. "Let's go into Bayrischzell for the evening. It's a lovely town."

"What about your appointment?"

"I don't have to be there until ten tonight. Plenty of time. I know it's not much of a compromise, but what do you say?"

Zoey glanced in the general direction of the town. "Are you sure it's safe?"

"I wouldn't have asked if it wasn't," replied Sascha.

A smile returned to Zoey's lips. "I'd like that. Thank you, Sascha."

Chapter 20

A certain kind of thrill ran through Zoey's chest as Sascha pulled the car to a stop in a parking spot in Bayrischzell. He'd barely put it into park before Zoey threw the door open and launched out. Her first time in the town. Her first time in what felt like months away from the safe house. Fresh air had never smelled so sweet.

"I thought you'd be happy to get out, but I didn't think you'd be this happy," said Sascha, stepping out of the car. "I don't think you've stopped smiling since we left the safe house."

"Are you joking?" grinned Zoey. She was shaking. She would have danced if she'd trusted her balance more. "Getting out feels better than you could ever believe."

Sascha laughed but didn't respond. There was a dryness to the sound, and Zoey faltered, wondering if she'd said something wrong. She pushed her door closed and stepped up beside Sascha, falling into step next to him. If she'd said something to upset him, she had a feeling it wouldn't upset him for long. He didn't seem the type to brood over something.

Zoey pressed her lips together and reached out, resting her hand on his forearm. He paused and turned to her, brows marginally raised in what Zoey could only call surprise.

"I really appreciate this," she said. "Thank you."

Sascha's face softened as he smiled. "Of course. I'm happy to do it."

Zoey grinned, her hand sliding away from Sascha's forearm as she looked around. Mountains reared tall around them. She breathed a happy sigh, the cool evening air settling in her lungs. There was a kind of protection emanating from them, as though their very presence formed a safe haven around the town. Maybe they did. Zoey lowered her gaze from the mountains to her immediate surroundings, trying to take in everything. Solid, cream buildings with their red roofs and timber balconies settled a kind of clean idyll in the air. Again, Zoey found herself struck by the safety of the area. She followed Sascha across a footbridge that crossed over a small stream, stopping in front of a three-story building. Great flowerboxes stood outside its doors, overflowing with colorful garden flowers. On the first, second, and third floor balconies, more flowerboxes burst with their own red, pink, and purple flowers. Zoey smiled. She could just catch a whiff of their gentle smell. The amount of life and color was almost overwhelming. Her eyes flickered across the front of the building, and she turned to Sascha.

"Gasthof zur Post. What does that mean?"

"Hm? Oh." Sascha slid his phone into his jeans pocket. "It's just the name of the place. It's a guesthouse. Want to eat here?"

"Erm. I don't know." She shifted her weight. "Was there somewhere you had in mind or somewhere you wanted to go?"

"Well, I had somewhere in mind, but if you'd like to eat here, that's fine, too."

Zoey balked. Why did it always feel like there was pressure when asked to choose somewhere to eat? She realized with a jolt how much she missed Chinese takeaway.

She shook her head. "Please don't do this to me. I hate choosing places to eat."

A smile flitted across Sascha's face. "Well then, we'll go for mine tonight. Stop here another night?"

"Sounds perfect," replied Zoey, breathing a sigh of relief and falling back into step beside him.

A kind of appreciation settled in her chest as she noticed Sascha sidestep a fraction to make room for her on the inside of the footpath. The roads were nearly silent, but Zoey couldn't help but feel touched by his gesture.

"You really hate deciding where to eat that much?" asked Sascha.

"Well, if the food were bad or someone didn't like what they got, it would be my fault for deciding to eat there, so I feel like that ends up being my fault," replied Zoey.

Sascha hummed. "Odd."

"What do you mean?" asked Zoey.

She looked past Sascha and paused as they approached a church. Its dark roof marked it out from the other buildings around it. There was a quiet kind of elegance to it. A fineness. Green moss settled on the stone wall surrounding the churchyard's perimeter. The same splash of color touched a few of the exposed grave headstones. Peaceful.

"I forget sometimes that not everyone lives on their own," shrugged Sascha, leaning his elbows on the stone wall surrounding the graveyard.

"Does it ever get lonely?" asked Zoey, pausing beside him.

"Sometimes," he replied. He glanced at her and breathed a quiet, humorless laugh. "All the time."

Zoey tilted her head, sympathy rising in her chest, and just for a second, she wanted to press him for details. His eyes had locked back on the church, a faraway expression in them. Reminiscent. Thoughtful. She had a feeling that there was more to Sascha's small reply than he had said. A huge amount more. But she didn't think he'd want to be pressured for more information. Maybe soon she'd have the courage to ask him. But not tonight. It was too personal. Silence stretched between them, awkwardness forcing its way in. She changed the subject, grappling for something to say. "These mountains, do they have names?" Zoey fought the urge to groan. Stupid question. Why had she chosen to say *that*?

"'Course they do," replied Sascha, the smile springing back to his face as he straightened. "The one looming over the town is Wendelstein."

"Is it the highest mountain in Germany?" asked Zoey. She'd started on this track, she might as well finish it. At least it had eased the awkward pause in their conversation.

"No. Not by a long way. The highest mountain in Germany is Zugspitze. It's much higher than Wendelstein."

Zoey, smiled, the expression feeling soft on her face, and looked back to the mountains surrounding them. "I'd like to see it one day."

"I can take you if you'd like. Provided you come to the summit with me. I hope you're not afraid of heights."

"Never have been, so it's a deal," replied Zoey.

The conversation was comfortable again, and Zoey felt her chest warm. Making plans for actions she somehow knew would never occur. But there was an idyllic nature to the words. The creation of a kinder future in a kinder world. She paused as Sascha led the way into a beer-garden with outdoor seating. A few garden lights, strung along low branches of the garden's blossom-coated trees, cast a soft glow to the early evening. A menu was posted outside the restaurant's door.

"Take a look at the menu," said Sascha. "Beer or wine?"

"Wine, please," replied Zoey, stepping past him to look at the posted menu.

"You're in Germany, and you want *wine*?" Sascha sounded scandalized. "Tasteless."

Zoey laughed and rolled her eyes. "Beer, then."

"Better choice," he grinned. "Back in a tick."

"Sascha, wait I –" Zoey bit off the rest of her sentence as he vanished inside the restaurant.

She raised one hand and tapped her upper lip, and her eyes darted to the posted menu. Words about six feet long with far too many vowels and umlauts stared at her. She grimaced. If it were French, she might have fared slightly better, but this? This looked like nonsense. Grimacing, she scanned the menu for any German cognates that might resemble their English counterparts. Nothing – nothing that made any amount of sense, anyway. Was there any point in trying to scan for German words that might resemble ones she knew in French? Again. Nothing.

Turning away, Zoey looked around. Maybe she'd fare better at finding a seat for them. God, she hoped there were English menus. She spotted an open table near the center of the garden and made her way toward it, settling on the edge of the bench. She leaned back, elbows on the table. Her leg throbbed a little from the strain. She hadn't walked this far since she and Sascha had arrived at the safe house. Even their evening walks hadn't taken them quite this distance.

This was the first time since the night she'd been taken that she'd been alone in public. She could get up and leave now. She could blunder her own way back to England. She could. But she didn't. Staying with Sascha was safer than striking out alone. Zoey's eyes drifted down. There was a part of her – a very small, extremely guilty part – that didn't want to leave. In spite of herself, in spite of all the reasons she shouldn't, she enjoyed Sascha's company. Twisted and backward as that must be.

Her gaze settled on the door to the restaurant, and Sascha stepped outside, one glass of beer in each hand and official menus under his arm. The early evening sun caught on him. It turned his hair golden, accentuated his sharp features in all the best ways, and practically highlighted his confident stance. For a second, Zoey couldn't tear her eyes away, and she swallowed hard. Sascha was truly, devastatingly handsome.

A flush leaped to her cheeks, and Zoey tried to beat it back before Sascha looked in her direction. Handsome or not, she was in no position to think of him like that. Just the same as her harebrained thoughts of kissing him from earlier that afternoon. He was an assassin. She was, well, she was herself. Zoey Blackmore. They belonged to two different worlds. In spite of herself, she remembered the feeling of his soft exhale against her skin from earlier in the day. The way a chill had flushed through her body, and how her blood had come alive.

No right. She had no right to think like that. No right to think of kissing him. It was disrespectful to him and everything he'd done for her. Sascha was getting things together for her passport. He was her guide through this. He wasn't someone she needed to think of in any other light than that. Just a friend.

Then those blue eyes landed on her. She took another deep breath, trying to force her blush away. Sascha was her best shot – no pun intended – at getting home. An ally. A friend. Nothing more.

"Do you mind if we move over there?" asked Sascha, handing her one of the pints of beer and nodding to a table further away.

"To that table in the corner?" asked Zoey, glad he had spoken. His voice seemed to have broken the spell her mind wanted to cast.

"Yes."

"Sure. But why?" she asked, getting up.

"I prefer to have my back to a wall or be in a corner in a public place. Makes me feel a bit safer."

"Being in a corner?"

"I can see more of what's going on around me, and it means that no one can get the drop on me from behind."

"Does it get tiring?" Zoey slid onto the bench at the second table and took one of the unintelligible menus from Sascha. "Not being able to really relax, I mean?"

Sascha shrugged, half leaning a shoulder on one of the window flowerboxes. "I'm used to it. I was trained to think and live this way."

"It's not something I could do," said Zoey, taking a sip of the beer. It was pale amber, but still heavy with a strong hoppy taste.

"It's something I hope you never *have* to do," replied Sascha. He pointed to the beer. "What do you think of that?"

Zoey grinned and eyed the glass. Even so, she couldn't help feeling a little skeptical of it. "It's nice. But strong. Stronger than I expected, if you go by the looks of it. I'm not a big beer drinker, though. Quick question."

"Hm?"

Zoey fiddled with a corner of the menu. "Do they have English menus? Trying to read German when I don't know any is a bit tricky."

Sascha paused, his glass halfway raised. "Oh. I'm sorry, Zoey. I forget sometimes that you don't know German."

"Not a word," replied Zoey.

"I'll translate. I don't want to draw a lot of attention by asking for the English version of the menu."

Zoey waited until Sascha had raised his glass and was halfway through drinking before she spoke. "Or you could just order me something so aggressively German that I learn the language through assimilation."

Sascha snorted into his drink, the sound caught somewhere between laughing and trying not to laugh. He wiped his chin. "Thank you for that, Zoey."

She grinned. "You're welcome."

"I'll order for you, but you've just made a dangerous proposition. I hope you realize that. This would be a great opportunity for you to learn some simple words."

"Oh, joy," she replied, trying to keep the touch of sarcasm out of her voice. "Much as I'd like to learn some German, I didn't think I'd be in for a lesson *tonight*."

"I hardly think your school teachers would bring you beer to lessons," replied Sascha, one eyebrow rising a fraction. "I *can* teach you some German if you'd like."

"I –" Zoey smiled and breathed a tiny laugh. "Are you just multitalented?"

Sascha shrugged, the corners of his mouth twitching up. "Jack of all trades, master of one."

"I'd like to learn *some*. Seeing as I'm here. What's the German word for 'beer'? No doubt something exceedingly long and impossible to say."

"Truly a staple word of the German language," Sascha laughed, a smile settling on his lips. "Bier."

"You're joking? So, it's a cognate? Why did I not see that on the menu?"

"It's not written as a cognate on the menu. The beers on the menu are listed under the brand names themselves."

"Well, that's helpful," said Zoey, folding her hands together on the tabletop and sitting back as a waiter approached their table. She was more than content to let Sascha take the lead here.

"Ein Almschnitzel, ein gebackener Camembert, und zwei mehr Tegernseer helle Biere, bitte," said Sascha, passing both menus up. "Danke."

Zoey stared at him, only vaguely noticing the waiter respond and leave them once again. Even during classes, she'd been fascinated by the students who could slip to and from languages as easily as breathing. A touch of jealousy raised its head.

"How many languages do you speak?" Zoey asked.

She wondered if he'd need a second to pause and reset to English. She'd seen students do that during classes before, as though they needed to shake off the second language in order to return to their first.

"Nine," replied Sascha.

Zoey resisted the urge to sigh. Of course, he hadn't missed a beat. "Which ones?"

"Slovene, German, English, French, Spanish, Italian, Russian, Arabic, and Mandarin. I speak others as well, but those are the ones I'm fluent in." A smirk pulled the corner of his mouth, and he raised one hand. "I also know sign language, which comes in pretty handy."

Zoey stared at him and sighed hard. In spite of the awful pun, she found herself fighting a grin. Beat it back. She couldn't give him the satisfaction of laughing.

"That was awful. Truly."

"Come on, I've got a great sense of humor. You could almost say it's killer."

Zoey bit her tongue and planted her hands on the table as though she was going to stand. "Sascha, this has been great, really. I was looking forward to working with you to get back to England. But after that, I'm going to have to insist that I swim the Channel rather than listen to another round of puns."

"Oh, come on, Zoey, I think that one was rather good. You know, I've always thought that if I didn't professionally kill people, I'd make quite a comedian. I certainly know how to split ribs," he said, grinning.

Zoey grinned, shaking her head. "I'm going to throw this glass at you if you don't stop. But, seriously? A comedian?"

"No, not really," scoffed Sascha, taking another sip of beer. "I'm only funny sometimes because I've done horrible things, and humor is a coping mechanism." "So what *would* you want to do?" asked Zoey, resting an elbow on the table and propping her chin in her palm. "If you weren't . . . well."

"If you don't want to say the word, just call me a contractor," said Sascha, a small, rueful smile on his face. He nodded at the flowerbox beside him. "Florist."

"*Florist*? Are you serious?"

"I love flowers. I love working with my hands. The way people use flowers to convey emotions they can't bring themselves to speak. For those feelings to be spoken through petals and physical, tangible beauty using the language that flowers speak – it's something truly incredible. I remember . . ." He paused, expression turning cautious for a moment. Then the expression faded, replaced with the smile that had been there before. "When I was a boy, my father took me to the florist's shop in the village to collect a bouquet for my mother in the hospital. The smell of the place. So clean and green and full of life. I've never forgotten it. From that day on, I wanted to open my own flower shop. Spend my days making bouquets and arrangements for all moments of life. The good and the bad."

"I feel the same way about dancing," said Zoey, the words tumbling from her mouth with ease. "It's art and emotion brought to life. It's passion, love, beauty, sorrow, and all the sense of humanity flowing in motion with music. I miss it. A lot."

"You'll get back to it. I know you will."

"I just hope you're right." Zoey swallowed, an unexpected lump rising in her throat. She changed the subject. "Your mom. You said she was in the hospital when you were young?"

Sascha nodded. "Yeah. She died when I was about ten. Some sort of cancer. Dad died in a car crash only a few months later. It was just me and my two sisters from then on. They vanished a couple of years after we moved to Ljubljana. I never found out what happened to them."

"I'm sorry."

"It was a long time ago, Zoey." Zoey sighed, and she grimaced, feeling like she'd dampened the mood. She rubbed the side of her neck, wishing her fingers would contact cold metal again.

"You do that a lot," said Sascha.

"What?" asked Zoey.

"Rub your neck or collarbones. Why?"

Zoey laughed quietly and shook her head, gaze dropping to the table. "I, ah, I used to wear a necklace. Rona and Hailee got it for me a few years ago. It was beautiful. A little pair of dancing slippers on a gold chain. I wore it every day. I feel odd without it. I miss it."

"What happened to it?" asked Sascha, taking another sip.

"I . . . I lost it."

"Seems uncharacteristically careless."

Zoey felt her smile slip away before she could stop it. "He – Ewan – ripped it off when I woke up the night after they took me, and they threw it away. It's stupid, really. It was just a necklace. I can get another. But I always felt as though I danced better with it. I'm a bit scared that when . . . if . . . I dance again, that'll have changed. I'm worried about my leg as well. I don't know if I'll be the same. Maybe this injury won't affect me at all. Maybe I'm being stupid. I don't know. I'm rambling, I'm sorry."

"That injury on your leg will never stop you," said Sascha with a soft smile. "You'll see. I'm certain of it."

Warmth spread through Zoey's chest, and she took another sip of beer to cover her blush. "And I'm sure we'll see you open that flower shop one day."

Sascha paused, an expression of something like surprise catching at the sides of his mouth. Then he smiled, and the chill in his blue eyes melted clean away. A red poppy behind him suddenly bowed its head in a gentle summer breeze, blood-colored petals brushing his temple. Zoey froze, feeling something bright settle in her chest, somewhere down between her ribs. That image, she thought, might be ingrained in her mind for the rest of her life. The vibrant, scarlet petals brightening the blue in Sascha's eyes to an intensity that was almost unbearable. The gentle breeze sent a few white petals swirling down from the summer blossoms in the trees, and Zoey didn't pull away as Sascha brushed some of them from her hair.

~ ~ ~ ~ ~ ~

A sigh escaped Zoey's mouth as she stepped back inside the safe house. She'd grown used to the place, perhaps even a touch fond of it. She blinked hard. Her head was a little foggy after dinner – maybe the beer was hitting harder than she'd thought it would. She turned as Sascha flipped the living room lights on. The lighting seemed softer, hazier than she remembered it being. "I should get going soon," said Sascha.

Zoey turned. Sascha lingered still in the doorway, leaning on the doorframe. The keys hadn't even left his hand. Seriousness pressed its way back in.

"Do you need to get anything before you go?"

Sascha shook his head, lifting the right side of his sweater. "Already prepared."

An involuntary swallow seized Zoey's throat as the grip of a handgun came visible, holstered between his black undershirt and waistband. Her gaze lingered, and she realized there was something else. His black undershirt wasn't a shirt. It ended a few inches above his waist, his actual, blue shirt just visible below it. She'd seen these before in war films and worn by police on the news.

"Bulletproof vest?" she asked. "Have you been wearing that all evening?"

"No, I slipped off and changed while you were standing there," smirked Sascha, lowering his sweater.

"*Ha. Ha.* Very funny. How long will you be gone?"

"I'm not sure. Maybe a few hours or all night. You'll be fine on your own."

Zoey tilted her head, resting one hand on the table in the foyer. She couldn't quite tell if what Sascha had just said was a statement or a question. She brushed a few strands of loose hair over her shoulder. It was growing. At last.

"Yeah, I'll be fine," she replied.

"Good," replied Sascha.

Silence fell. A flicker of amusement wavered in Zoey's chest. She wanted to break the quiet, but, in the very same moment, she wanted it to remain. She wanted it to stretch without ending. In spite of the bulletproof vest under Sascha's shirt and the gun at his hip, Zoey found that it wasn't an uncomfortable lull.

"Well. No sense in me standing here," he said, standing upright. "There's food in the fridge if you get hungry later on tonight for any reason. You know the television upstairs works, but just be wary of those clown films."

"What about actual television? News and stuff?" asked Zoey, her attention piquing. It would be nice to be able to listen to the news for a night. Catch up with the world – remember that there *was* a world.

"I'm afraid there's no cable connection. Annoying, I know, but I don't normally stay here as long as we have."

Zoey nodded. She couldn't help feeling a little disappointed. Maybe there was some way that she could get to the internet through Sascha's phone. As soon as the idea surfaced, she beat it down. The phone Sascha had lent her was a skeleton. If there was any way to access the internet, she wouldn't find it.

"There should be some English books on the shelves near the television as well. When I go –"

Zoey laughed. "Lock the doors and windows, don't answer the door to anyone, and don't answer the phone? Make sure I turn away any suspicious old women offering me apples? I know the drill, Sascha. I'm the oldest of three girls. I've been told this, and I've told it to my sisters in turn."

"What can I say?" shrugged Sascha. "Leaving at night makes me more anxious.""You're fretting," said Zoey.

Sascha hummed, sounding amused, then seriousness fell over his features. The softness to his expression vanished, and Zoey stopped leaning on the table. She straightened, her balance shifting to the balls of her feet. Sascha was all sharp edges and angular features again – just the same as the night she'd met him.

"They wanted to have the meeting with you at ten tonight, didn't they?" asked Zoey as the atmosphere between them veered away from comfortable.

"Well. Not exactly. I want to get there no later than ten so that I can get a good look at the area and not have any surprises. It's going to be a late night."

"Should I wait up?" asked Zoey.

Sascha tilted his head, and Zoey couldn't keep her eyes from darting away. That unreadable expression unsettled her. Her heart beat a little faster in her chest, and she rummaged for a way to dispel the sudden tension.

"No," he replied, turning away.

"Sascha," said Zoey, a flash of fear leaping to the front of her mind.

"Hm?"

"What if you don't come back?"

"I'll come back," said Sascha, a smile pulling at the side of his mouth as he turned away. "You won't even notice I'm gone."

A rush of emotion – emotions Zoey didn't quite want to name – surged up in her chest. "Sascha?"

"Yes, Zoey?" he asked, pausing at the door.

She folded her arms. "Be careful."

Sascha's hard look faltered, and a fragment of a smile crept into his eyes. "I will."

Stillness hit Zoey like a hammer blow as the door closed behind Sascha. The house felt hollow. Outside, she heard the car start and gravel crunch as it turned around. Final silence. Only the humming of the fridge broke the quiet. Zoey glanced at the clock above the oven. It wasn't even nine. She bit the inside of her cheek. Why did she feel so anxious? She'd been without Sascha before now – without even knowing it. There was no reason for her to feel more worried tonight. Was it just because she knew he was meeting someone to discuss her passport? She exhaled hard and ran a hand through her hair. Might as well go upstairs. There wasn't much for her to do here aside from wait for Sascha to get back.

Zoey made her way up the stairs. Her steps were so much steadier. She glanced around the upstairs living room and spotted the television remote on the coffee table. She turned toward the shelves on either side of the television and scanned the DVD's there. Nothing looked even remotely English. She sighed. She didn't know why she'd expected there to be anything new this time. All the same, she pulled one from the shelf. *Das Labyrinth des Schweigens*. It sounded . . . very German. Pressing play on the DVD player and turning on the television, she settled on the couch and allowed her mind to drift.

In the back of her mind, a memory surfaced. A moment between her and Rona. *'Be careful.'* Rona always laughed at her when she said those words. She'd told her they were a dressed-up way of saying *'I care about you.'*

Maybe she was right.

Zoey reached back and pulled a throw blanket over her legs as the film started. *A dressed-up way of saying, 'I care about you'.* But that raised a whole new set of problems. Did she care about Sascha? Of course she did. After everything he'd done, everything he'd told her, she wasn't sure there was any way she couldn't feel as though she cared about him. He was helping her get home. He was kind. She liked his company.

Zoey tilted her head, trying to follow the storyline and characters on the screen, but her thoughts kept turning back to Sascha. She'd thought about kissing him earlier. *Wanted* to kiss him earlier. For a split second, she wondered what his lips would feel like against hers. She sighed sharply and adjusted the way she sat on the couch, willing herself not to think about it.

She turned and rested her chin in her hand, again, trying to refocus on the film. Something about a lawyer. A lawyer who, if she squinted, would look very like Sascha. Zoey frowned and leaned forward, turning off the movie. As far as anything even remotely involving romantic interest went, Sascha was the most off-limits person in the history of off-limits people. She mustn't let her thoughts run away with her.

Chapter 21

It was the vibration of her phone on the wooden nightstand that woke Zoey. Overcast light filtered in through her bedroom window. She groaned and covered her eyes with one arm. It couldn't be past six in the morning. The light had that early, soft quality to it. Gentle rain tapped the glass. Zoey rolled over, pulling her blankets closer around her shoulders. There was a quiet sound from downstairs. Not one Zoey could place. Still half asleep, she lifted her head and tapped her phone screen. A cold bolt of fear dashing through her. One text. No one texted during the night unless it was urgent. Much less at just past five-forty-five in the morning.

Sascha, 5:47 AM: *Back*.

Blinking fast to clear the sleep from her eyes, Zoey grinned, her anxiety fading. He was back. News on her passport! She was going home! Zoey raised her fingers to respond to the text, then stopped herself. Sascha had gotten back an hour ago. He was probably asleep. Then . . . no. He wasn't asleep. Zoey could smell coffee. She sat up and swung her legs out of bed, a yawn pausing her movement. She wouldn't get back to sleep now. She was too awake. Downstairs, home had to be just a conversation away. Rona, Hailee. They were within reach of her going *home*.

She pulled on a fresh shirt, giddy with excitement, and dashed downstairs, resisting the urge to take them two at a time. Her leg was getting better, but it was definitely not ready for that much strain.

At the bottom of the stairs, she stopped. Sascha was sitting in the center of the living room couch, a rust-colored mug in one hand. Zoey paused, a small smile curling her lips. A second mug was on the table. Toward the center of the table sat Sascha's laptop, open as though inviting her to come and have a look.

As she spotted the rest of the items on the table though, her smile faltered. A handgun, muzzle still trapped in a black plastic holster lay on the table, within Sascha's reach. His bulletproof vest was draped across the back of the couch. She shook herself. She shouldn't, she mustn't, be surprised about this. This was part of what Sascha was and what he did. It wasn't something she needed to feel concerned about.

Zoey cleared her throat. "Good morning."

"I wondered if coffee might bring you down," chuckled Sascha, turning and smiling at her. "I know it's earlier than you usually get up."

"Tea would have worked better. Nothing to attract the English attention like a cup of tea," she teased, any wariness she'd felt at the sight of the gun slipping away with Sascha's smile. "How'd everything go?"

Sascha's gaze slipped away. "It went. I've got good news and bad news. Which do you want first?"

"The bad," replied Zoey. "Always best to get the bad news out of the way first."

"Too true. Sit down," he said, closing the folder.

"What is it?" she asked. She settled on the couch beside Sascha. A cold weight of foreboding settled around the base of her spine, and she eyed the laptop on the table. Nothing. It was just open to the home screen.

Sascha rested his elbows on his knees. "OMNI knows I'm in the area. I got a message from them this morning. They want a meeting with me."

A bite of fear seared its way through Zoey's chest. "Why?"

"I don't know yet, though it's likely that they want to hire me for something. I have a funny, gut feeling that they'll want to hire me to find you."

"When?"

"A few weeks from now. They haven't given a date yet."

"Can you tell them you don't want to meet?"

Sascha laughed quietly. "You don't say 'no' to OMNI. You refuse them, you end up dead. I'd prefer not to die."

Zoey looked at the carpet. Had she somehow given them away? This was a safety concern for them both. If OMNI knew she was here . . . that she was with Sascha . . . she didn't know what might happen. What they might do.

She raised her gaze back to him. "Do you think they know about me? That I'm here?"

"No," said Sascha, shaking his head. "If they knew, I feel sure that there would have been some concentrated effort to get you back. Or to get me out of the way."

"What do we do?" asked Zoey.

"We continue what we've been doing. Lying low, let work on your passport continue. The biggest problem is, I can't move until after this meeting – certainly can't go to England in the next couple of weeks. It'd be too suspicious."

Zoey swallowed. "What if, once we get the passport, I leave alone from Munich?"

Sascha snorted, sounding derisive. "On your own? OMNI will still be watching the airports for anyone matching your description. They only lost you a short time ago. Their operatives haven't come off high alert yet. Not by a long shot. I'm sorry, but no. It's not a good idea. They'd have you back before you even left the airport."

"What about a disguise?" asked Zoey. "You wore one at Charles de Gaulle."

"There's too many factors that can go wrong with disguises," replied Sascha.

"Don't you think you're underestimating me a bit? I'm not helpless," snapped Zoey. She bit the inside of her cheek as the words left her mouth. Blood drained from her face. She hadn't meant to say it. Maxwell couldn't stand it when she, Rona, or Hailee got sharp with him. Her mind flashed the memory of Maxwell slamming his hands on the kitchen table and shouting so viciously at her that she'd cried after some smart remark. Backtrack. Backtrack now.

She choked out her words. "I'm sorry. I didn't mean to say that. I don't know why . . . It's early. I'm still half asleep. I'm sorry."

Sascha shook his head and yawned. "I wish I *were* underestimating you. I have no doubt you could navigate an airport under normal circumstances, even wearing a disguise. But these aren't normal circumstances. Against OMNI, you *are* helpless. To them, you're a chess piece. They're a big, powerful corporation with a lot of people on hand, people who are actively hunting you. Without someone to watch your back and give you help where you need it, I think they'd find you."

Zoey looked away, guilt for snapping at him making her crawl in her own skin. She fixed her eyes on her knees. "I'm sorry."

Next to her, Sascha sighed, the sound soft. "Don't apologize. You're frustrated. I know how you feel. I've been in situations like this myself. Nothing is moving fast enough and everything you're trying to do relies on other people. All I ask is that you understand I'm trying my best to keep both of us safe. If we rush this, we risk us both getting caught. I would die a horrible death, and you'd end up someone's property. Neither of which I want to see happen."

Zoey nodded, swallowing hard. She risked a glance at Sascha from her peripherals. He didn't look angry. He looked concerned – that furrow between his brows was back, and the area around his mouth seemed drawn.

"I understand," she said. Her voice was smaller than she'd expected it to be.

"Want to hear the good news?"

"I'm surprised you still want to give it to me," replied Zoey, letting a fragment of humor creep in.

"I'm not vindictive like that. You should know that by now," said Sascha, the strained expression fading. He leaned forward and clicked on one of the home screen's icons. "Have a look at this. Work on your passport's come a good way. Still more to do, but it's getting there. It really won't be long now before it's finished. My contact secured you a temporary address in Paris. You've just finished a summer abroad through University of London, and you're on the way home. They also pulled an address in London for you in case anyone asks. Different city of birth. I gave a false birthday for you as well. According to this, you were born in February in 1996."

"Think I can pass for a bit older than I am?"

"I think you can make it work."

A laugh formed in Zoey's chest, but she didn't let it free. She scrolled to the next page. "Is that . . . ?"

"Ah. There's the template proof for the counterfeit passport. My contact said it shouldn't take much longer to finish now. Speaking of, do you mind if I rip one of your social media pictures and photo shop it a bit to make it usable?"

"I – of course, I don't mind."

"Perfect. That's one of the last bits of information my contact needs. After that, they'll get to making the real thing – well, the forged thing. Not long now."

"You're fantastic, you know that, don't you?" said Zoey. She bit the inside of her cheek as she flushed. All the blood that had drained from her face earlier came rushing back. She was in the business of saying things she didn't mean to this morning. "Sorry. Again."

Sascha laughed quietly and leaned back against the far armrest of the couch, taking a sip of his coffee. "You apologize more than I ever thought humanly possible."

Zoey reached for the second coffee cup on the table. The mug was still lukewarm. "Comes from growing up feeling as though you have to apologize for everything."

"Yes, Maxwell has that effect."

Zoey looked at Sascha, her eyes narrowing. There it was again. Something odd. Something unsaid. Some trace of familiarity. "That's several times you've done that now, you know?"

Gray eyes met blue over the rim of Sascha's coffee cup. Zoey took a sip of coffee as one of Sascha's brows rose. Was he prompting her to go on? She raised one of her own brows and waited for him to lower his mug. He didn't. Either he wasn't going to answer, or he was trying to drown his silence in an eight-ounce mug. Zoey gathered her courage together and leaned back on the armrest on her own side of the couch to face him head-on.

"Why does it sound like you know him?"

"In my sphere, there's only a few people that one can . . . oh, never mind. I've been honest with you. I'm not going to start lying now." Sascha put his coffee mug back on the table. "Zoey, your father trained me. I used to work for him."

Zoey coughed, coffee catching in her throat as she tried to swallow. Cold shock swept over her. "*What*?"

Sascha sighed and looked away. There was an annoyed kind of expression in his eyes, but Zoey had a feeling it wasn't directed at her. He took a deep breath and lifted his head. He went silent, and Zoey was on the verge of probing him again. They'd worked together? Why hadn't Sascha told her this before?

"It's a long story, but I'll try and keep it as brief as I can. Very few people know this story, and if you repeat it to anyone, Maxwell and I will both deny it. As far as most people are concerned, what I'm going to tell you never happened. Do you understand?"

"Yes," replied Zoey. She rubbed her chest, torn between asking questions and letting Sascha talk.

Sascha leaned forward, elbows resting on his thighs and fingers lacing together. When he spoke, he kept his eyes on the floor.

"Your father found me when I was thirteen. My parents had both died by then, and my sisters were gone. I was alone in the world, surviving on side jobs and petty crime. I saw Maxwell for the first time in Ljubljana. He was well-dressed, and I decided I'd try and get some quick money from him. I pulled a knife on him. He pulled a gun on me. He disarmed me, but instead of calling the police, he bought me food. It was the first time I'd eaten in days. I've never understood why Maxwell did what he did that day, and I don't think he does either. In any event, he made me an offer.

"He said if I came to England with him, he wouldn't tell the police about my attempted theft. If I refused, well, it was off to the police. The idea of being thrown in jail is terrifying for a thirteen-year-old, so I went with him." Sascha ran a thumb along his lower lip and sighed. "He fed me, housed me, gave me a life, even made me part of his shadow organization in the SAS."

"So, what happened?" asked Zoey. "Why did you leave him and the SAS?"

Even though Zoey saw Sascha's mouth twitch in amusement, she could see a glimmer of resentment in his eyes. She tilted her head, inwardly willing him to go on. It was like a dam had broken inside Sascha, and she wasn't about to interrupt him.

"Do you know what it's like to kill someone, Zoey?"

"No," replied Zoey, the single word tiny and fragile.

"I learned what it was like at sixteen years old. Because your father told me to. He told me I was doing the British public a favor. That I owed him for the kindness he'd offered me. And that's what it was like for the next three years. Train. Go out. Kill people on Maxwell's orders. Repeat. When I turned nineteen, I thought I had the freedom to choose my own path. I wanted to go into the Royal Marines. I wanted to do something *good*. But Maxwell wanted something different for me. I was an expensive investment, so your father tried to lock me into a contract of his making with the secret services. Their perfect clandestine agent. Covert killer of dangerous opponents at the behest of the British government. Maxwell and I had an argument, and he blackmailed me. He used my lack of citizenship status and the crimes he'd had me commit against me. If I refused him, he'd reveal all of my information to anyone looking for me. I'd already assassinated people internationally, and I'd have been facing the death penalty in some countries. Still am. In the end, he made me an offer. If I carried off my next mission successfully, he'd reevaluate my future. Let me have a fresh start. That was when everything hit the fan."

"What happened? On your mission, I mean? It had to be bad to make you finally run from him."

Sascha turned to her, and Zoey's chest ached. She'd never seen him like this. His expression was so painfully guilt-ridden.

"I killed a child." He paused and pinched the bridge of his nose. "Maxwell and his team gave me bad information. Looking back, I'm almost certain it was deliberate. Based on the information they gave, the girl was never supposed to be in the house. But she was. She was only ten. It was supposed to only be her father on the property. I'd already killed her father, and I heard a noise in the hallway. I didn't think about it, I just . . . shot. The next thing I knew, I'd killed a father and a daughter, and I'd botched a high-profile mission. It gave Maxwell the leverage he needed to lock me into his contract. So I bolted."

Zoey's chest constricted, and she reached out for him, resting a hand on his wrist. "Sascha, I'm so sorry."

Half his mouth slanted up in a humorless smile. "It's not your fault, Zoey."

"What Maxwell did. Everything. Using you, blackmailing you, the high-profile missions. That all *had* to be illegal. Didn't anyone know? All the people he works with? Did they know what he was doing? Know that you were with him? Surely, someone in his organization would have spoken out."

"It was extremely illegal, and they all knew that. They just didn't care. Even if anyone had cared, they'd have been too afraid to say anything. They'd have washed up on a riverbank with no teeth and no fingerprints. Like I said, I was Maxwell's expensive investment. It's easy to make someone into whatever you want them to be when there's no record of them existing, and I was a boy without immigration papers. I was a tool to be used. Nothing more."

"I can't believe he never mentioned you . . ."

"He had no reason to. He concealed his true identity from you and your sisters for years, and I was his greatest failure. An embarrassment to his record. Trained and honed for years to be a . . . well." Sascha gestured to himself. "Something intended to keep other people from getting their hands dirty."

"But after you ran, why did you continue being . . .?" Zoey let the sentence hang. She couldn't quite bring herself to complete it.

"A killer?" asked Sascha.

"That," replied Zoey, looking away, glad he'd supplied the word.

"After I left England, I knew I had to play to my strengths if I wanted to stay alive and stay out of your father's hands. My strongest skills, well, I'm sure you can guess."

Zoey bit the inside of her cheek. "What he taught you."

Sascha inclined his head, half-nodding. "In spite of my efforts, I ended up being what I am. What eases me about it is that I am still free. I am my own person, and my choices are my own, however monstrous those choices may be. I still have the freedom to not let that hammer fall. If you had to kill, wouldn't you prefer it be your choice, your own decision, rather than orders you had to follow?"

Zoey looked down, staring into her mug. She couldn't look at Sascha. Guilt that wasn't her own settled down in her chest and weighed heavy.

"He trafficked you," said Zoey, more to herself than to Sascha. "He runs a shadow organization that directly combats human trafficking, and . . ."

"Believe me, the irony isn't lost on me."

Zoey shook her head slowly, her gaze fixed on the pale carpet. "If you hate him so much, why did you help *me*? You had to know I'm his daughter. Blackmore isn't exactly a common name."

Sascha sighed hard. "I don't hate many people, but him I make an exception for. But, Zoey, listen to me." A spring in the couch creaked, but Zoey didn't look at Sascha. She couldn't. His thigh pressed against hers. "Your father puts people in danger. It's what he does. But no one else should have to suffer for his decisions. Our paths crossed by chance in France, but when I saw you and recognized you, I couldn't leave you there."

Zoey fought to keep her lower lip from trembling. "I'm sorry for what he did."

Sascha's hand settled on her forearm, his thumb tracing circles on the inside of her wrist. "Look at me."

Zoey barely heard him. She couldn't look at Sascha without guilt turning her insides molten. She shook her head in disbelief. How could Maxwell have done this? How could he have used –

Her thoughts juddered to a halt as she felt Sascha's free hand take her chin in a gentle but firm grip and turn her head toward himself. Zoey froze entirely. His face was only inches from her own. She stared into his eyes, unable to look away. As caught in his gaze as a deer in headlights. Immediately, that wild, frantic urge to kiss him raised its head. It would be so easy to just lean forward and . . . Zoey swallowed hard and fought to shove the thought away, but it stayed, and she had to hope Sascha couldn't feel her heart racing. His other hand was still on her wrist, his thumb tracing those tiny, insistent patterns that set her skin on fire. There was no way that he couldn't feel her pulse hammering in her veins.

"What happened between Maxwell and I is our business. It's not your cross to bear, and I won't hear you apologize on *his* behalf. For even thinking of it, you have more grace than he could ever wish for."

Zoey breathed again as Sascha leaned back, his hands dropping away and leaving trails of heat on her skin. Suddenly, there was space between them again. She offered a tiny laugh and looked away, adjusting her grip on her coffee mug. She'd forgotten she was holding it. How had she not dropped it?

She cleared her throat. "I have to ask, is the fact that you know my father why you've been being so nice to me?"

"What? No," Sascha snorted, blue eyes widening and a shocked smile settling on his mouth. "I've been nice to you because I like you. I enjoy your company. God above, you'd know if I didn't."

Zoey laughed, flustered, and she glanced into her coffee mug, trying to avoid Sascha's eyes. She could feel the blood rushing to her ears. She grimaced as she looked back up at him.

"Why didn't you tell me about Maxwell before?" she asked.

Sascha paused, and for a moment, he looked embarrassed. "Frankly, Zoey, I didn't want to bring it up. I know you were wary of me when you first arrived, and I thought that telling you about this might upset you even more. It's also not really something that I talk about lightly. I normally try and pretend it never happened. Forgive me?"

Zoey smiled at him. She couldn't help it. Sascha looked so vulnerable. So human.

"I suppose I'll be able to find forgiveness in due time," she grinned. "Another coffee?"

"Please," he replied, holding his mug out to her. "There should be some decaf left."

"Ah, yes, the personal war on caffeine continues," she replied, getting up. "Are you sure you don't want anything a bit stronger after being up all night?"

Sascha laughed. "Thank you for the offer, but I can't stand caffeine. Makes me shake. It always has."

Zoey shook her head and walked to the kitchen, refilling Sascha's mug. "Want anything in it?"

"Black is fine," replied Sascha.

Zoey scoffed and returned to the couch with a full cup. "Disgusting. I don't know how you drink it like that. I'd be sick if I tried."

"Clearly you don't have as refined a palate as I do," replied Sascha.

"You mean as ruined as yours?" she grinned, passing his mug back to him.

"Keep teasing," he said with a smile, settling back and resting his feet on the coffee table. "See where it gets you."

Zoey laughed softly and leaned back against the couch arm, stretching her back. She sighed as she heard the joints pop in a satisfying way. From her peripherals, she just spotted the side of Sascha's fingers tightening on his mug as though he was uncomfortable. She tilted her head to ask what he was thinking, when he rolled his shoulders and leaned forward.

"How's that injury of yours doing now?"

"A lot better. There's not much pain anymore. I think it's nearly healed."

Sascha hummed softly, pulling the large drawer containing first aid gear out from the coffee table. "I think those bandages are ready to come off permanently."

Zoey glanced at her thigh and pursed her lips, then replaced her coffee mug on the table. "You know, I think you're right."

Chapter 22

Maybe it was nothing. Sheer restlessness. Maybe it was facing the reality of what had been uncovered beneath the bandages – a livid mess of red, barely healed skin. In any event, Zoey couldn't sleep. She couldn't relax. She couldn't get the image of the shiny, new scar tissue across her thigh out of her head. She felt naked without the bandages now, somehow. She'd got used to them. They'd been a buffer for what lay underneath. She took a deep breath and rolled onto her back, staring blankly upward and wishing she had her own phone to scroll through mindlessly and lull herself to sleep. A podcast. A video. Anything. But she didn't have her own phone. She had the shadows of moonlit trees dancing against the wall. She yawned, tiredness pulling at the fringes of her mind, but every time she closed her eyes, any semblance of wanting to rest faded away, leaving only frustration in its wake. She drew another deep breath and grabbed a second pillow, covering her face and trying to force herself down into sleep. Fleetingly, she wondered if maybe if it was darker, she'd be able to sleep better. A vain hope.

Rona and Hailee's faces danced in front of her closed eyes, and sleep refused her. Sighing hard and pulling the pillow off her head, Zoey stared at the ceiling a moment longer. The moonlit trees bowed and waved ever so slightly. They seemed to be mocking her, somehow. The world at peace, asleep, and she was still awake, tossing and turning. Zoey shook her head and got out of bed without any sort of plan. She grabbed her phone and turned on the flashlight function, not quite wanting to turn on any of the overhead lights.

Maybe putting on the television would help. But that would probably wake Sascha. She didn't know how light or heavy of a sleeper he was. Light, she was willing to bet.

Maybe a cup of tea? A drink that tasted like home. But also a drink that was almost as caffeine-heavy as coffee. Probably not the best idea for getting back to sleep. But it would make her feel that bit closer to Hailee and Rona. It would taste like *home*. A kind of certainty settled in her chest. That was what she wanted.

Keeping her still uneven steps light, Zoey slowly opened her bedroom door. She didn't close it behind her. Just on the off chance the actual closure was loud. She started toward the stairs.

The house was pitch dark. The only movement, a low hum of electricity, which wasn't really movement at all. Rather a constant background noise that felt like movement. Holding the banister, Zoey descended the stairs. At the bottom, she glanced in the direction of Sascha's bedroom. No light shone from underneath the door. She was suddenly glad that she'd decided against putting on a film or turning on the overhead lights. She'd hate to disturb him. God, how different this was. If she were home, she wouldn't care one bit if she woke Hailee or Rona.

But Sascha wasn't Hailee or Rona. He was . . . special. For lack of a better word.

Would boiling the kettle wake him up? Zoey scoffed to herself. That was such a quiet noise though. Hardly louder than the sound of the fridge running. She rounded the end of the kitchen bar and turned the kettle on, trying to content herself to wait for the few minutes it would take to boil. A few minutes. Only a few minutes. And yet she couldn't force herself to be still. Even for those few minutes. She had too much jittery energy coursing through her.

Moonlit trees beckoned through the glass door at the back patio, and Zoey turned to them, their movement captivating down here, where upstairs, it had only been irritating. Leaving her phone on the counter, she crossed the dark living room to the patio door and looked out. Zoey smiled and breathed softly. She couldn't remember a time she'd seen so many stars. She pulled the door open and stepped out, eyes fixed upward. Thousands of distant, twinkling suns embedded in the night sky winked back at her. Zoey grinned to herself, a tiny, childish part of her couldn't help finding this magical. She narrowed her eyes marginally, straining to see more. For a second, she thought she might have seen the cloudy outline of the Milky Way, but she blinked and the image was gone. All her restlessness and tension drained away. It was just her, the moon, and the stars.

Eyes up, she settled down on the patio wall. Could Rona and Hailee see these same stars? These same patterns in the dark? Yet another thing she wished she'd paid more attention to. How could she have known she'd ever want to know about stars? Know where the constellations were so that she could at least be assured she and her sisters could see the same heavens. Surely, the views of the night sky couldn't be *that* different between England and Germany, could they? She wished she knew with certainty. It would be nice, comforting, if they could at least share a night sky. Zoey took a deep breath and watched a shooting star flash across the dark. She missed them. So much. She dropped a hand to her thigh. And she wouldn't be going home the same. What would Hailee and Rona say when they saw what had happened? There was no hiding her injury.

"Zoey?"

She turned, her heart sinking. Sascha stepped out, tucking something into the back of his waistband. He paused a few steps away, head tilted to one side.

"I'm sorry," she said, the apology falling from her mouth before she could stop it. "I woke you up."

"Woke me up?" asked Sascha, smiling slightly. "I've been awake."

"But your light was off?"

"I like the dark," replied Sascha with a shrug. "What are you doing out here?"

Zoey scoffed quietly and tipped her head back up to the stars. "You're going to laugh at me."

"I won't. Promise," said Sascha, sitting down beside her.

"I keep thinking about Rona and Hailee. I can't sleep, and I came down for a cup of tea. Then wandered out here. It felt peaceful."

Sascha stayed quiet, and Zoey pursed her lips. It sounded so ridiculous now that she'd said it out loud. She'd thought about her sisters so much and so hard that she couldn't sleep. Who in their right mind would think that the next logical step was coming outside and staring at the stars? Zoey rubbed her feet together and shuddered, the chill of the ceramic tiles and the night's coolness finally getting to her. She should have thought to pick up a pair of socks.

Beside her, Sascha stood without a word and walked back inside. Zoey turned to watch him go, black gunmetal flashing just above his waistband as he walked. Was he really leaving? Without another word? Well. He *had* promised not to laugh. Zoey swallowed and looked back up. The childish magic she'd seen in the glittering night sky fizzled and died. All at once, she wanted nothing more than to go back upstairs and sit in the dark and the silence, her blankets pulled up over her head to block out the moon and all the stars. She pulled her feet up to sit cross-legged and waited. For what exactly, she wasn't sure. For enough time to pass, she supposed. So that Sascha wouldn't think she was just following him inside. So that he might go back into his bedroom, and she could slink quietly back upstairs.

A blanket landed in her lap, and Zoey jumped, a small smile settling on her lips as she lowered her eyes from the stars to Sascha. He carried a second blanket on his arm – Zoey recognized them as the throw blankets from the living room – and an orange mug in each hand.

"You're welcome to your caffeine this late at night. I'll stick with something that won't keep me up until dawn," he said, offering one of the mugs to her.

"I thought you'd gone back to bed," said Zoey, taking the mug and moving over to make room for him to sit.

"Tonight is too pretty to waste," he said, settling beside her, gazing upward. "And you're right. It *is* peaceful out here."

Zoey smiled and pulled the blanket around her shoulders, the mug warm in her hands. She lifted it to her nose and breathed, the familiar smell of *home* curling in her nose. She blew on it and took a small sip. Sascha made a decent cup of tea. Something she was glad of now more than ever before.

Slowly, Zoey tipped her gaze skyward again. "Are they the same as the ones over England?"

"The stars?" asked Sascha, lifting his own mug to his mouth.

Zoey caught a faint smell of something floral as Sascha moved and knew it had to be some of his blue tea. "Yeah. Stupid question, I know, but I've never really thought about the stars much. It'd be nice if . . . you know. I'd like to think they at least look the same."

"They're the same," nodded Sascha, "A few differences in view here and there, but more or less identical skies."

Zoey nodded silently and breathed out. The same skies. At the very least, she could see the same stars as Hailee and Rona. This much they could share, even hundreds of miles apart. It was a relief somehow. The tiniest sliver of connection.

"I can't stop thinking about them," she said, the words slipping like water from her mouth. "Tonight just feels worse than other nights."

Sascha laughed softly. "They're your North Star."

"My what?" asked Zoey.

"It –" Sascha glanced into his mug and smiled. "It's something my mother used to say. Everyone has a North Star. Something they use to find their way when they're lost. Something they never lose sight of. Keeps them going in the dark. Hailee and Rona are yours."

Unexpected tears pricked the backs of Zoey's eyes, and she looked back up at the sky, taking a deep breath to cover her emotion. "Where's the North Star?"

Sascha hummed and fell silent for a moment or two then pointed. "There. It's in the Ursa Minor constellation."

"You know the constellations?" asked Zoey, turning to him. "Is there anything you don't know about?"

He smiled. "My mother would take me and my sisters out on clear nights and tell us about them. I used to know all the ones visible over . . . over our village. Now I can only remember some of them. That one, there, beside Ursa Minor, is Ursa Major."

"They're the bears, right?" asked Zoey.

Sascha nodded. "The great bear and the little bear. There was a story about how they became constellations, but I can't remember it."

"You mean you forgot?" asked Zoey, taking a sip of her tea.

Sascha laughed quietly, his head tilted back. "We all have flaws. If my worst is forgetting ancient legends, I'd say I'm doing quite well."

Zoey smiled, returning her gaze to the stars. "What's your favorite constellation?"

"Tough question. I don't really have a favorite, but on a whim, that one." Sascha pointed. "See those three stars in a straight line? Part of the Orion constellation."

"Orion's the hunter, right?" asked Zoey.

Sascha nodded. "Yeah. It's an easy constellation to find, and . . . I have a morbid sense of empathy with him, I suppose. Not sure I'd exactly call it my favorite though."

Zoey turned to Sascha. Pale moonlight made him look ethereal, his eyes almost reflecting silver back up to the heavens. She tore her eyes away and forced herself to sip her tea. Sascha the hunter. It wasn't a thought she particularly liked.

"What about a favorite star?" Zoey asked. "Is yours the North Star?"

"Not quite. It's . . . give me a moment . . . there." Sascha pointed. "It's faint at the moment, but at the right time of year, it's one of the brightest stars in the sky."

Zoey narrowed her eyes, straining to see. "What is it?"

"Altair. The eagle star. Part of the eagle constellation."

"What's that one called? The eagle constellation, I mean."

A strange expression swept over Sascha's face. If Zoey didn't know better, she'd have called it longing. A heartbroken, desperate kind of longing. He fell silent, and Zoey resisted the sudden urge to move closer to him, to press her leg against his.

"Aquila," he said quietly, speaking in a tone Zoey couldn't quite decipher.

Zoey stared where Sascha had pointed, memorizing Aquila's place in the sky. At least when all this was over and she was home again, she'd have some shared focal point with him. Some shared, silver image in the night. Aquila. She solidified it in her mind, and the warmth that had settled in her chest days ago burned hotter.

"What's your North Star?" asked Zoey.

The cool, night air stilled, and she turned to Sascha, suddenly afraid she'd asked the wrong thing. Maybe she had. Expression drained slowly out of Sascha's face, but his eyes were still fixed on Aquila, staring at it with such intensity, Zoey had to half-wonder if he was waiting for a real eagle to materialize out of the cosmic dust and take wing through the night sky. She swallowed. Aquila was *his* constellation. Even if he hadn't said it aloud, nothing else could account for the heartache in his eyes. The breeze lulled, almost falling silent, as though waiting for Sascha's answer. Zoey almost looked away from him, suddenly feeling as though she was intruding on a very private moment. But she didn't. Perhaps couldn't. She wasn't sure.

He took a long drink from his mug. "I wish I knew how to answer that. Do you think North Stars can change?"

"It's not my family legend," replied Zoey, pressing her shoulder to his. "What do you think?"

"I think it would make sense for them to change every now and again. What's important to you as a child shouldn't be important to you as an adult. Goals change. Mine . . ." Sascha lowered his mug. "Mine used to be my sisters, too. But they're long gone. I think my freedom has become my North Star. God, that sounds awful saying it out loud."

"No, it doesn't. I think that makes sense," replied Zoey, sitting upright. "Your freedom is still something for you to hold onto, isn't it? Something that guides you in the dark?"

Sascha turned to her, a small, thoughtful smile on his face. "It is."

"Then I'd say that's a perfectly valid North Star," said Zoey, looking up and grateful that the night hid the unexpected blush that colored her cheeks.

She stayed still, feeling Sascha's eyes lingering on her for a few moments more. Then he looked back up at the sky, too. Zoey narrowed her eyes, peering into the diamond-studded darkness overhead, then lifted her hand and pointed to another cluster of stars.

"What's that one?"

Sascha leaned forward. "If you're pointing to the one I think you're pointing to, that'll be Andromeda. I *think*."

"And what's that one supposed to be?" asked Zoey, adjusting the blanket around her shoulders.

"Now you're really testing my memory," grinned Sascha.

Chapter 23

A light, early morning rain pattered against the windowpane in Zoey's bedroom. She took a breath and toweled her wet hair in an attempt to dry it. A vain struggle. It would have to air dry. She draped the towel over her shoulders and pulled a fresh shirt and a pair of jeans from the drawers in her nightstand, mentally thanking Sascha for buying them for her when she first arrived. She glanced at the door. Downstairs, she could hear Sascha moving around, and she smiled without meaning to. His company was so . . . easy. It felt natural. So natural that she almost forgot she'd been here for several weeks. How had it already been weeks? It felt like both an eternity and only a few days.

As she dressed, she took a deep breath, nerves clamoring in the back of her mind. What she wanted to ask him wasn't a big deal. She had to tell herself that. She played with the hem of her shirt, gathering her resolve, then turned and made her way downstairs. One request. That was all she had. The worst Sascha could say was no. She had to keep telling herself that. He wouldn't rage. He wouldn't storm. He wouldn't behave like Maxwell.

Zoey paused a second to sit down on the bottom step, her thigh throbbing. She took a breath and rubbed at it hard, watching as Sascha rinsed a used plate with one hand and texted with the other, hands totally independent of each other. She rolled her eyes, pushing herself upright. A show-off even when he thought no one was watching. Sascha glanced up and flashed a quick smile, and Zoey grinned in response.

"Hey," she said, crossing the living room and leaning on the bar. "Question."

"Ja?"

Zoey clicked her teeth, her heart sinking a little. "Oh . . . can we please not do this right now? I've got something I need to ask you."

"Nein. Ein deutscher Satz pro Tag, Zoey. Die war unsere Einigung."

Zoey sighed heavily, not fighting to keep the deepness out of it. She could have sworn she saw a flicker of amusement in Sascha's eyes. Glancing at the ceiling, she thought back over the words Sascha had already taught her. She'd asked for this at dinner in Bayrischzell.

This was a monster of her own making. Even still, one of the dictionaries from upstairs would be a godsend at the moment. She wished she'd grabbed one on the way down.

"Ich habe . . . I can't remember the word, Sascha."

He slid his phone into his pocket, rested the clean plate in the drying rack, and leaned on the kitchen counter, eyes dancing. "Ich habe ..."

"Sascha, come on."

One blond eyebrow lifted, and Zoey fought the urge to throw her hands up in defeat. Curse the day she'd asked him to teach her German.

"Ich habe eine ..." Frustrated, she snapped her fingers. If only it was so easy to recall a word. "It's the word for question."

"Das Wort fängt mit '*F*' an."

"Frage! Thank you, yes. Frage. One of those."

"Gut. Ein ganzer Satz jetzt, bitte," replied Sascha, grinning.

Zoey took a breath. She should have expected this, really. "Ich habe eine Frage."

"Und sie ist?"

"Sascha, that's not fair," replied Zoey, unable to keep a laugh out of her voice. "I had a struggle trying to get four words out."

Sascha's smile softened. "What's your question, Zoey?"

"Well . . . it's not really a question." Zoey leaned forward, resting her elbows on the kitchen counter. "I want to call Rona. I've been gone for weeks. They need to know I'm alive. Rona and Hailee have to be losing their minds by now. I know you said it would be dangerous, but there's got to be some way to get in contact with Rona or Hailee without telling them where I am. Maybe?"

"Ich wollte meine Schwester anzurufen," nodded Sascha. A hint of reservation crept into his eyes, and he inhaled through his teeth. "I don't know, Zoey. We've been doing well keeping you undercover here. Any international call to any of your family members' phones could ping in OMNI's systems and give them some idea of where you are. It's the kind of thing they're looking for."

"I just want them to know I'm alive. That's all."

Sascha glanced away, that reservation still around his eyes. Heart thundering, Zoey gathered her nerves and slowly reached across the counter, settling her hand on his. Sascha looked up sharply, but he didn't pull away.

"Please," she said.

Sascha's eyes flashed almost imperceptibly, and finally he nodded. "Give me a few hours. I'll have to set some things up for it. We'll need to get another burner for you to use, and we might have to make a bit of a drive."

Zoey breathed a sigh of relief, and she smiled at him, squeezing his hand once before she pulled away. "I thought we'd be using payphones?"

A grin flashed across Sascha's face again, a teasing look gathering in his eyes. "Are you from the Stone Age? Payphone! Honestly. I didn't think you'd even know what one is."

"I'm not *that* much younger than you," replied Zoey, fighting a grin. "And thank you, but they still have telephone boxes in England. I know what payphones are. Why use another burner? That'd be our third one."

Sascha's smile faded. "Burner phones are harder to trace. If OMNI were to intercept the call, it could be traced, but it wouldn't give away exactly where we were."

Zoey pressed her lips together and nodded. "There is a small problem."

"Naturally."

"I don't know her number. Not from memory, anyway."

One side of Sascha's mouth crooked up. "That won't be a problem. I can pull some strings. That sort of information isn't difficult to find."

Zoey sighed and shook her head, resting her chin in her hands. "Sometimes I forget you're a criminal."

"Criminal?" A small chuckle rumbled in his chest. "I am an *assassin*, Zoey. And quite a successful one at that. I like to think I'm a step above common 'criminal'. Have some class."

"Alright, alright," sighed Zoey. "Master criminal? Is that any better?"

"A bit," replied Sascha, his mouth quirking into a full smile.

Zoey couldn't help returning his smile. She also couldn't help the way that her heart constricted and chest warmed at seeing the brightness in his eyes and the softness in his expression. How was she supposed to not feel this way when he smiled? There was just something about seeing those harsh edges fade away into something viscerally human that was so comforting. How many people had seen him smile like this? How many people had seen the man beneath those sharp eyes and cutting edges? How many people had sat and watched stars with him? Not many, of that, she was sure.

Then she realized Sascha's stance. Leaning forward, head tilted, one eyebrow raised. Humor lingered around the corners of his mouth.

"Did you hear me?" he asked.

Heat flushed Zoey's face. Studying him so hard she hadn't even heard what he'd said. Daydreaming about their night of stargazing from a week prior. If that wasn't embarrassing, she didn't know what was.

"No. Sorry. I was miles away," she said, desperately trying to beat back the flush that rushed her.

"Clearly," he replied. "I asked if you wanted to go armed or not."

Zoey glanced away, one hand rubbing her neck and collarbones. Her other hand curled into a fist on the countertop. Shooting. Being put in a situation where she might have to do intentional harm to something that wasn't a tree or target box. Protecting herself was something she'd wanted, until she actually shot the gun in practice. That was when the flashbacks of *that* night came back. For that reason alone, she'd avoided shooting except when Sascha had asked her to these last few days.

Sascha's hand settled on her wrist, squeezing softly and his thumb tracing mindless patterns on her skin. Her blood burned in the wake of the movements. Zoey took a tiny breath as she locked eyes with him, trying to wipe emotion away from her face. Sascha was her *friend* and nothing more. This was just a result of her being around him and only him for so much time. That was all. It had to be.

"You don't have to if you don't want to," said Sascha, his hand sliding away.

Lines of heat lingered on Zoey's skin, and she almost reached after him. She forced herself to shove the urge away. What was *wrong* with her?

"Are you sure?" she asked.

Sascha shrugged. "I'll stay close and help you if you need me. Did you want to make the call today? Or try another day?"

"I'd really hoped to do it today," replied Zoey, giving a sheepish smile.

Sascha glanced over at the clock on the oven and nodded. "We have enough time. Let me get on my laptop, and I'll see if I can snag Rona's phone number."

"Is her phone number exposed in her personal information as well? Like everything about me is?"

Sascha paused a second, then nodded. "OMNI's still looking for you and your sisters, but I doubt they'd call Hailee or Rona. It'd give Maxwell an edge on where to find *them*, which really isn't something they want." "That doesn't really set me at ease," said Zoey, her gaze dropping to the kitchen counter.

"I know. This will all come right, Zoey. I promise."

"Don't make promises you can't keep, Sascha," said Zoey, smiling half-heartedly at him.

Sascha tilted his head, a thoughtful expression settling around his eyes. "I don't."

~ ~ ~ ~ ~ ~

Excitement and fear somehow seemed to run close together. Zoey took a deep breath, exhaling slowly. Just outside Linz, Austria. This was where Sascha had chosen to make this call. Just over two and a half hours from the safe house. Her heart beat a little faster in her chest. She pressed her lips together and clasped her hands tightly together on her lap to keep them from shaking. Rona. Soon. She'd be talking to Rona. Outside her window, the late afternoon light flickered through a thick, dark pine forest as they moved along the road. She took another heavy breath. Maybe she was just overanalyzing everything. Hyperaware.

Eyes. She could feel eyes on her. Zoey looked over and caught Sascha watching her.

"You should be watching the road, you know," she said, leaning back.

"Hard to do that when you're vibrating in your seat," chuckled Sascha. "Excited much?"

Zoey breathed a laugh and turned her gaze back out the windshield, watching the scenery pass by. "Yeah, just a bit."

"I can be right beside you or stay at the car. It's your call."

"Thank you," replied Zoey. She pressed her lips together again. "Sascha, what if something happens? What if someone recognizes me? Or you?"

"They won't."

"How do you know?"

"We won't be making this call anywhere near people. We won't be going into the city. I wouldn't take that kind of a risk. At least not in this case, I wouldn't."

"You took a risk helping me."

Sascha glanced over, expression unreadable. "That was a calculated risk."

Zoey shook her head and laughed. "Good thing you're better at math than I am."

Sascha chuckled softly and turned the car off the main road into an empty slip road near a scenic overlook. Beyond a thin band of trees, Zoey could just make out a river, mountains rising high on the far side of the water. She darted a nervous glance at Sascha. Was this it? Somehow, she'd expected something just a little *more*. Maybe a sheltered building. A secret place hidden back from the road. This was so . . . normal. Her gut told her that that was exactly why Sascha had chosen it.

Turning, Zoey reached into the backseat for the burner phone Sascha had bought earlier. It was still in its box, unopened. A hand closed around her wrist, stopping her before she could pick it up. She turned back to Sascha.

"What?" she asked.

"Don't touch it bare-handed," he said seriously. "Anyone finds that phone, I don't want your fingerprints on it."

Zoey sat back in her seat. "How likely is it that someone will find it?"

"Never can tell. Best to err on the side of caution. Here."

She paused as Sascha held out a pair of black leather gloves to her. "Isn't this a little excessive?"

He gave her an odd look, head canted to the side. "I think it's exactly the right amount of caution. If someone finds that phone with both of our fingerprints on it, it won't take them long to put the pieces together."

Zoey nodded, catching the seriousness in his eyes. "Okay."

"Thank you."

He reached onto the backseat, picked up the phone, and turned it on. Zoey watched him focus a moment, waiting for the phone to connect to a network.

"No gloves for you, then?" she asked, sliding them on. Too big for her hands. They had to be Sascha's.

"No. If the phone just has my prints on it, that's not too big of an issue. I'm sure there must be hundreds of phones in the Danube with my fingerprints on them by now."

"Make a habit of tossing phones in rivers?"

Sascha chuckled but didn't reply. Then she realized he was holding something out to her. A piece of paper. Numbers. Zoey swallowed. Rona's phone number. It had to be.

"Zoey."

"Yes?" asked Zoey, holding Rona's phone number tight in her gloved hand.

"We've got one shot at this. If this phone call doesn't go through, we can't try again. Do you understand that?"

Swallowing, Zoey nodded. "What if she doesn't answer?"

Sascha looked up from the phone screen. "Leave a short, and I mean *short*, message. For both of our safeties don't tell her where you are, don't tell her how you got here, don't tell her where we're staying, and for heaven's sake, don't mention my name."

"Okay. Got it. So, if she answers, what *can* I tell her?" asked Zoey, biting her tongue as she heard how sharp the words were.

If Sascha noticed it, he gave no indication of it.

"Tell her the important things. That you're safe. That you're trying to get back to her and the rest of your family. If she asks you anything about where you are and who you're with, please, don't answer her. If she picks up the call, you have to keep it to under three minutes. That's all the time I can safely give you. Do you understand?"

Zoey nodded, flexing her fingers in the gloves. "I do."

"Okay," replied Sascha, settling the phone in her hand. "You'll get better reception outside."

Zoey nodded again, words suddenly failing her. She swallowed hard and pushed her way out of the car, breathing in the cool forest air. Dimly, she heard Sascha get out of car, too, the car door thudding closed. Slowly, she swiped the phone screen up. Rona. Touch screen gloves, evidently. In just moments, she'd be hearing Rona's voice again. It felt like years since she'd spoken to her sister. She took a deep, steadying breath, and typed in the number.

The phone rang.

Once.

Twice.

Zoey clenched her jaw, struggling to keep her emotions in check for a moment more. Answer. Answer. All she wanted was to hear her sister's voice. That was it. Just to tell her that she was alive. Rona practically lived next to her phone. Where was she?

Three times.

A fourth ring.

No. Rona *had* to answer. She had to. There was no reason for her not to. Zoey ran her thumb along her lower lip, fighting to keep it from trembling. She looked over her shoulder at Sascha. Her face must have shown her emotions. He stood upright immediately, shifting from where he had been leaning against the car.

A fifth ring.

The start of the voicemail prompt.

Emotion choked in Zoey's throat. Real, physical pain burned hot in her chest. She covered her mouth and barely felt Sascha settle a hand on her shoulder. She'd been so certain that Rona would answer. So certain. The empty space where her necklace had hung seemed suddenly more noticeable. Zoey pressed her lips together hard, waiting for the inevitable beep, prompting her to leave a voicemail. Why hadn't Rona answered? Had she just not recognized the number? Was that why she hadn't picked up? Was she out? Was she . . . was she in trouble, too?

A gentle squeeze to her shoulder jerked her attention back to Sascha. "Leave a voicemail for her. She'll at least know you're alive."

"Can we try again?" asked Zoey, not making any attempt to keep the plea out of her voice.

Sascha shook his head slowly. "No. We can't risk it."

"Please."

"No, Zoey," he said, his voice still low and patient. "I'm sorry."

Zoey nodded, clutching the phone with both hands as the cue to leave a voice message droned clear through the earpiece.

"Rona. Rona, it's Zoey. I don't have long. I just wanted, needed, to call you. I'm – I'm alive. And I'm safe. I'm with –" Zoey cut herself off as Sascha's hand tightened like eagle talons on her shoulder. "– I'm with someone who's been helping me. Looking after me. I'll be home soon, Ro. I promise. I'll be home soon. I don't know when. But I'm coming. I love you and Hailee so much. Please, try not to worry. I'll be home as soon as I can."

Drawing a shuddering breath, Zoey pressed the *end call* button. Immediately, she turned to Sascha. *What now?* She wanted to ask. But she didn't. She shook her head and looked at the ground, passing the phone wordlessly to Sascha. He paused, then took it from her. Blinking away tears, Zoey stared into the distance, neither taking in nor really seeing the darkening forest. There was a small shuffle of activity behind her, but she paid it no mind. Sascha hadn't commented on it. She didn't see any reason to pay it attention. There was a quiet splash moments later. Still, Zoey barely registered it.

Rona hadn't answered. That was all that mattered. Rona hadn't answered. And Rona couldn't call her back. Zoey covered her eyes, part of her wanting to hide away, part of her wanting to block out the gentle oranges and pinks of the oncoming sunset that danced across the tops of pine trees. She had missed her only chance to talk to her sister. She wouldn't get another.

Chapter 24

Rona swallowed hard. This was her first time in Charity's office. She couldn't help feeling like an insect under a microscope. Or like she was sitting in a very awkward therapy appointment. Maxwell sat at Charity's desk, Charity behind him, one hand on his shoulder. Rona couldn't help feeling nauseous to see it. Maxwell wasn't supposed to have human connections. His index and middle finger rested on the black screen of Rona's phone. Rona glanced at Flynn beside her, who looked as strained as she felt.

"So," Rona said, breaking the silence. "It *is* Zoey, right? It's not someone just pretending to be her?"

"Flynn, you said you didn't find interference on the voicemail?" asked Maxwell.

Flynn shook his head. "I scanned for everything I could think of. As far as I can tell, that's Zoey."

"And she's still with Sarajevo," said Charity. She practically spat the last word.

"But he's keeping her alive for now," said Maxwell. "There's no way for you to trace the origin of the call, Flynn?"

"I don't think so. I can tell from the number itself that it's a German number, but the phone seems to have been destroyed since the call was made."

"He does entirely too well at being a step ahead," sighed Maxwell. "Keep looking into it. Let me know what you find."

"Yes, sir."

"Can I have my phone back now?" asked Rona.

Maxwell didn't reply, simply held her phone out to her as he turned to Charity. It was all Rona could do to not snatch it from him. If he hadn't ripped it from her hands when the call came through, she could have talked to Zoey. She could have found out where she was. She could have brought her home. Rona took a steeling breath and left the office, resisting the urge to slam the door behind her.

"You alright?" asked Flynn, matching her stride as they walked toward the stairs.

"No. I don't understand," sighed Rona. "Why didn't he let me talk to her? Why didn't *he* talk to her?"

Flynn sighed. "Rona, I don't know much about Sarajevo, but from what I've read in his file, he's . . . pretty evil. He's got a list of murders miles long to his name. Politicians, CEO's, ordinary people. He doesn't discriminate, and there's no telling what he could have been doing to Zoey on the other end of that call. He could have been torturing her. It was safer to not answer."

"Don't say things like that," snapped Rona. The footage of Zoey being punched and kicked instantly played out in Rona's head, and she shivered uncontrollably. Torture wasn't out of the question.

"I'm sorry. But that's the reality of it," replied Flynn. "We just have to trust Maxwell to call the shots at the moment."

"At the moment?" Rona scoffed. "He always has."

"If it's any consolation, he's the same at work."

"Good to know he never changes," sighed Rona, turning the corner at the bottom of the stairs into the living room.

In spite of her emotions, Rona half smiled. Hailee was already there, perching on one of the chairs and looking entirely too innocent.

"When did you get in here?" asked Rona, leaning on the doorframe.

Hailee scrambled to her feet. "What did he say? Was it really Zoey?"

"How did you know Zoey called?" asked Rona.

"I listened through the door off the kitchen. Maxwell wrestling your phone out of your hands and all of you bolting upstairs wasn't subtle."

Rona hesitated, then nodded. "It was Zoey. But I don't know what he's thinking of doing next. I don't think there's any way for us to find her through the phone call."

"Excuse me, Rona," said Simon, squeezing past Rona as he walked behind her from the kitchen, carrying three mugs.

"So, there's no way at all that we can find anything out about Zoey? Other than she's alive?" asked Hailee.

"No," sighed Rona, rubbing a hand across her face. "I'm so sick of this."

She caught the exchanged glance between Simon and Flynn. At least Flynn had the decency to look a little embarrassed about it.

"What aren't you two saying?" asked Rona, her temper fraying.

"Nothing we *can* say right now, Rona. I'm sorry," said Simon, offering her a mug of tea.

Rona took the mug, tempted to throw it back in Simon's face. Instead, she shook her head and sat down heavily next to Hailee. Her younger sister stared silently into the tea as though she could divine answers from it.

"You alright?" asked Rona.

"I just wish we knew when she was coming home."

Rona's heart constricted. Hailee's eyes were watery and rimmed red.

"We'll have her home soon," replied Rona. "I promise."

"You've been saying that for weeks," muttered Hailee.

Unexpected temper flashed through Rona's blood. "It's not *my* fault she's not home yet. Christ! I can't do anything to help, and I don't know *how* to help. If I could do something, I would do it."

Silence rang louder than shouts. Rona took a steeling breath. Hailee flinched away and returned her gaze to the mug in her hands. Flynn and Simon had gone quiet.

Maxwell cleared his throat from the bottom of the stairs. Rona turned, not sure whether to feel relieved or incensed that he'd come down. She stood up, desperate for something to *do*, even if it was as simple as moving from sitting to standing.

"Actually, Rona," said Maxwell. "There is something you can do."

"What is it?" she asked, taking a few steps toward him. There was something in his voice. Something conniving and calculated. But getting Zoey back meant more than her father's bad temper.

"Come with me," he said, tightening his loosened tie.

~ ~ ~ ~ ~ ~

Listless. Zoey knew she'd been quieter than usual since her phone call to Rona earlier that evening. But she hadn't expected this sudden rush of ennui to smother her. She hadn't left her room since they'd come back. She hadn't wanted to. Almost couldn't. Moonlight streamed in through her window, the silvery trees waving gently. But Zoey rolled away from them, facing the door. Her chance to talk with Rona was gone, and it would not resurface. Part of her wanted to try re-dialing Rona's number on the burner phone Sascha had given her when she first arrived, but the international dial code was so long she hadn't had a chance to memorize it. It would also be such a violation of Sascha's trust. Something she couldn't bring herself to do, even if she'd known the number.

That didn't stop her still wanting to talk to Rona, just to hear her voice, and somehow, that had all fallen apart in front of her. She couldn't help but feel grateful to Sascha for having given her space. He'd knocked earlier, to ask what she'd wanted for dinner, but... Zoey swallowed. She couldn't eat. Not after this. A weight of gratitude to Sascha opened in her chest. He hadn't pressed. Just told her that he'd leave something in the fridge for her.

Her stomach growled insistently, and Zoey breathed in and sat up. She *should* eat something, really. But how could she when she felt like this? Crushed. Devastated. Would Rona even get her voicemail? Or would she just delete it? She'd been so close.

Moonlight shivered against her bedroom door, and Zoey glanced over her shoulder. In her peripherals, she caught sight of the distant stars.

Stars.

The same stars over Rona's and Hailee's heads.

Any food she'd wanted could wait. She needed to be outside. Now. She stood, pulled a pair of socks on, then opened her door quietly and tiptoed down the stairs.

Cool night air chilled her, and Zoey pulled her shirt a little tighter around her shoulders. Even through socks, the patio tiles felt like ice underfoot. Who'd given summer the right to feel this cold? It didn't really matter somehow. She tilted her head upward, eyes scanning the glimmering sky.

North Stars. That was what Sascha had called Hailee and Rona. Her North Stars. So where *was* the North Star? Which one was it? She hissed a breath through her teeth. They all looked the same. She blinked quickly, sudden, desperate tears pricking her eyes.

Then she caught sight of Aquila. Suspended in the night sky just above the horizon. Sascha's constellation. She forced herself to take a deep breath and nodded to herself, letting her gaze linger on Aquila as she collected herself. If she could find Aquila, she could find the North Star. She lifted her gaze from the horizon to the stars above. She sat on the edge of the patio wall as her eyes landed on Orion.

So, she could find at least two of the constellations. But where was the North Star? She swallowed, eyes flitting between tiny pinpricks of light.

"I wondered if I might find you out here."

She turned. Sascha stood in the doorway, dressed only in pajamas, one shoulder leaned against the doorframe. Zoey inhaled sharply and tried to offer a smile, then exhaled with a heavy sigh, her shoulders falling forward and her eyes lowering to the dewy grass.

"I can't find it," she said, grimacing and talking through clenched teeth. "I don't know why it's so important. It's not. Not really. We're seeing the same stars, and I know it's up there. But . . ."

"It takes practice," said Sascha quietly, rounding the end of the patio wall and sitting down. "Let me help. North Star, right?"

Zoey nodded and returned her eyes to the night. "I just wanted so much to hear their voices. To be able to tell them myself that I'm okay."

"And you will soon, Zoey. Before you know it, you'll be back with them. I promise."

Zoey paused, her eyes prickling for a different reason now. She sniffled and half-turned away, pretending to look in a different area of the sky. How did Sascha always know the right thing to say? The right thing to make her fears ease and her heart race in the best way.

One of Sascha's knuckles settled under her chin, and Zoey flushed dark as he gently turned her head back.

"There," he said, pointing. "See it?"

Eyes searching desperately, Zoey shook her head. Her mouth ran dry as Sascha pressed their cheeks together and nodded toward his finger. Heat swept through Zoey's body, blocking out the night chill. How was she supposed to find a star when Sascha was closer now than he'd ever been before? When the beginnings of stubble on his jaw prickled her skin? When all thinking short-circuited? Then, in spite of Sascha's closeness, at the end of a curving line of four stars, Zoey spotted it. A star brighter than the others surrounding it twinkled down at them.

The tightness in Zoey's chest eased. She swallowed, and it felt like she breathed for the first time in hours.

"Thank you," she whispered, sitting upright.

Sascha smiled. "There's a trick to it, you know?"

"Oh yeah?" asked Zoey, smiling shakily.

"Yeah." Sascha reached into his pocket and pulled a small, black box free. "This."

Zoey's thoughts crashed to a juddering halt, and she breathed a tiny, nervous laugh. "I hardly think jewelry would help me find stars."

"Ha! In most cases, no." Sascha passed it to her. "I saw this when I was in Switzerland last week, and it made me think of our conversation from the other night. I was going to give it to you when we got you back to England, but I think now works just as well."

Hand shaking, Zoey opened the box. She pressed a hand to her mouth, and tears welled up in her eyes. Inside the box lay a silver chain, and on it, a simple silver pendant engraved with the pattern of Ursa Minor. A tiny, white gem of the North Star glittered at one end of the design, glinting under the moonlight.

"Now you can always find it."

"Sascha," breathed Zoey. She blinked fast and tilted her head skyward to take a breath. When she was sure her voice would be steady, she turned back to him. "I don't know what to say."

Sascha tilted his head back to the sky. "I know it's not the necklace you lost, but maybe it'll bring you some comfort until you get back to England," he said softly.

Zoey stared at him in silence. She tightened her fingers around the box, clutching the stars in her hands. She couldn't have looked away if she tried. Even if she *could* . . . she didn't want to. Moonlight streamed down from above, pure and silver, and Zoey swallowed thickly. Sascha's eyes flickered to her, and his tiny smile warmed. Under that pristine light, the harsh angles and sharp edges of Sascha's features rolled back, and his blue eyes softened. The urge to kiss him rose in Zoey's chest again. Something less impulsive and wild than it had been weeks ago. It thrummed just below the surface of her skin, almost overwhelming in its insistence. In another life, in another world, she *would have* kissed him.

But she didn't.

Instead, she reached out, one hand settling on his. Sascha turned fully to her, an unreadable expression in his eyes.

"Thank you," she said, the words falling from her mouth in a whisper.

Slowly turning his hand over, Sascha intertwined his fingers with hers. Zoey could hardly breathe. She squeezed his hand tightly, trying to drown out the sound of her blood surging in her ears.

"Let's not lose this one," Sascha replied, his voice just as low as hers had been.

Chapter 25

"Better!"

Zoey landed her kick, feet shoulder-width apart, her hands up in fists protecting her head. She narrowed her eyes, one side of her mouth curling up at Sascha's praise. She sprang backward as Sascha lashed out at her shoulder with a left-handed jab. She blocked, the impact from his fist running down her arms, and watched his hand to make sure it was falling away from hitting her. A shadow fell over the other side of her face. An impending attack that was both felt and seen in the seconds before it struck. Zoey cringed away and raised her arms to block, eyes squeezing shut and waiting for impact.

In front of her, Sascha chuckled and tapped one of her fists. Zoey opened her eyes and straightened, not realizing she'd folded inward on herself.

"You're still not preparing for that second attack," said Sascha. "Always be aware that your opponent may try a follow-up attack if you block their first. Sometimes the first is just to divert your attention."

Zoey dropped her hands to her sides, shaking the tension out of her shoulders as Sascha lowered his hands as well. A truce for now. Zoey took a steadying breath and backed away from Sascha half a step. She was still getting used to him being in her space and her in his. Still getting used to the way his touches seemed to linger on her skin long after any contact had vanished.

"I know, I know, but just remember, you've been fighting hand-to-hand for years," said Zoey. She tightened her ponytail. "I've been sparring with you for – what is it now? – two weeks?"

"And showing not bad promise as a student," replied Sascha. "Remember to keep some body weight behind punches and kicks. It'll increase the power behind the movement."

"'Not bad promise'," snorted Zoey. "It's not exactly praise, but I'll take it." "It's the closest to praise you'll get. Remember, too, you're fighting much too clean. Punches and kicks anyone can expect. Scratches, soft tissue, and eye gouges are going to be your best friends. And I know first-hand that you've got a decent ability to bite."

Zoey grimaced and laughed. "I don't really want to bite you again."

"Well, you won't always be fighting me, will you? You may need to sink your teeth into someone else at some point."

"Is that so?" asked Zoey. "How's *this* then?"

She launched at him, aiming to get her arms around his middle and send them both sprawling in the grass. But Sascha was simply no longer there. Zoey caught a flash of movement out of her peripherals and landed hard on her side, coughing and wheezing for breath.

Sascha's shadow fell over her, and he raised an eyebrow. "Really?"

"Oh, come on," said Zoey, brushing herself off and standing. She rubbed her ribs with a rueful grin. "You never saw it coming."

"Zoey, I'd have known that was coming even if I were both deaf and blind."

"You really know how to encourage someone, you know," snorted Zoey.

Sascha shrugged, one side of his mouth lifting. "It's a skill." Zoey laughed and took a few steps away from Sascha, taking in the bright afternoon. The meadow grass was soft underfoot, and the sky overhead was glorious. A few white clouds scudded across the blue backdrop, a warm sun beating down. Zoey stopped beside a rock jutting out of the ground and grabbed her water bottle from where it stood on the stone, wiping a few beads of sweat from her forehead. An eagle took off from a distant tree, rising effortlessly into the sky, and Zoey wondered if it was Baldr or Morana.

Watching the eagle ascend, Zoey took a long swig of water, and her mind went back to the events of the last two weeks. Two weeks since Sascha had come back from Innsbruck with news about her passport. Two weeks since she and Sascha had taken the bandages off her leg. One week since her failed phone call to Rona. She lifted a hand to her necklace and turned, flashing him a quick smile. In these short weeks, he'd done as he'd promised and more. Kept her informed about her passport as much as he could, helped teach her self-defense, taught her some German. She'd wanted to ask him to take her to Munich when he went, but somehow even asking the question seemed a bit too much like tempting fate. Particularly her disastrous phone call to Rona. All the same, she turned back to him, a thoughtful smile lingering around her mouth.

"What are you smiling about?" he asked, picking a stalk of tiny, purple, alpine flowers and tucking them behind his ear.

Zoey laughed and something in her chest flushed warm. "Really? Mid-sparring and you're stopping to make flower crowns? What is that, a bluebell?"

"Harebell," chuckled Sascha, tucking the flower more firmly over his ear. "Same family. Legends say witches used them in magic potions to turn themselves into hares."

Zoey couldn't quite wipe the smile from her mouth. "Well, thank God we don't have a rampant witch population. Can't imagine what a ton of witches turning into hares would do to the local wildlife. You know, two weeks we've been doing this, and I have yet to even get close to you, aside from blocking. Let alone actually land anything on you."

Sascha shook his head. "I'm an assassin, Zoey. I've been in this business for several years now. My livelihood is killing people. I'd be a pretty piss-poor killer if I let someone with your amount of experience get me."

"Well, I suppose you have a point," she replied, passing him his water bottle.

"The reassurance is that I doubt you'll ever have to fight someone with my level of experience. At the best, you can protect yourself in a dark alley. At the worst, you could potentially defend yourself against someone like Ewan long enough to get away. Remember, your job isn't fighting back so much as making an opportunity to get away."

"Speaking of," said Zoey, lowering her hands to her water bottle and fiddling with the cap. "Has OMNI contacted you again to, you know, cancel the meeting or anything?"

"No. The meeting is still on."

"When?"

"Couple of days away."

Zoey choked on the water she'd just sipped. "What? I hadn't realized it would be so soon . . . What will you have to do?"

"I don't know yet. Meetings like this are often incredibly covert. I won't know where the point of contact will be until closer to the time."

"What if it's somewhere like Australia?" asked Zoey.

"They won't pull me to Australia on short notice," replied Sascha. "Austria, maybe. Not Australia."

Zoey turned to face him. There was something in his voice that sounded thoughtful. Zoey swallowed, a question lingering on her tongue. She debated not asking, but what good would that do?

"What about me? If you have to leave for several days, what do I do? I still can't travel anywhere that isn't continental Europe."

Sascha winked and raised his water bottle. "Oh, I think I might have a remedy for that at long last."

Zoey's jaw dropped, and a wave of emotion rushed her. "Is my –?"

Sascha laughed and backed away a few steps. "Your passport *is* ready. Now, don't be angry. I only got the message myself this morning. I was going to surprise you tonight over dinner."

A breath of relieved laughter leaped from Zoey's chest as she covered her mouth. Tears sparked at the corners of her eyes. *Home.* She was going home. Home to Rona and Hailee. Home to her family. And in just a day or two. She looked at Sascha, the sunlight catching him at a different angle. He seemed softer, and the expression in his eyes was gentle. Zoey couldn't look away, and her heart skipped a beat in her chest. He had done it. This incredible man had paved her way home. He'd had no reason to help her, but he had anyway. Emotion took over, and Zoey launched at him. She wrapped her arms around him, burying her face in the fabric of his shirt, then laughed as she felt him tense and raise an arm between them to fend off what he must have thought of as a continuation of their earlier sparring.

"Thank you," she said, rising onto her toes and resting her chin on his shoulder. Zoey smiled as the arm Sascha had brought up between them dropped. There was a pause, and Zoey had to wonder how long it had been since Sascha had been shown any genuine affection. He seemed frozen. Then Zoey felt a laugh rumble in his chest, and he relaxed against her. Zoey closed her eyes and pressed just a fraction closer to him. A warmth that had nothing to do with the summer sun on her back spread through her body.

"I promised you I'd help."

Zoey dropped her grip to his upper arms, leaned back a fraction, and punched him squarely in the shoulder. "You're an arsehole for not telling me earlier though."

"I'll take that as a token of your appreciation, then I suppose?" He rubbed his arm and grinned. "Hopefully, the arrival of your passport will cover my transgression."

Zoey hummed, feigning a thoughtful expression. "It should make up for that. Do we have to go and pick it up, or will your contact send it to us?"

"I'll have to go and get it. I could go tonight if you want."

"Can I come?" asked Zoey, the question leaping from her mouth before she could stop it.

Sascha hesitated, a pensive look falling over his face. "I don't know, Zoey. This may not be the right time to think of leaving here."

"You've been out loads of times. Please, Sascha. This is my *passport*. We'll be leaving here after I get it anyway."

Sascha tipped his head. "You're not wrong."

"Will you be meeting your contact at Innsbruck again?"

He nodded. "My contact's based in Innsbruck. He won't meet anywhere else."

"Then it's not far. Only a couple of hours south of here. *Please*. I won't get in the way."

Sascha stared at the hillsides for a long moment, and Zoey fought the urge to start begging. Her passport. Going home. Sascha knew how important this was, so why hesitate now?

Then Sascha sighed. "Alright. Pack any personal items. If things go south and we need to make a break for it, we won't be coming back here."

~ ~ ~ ~ ~ ~

A cashmere sweatshirt, jeans, and ankle length boots seemed an odd choice of body armor. Zoey glanced over at Sascha in the driver's seat as he negotiated the roads leading through Innsbruck. A small frown fell across her lips. The casual look of his clothing was deceptive. Under his sweater, she knew, there was a snug-fitting bulletproof vest and a handgun. The weight of her own handgun, wedged between her jeans and hip, was unfamiliar – alien and threatening. Zoey ran Ursa Minor along its thin chain, her mouth dry, as she remembered their shooting session from earlier in the afternoon. She'd been able to land several more shots on the target. Only one of them had vanished into thin air. Sascha had offered a stiff nod and reminded her about needing better trigger control and waiting half a second longer to make sure she was on target before she fired.

Now, all firearms and ammunition, save the two she and Sascha carried, were tucked away in the rear of the car. Zoey's own backpack was nestled in the backseat beside Sascha's. Zoey ran a hand along her chin. The safe house had been left a skeleton, all sheets washed, all surfaces wiped down, and the entire place deep cleaned. It was as though they'd never even been there. Expecting the best but preparing for the worst. Zoey wished she'd been able to catch a glimpse of Baldr and Morana before they left the safe house, but neither eagle had put in an appearance.

Zoey shook her head, thoughts returning to the present. Maybe she should have let Sascha do this alone. But it was too late to back out now. Besides, she'd asked – more or less begged – to let her come with him. She turned to look out the side window. Evening clouds hung low, but Zoey could just make out the sloping outlines of the mountains surrounding Innsbruck. Earlier, she'd spotted layers of snow still holding to their peaks.

"Where are you meeting them?" asked Zoey. Conversation. Anything to distract herself from her mounting anxiety.

"In der Altstadt," murmured Sascha, navigating a corner.

"What?" asked Zoey. She'd caught the German word for 'city' but wasn't sure what Sascha really meant.

"Oh. Sorry, my mind was elsewhere. The historic part of the city. It's a relatively popular tourist hub, so quite a few people, even late in the day. Crowds, narrow side streets, and lots of open-fronted shops. It's an easy place to cause confusion if something goes wrong. Most old cities, you can even get on the rooftops to get away from a situation if you need to."

"Think it will?" asked Zoey. "Go wrong, I mean."

"Shouldn't. But I'd prefer to be safe rather than sorry. A good location can be a huge help in any situation."

"What do you want me to do while you're getting the passport?"

"It might be for the better," replied Sascha, navigating another sharp turn. "If you stayed close to me. Near but out of sight. Then I'll be at hand if anything happens. If something happens and we get separated, text me and I'll find you."

Zoey nodded. "What about OMNI? Any word about where they are?"

"I got a message earlier that they're concentrating operatives in Vienna."

"That's not close to here, is it?"

Sascha shook his head. "Opposite side of Austria."

"Am I . . . am I going to that with you?"

"Absolutely not." Sascha glanced away from the road. "You'll only come anywhere near Vienna if things fall apart here and we can't go back to the safe house. Clearing everything out tonight was just a precaution."

Zoey turned to look out of the window again. She had to wonder if he was worried about getting her passport and meeting with the very group that wanted to traffic her within days of each other. Now that she was here, with him in Innsbruck, this ordeal seemed like the riskiest undertaking she'd ever ventured.

They drove past a cluster of people gathered on the pedestrian path beside the road. In spite of everything, a small smile crossed Zoey's face. They looked about her age. There was something bittersweet about seeing them. They looked carefree. Unburdened. In her peripherals, Zoey noticed Sascha's expression. Other than the pinched look around his mouth, he looked emotionless. Zoey knew that micro-expression by now though.

"Are you worried?" she asked. "You look like you're thinking. Hard."

"No. Worry can be a paralytic. I am measured and cautious, but not worried."

She looked back out of the front windshield. "You see the world so differently to me."

Sascha laughed, but there was no humor in the sound. "That's what this lifestyle will do to you."

Zoey rubbed her upper arms. "Do you think I might get recognized?"

"It's a possibility," replied Sascha. "Oh. Hold that thought. Parking."

A breathy laugh escaped Zoey's mouth as Sascha pulled the car into a roadside parking slot. The street was quiet, even though it was just off what seemed like one of the main roads through the city.

"No parking garage?" asked Zoey, getting out once Sascha had turned the car off.

"Absolutely not," replied Sascha. "They're great places for getting cornered. Terrible for making quick exits from. Be right back. I need to pay for the parking."

Zoey shook her head and pulled her sweatshirt a little tighter around her shoulders. In spite of being the middle of summer, the air was chilly. Immaculate, three and four-story buildings rose up on either side of the street. There was a sense of the ornate, of age, to them as well. Buildings out of their time. Stores and businesses had taken over the ground floor of many buildings, but, as Zoey looked up, she noticed lights shining on the upper floors, and had to wonder if people lived in those spaces. A small smile pulled at her mouth, and she couldn't help a pang of unprecedented homesickness.

Sascha rejoined her. "Might I remind you, you wanted to come. If I remember correctly, nearly begged me to let you."

Zoey stepped up next to him as he started walking. "Yeah, I know. I'm still apprehensive, though. Maybe someone might tell OMNI that you and me are in the same area on the same night. Someone might try and take me to them."

"Is this your way of telling me you regret coming?"

"Not exactly, but now that I'm here, I'm realizing how risky this is," replied Zoey, hearing a note of unease creep into her own voice.

Sascha nodded. "It is a risk. Not one I would have taken if I were in your position. But it's too late to jump ship now. So the only thing you can do now is focus and, irritating as it may sound, try not to worry."

Zoey laughed in spite of herself. "'Have you ever tried just not worrying?' Thank you, Sascha. I'd never thought of that before. Wonderful advice. By the way, how are you *not* worried about being recognized? You're an international hitman –"

Sascha cleared his throat. "Assassin. Thank you."

"Assassin. Hitman. They're the same, aren't they?"

"Assassin sounds better. It's more professional."

Amused exasperation surfaced, and Zoey shook her head. "Bottom line, you bump people off for profit."

Sascha gripped his chest, one hand covering his heart. "You know, I'm wounded, Zoey. My work runs deeper than money. How base of you. My choices revolve around the dichotomy of free-will versus determinism. Fate and circumstance. Survival and –"

Zoey elbowed him. "So, there's *no* money motivation there, at all?"

Sascha shrugged. "Yeah, alright. I do it for money as well. We can't all be saints."

Zoey's smile faded, and she tucked her hands into her sweatshirt pockets. She'd never asked Sascha much about his work, and tonight, she was certain, was not the right time to start. They stopped at a pedestrian crossing, and Zoey looked up at Sascha, his features sharp under the overcast light of early evening. He looked the picture of calmness, and Zoey swallowed. There were two sides to him. There was the side she had come to know, the one who made her laugh, told awful puns, was conscientious, taught her things, and made sure she was comfortable. The other side she had seen only once. The side she'd met in her first encounter with him. The side that had shot Bouncer in France, that had asked her to look away before he fired, that had told her the truth about herself and her family with brutal honesty. Zoey took a step forward as the pedestrian crossing light flashed. She wasn't sure which side was next to her now.

It was a rabbit hole she wasn't sure she wanted to go down at the moment.

Zoey looked up. The tall, antiquated buildings of Innsbruck's historic center reared up. The streets here were narrower. She could worry about Sascha's true nature later on. Zoey took a step away from him as they turned onto one of the narrow streets. Even in the early evening, there were still a fair amount of people around.

"Split off from me," said Sascha in a low voice. Zoey resisted the urge to move closer to him to hear. "Stay near but far. This won't take long. Then we can get you out of here."

Zoey gave a tiny nod. She stopped and turned to look in the window of a jeweler's, trying to do as he asked. Near but far. How exactly she was supposed to do that, she wasn't sure.

Trying to make it look as though she was nothing more than a tourist, she looked at some of the products in the store window. Hailee would love some of the rings. Catching sight of the price, Zoey hissed through her teeth. Even home in England, where she had some income, these would have been far too expensive to buy. Trying to keep her movements casual, she looked back in the direction Sascha had gone. Gone was a good way to put where Sascha was. She bit the inside of her cheek to keep from swearing. She'd meant to at least keep him in sight. It would have been interesting to see him at work. Safer, too. Zoey frowned, beating back the rush of fear that had threatened her chest. She didn't need Sascha around her all the time. They'd find each other soon enough. She couldn't help feeling a little disappointed though. She'd wanted to be able to watch her passport change hands. Then going home would feel all the more real.

Chapter 26

Steps slow, Zoey moved along the streets. The shops here were similar to the ones in Hereford's historic district, but these buildings stood on a much grander scale. How long had Sascha been gone now? She glanced down at her phone screen. Fifteen minutes or so? Zoey turned her attention to the café seating lining the sides of the street, scanning for any sight of Sascha's blond hair. Nothing. A small smile pulled at the side of Zoey's mouth. She had a feeling she could walk right past him and not notice him. It seemed that Sascha's superhuman ability of entering and leaving an area without disturbing anything wasn't confined to just home. Home. She felt her smile falling away. *Home.* That was one word she'd been trying to avoid. The safe house wasn't home. It never would be. It was an empty shell of a place. So, why was it that she'd been happy there? Happier than she'd ever felt in Hereford. It didn't make sense.

Maybe it didn't have to.

Zoey shook her head. Another rabbit hole she couldn't afford to go down this evening. She lifted the phone Sascha had given her weeks ago once more and started typing a message.

Where . . .

Watched. Zoey stiffened, prey instinct kicking in, sharp and vivid. She was being watched. She lifted her head and looked down one of the narrow side streets. A few people walked along the lane, passing under a building that had been constructed to arch over the street. One man lingered at a shop window, smoking a cigarette. A woman walked quickly down the street, high heels clicking on the old stone. Nothing. Nothing out of place. Zoey swallowed her nervousness and finished typing her message to Sascha.

. . . are you?

Sliding the phone back into her pocket, Zoey moved on, a shiver running down her spine. Sascha couldn't have gone far – something Zoey was glad of. There was still that lingering feeling of unease, and she wanted him nearby. But again, there was nothing out of the ordinary. Nothing at all. Just people going about their business. There was *nothing* nefarious in that. So, why did she feel so rattled? Zoey paused as she approached a large junction of pedestrian streets. Small alleys ran between the high buildings, colorful frescoes brightened large portions of building walls. Flower baskets hung from one building's windows. There was nothing dangerous here. Zoey scanned the crowds of people again to see if she could spot Sascha's blond hair. She checked her phone. No response. He must still be busy. Silently, she begged him to not be much longer.

Exhaling, Zoey turned, arriving on another street lined with cafes and restaurants. More people crowded the streets here, and she relaxed, tension easing from her shoulders. Crowds were supposed to be safer, weren't they? She stopped at another shopfront, trying to look natural as she calmed down. Why was it that whenever trying to do a normal thing was necessary, it became much harder? She wasn't sure how much more of this hunted feeling she could stand.

A shadow fell across her.

"Thinking of a watch?"

"Just looking," replied Zoey. Her heart dropped.

The voice hadn't been Sascha's. Similar, but not his.

English spoken.

English replied.

Heart racing, Zoey froze. Her limbs fell numb. Her handgun rested, useless, in its plastic holster tucked into her waistband. Could she have even reached for it on this crowded street? How much attention would *that* attract? She turned to face the man who'd materialized next to her, as though appearing out of thin air. Tall, equally as tall as Sascha, with dark eyes and red hair. There was something about his expression that seemed almost friendly. Nothing about him stood out. He was dressed in casual clothes and an open-fronted coat. He blended in. Just like Sascha did.

And she knew him.

She'd met him in France all those weeks ago.

She had the nightmares to prove it.

She knew that red hair and those frigid eyes.

Erik Ardennes.

"And what brings you to this part of the world, Zoey Blackmore?" he asked.

He remembered her. Of course. How could he not? He'd known her then in Paris. He'd know her now. Zoey shook her head. She'd already given herself away. Her phone vibrated several times. An incoming call. She didn't dare answer it. Erik sneered and leaned in closer, his sickly kind expression falling away.

"I think you and I need to take a little walk, don't you? It's been a while since we've had a chance to see each other," he said, a feral smile rising to replace the mocking one that had been there before.

"No," snapped Zoey, taking a step back.

Her hand twitched as her phone buzzed with a second phone call. She wanted to reach for it. Desperately. On the other side of that phone speaker lay a lifeline. But she couldn't grab it. There was no telling what the consequences would be. Erik could shoot her before she ever even answered it. He could take it from her and find out Sascha was with her.

"I think you *really* should come with me," he replied, opening his coat just enough for her to see the grip of a handgun exposed above his waistband. "Let's go."

Zoey snapped back to her senses as he touched one hand to her lower back. Adrenaline kicked in. Anger rose. Get away from him. Think of something. But she couldn't move now. He'd be expecting her to run. She lifted her chin a fraction, locking her jaw. Play his game for the moment. Find an opportunity to get away from him. She turned the way he shepherded.

"You're a long way from where we lost you," Erik murmured, his hand tightening against her shirt. "We've been very concerned."

"And who exactly is we?" asked Zoey, narrowing her eyes.

"My employers. The gentleman who shelled out a considerable amount of money to purchase you. He's been sick with worry since you went missing. Anything could have happened to you. After what happened with your first handlers, The Czarina thought you needed to be looked after by someone more professional, so a few coworkers and I volunteered to comb Europe to find you."

Zoey's upper lip curled. "And how exactly did you find me?"

Erik chuckled, a deep, threatening sound that lacked any humor. "You should be more careful with your voicemails, Zoey. OMNI has better tech than your dear old dad and the SAS could ever hope for. We triangulated your location based off that little phone call, then sent a few operatives to the German-Austrian border. We had a feeling you'd surface eventually, and we were right."

Zoey nearly froze. This was all her fault. After all of Sascha's careful work, she'd given herself away. In her pocket, her phone vibrated again. A third phone call. Her hands balled into fists. They were leaving the crowds behind. Erik shifted the pressure of his hand, and

Zoey turned with him. A side street. Dark. Empty. Perfect. Sascha hadn't taught her how to defend herself for nothing. If there was ever going to be an opportunity, it was now.

Teeth bared; Zoey spun. Her raised elbow cracked into the side of his head. She hissed as it connected. The reality of hitting someone sunk in. Not in reaction. Not a sparring session. She hesitated. Erik stumbled, bending down, one hand clamped to his cheek. He glared up. Zoey caught the malice in his eyes. Erik would hurt her. If he got the chance. She mustn't give him that chance.

Now or never.

Zoey lunged forward and grabbed the back of Erik's head, clawing at his hair. His hands fumbled for her wrists. She drove her knee up, slamming his forehead. Once, hit. Second time, miss. Third time, a miss. He surged forward. Zoey lost her breath as her back crashed into the wall behind her. She let go, strands of red hairs caught between her fingers. Shove at his shoulders. Kick out at his legs where she could. He released her wrists and stood fully. Zoey reached back and caught him with an open-palmed slap. Writhe away from him. And . . . Erik stood between her and the closest end of the alley. Escape was cut off.

He stood straight and shook his head, and Zoey backed away a few steps. The far end of the alley was open behind her, but could she make it? Could she outrun him? He started at her again. Zoey lashed out with her left hand, fear lending strength. Knuckles caught the side of his mouth with a *crack*. Zoey screamed and shook her hand. Pause. Erik turned his head and spat. Blood spatters landed on the pale pavement. Pain throbbed up from her knuckles. Erik reached into his coat and withdrew his handgun. Seconds dragged out. Zoey felt numb. He was armed now. What should she do? What had Sascha taught her?

Don't panic.

Erik was moving again. His arm lifted.

Don't panic.

Advancing. Weapon pointed at her.

Panic.

She only had one good hand. Her legs trembled. She stumbled back a step, raising her uninjured hand to slap him. To punch him. To claw at his face. Anything. Desperation snared her throat tight in its grasp. Erik caught her wrist. Cold metal pressed up against her chin. Zoey screamed.

Sascha had taught her how to get out of holds.

But she couldn't remember.

Not holds like this. Not with a gun pointed to her chin.

The pattern of light and shadow shifted overhead. What did she do now? React. Somehow. But she couldn't. She had a weapon at her side. But she couldn't make herself reach for it. She couldn't. Erik snarled, his gaze furious. Blood stained his teeth. Zoey lifted her throbbing hand, prying at his fingers around her wrist. Then something hard and metal cracked against the side of her head. She both felt and heard her teeth clack together. Blood washed over her tongue. Stars and black spots dazzled her eyes. Feeling numb she collapsed sideways, elbows and hands smacking against the hard pavement.

Fighting to push herself up, Zoey looked around in a daze. Still her vision swung back and forth between black and colorful. Erik approached her, but she was powerless to keep him away, all her limbs felt so heavy and useless. She could barely see. Nausea gripped her stomach, and she was certain she was going to be sick. She raised her gaze beyond him, a shape catching her attention. Standing atop an adjacent roof, leaning over the awning, was a figure. She recognized that stance.

Sascha. Sascha was here.

Warm relief washed over her. A kind of relief unlike anything she had ever known before. Safety.

Then one of Erik's hands covered her nose and mouth, slamming her head against the wall behind her. A feverish chill ran through Zoey's body. She felt like she'd been dunked in cold water. She snapped blindly, teeth closing on empty air. She clawed at his arm. Anything to get him off her.

Erik's hand tightened.

Stars blurred her vision, and air choked in Zoey's throat. She tried to scream, scraping at his hands, but the sound jammed airlessly, no sound leaving her mouth. Vaguely, she felt something sharp and stinging stab through her clothes and into her arm. She choked, eyes drifting to Erik for a second. His mouth curled into a vicious sneer, and Zoey lifted a weak hand again to try and pull him off her. Blackness ringed her vision. Through failing eyes, Zoey looked back at the rooftop. Sascha was gone. Coming. He was coming to help her. He'd come. He had to. Colors melded together, sliding away into black, and her vision closed.

Chapter 27

The headache was what woke Zoey. Before she even opened her eyes, there it was. Pounding. It made her eyes ache and ears ring. Painfully, Zoey opened her eyes. Everything hurt. She groaned and blinked a few times to clear her vision. This room. It was unfamiliar. Definitely not the safe house. The dark wood walls made the room feel like a cave. Outside the single, small window, darkness pressed in. A kind of slow fear sparked in her chest. Even if Sascha had somehow managed to find her while she was unconscious, this didn't seem like the kind of place he'd bring her. And, some deep gut feeling told her, he would have been here when she woke up.

Carefully, Zoey sat up and assessed herself. Her left hand throbbed and ached, and she groaned, hugging it to her chest. Her shoes were still on her feet. There was no weight of a weapon at her side. That was gone. No cell phone in her pocket. That was gone, too. She swallowed hard and looked around the room. It was bare, save the bed where she lay and an empty bedside table.

Sascha wouldn't have taken her phone. Even if he had taken it off her person, he would have left it somewhere she could find them. Zoey swallowed and exhaled shakily. She rubbed a hand across her forehead. This could only mean one thing.

Erik. She was here because of Erik. She drew a slow, shuddering breath and stood, her head swimming and vision washing in and out for a second. She grappled for support, clutching at the bedside table until her head cleared. Sascha valued his freedom more than anything. If it was a choice between him staying free and helping her again . . . she knew which one he would choose.

A crushing kind of defeat rippled through her chest.

How stupid she'd been to think he'd come for her.

She was on her own.

The doorknob rattled, and Zoey jerked her head up, ignoring the way the room spun to catch up with her vision. She dropped her hand back to her side and stood unsteadily on her feet as the door swung inward. Her stomach dropped as Erik stepped through, but she couldn't help feeling a tiny flicker of satisfaction as she caught sight of a bruise at the side of his mouth.

Two other men she didn't recognize followed Erik into the room. Zoey paused to take in his two companions. The first was a shorter, sturdy-looking man, with dark features. The second, a tall and incredibly thin man with dark hair and a scraggly beard. He stared at her with unreadable brown eyes.

"Hello, Zoey," Erik said. "Lovely to see you back on your feet."

Be strong. She was on her own now. "Where am I?"

"Cuts to the chase, doesn't she?" asked Erik, grinning at the blond man beside him. "Zoey, may I introduce you to two of my colleagues?"

"Do I have a choice?" she asked.

"No." Erik gestured to the smaller man at his side. "This is Marcus Yaroslavl."

Marcus offered an oily smile, and Zoey couldn't help but take one step back. There was something horribly menacing about him, something even more so than Erik or the other man at Erik's side.

"Pleasure to finally meet you, Zoey Blackmore. We've heard a great deal about you in our sphere. All of us have been waiting anxiously for you to finally make it to your destination. It's an honor to be one of your final *escorts*," he said.

Zoey fought not to curl her lip at the way he said his last word. These men were here to traffic her. Traffic her into . . . she swallowed down the bile that rose in her throat.

"Easy, Marcus. Let's not frighten the poor girl. I'm sure there'll be plenty of opportunity to do that later," said Erik, a small smile playing on his lips. "The silent one here is Varek Houston. I have a feeling you'll be seeing a lot of him when we finally get you up with Lord Marion. He's Marion's personal problem solver."

Varek tilted his head, looking at Erik from the corners of his eyes. "That's enough about us now, Erik."

Zoey took a shallow breath. Ardennes, Yaroslavl, Houston. None of the names sounded natural. They were all locations. Just like Sascha's. Were these men like him? Assassins, too? She had a horrible feeling that they were. If so, these were not amateurs.

"Why am I here?" asked Zoey. She already knew the answer, she was sure of it, but the question still left her mouth.

Marcus laughed low in his throat and leaned on the door jamb. Erik stepped forward, a small, derisive smile on his face. Even one side of Varek's mouth curled up. The air filled with a sense of mockery. They were enjoying this. All of them. Zoey's insides boiled, turning quickly to nausea. She was twenty. Barely an adult in the world of traffickers, assassins, and killers. A world she never imagined even existed. And they were laughing at her.

Erik grinned at Marcus and Varek, then turned his eyes on Zoey. "Now that we've tracked you down, we'll be delivering you to Lord Marion. Originally, we wanted to show you off to The Czarina for a few days, but even she agrees that you're too valuable an asset to allow another chance of getting away."

"Where am I going?" asked Zoey, already certain they wouldn't tell her.

"Does it matter?" asked Marcus.

Zoey looked at him. She recognized those words. Bouncer had spoken them to her weeks ago. Before she'd met Sascha. Sascha. What would he do in this situation? What would he tell her to do? Fight her way out? Not a chance. There were three of them and one of her. Escape in the middle of the night? How much more of the night did she have left? Even if she did manage to get away from them, how long would she last before she was caught again? Was running just prolonging the inevitable? No. She couldn't think like that. Sascha wasn't coming for her. That was fine. She still had to get away for the sake of her sisters. She'd find a way out of here on her own merits. It was just going to be harder than if she'd had Sascha at her back.

Zoey tilted her head at Marcus, Erik, and Varek. "No. I suppose it doesn't."

A bright smile crossed Marcus's face, but Erik and Varek exchanged a look, as both their eyes narrowed.

"Actually, Zoey," said Erik, motioning to Marcus. "Before we get going, we had a few questions for you. There are some, ah, gaps in our timeline. Come with us."

Zoey hesitated as Erik turned and stalked out of the room, followed by Marcus and Varek. The door stayed open. She took a breath and walked out of the tiny bedroom. She looked around as soon as she entered the rest of the house. If it could even be called that. It was a single room, the kitchen and living room conjoined. One couch and two chairs took what little space there was in the living room. They all looked aging and moth-eaten. The entire place stunk of dry rot. A sleeping bag was rolled up on the couch. There was another door off the kitchen. Zoey assumed it was a bathroom. There would be no escaping through there. Large glass doors formed the front wall of the house, with nothing beyond save the pitch dark. That was her exit. It could be her only exit. She just had to figure out how to get past Erik, Varek, and Marcus to reach it. Varek crossed the room to stand between her and the door. Marcus moved to stand near one of the chairs.

"Don't even think about it, Zoey," said Erik. "Varek and Marcus will be on you before you can blink. Unlike your previous escorts, we have permission to break some bones if we have to. And I don't think you'd get very far on a broken leg. Come here."

Zoey swallowed thickly and turned away from the door. Best not to even think about it right now. Not with them all watching and waiting. Erik stood at the kitchen counter, two items on the surface beside him. Familiar items. Her handgun and her phone. She fought to keep her breath from hitching.

"Where did you get these?" asked Erik, giving a cruel smile showing too many teeth. A smile that looked horribly feral.

"I found them," said Zoey. Even if Sascha had abandoned her, she wasn't going to give him up. That was their first agreement. That they'd never tell other people that they'd ever met. He'd been kind to her. She'd keep her promise. She owed him that.

Across the room, Marcus barked a laugh.

"Found them?" asked Erik, lifting the handgun.

"Yes," nodded Zoey.

"I don't believe you."

Zoey fought to keep herself steady. Panic threatened her again. Was he going to shoot her? Erik turned the weapon in his hand and smiled, shaking his head.

"You see, Zoey," he said. "This weapon is special. *This* is a ghost gun. There's no serial number. No way to track where it was made or who it belongs to. They don't belong to just anyone. They belong to men like me, Varek, and Marcus. So, unless you stole this from an assassin – which I highly doubt – you're lying. Where did you get it?"

"I found it," said Zoey. She'd started this lie now. She had to run with it. "I don't remember where."

"I see," nodded Erik, his voice horribly gentle and filled with false kindness. He set the gun down, and Zoey breathed. "Now, Zoey, this phone. It's also very interesting. Not the kind of phone a girl would have at all. No photos, no apps, nothing to give away what it might be. Not even a brand. Did you *find* this, too?"

Zoey's mouth went dry and she felt the blood drain from her face. "Yes."

There were still texts between her and Sascha on there. Phone calls. His contact information was still there.

"We thought about going through this while you were asleep, but seeing your face now makes waiting worthwhile. You see, we've heard the precious, little voicemail that you left for your dear sister. We know someone's been helping you. Who gave this to you?"

"I – I found it," said Zoey, hearing the quaver in her own voice. As though she could sound any less convincing. "No one –"

Varek straightened in her peripherals, and the words died in Zoey's throat. Erik smiled again, the feral note slipping back into his expression.

"I know. I know. You found it, didn't you?"

Zoey wanted to ball her hands into fists. To look away. To run now and make a break for it. But she couldn't. She mustn't. She blinked fast. Protect Sascha.

"That's right," she said.

Erik racked the top of the handgun back and smiled. Zoey shivered. She'd heard a bullet slip into place. Fully loaded and ready to go. Erik turned to her and grinned, showing far too many teeth once again.

"Who's been helping you, Zoey? I'm not an idiot. You couldn't have made it this far on your own."

Zoey shook her head. "No –"

The muzzle swung toward her, and Zoey saw Erik's finger fall to the trigger.

"I can shoot you without killing you, Zoey. Very, very easily. I can make this hurt for a very long time until we get the truth. We're alone on this mountain and nobody will hear you screaming. Don't make me ask again. Who has been helping you?"

Zoey stood very still. Permanent injury. Disfiguration. Was she willing to risk that for Sascha? And yet, he'd already risked more for her. He'd never tell anyone if he were in her position now. Something furious rose in her chest. She'd never give him up. Not to Erik. Not to anyone. She'd promised him. Just as he'd promised her.

She met Erik's terrible brown eyes and shook her head.

"I'm getting irritated," he said, lowering the gun to aim at her shins.

The phone on the kitchen counter rang.

Zoey froze. Only one person had that phone number. She stared at Erik. His eyes were on the phone, the handgun lowering slowly to his side. The entire room fell still and tense. The darkness outside seemed to have pressed into the room itself.

The lights flickered and cut out.

Glass shattered. Something flashed in the corner of Zoey's vision. Light, dazzling white and blinding. A sound like a bomb exploding rocked the house. Another blinding flash turned Zoey's vision white, and she stumbled forward, barely catching herself on the kitchen counter. A second bang set her ears ringing. She could smell something acidic. The air practically tasted of gasoline. Glass shattered again, louder this time. She bolted toward the front door but slipped on a piece of broken glass. She crashed against the floor on her hands and knees. Shards of glass pierced her hands. Seconds later, three patches of bright, orange flames flashed across the floor, scattering like spilled water and devouring the wood and carpet. Varek shouted something unintelligible as he tried to dive toward the couch. Another gunshot split the night. Varek crumpled to the ground, holding his ribs, blood staining his shirt black in the flaming half-light.

Erik swore loudly. Zoey turned from where she was on the floor. Outside, another gunshot split the night. Erik screamed, a horrible, agonized sound. Warm wetness spattered Zoey's face like summer rain. Hot iron tang followed it. Metal clattered as Erik dropped his weapon, and it scudded away across the floor. Zoey pushed up to her hands and knees and spun to look at Erik. She wished she hadn't. His hand was a mutilated mess of fingers and blood. Zoey screamed and looked around desperately, trying to find the doors. The smoke was already dark and thick, and her eyes and ears didn't want to work properly. She heard the window in the bedroom blow out, and more heat bloomed as another fire ignited. Any way out through the bedroom was cut off.

Zoey coughed and stood fully, turning back to the living space. The only light came from the flames themselves. Erik was across the room, pulling Varek to his feet with his good hand. He turned to Marcus, who had taken temporary refuge at the base of the kitchen counter. Over the roar of the building flames, Zoey heard Erik shouting.

"Get Blackmore! Meet us outside!"

Zoey stared at Marcus. He was between her and the door. Marcus looked shocked, unable to comprehend what had just happened. Across the room, Erik and Varek wrestled the door open. Smoke billowed out behind them. Zoey coughed hard and looked around. If there had ever been a chance to run, it was now. She glanced downward and caught sight of a black handle near her foot. The gun Sascha had lent her. If she was going to get out of this, she'd need it. Not even considering the glass embedded in her hands, she snatched it, palms slippery with blood. And she hesitated. She was armed. Marcus wasn't. Whoever had ambushed them had to be nearby. She didn't have much time.

"Get out of my way," she snarled, raising the weapon.

Marcus lowered his head and spread his arms as though he was trying to catch her before she even moved. He wouldn't let her pass. She knew that. Zoey paused as she heard glass shatter again in the living room window. They, whoever *they* were, had arrived.

"I'll kill you if you don't get out of my way!" she shouted, dropping her finger to the trigger.

"Not going to happen."

Zoey felt her finger slip, and the handgun fired. Marcus stopped as though shocked by electricity. Red mist spattered out from the side of his head. He swayed in slow motion, then fell sideways, crashing to the ground, blood pooling at his head and spreading across the white linoleum. Zoey stayed frozen. Her entire body went cold. She'd . . . she'd fired and . . . The flames around her seemed to fade away. Her arm fell slowly to her side. This human, who had been alive only seconds ago, was . . .

The handgun was wrenched from her trembling grip. And hands. Hands were on her now, shaking her hard. In a daze, she looked up. A figure towered over her in the orange half-light, features obscured with dark goggles and a face covering. Not someone else. She'd never make it out of here with four people after her. Then the figure tore their mask down and ripped their goggles off. Blue eyes. Blond hair streaked with dark dye. Sascha. But he wasn't supposed to be here.

"Move!" shouted Sascha.

Sascha. Zoey blinked a few times. Hearing and function returned. She gagged and heaved, while her knees threatened to buckle. She stumbled, wanting nothing more than to sink to the floor. A strong hand caught her and hauled her upright. Zoey stared dumbly at Sascha. She didn't have words. Speech failed her completely. What had she done?

"Stop it!" shouted Sascha, somehow making himself heard over the fire. "You'll have time for this later!"

But she couldn't. She stared at Marcus's fallen body. She'd done that. She'd *killed* someone. She couldn't move. She stumbled as Sascha grabbed her shoulder and shook her hard.

"Zoey, move!" he shouted.

She couldn't move. Nothing in her body responded. Sascha tugged her, and Zoey stumbled after him as he bolted from the house, his grip tight on her upper arm.

~ ~ ~ ~ ~ ~

The sliver of moon overhead gave little light. Stars stared down from overhead, silent and distant. Stars. North Star. Where was it? Zoey blinked hard, scanning the sky for it. But she couldn't find it. Aquila, then.

"Zoey," called Sascha from ahead, interrupting her search. "We can't stop."

She returned her gaze to him. She could only see his vague outline ahead as she trudged the few paces to catch him. He was almost invisible in the dark. She panted, leaning on a thick pine tree to catch her breath. Her legs burned beneath her from the steep, uphill ascent. Her feet ached. Her hands still wept blood from the broken glass. The scar across her thigh pulsed and throbbed. She'd lost track of how long they'd been walking, unsure now if it was only a few minutes or if it had been hours. It was all she could do to keep putting one foot in front of the other. Part of her didn't want to. She inhaled deeply, smelling the leaf litter and decay on the ground. She couldn't quite rally herself back into movement. She wanted to block this night away. Let it fade out of existence and memory. To never think about it again. Never think of how a bullet fired from her own gun had caused a living human to drop like a stone, dead before he hit the floor. Never remember the spray of red that had burst from Marcus's head, painting the kitchen cabinets beside him. Zoey heaved another a deep breath, the smells of earth and fallen leaves flooding her senses.

No more footsteps.

Zoey lifted her head. Ahead, she could just make out Sascha's dark outline. Silently waiting for her to stir. Sascha. He had come for her. Again. When she hadn't expected him to. He had risked his life for her a second time. Even now, he didn't have to wait for her. He didn't have to chance his clean escape just for her. But he did.

Fighting the tremble in her lower lip, Zoey gathered herself again. She had to keep up with him. She owed him that. She mustn't let his risk be taken in vain. Somewhere nearby an owl hooted in the trees. Slowly, Zoey took a deep breath and forced herself to walk again. Sascha waited where he was until she drew even with him. She turned in the dark and locked eyes with him.

"Where are we going?" she asked, keeping her voice low.

"Somewhere safer than this. The car's not far now," replied Sascha, his voice equally quiet.

"What time is it?" asked Zoey.

"Four in the morning. It'll be light in a few hours."

Zoey nodded, hearing the unsaid part of his sentence. They didn't want to be anywhere near that ruined house when light broke. She swallowed and fell into step just behind Sascha as he struck off again through the night. How he could tell where he was going, Zoey had no idea. How he'd arrived and found her was another mystery. She didn't think she would ever know how he'd managed it. Was it really important though? In the dark, she watched him. Just as he had the first time she'd met him, he'd left her with more questions than answers. And just as he had been that first night she'd met him, he exuded that silent sense of strength. A resilience she'd never encountered before. In the gloom, she could make out his faint profile. He was all sharp edges and angular outlines again. Zoey forced strength back through her body. She needed to keep up with him. She would not let herself be more of a liability than she already had been.

Underfoot, the ground started to slope downward, and Zoey breathed a quiet sigh of relief as the pain in her burning legs eased a fraction.

"Try not to scuff your feet," said Sascha in a flat voice.

Zoey hesitated as she descended. The lack of emotion in Sascha's voice hit her hard. Harder than it possibly should have. She swallowed. She'd heard that tone before. In her father's voice. Disappointment. Sascha expected her to get them caught.

"Sascha," she said. *If they find us again, leave. Don't risk yourself again.* The words teetered behind her teeth, lingering on the edge of her tongue.

"Not now, Zoey."

The words Zoey had nearly said burned and died in her mouth. She swallowed them back and kept going, taking care to mind where she trod.

As the small morning hours wore on, Zoey lost track of time. Lost track of the times unseen branches scratched her face, lost track of the number of times she'd nearly fallen after stepping on unseen stones or fallen branches, and Sascha had been there to steady her. He hadn't missed a single beat.

Zoey breathed a sigh of relief as she spotted the outline of a road just ahead, wending its way through the Alps. Closing her eyes, she forged onward, following Sascha, as he led the way through thick underbrush in the final stretch to the car. Then, at last, they were out of the woods and beside the vehicle. She could have kissed the gravel on the slip road as they broke onto it. She hadn't realized how much of a relief it would be to walk on even ground again. As she reached for the door handle, she glanced at Sascha, the outline of his face gray now against the last vestiges of night. His expression was unreadable. Zoey dropped her hand to her side.

"How did you find me? Again?" she asked.

Sascha paused on the other side of the car, and a muscle in his jaw twitched. He took a low breath and fixed his gaze toward the mountain forest they'd come through.

"Erik. He posted a picture, one of you unconscious in that cabin, to our dark corner of the internet. I knew there was an OMNI-run safe house here. The dots weren't hard to connect," said Sascha, rage coursing through every word. He took a sharp breath. "Please, Zoey, get in the car. We can't be caught out here. I want to get you safe."

Zoey swallowed hard and nodded. Sascha wanted her safe. She wanted them both safe. She didn't want to risk an encounter with whoever might come to clean up what was left of Marcus.

~ ~ ~ ~ ~ ~

"One more flight of stairs," said Sascha. "Almost there."

Zoey looked up. She was exhausted. Fear had drained her. They'd driven all day. The sun had long since set. Sascha had stopped often and doubled back several times, keeping out of cities and sticking to backroads. It had stretched out the journey much longer than it should have been. Other than his wrapping her hands in bandages after tweezing shards of glass from them, he'd said nothing throughout the trip. Neither had Zoey. The car ride had been so tense. She almost hadn't dared to wipe Erik's dried blood from her face. Even though it was gone now, she could still almost feel it, cracking and breaking against her skin with every movement. Her eyes darted to Sascha. His jaw was still tense. Disappointed. Again, that word killed her.

The car was parked just below them on the street. Zoey breathed heavily and continued up the flight of stairs. Her feet ached and burned with every step. Merano. Italy. A country away from where everything had gone so wrong. Zoey knew without asking, that this was another safe house, nestled in a block of apartments in the center of the town. Unremarkable. Hidden in its normalcy. As she reached the landing at the top of the stairs, Zoey leaned on the wall, exhausted. The straps of her backpack lay heavy on her shoulders. She stepped in beside Sascha as he walked ahead. The sour taste of guilt settled in her mouth. She'd ruined everything. She should never have begged to come with him. She'd been a risk from the start. A complete liability.

"Stop," said Sascha, punching in a number code to one of the doors.

"Hm? What?" asked Zoey, raising her head.

"Blaming yourself. I can almost hear it." He moved aside and gestured to the open door. "This isn't your fault."

"It feels like it," sighed Zoey, stepping into the apartment.

Tiny. It was tiny. Dim. A studio. Walls painted a dark yellow. One bed. One bathroom. A tiny kitchen. A chair. A single, square window. The curtain was drawn.

"It's not," replied Sascha. "I shouldn't have let you come with me. I should have told you 'no'."

"You came for me," she said, turning back to Sascha. Her voice sounded thicker than she expected.

"I almost didn't," replied Sascha. "I was over the German border when I turned around."

"You shouldn't have. This was all my fault," said Zoey, rubbing her face. "I thought you wouldn't come. We agreed. That first day that if . . ."

Sascha inclined his head. "If you left, we'd deny that we ever met. That I wouldn't chase after you."

"Yes," replied Zoey, lowering her gaze to the carpet.

"I couldn't leave you. Not like that."

A thousand questions swirled in Zoey's head as she looked back up at him. Sascha set his bag down on the floor at the foot of the bed. She shrugged hers off her shoulders and let it slide to the floor. The air was thick between them. Zoey looked down as her lower lip trembled. There, on the tiny, silver pendant Sascha had bought her, were flecks of dried blood, standing out like black murder spots. Zoey clapped a hand to her mouth to steady herself, her stomach turning against her.

"Zoey?" asked Sascha.

From her peripherals, Zoey saw him take half a step closer, and she scrambled backward in spite of herself. Another horrible chill of guilt gathered in Zoey's stomach as she saw Sascha stop dead as though he'd been stung.

"Zoey, what is it?" he asked.

"Someone's dead," she said, her voice trembling and shaking. "I killed . . . Sascha, I killed someone."

"Oh, Zoey," sighed Sascha, sitting down and unlacing his boots. "No. No, you didn't."

Zoey turned. "What?"

"It wasn't you that killed Yaroslavl."

"But I – Sascha, I shot him."

"No. You didn't. Think."

Zoey scoffed in desperation. How much she'd tried to clear the images from last night from her mind. "I don't want to think –"

"I know. But do. You fired and Yaroslavl dropped. Right?"

"Right," nodded Zoey, the single syllable threatening to stop in her throat.

"Which way did the blood exit his head?" asked Sascha, standing again and folding his arms.

"Sascha! Please," sobbed Zoey, her shoulders shaking.

One of Sascha's brows lifted, no humor in his expression.

Zoey heaved a steadying breath and pressed her hand to her mouth. "The side. It came from the side."

"Exactly. I was to his right. If the bullet that had hit him had been yours, Zoey, his blood would have hit the cabinetry behind him not to the side of him."

"It wasn't –" Zoey swallowed. "It was one of yours?"

Sascha nodded once.

"How can you be sure? There was so much going on."

"I've been a marksman for a long time, Zoey. I know where each of my rounds lands, and I don't miss. Whatever guilt you may feel about Yaroslavl's death, it's not yours to bear. You've killed nobody. For anyone who died last night, let the blame for their death be on me, not you."

Zoey sat heavily on the bed and buried her face in her hands, sobbing a few quiet breaths. She hadn't killed him. She pressed her bandaged hands to her eyes, then lifted her gaze, lacing her fingers together in front of her mouth. Blood still hung, staining silver, around her neck. Sascha's hand ghosted her shoulder, and Zoey heaved a breath, glancing at him. Movements slow, he clasped the silver pendant between his thumb and index finger and held it for a moment. Then, without a word, he turned and rummaged through his black duffel bag, returning moments later with a sterile alcohol swab. Zoey reached up to take it from him, but he shook his head.

"Let me. You've dealt with more than enough blood."

Zoey inhaled, readying herself to protest, to tell him she could clean her own necklace. But there was a strange look in Sascha's eyes, and Zoey exhaled, her shoulders falling forward. She closed her eyes as he sat next to her, and the chain rubbed her skin as he gently clasped the pendant again. With each pass of his thumb, Zoey knew, more blood lifted from silver, transferring to the sterile wipe in Sascha's hand. Her throat threatened to close.

She took a breath to steady herself. "Did you know the other two men?"

"I know of them," replied Sascha, tossing the bloodied alcohol wipe into the wastepaper basket by the door. "I've known of Erik for some time. He contracted several years with OMNI for one of their higher-ups. I know Yaroslavl was freelance. Varek's a mystery. Last I heard, he was contracted with Lord Marion. I imagine Erik and Yaroslavl pulled him in to help."

Zoey swallowed, unsuccessfully stifling a tremble at the mention of Lord Marion. "It was him. Lord Marion. He was the one who bought me."

Sascha paused for a long moment. "That explains Varek."

"Are you still going to the meeting with OMNI?" asked Zoey. The single room seeming too small for both of them.

Sascha rested his chin in one hand, and when he spoke, his words were measured. "This has changed everything, Zoey."

Zoey watched him, wary. That wasn't reassuring. Which side of him was this? It wasn't the side she'd come to know. It wasn't his sharp side that she'd seen again last night. This was something else. Something uncertain. Something she didn't like. Something that made her heart constrict in all the worst ways. A sinking, sickening feeling.

"*What's* changed?" she asked. Her voice sounded harsh. Angry.

Sascha looked toward the curtained window. "Erik will tell his employer that he saw me last night. I probably ended his career last night, so he'll have a pretty hefty vendetta now. They'll know I'm the one who kept you safe, and they'll know that I'm the one who helped you in the first place."

"What are you going to do?" asked Zoey, standing slowly and folding her arms tight. She struggled to keep herself contained. He was going to turn on her. She was sure of it. It was in his voice. In the heaviness of his words. His own life and his own freedom had to mean more to him than hers.

Sascha turned, his eyes a fraction narrower than usual. "I'll thank you to not sound so accusatory. Do you remember what I said about OMNI all those weeks ago?"

"That no one says 'no' to them?" Zoey gathered herself.

Sascha nodded once. Zoey swallowed. They were discovered, and only one of them could walk away from this free. Sascha still had her passport. She should have known better. Sascha valued his freedom more than anything else. It was the reason he'd run from her father all those years ago, and it was why he would turn on her tonight. God, she'd been such an idiot to trust him. And yet, she didn't *blame* him. He was just one man. He could only do so much. So, why did it feel as though her heart was going to shatter? Why did tears feel so close to the surface? The promise of home was being torn away, and the time she'd spent with Sascha was tarnished.

He cleared his throat. "It's –"

Sascha's phone chimed, and he tilted his head, brows furrowed. Zoey shook her head. She hadn't sent him anything – how could she? Her own phone had been incinerated the night before. He scrambled for his phone, pressing a few buttons on it, then dug his laptop out of his bag. There was a sleekness to his movements, that made Zoey feel even more like she was balanced on a knife edge. He opened the lid and pressed a knuckle to his lips, illuminated blue by the laptop's light. Zoey caught his meaning. Quiet. Sascha's face settled into an unreadable mask.

A woman's voice, one that Zoey could only describe as being like the sound of running water, broke over the speakers of Sascha's laptop.

"Good evening, Mr. Sarajevo. I hope that this message finds you well, and you, too, of course, Zoey. I'm The Czarina. Head of the OMNI Corporation." Clamping a hand over her mouth to stifle any sound, Zoey sunk to the arm of the chair, strength in her legs evaporating. The foundation of safety was gone. They knew. OMNI knew. They knew exactly where she was. They knew who she was with.

Through the screen of Sascha's computer, the woman continued. "You know, I'd really hoped I wouldn't have to send this – prerecorded messages are such a hassle – but people are so tragically predictable. I'm sure you understand my sentiments, don't you, Sarajevo?"

Sascha tapped a key on the laptop. "Zoey, come here."

Zoey hesitated. She was about to see the person, the woman, who had done this to her. Who had sent her racing across half of Europe. Who had ripped her from her home. Heart beating faster than she ever knew it could, Zoey moved from the chair to sit next to Sascha on the bed. The video on his laptop screen was paused, not displayed on a browser or email platform that Zoey recognized. Her eyes swept the woman on screen. Beautiful was the only way to describe her. She was lounging in a chair, set against a white backdrop, black hair loose and flowing over her shoulders. Zoey swallowed. Brown eyes, eyes that should have been warm, leered out of the screen as though this woman knew exactly where she sat. The ruby lipstick the woman, this 'Czarina', wore matched the color of her shirt to perfection. There was power here. Control. Menace.

Sascha leaned forward and played the video.

The Czarina moved. Even her movements, languid, radiated authority. Her tone was gentle, as though she was speaking to a child.

"I'm going to keep this in English for your benefit, Zoey. I know you'll be listening. Sascha, it was deeply upsetting to me to hear Erik's report from last night. He told me he, Varek, and the late Marcus had darling Zoey in possession and that you came and took her from them. Erik tells me you killed Marcus and injured him and Varek. You can imagine my dismay when I saw my Erik's poor hand. He'll be lucky if he ever shoots again. I've worked with you before, Sascha, and have always been most impressed with your services, but I simply can't fathom why you'd come between my personal operative and a known target of my organization." The Czarina's expression changed, lethal now. "Then things fell into place. Zoey Blackmore's sudden and complete disappearance, your surfacing in Germany not long afterward – when it was rumored you were on your way to Slovenia – and finally, your appearance together last night. Rather a far-fetched series of coincidences, don't you think?"

Zoey looked at Sascha. His face was impassive. She moved, overcome by a desperate need to sit behind him on the bed, as if putting a barrier of protection between herself and the woman on the screen.

The Czarina straightened, folding her fingers at her chest. "I know you're with each other. I know you, Sascha, had a major hand in her separation from my agents. I know you've been deceiving me. But I am a forgiving woman. I have not yet taken the liberty of cancelling our meeting, and, as far as I am concerned, it still stands. If you bring Zoey Blackmore to me in Vienna by twelve noon tomorrow, I will forgive this little indiscretion of yours."

Again, Zoey looked up at Sascha. His expression was shadowed by the laptop's cold light. The Czarina leaned forward slightly, head tilting. Zoey couldn't help feeling that her eyes were fixed on both of them.

The Czarina spoke again. "If you choose not to come to Vienna tomorrow, this is what will happen. Zoey, my men will find you, they will bring you to me, and I will personally deliver you to your new owner. He's paid a high price for you, and I intend to see that he gets his merchandise. Customer service is a priority for my company. Sascha, if you choose to run, I will find you, and I cannot emphasize this enough, I *will* find you, I will skin you alive and feed you to my dogs. Think hard on what you will do, Mr. Sarajevo. I await your answer."

The video ended, and the laptop screen faded black.

Chapter 28

Sascha let out a low chuckle, and Zoey turned to him. She felt nauseated.

"What are you laughing about? She's sick! That whole thing was . . . She . . ." Zoey shook her head, words failing her. How could people like that exist?

"'Feed you to my dogs'. That one's good. I haven't heard that one in years."

Zoey stared at Sascha. There wasn't even a trace of fear in his eyes. "You're not worried? That didn't scare you *at all*?"

Sascha shrugged. "It's nothing I haven't heard before. People like her love to threaten when they feel their control slipping away." Zoey turned away, holding her head in her hands. The ultimatum this woman had given Sascha . . . surrender her or be killed. There was no way he wouldn't take it. This was over. The mattress creaked as Sascha stood, and Zoey stayed perched on the edge of the bed. She sucked a breath in through her teeth and watched him, fighting back the tears that pricked at her eyes. Had she not known him better, Zoey would have missed the marginal tilt of Sascha's head. She exhaled hard, a sigh leaving her with a shudder.

Steeling herself, Zoey made eye contact with him. "It's okay. I'll find a way to get loose."

"Pardon?" asked Sascha, folding his arms.

"That ultimatum she gave you . . . I know you're going to hand me over. I'll find a way to get away from this Lord Marion on my own. Poison him if I have to. That's the woman's weapon, right?" Zoey fought the absurd urge to laugh, remembering one of Sascha's earliest comments to her. Her voice broke when she spoke again. "What I mean is, I'll be okay. I'd do the same if I were in your shoes."

"Then let's be glad you aren't in my shoes. I didn't get the chance to finish what I was saying earlier," said Sascha. He took a step closer to the bed and reached in his pocket. "Are you ready to go home?"

Zoey's mouth fell open as Sascha pulled her passport from his pocket and tossed it to her. She, miraculously, caught it with shaking fingers. For a moment, she couldn't tear her eyes away from it. She swallowed hard, then looked up at Sascha through a watery haze. Her chest swelled with every possible emotion. He gave her a small smile, his eyes softening a fraction. Then Zoey was on her feet, passport left behind on the bed. She wrapped her arms around him, the side of her face pressed against his chest. She could hear his heartbeat, slow and steady.

"I don't understand why you'd stick your neck out for me. I'm no one special," she said, pulling him tighter.

Sascha chuckled, his arms coming up and pulling her tight to his chest. "Not special? I beg to differ."

Zoey pulled back a bit and tipped her face back to look at him, a chill running down her spine as his soft laugh vibrated through her chest. "You came after me, even when you knew it would expose you. You're up against a worldwide corporation, and you're still willing to help *me*. Why?"

Blue eyes met her own, and Zoey's breath caught in her throat. There was something in Sascha's eyes. Some depth she hadn't seen before, as though he had waited until now to show it to her. One of his hands slipped into her hair, his thumb tracing her cheek, and Zoey fisted her hands in his shirt. Her blood rushed hot in her body. His other hand lingered at her lower back.

Sascha tilted his head, his eyes unveiled. "I thought it was obvious. I *care* about you, Zoey Blackmore. You're special to *me*. You and all that you mean to me are not things I intend to just throw away. I promise you this, Zoey, Lord Marion will not get his hands on you. Not as long as I'm alive. And if, somehow, he does, I would tear the world apart to make you safe again."

"I –" The words stuck in Zoey's throat. She mustn't say them. She'd spent so long trying to stifle the words to voice her feelings. But she couldn't *not* say them. "I care about you too, Sascha."

Even as she spoke, she had to wonder if what she'd just said ran the risk of damning her later. Then an expression settled behind Sascha's eyes, an expression Zoey couldn't place, and that small smile lifted one side of his mouth. If her words damned her, it would be worth this. All that mattered was the fast thrum of her pulse in her throat, the slow, comforting beat of Sascha's heart in his chest, how close she was now to him – a rock in this unsteady world.

Handsome.

She pressed her cheek against his hand. Weeks ago, she'd thought him handsome. She'd been right. Sascha *was* handsome. But it was a kind of handsomeness that didn't come from his looks alone. Not from those high cheekbones or short blond hair. Not from his graceful movements or careful words. It was from something else. From something lodged deep behind those sharp blue eyes. In that dark little room, time stood still. Her lips parted, and she could have sworn Sascha's eyes flickered away from her own and he leaned incrementally closer. Emotion washed over her – unlike anything else she had ever felt before. A barrier fell, and heat surged through her chest. She shifted her weight into her toes, leaning up toward him. His return movement was subtle. A second, tiny shift forward in his weight, his nose almost brushing hers.

Zoey tightened her fingers against Sascha's shirt, and when she spoke, her voice left her mouth in a whisper. "What happens now?"

"We start for England, going to Portsmouth from Cherbourg via Paris," replied Sascha in the same quiet tone. "They'll be watching airports, not ferry ports. We can't outman them. We have to outthink them."

A cold chill gripped Zoey, flushing the warmth of the moment away and bringing her back to the present. Merano.

"Are you sure about not meeting with her?" asked Zoey, tilting her head toward Sascha's laptop. Her. It was strange to finally have a face to the spectral danger that had lingered over her head for the past weeks.

Sascha laughed quietly. "Positive. I've already betrayed them. What I can do is salt the wound and stand her up like a cheap date."

"You're insane."

Sascha tilted his head and shrugged. "Maybe."

He pressed his forehead gently against hers, and Zoey found that she couldn't breathe. She couldn't help but notice how his eyes, crystal blue at their fringes, deepened to ocean blue at the center. Why was she noticing this? Why did it matter? She didn't know. All she knew was that it *did* matter. She wanted to capture this moment in time and hold it frozen for the rest of eternity.

"What do you need me to do?" she asked.

Sascha's lips parted a fraction and his hand lingered on her cheek. His hand at her back tightened a fraction, pulling her closer against him. Then his laptop chimed in the background, and he sighed, stepping away. Zoey wanted to reach out after him. To bring him back to where he had been moments ago. But she didn't. The moment was over.

"For now," said Sascha, stepping back, his hands falling to his side. "I need you to get some rest. I don't have a plan yet, but I'll have one by morning."

One bed. Zoey looked at the chair. After all Sascha had done, it was only right that she slept there tonight. She took a step toward it.

"Zoey."

In the dim room, she turned back to him. He gestured to the bed.

"There's only one bed," she said, her cheeks flushing.

Sascha blinked. "Yes."

"Both of us?" asked Zoey.

"I won't be sleeping tonight. You take the bed and get some sleep for both of us."

"Will you be alright?"

He smiled. "I'll be fine. I've been trained to go without sleep for days at a time."

"Sascha –"

"Don't start a fight you can't win, Zoey," said Sascha, a smile working onto his face. "I'll hear no protests about this. You sleep. I'll stay awake."

"Thank you," she breathed.

"And, Zoey," said Sascha.

"Yes?"

"Try not to get caught again. We really can't keep meeting like this."

In spite of the night and the one preceding, Zoey smiled. "I won't."

Again, that warmth swelled in Zoey's chest, rising through her blood to a nearly unbearable level. She turned away and ducked into the bathroom. Heart still pounding, she turned on the water for a shower. She couldn't ignore it anymore. The way Sascha's voice calmed her. The way his hands set her skin on fire. The way, as she'd leaned up toward him tonight, she'd been hoping for something more than a lingering, wistful stare. Feelings for Sascha. They'd arrived despite her fervent, internal protests. Sascha was more dangerous than anyone she'd ever met. And yet, he was kinder than anyone she'd ever met. Kinder than his lifestyle should allow. Zoey tested the temperature of the water and breathed in through her nose, out through her mouth, desperately trying to calm her heart.

And the horrible, ugly opposite side of the coin raised its head. Even if she felt something for him and he for her, his world wasn't the kind of world that allowed for emotion – that much, Zoey knew. And soon, once they reached England, their time would be over.

She glanced over her shoulder at the bathroom door. Was there anything wrong, really with savoring the last few days she had with him? No, she didn't think there was.

~ ~ ~ ~ ~ ~

Zoey groaned and rolled over on the backseat of Sascha's car. They'd left Merano while it was still dark. She wasn't sure if it had been four or five in the morning when they'd quietly crept downstairs to the car. Rubbing her eyes, Zoey glanced at the clock on the car's dashboard. Almost nine in the morning. She raised her gaze to look at Sascha in the front seat. His eyes were on the road. He seemed utterly unchanged from last night. Zoey wasn't sure she'd ever forget the image of him perched on the edge of the bed, staring toward the door, gun in hand. He was still looking ahead with steely determination. Even the overcast skies above didn't seem to have phased him.

"Good morning," he said.

Zoey shook her head, an amused smile rising of its own accord. "How did you know I was awake? You didn't even look in the rearview."

"I didn't need to. Your breathing changed a few minutes ago. Coming up front? I've got coffee up here. I grabbed another burner phone for you, too."

Zoey stretched as much as the backseat would allow and sat up, squeezing over the center console, careful to avoid knocking over the coffee, and taking her place next to Sascha in the front seat. She stretched a second time, unable to help feeling satisfied as a few of her joints popped. Sascha tapped his thumbs against the steering wheel and shifted his shoulders.

"You hate that sound, don't you?" asked Zoey, grinning. She debated popping all of her knuckles to see how Sascha would react but decided against it. She reached for one of the coffees instead, relieved that the bandages on her hands were gone. Deep scratches remained on her palms, but the bleeding had stopped.

Sascha shook out one of his hands. "Like nails on a chalkboard. I wouldn't drink that one."

"Why not?"

"It's mine. Unless you like decaf coffee and want to swap spit with me, I'd go for the other one. If you want to, though, that's fine as well."

"Are you ever going to give up your personal war on caffeine?" Zoey laughed, setting the cup back in the holder and picking up the second one. "Much as the idea appeals to me, I think I'll pass for now. Where are we?"

The terrain had changed. Zoey couldn't help but feel a surge of disappointment. The skyscraping, snowcapped mountains of Merano, Innsbruck, and Bayrischzell were gone. A sudden desperate need to see them one last time burst in Zoey's chest, and she turned to look out the rear window for a final glimpse of their sheer, jagged peaks. There they were. One final look. She could just see their snowy summits, the sharp outlines dark against the gray sky. Then, Sascha's car crested a rise in the road, and the Alps vanished behind the foothills. Zoey stayed where she was, just staring and thinking. A chapter in her life felt as though it had closed. Bittersweet. A chapter that was both amazing and horrific. She wondered if she would look at these memories fondly later. Then the image of Erik's mutilated hand appeared in her mind's eye, and she shuddered. That was one memory of many she would much rather forget. Turning around, she sat back down in her seat. Memories of last night would forever be burned into her mind, her memories with Sascha . . . those were memories to be preserved.

"I find that leaving the Alps always makes me want to go back," said Sascha. "We crossed the border from Austria back to Germany a little while ago. We're near Kempten."

"I'm not exactly great with German geography, Sasch," said Zoey.

"'Sasch'?" He laughed and turned to her. "Alright then, *Zo*. What, that one extra letter just too much for you?"

Zoey shrugged. "It's a bit quicker. What? Never had a nickname?"

"Nothing nice." A smile softened the angles of his face. "We're about seven hours from Paris."

"Begs my question. *Why* are we going back to Paris? Won't they be watching the cities and airports?"

"They will. Like I told you last night, we won't be leaving by air. We'll be leaving by ferry. Coast to coast rather than city to city. It's the less obvious method of travel. Now that we've been spotted, OMNI operatives will be on guard almost everywhere. If we're seen, it'll be easier to shake them in a big city. I also need somewhere with good internet to make reservations for the ferry crossing. I'd prefer to stay somewhere in the middle of nowhere, but there's no guarantee if I'll even have phone service to hotspot my laptop if we do that."

Zoey hummed and drummed her fingers against the disposable coffee mug. "Paris brings back some bad memories for me."

Sascha's hands gripped the steering wheel a little tighter. "I understand. It's where they first brought you. Paris is a beautiful city though. It would be a shame to have it tarnished forever by what they did to you."

She tilted her head and watched Sascha, trying to fight down the smile that wanted to rise. She wondered if he, like her, didn't want their time together to end. She wanted to get back to her sisters. She wanted that more than anything. To know that they were safe. To let them stop worrying. Yet, at the same time, she wanted to spend more time with Sascha. More time knowing him. If only there were a world where both were possible. Defeat settled in her chest. There was no such world.

Shake this feeling. Zoey grappled for something to say. They had seven hours in the car together ahead of them. Might as well make use of it.

"Question," she said.

"Answer."

"You said when we met that Sascha Sarajevo is the name you use. Is it your real name?"

Sascha laughed and shook his head a fraction. "My birth name is Sascha." He paused. "I chose the name 'Sarajevo' for the city. A lot of us do it. It's why so many assassins sound so pretentious. Sarajevo, Houston, Ardennes, Yaroslavl. They're places that mean something to that person."

"So, what does Sarajevo mean to you?" asked Zoey.

Sascha was a little quieter when he spoke, and Zoey wondered if she'd crossed an invisible barrier. "My first independent mission as an assassin took place there."

Zoey paused before she spoke. "Something happened there, didn't it?"

Some emotion flashed through his eyes. There and gone in an instant. He looked back at the road. The atmosphere in the car ran tense. "I made a mistake there. A petty, vindictive mistake. I let my emotions get to me during that first mission, and there were consequences. People got hurt. They deserved it, but it still shouldn't have happened. It was all my fault, so I called myself Sarajevo as a reminder to never let something like that happen again."

Zoey quickly turned her attention back to the road. Guilt. That was the expression she'd seen. It was one she knew all too well, herself.

"I shouldn't have asked," said Zoey, keeping her gaze out the front windshield. No more questions. There was no telling how close she was to venturing into territory that was still too personal for him. Zoey frowned. It had to be distressing to have so many things he was unwilling to talk about. So many secrets. So much about him she'd never learn.

"You didn't know," replied Sascha. "Only a few people know how I feel about that city and what happened there. But thank you." "What for?" asked Zoey, turning back to him.

"Not apologizing," he grinned. "That's a step in the right direction for you."

Zoey laughed. "Constant apologies are a byproduct of existing in the same space as Maxwell Blackmore."

Sascha laughed, and Zoey relaxed. The atmosphere in the car was easy again. Content. Outside, a few early morning clouds scudded the brightening sky. A contrast to the looming shadow they were running from. Zoey felt resolve steel itself in her chest. Paris lay ahead, and beyond, England. Home.

~ ~ ~ ~ ~

How long, exactly, could someone knock on a door without realizing they weren't welcome? Rona narrowed her eyes and glared at the door to her bedroom. At least five minutes, apparently. She was in a foul mood. Had been for days. The longer they went without news about Zoey, the angrier and more agitated she felt herself becoming. It had got so much worse after the disastrous way Maxwell had handled Zoey's voicemail. Rona marched across her bedroom and ripped the door open.

"What is it? You couldn't just text?"

Flynn's grinned brightly. "You're alive! Haven't seen you in days. Honestly, I wasn't expecting you to open up."

Rona folded her arms and leaned in the doorway. "What do you *want*?"

His smile only brightened further. "It's Zoey. My program pinged her in France."

Rona's mouth fell open, and she grappled for words. "What?"

"Come on. Let me show you what I've got. Your dad's already here. He's up in the office."

"Is she okay?" asked Rona, stepping out into the courtyard and forgetting to close her door.

"She seems to be," nodded Flynn, reaching back and tugging the door shut.

"Is she still with . . .?" Rona let her sentence trail off, flashing an anxious half smile at Flynn as he opened the door into the farmhouse for her.

"I'm not sure. I wasn't looking for him, and I've only watched a second or two of the footage. Not the whole clip. So far, I've only seen Zoey. Your dad should be able to confirm whether Sarajevo's there though."

Rona swallowed and started up the stairs to the second floor, glad that Simon and Charity had taken Hailee out into Conwy. At least this way if something was dreadfully wrong, Hailee wouldn't have to see the brunt of it. Rona took a deep breath and pushed open the door to Simon's office. Maxwell stood behind the desk; his face illuminated blue by the light of the computer. For a split second, his eyes looked utterly colorless, and Rona balked. She felt Flynn hesitate behind her and forced herself to walk onward.

"Nicely done, Flynn," said Maxwell, lifting a cup of tea.

"It's her? It's Zoey?" asked Rona, walking forward. Her feet felt both weighted and light, held in a dreamlike paradox.

Maxwell gestured to the computer screen, and Rona stepped around the edge of the desk. A surprisingly high-quality video dominated the screen, and Rona couldn't breathe. Zoey. Zoey, alive. Zoey, standing tall outside a black sedan with a bright smile on her face. Rona had to resist the urge to reach out and touch the screen. She couldn't, she mustn't, not with Maxwell standing there.

She swallowed again. "Where is she?"

Flynn leaned around the other side of the desk. "Paris."

"Is *he* there?"

Maxwell reached forward and tapped a button on the keyboard. The recorded clip rolled in silence, and Sascha Sarajevo emerged like a wraith from the car. Rona swallowed hard. He moved with a frightening kind of fluidity. A manner of moving that echoed Zoey's. But on him, it was somehow warped. Infinitely more lethal. Silently, Rona urged Zoey to run. To bolt before he rounded the front of the car. But Zoey waited for him, bright smile still on her face. Sarajevo gestured, and Zoey laughed. Together, they exited the frame, one of his hands on Zoey's lower back. Rona blinked fast and looked at Maxwell.

"I don't understand."

Maxwell shrugged. "Sarajevo's charming. One of the reasons he's as good as he is at what he does. Remember what we talked about a few weeks ago?"

Rona's mouth ran dry. "Yes."

"Still think you'd be alright going over there?"

"I . . ." Rona looked at Flynn then down at the desk.

"I'd be with you," said Flynn.

Rona searched his face in silence for a long moment, and a rush of intertwined affection and appreciation swept through her chest as his hand rested on hers. There and gone in an instant.

"Zoey would trust you more than me," said Maxwell. If he'd noticed Flynn's touch, he didn't comment on it. "And if I sent a team in to pick her up, I'd be willing to bet a few thousand of any currency that not all of them would come back."

"Do you think me going is the only way?" asked Rona.

Maxwell paused. "It may be the only way to keep people from dying, Rona. Sarajevo's a dangerous man, but Zoey's still alive, and, much as I hate to say it, they appear to have some form of connection. I think you stand the greatest chance of getting Zoey home. Or at least away from Sarajevo."

Rona took a deep breath and steadied her shaking hands. "Okay. I'll do it."

"I commend you for that, Rona," Maxwell nodded. "This breaks all our normal protocols, but it's the best option we've got, and it's our best shot at getting both Zoey and possibly Sarajevo, too. Remember, I told you some of this is going to be an appeasing game. Stepping into Sarajevo's ring means doing things his way."

"I remember," nodded Rona, her heart rate spiking in her chest.

"Good. You and Flynn will go there first. I'll follow behind with a team. Here's what you'll need to do."

Chapter 29

Relief. It was all Zoey could feel now that she and Sascha were in Paris. Finally finished driving. Evening had drawn in, the sky turning lilac. Their hotel was nestled down a narrow side-street. It was nothing remarkable. Nothing overly expensive or cheap. A chain hotel. Average.

"So," said Zoey, cautiously peeking out of one of the windows. Their room overlooked a quiet, one-way street below. "Why here and not a safe house?"

Sascha didn't turn from where he was unpacking his bag on the bed. "There are hundreds of hotels in Paris and hundreds of hotel rooms. There are only a handful of safe houses. In a place like Paris, we're better off using a hotel. If I were looking for an assassin travelling with a companion in a large city, I would look in the safe houses first. I would then look in the most expensive and the cheapest hotels. This one is an average price point. Here, we have less chance of being found. I would have asked for a room with two beds, but that would have made it look too suspicious for my liking."

"You really have to think about all of that when you're choosing a hotel?" asked Zoey. She took a cursory glance around the room, beating down a wave of memories about Groper and Bouncer that threatened to rise. The generic artwork, the white bedclothes, even the smell brought back a wave of anxiety.

She shook herself and rested her hands on her hips, turning back to Sascha. Almost immediately, her nerves eased. She was here with Sascha. She was safe.

"Yes," he replied. "I don't think anything of it anymore, Zoey. They're habitual precautions for me."

Zoey shook her head. "I could never get used to that."

"I hope you never have to," replied Sascha, turning. Something like a smirk settled around his mouth. "There's only one bed. Looks like we'll have to sleep together."

Zoey turned, an unbidden smile taking her by surprise. A rush of confidence seized her, and she took a few steps toward him.

"Is that a threat or a promise?" she asked.

"Do you want to find out?" replied Sascha.

Zoey's heart thundered in her chest. "Maybe I do."

Sascha laughed quietly and shook his head. "I'll book the ferry later this evening, but, for now, we've been in the car all day. Want to stretch your legs or do you want to stay here?"

"Don't you think we'd be seen?" asked Zoey, perching on the edge of the bed.

"There's over two million people in Paris alone, Zoey. Twelve million in the region. Those numbers are good enough to ensure we aren't found." He smirked and tilted his head toward the windows. "How about it?"

"It's not like you to gamble. Calculated risks and all that," grinned Zoey.

"I love this city," replied Sascha, lifting his gaze toward the window, a small, genuine smile on his face. "I know how afraid you must have been when you last came through here. I want to change your impression of it."

Zoey couldn't help smiling as she watched him. She heard the unsaid part of his sentence. *I want you to love it, too.* He didn't have to say it. She already knew what he meant. This could be one of their last nights together. This was Paris. There were better places to spend this evening than inside the most average of average hotel rooms.

"If your first mission had been here, you could have called yourself Sascha Paris," she said.

"I couldn't have done that."

"Why not?"

"That's a stripper name."

"Sascha!" grinned Zoey, heat flushing her cheeks.

He laughed and shook his head. "Well? Shall we?"

"Let's do it," replied Zoey.

Sascha reached a hand out. Zoey hesitated, her surge of confidence suddenly evaporating, even though a deep, warm sensation flushed through her chest.

One side of Sascha's mouth pulled upward. "Come on, Zoey. Humor me."

Zoey smiled and placed her hand in his, slipping their fingers together. Warmth spread through her chest down to her toes, and she fell in beside him as they exited the hotel room.

~ ~ ~ ~ ~ ~

Zoey had to admit it. Paris was beautiful by night. The night sky and the stars were obscured by the amount of artificial light, but it was warm, and the city felt *alive*. People still roamed the streets, cars still swept up and down the roads. Totally unaware of the killer in their midst. Zoey tightened her grip around Sascha's hand. He wasn't a killer right now. He was just Sascha. The Sascha she knew. They'd grabbed something to eat in a small café earlier that night and had been walking the streets ever since. Zoey turned to look at Sascha. There was a small smile on his face, and a kind of relaxation to his strides that she remembered from their time in Germany. He looked happy.

"I can see why you love it here," said Zoey, matching Sascha's steps as he led the way down a ramp to walk along a pathway beside the Seine River. He seemed to know exactly where he was going. She tilted her head as they passed a group of boats moored at the riverside. She couldn't tell if they were houseboats or not. In any event, there were no people around. This area of the riverbank walk was quiet. Even though Zoey could hear cars on the road a short distance away, they seemed in a different world. At this moment, it was just her, Sascha, and the night. She tilted her head back to try and scan the sky for stars again, but it was too overcast to make anything out, clouds reflecting back a red haze and nothing more.

"It's a beautiful city," he replied. "One of my favorite places in the world."

A small smile appeared on Sascha's face, and Zoey couldn't stop the one that rose to her own. Under night's gentle light, Sascha couldn't have been more removed from the sharp, harsh man she'd met a month ago. There was a warmth to him now.

"When did you first come to Paris?" asked Zoey.

"I've been here several times over the years. I used to live here. It was . . . it was the first place I stopped after the incident in Sarajevo. I learned to love the city. Learned to listen to it."

"Listen to it?" asked Zoey.

Sascha nodded. "Every city has a rhythm. The moment you tap into one city's, you can tap into it anywhere. Knowing how a place moves and how people behave has saved my life more times than I can count."

"How do you do it?"

"It's something you feel. A way of moving yourself and through the people around you. It's less about *doing* and more about *feeling*. The energy of the place. An overall hum."

"I doubt I could ever do it," replied Zoey.

"Of course, you could," said Sascha. "You're a dancer. You haven't noticed it yourself, but you've already been doing it out of instinct."

Zoey stopped as Sascha gave her hand a gentle squeeze and motioned across the river. From their position, there was an almost unobstructed view of the Eiffel Tower. The metal structure suddenly came alive with thousands of twinkling lights. Zoey grinned, a little breathless. She hadn't known it lit up at night. There was something mesmerizing about the yellow lights shining and flickering from inside its iron frame. Like tiny, earthbound stars. She pressed a little closer to Sascha. Then his arm was around her shoulders, pulling her flush against him. Heat pooled in Zoey's cheeks. His move had nothing to do with protecting her from danger. It was just . . . closeness. Closeness for closeness's sake. She looked up at Sascha to find him already smiling at her. There was such a softness in his eyes, and Zoey felt her chest constrict. She couldn't breathe.

The words were out of her mouth before she could stop them. "I'm never going to see you again after this, am I?"

Sascha drew a sharp breath, and the expression in his eyes faltered. A small smile flashed across his face. Zoey held his gaze. Inwardly, she begged him not to lie. She needed to know.

"Of cour . . ." Blue eyes drifted sideways, and he shook his head. "No. Not because I don't want to, but because it would be too dangerous for you and your family. When you get home, you and your family *have* to go underground. Conceal yourselves so well that even I can't find you. Make sure Lord Marion can't find you. And when we part ways, I will lay a false trail for OMNI. If I were to go back to you, they'd find you. I will not let that happen."

Zoey couldn't help the way her bottom lip trembled. Going home meant leaving Sascha. It was something she'd always known. But she hadn't expected the reality of it to feel this crushing. She leaned forward and pressed her forehead to the crook of his neck. He was unlike anyone else she had ever met. He always had been. Some deeper knowledge, some instinct that lived in her chest, told her that he always would be. There would be, there could be, no one else like Sascha.

A bittersweet sensation shuddered through Zoey's chest as one of Sascha's hands came to rest on her lower back. She flushed as his other hand slipped under her chin and tilted her head up. Gray eyes met blue. Sascha stayed silent. Zoey held his gaze. How many people could do this? How many people could look him in the eye and not feel fear?

She took a shallow breath, trying to ease the tension in her chest. "I'll miss you."

"Oh, Zoey. And I'll miss you," replied Sascha, his voice low.

Sascha's thumb traced her cheekbone, and Zoey swallowed hard. Her mouth ran dry. Move. Do something. Zoey's hands shifted of their own accord, one resting on Sascha's shoulder, the other resting on the short hairs at the back of his head. One of his brows twitched upward, and a micro expression flashed across his face. Zoey pressed close against him, chest to chest.

She stood on her toes. "Remember me?"

Sascha leaned down a fraction. An almost imperceptible movement. Zoey wouldn't have noticed it if she hadn't already been so close. Their noses were a mere whisper away from touching.

"How could I not? You have engrained yourself in my heart and my soul. You have made me remember that I am a person who is still capable of doing good. That I am more than just a means to an end. You're my North Star, Zoey."

Zoey nearly swayed on her feet. She adjusted her grip on his shoulder for balance, and she could have sworn his arm at her lower back tightened in response, pulling her closer still. And she froze. Her lips were breaths away from his, and she couldn't move.

A laugh rumbled inside Sascha's chest, and he closed the distance. Warm lips fell against her own. Zoey's eyes closed on reflex. Her mind cleared. The feel of Sascha's lips on hers wiped all thoughts away. It was just a press, just lips against lips, and yet, she'd never felt more alive. Her blood rang in her ears. There was no more Paris. No more OMNI. No more night. No more time. There was only Sascha. His lips on hers. The way he smelled of gunmetal and fresh cut flowers. He leaned closer, pressing their lips more firmly together and deepening the kiss. Zoey bent backward, letting his arm support her. There was emotion here, rushing and surging under her skin. For emotion to take root and bloom here – it didn't make sense. Winged Cupid was indeed painted blind. She linked her hands together behind his head and adjusted her position. There was nowhere else she'd rather be. Not home. Not Bayrischzell. Just here, toe to toe with him. Preserve this moment. This was stillness in a world that moved.

Gray eyes opened as Sascha pulled back. Zoey took a breath, words not coming. Did they need to? She met his eyes, and she knew. This moment, their moment, could be understood between them without words. Tears pricked the backs of her eyes. She would never see him again. Zoey closed her eyes, refusing to let the tears fall. Don't ruin this. She stood taller, pressing her forehead to his. She could still feel the pressure of his lips on hers. The memory of contact. It was something close to bliss. As gray eyes met blue,

Zoey knew. A part of her heart belonged to Sascha. A part she'd never meant to give away. It always would. The precious idea of meaning something more to him and him to her. Something in her chest had ignited with Sascha at the source. The image of Aquila flashed in front of Zoey's eyes, a star-studded eagle suspended against an ink-black sky. Sascha's constellation. The man who named eagles, who picked them out in the pattern of stars.

"Part of me wants to lengthen the time we have together," sighed Sascha, his voice soft and low.

Zoey's breath caught as he brushed her cheek with the back of his hand. She could smell metallic heat on his fingers. She recognized the acridity of it. It was the same smell that filled the air after shooting. Had it always clung to him like this? Time began moving again. She wished it would slow down.

"I know what you mean," she replied, fighting to keep her voice steady.

Sascha leaned back. "But your family needs you home, and there's no world in which we can have everything we want."

The corner of Zoey's mouth trembled now – as she knew it would – and she looked away, resting her eyes on the iron tower that dominated the Parisian skyline. Thousands of captured stars glimmered from within its frame. Sascha's hands were still warm on her back and cheek. She swallowed and turned, resting her back against his chest to face the river and the tower. His arms circled her, and Zoey had to force down the lump that rose in her throat. Safe. She couldn't remember a time she'd felt so safe.

~ ~ ~ ~ ~ ~

It was late by the time Zoey ascended the stairs behind Sascha and entered their hotel room. She disentangled her fingers from his and unzipped her backpack, fishing for a change of clothes.

"Shower?" asked Sascha, pulling his laptop from its bag.

"I was planning on it," replied Zoey.

He nodded and rested his laptop on the hotel room desk. "I'll probably be asleep by the time you get out. Can I ask you to do something for me?"

"What is it?" asked Zoey, pausing.

"We're in an unfamiliar place, and I don't want both of us to sleep at the same time. Can you manage to stay awake an extra three and a half hours? There's a chance we may be spending an extra day here, depending on how full the ferries are. If so, I'll need to be alert enough to keep an eye out for our safety."

Zoey raised one eyebrow. "You only sleep for three and a half hours?"

"Thereabouts." Sascha shrugged. "It's fine if you don't want to. I can manage a day or two more without sleep."

"Sascha," said Zoey. She bit back the stupid urge to drop a term of endearment. "Sleep. Please. I can keep an eye on one room for three and a half hours. You've already done so much. I don't want you going without sleep."

Sascha breathed a laugh and nodded, his shoulders dropping a fraction. "Alright. If you hear anything or suspect that's something's wrong, just wake me up. I'm a light sleeper. The handgun you've been using is in the front compartment of my duffel if you need it."

Zoey nodded and disappeared into the bathroom, shutting the door behind her. The idea of raising a gun to harm someone... Marcus's face rushed back in her memory, and she felt nauseated. Even though she hadn't actually shot him, if Sascha hadn't, she *would* have. The idea of hurting someone. It wasn't an idea she relished. And yet, she would have done it. Zoey glanced at the bathroom door, letting the shower run and giving the water time to warm. Turn her thoughts away from the implications behind Sascha's words. They were in a dangerous position, that was a given. If she had to hurt someone to get home... Home. She faltered. England. Where they would part. She would go back to her life. She swallowed. Would life be the same when she got back? Would she be the same? Somehow, she didn't think so.

A few minutes later, trying to keep her steps light, Zoey pushed the bathroom door open and stepped back into their room. The lights were off. The bedside lamp closest to the bathroom was the only one left on. Zoey wrung her hair out again, trying to shed the last drops of water. It was still damp, but she hadn't wanted to use the hair dryer at risk of waking Sascha. She looked at the bed and couldn't help smiling. She'd never seen Sascha sleep before. Not once in the time she'd known him. She had seen him feign sleep on the very first morning she'd spent with him, but she'd never seem him truly sleep. He lay on his back, one hand across his stomach, the other behind his head. His breathing sounded low and relaxed. She shook her head a little and slid onto the bed beside him, being sure to keep some distance between them. She didn't want to wake him up, and she wasn't sure how he would react to another person appearing as he slept. Zoey watched him a moment more, and her brow furrowed. How many people could say that they'd done *this*? Kissing him was one thing, but this, this felt like something else. This felt like trust. Her breath caught a little. She trusted Sascha, she knew she did. It had taken a long time to build that feeling, but she did. She ran a finger along her lower lip, remembering the pressure of his kiss. Never before had she known the kind of raw emotion that had taken hold tonight.

Beside her, Sascha moved, rolling onto his side to face her. Zoey couldn't help trying to memorize his face. In a few days, memory would be all she had of him. Blond hair fell across his forehead. One of his elegant hands lay open on the bed. He looked younger, his face not so drawn with tension, and his constant guard down. Her chest ached.

Chapter 30

Morning drew in, bright and cheerful. Chatter and vehicle engines sounded loud in the street below. Zoey groaned and refused to open her eyes. The windows must be open. While groggy, she was cozy and comfortable. Sascha had woken up exactly three and a half hours after he'd gone to sleep, and Zoey couldn't say how grateful she was. To push through those extra few hours had been more difficult than she'd imagined. Maybe, after everything, she'd been more tired than she realized. She turned away from the open windows, curling around one of the pillows and burrowing her face between them, trying to recapture the warm comfort of sleep. One of the pillows laughed.

"What are you doing?"

Zoey's eyes flashed open, and she felt herself blush darkly, heat catching her cheeks before she even lifted her head. She swallowed her embarrassment and looked up. She had pressed flush against Sascha's side, thrown one leg over his thighs, an arm over his stomach, and was trying to press her face between him and the mattress. She swallowed, grappling for a response.

"Trying to go back to sleep," she mumbled. She wished the floor would open up and swallow her.

"Do you always sleep like this?" asked Sascha.

"Like what?"

"Like some kind of demented octopus. You've been wrapped around me almost all night."

As if she could have blushed any hotter. The word 'mortified' had never felt so relevant. "I have *not*."

"Oh, you *have*."

Zoey looked away, trying to collect herself. "God, Sascha, I'm so sorry."

He laughed and leaned a little closer. "I never said I minded."

Zoey tipped her face up to look at him. Amusement danced in his eyes, and Zoey's mouth ran dry as he put an arm around her waist, pulling her closer still to his side. Then he smirked, a wolfish grin lingering behind the expression.

"What's that look for?" asked Zoey.

"What I do mind is the snoring."

Zoey swatted him on the chest, unable to keep from smiling herself. "Stop! I don't!"

Sascha laughed. "Like a sawmill."

"Shut up," snorted Zoey. Sascha's quiet laugh was contagious. "We can't all sleep like Greek gods."

"Clearly." His smile softened. "I've got us on a ferry out of Cherbourg tomorrow afternoon. Do you want to stay here another night, or do you want to go ahead and clear the area?"

"What do you recommend?" asked Zoey, propping herself up on one elbow.

"Paris is bigger," replied Sascha, tipping his head. "Something goes wrong here, there's still an escape route. Something goes wrong in Cherbourg, we've got to stay in the area. My vote goes to Paris. We leave early tomorrow morning, and we can make it to the ferry in plenty of time."

"Then I'm with you," replied Zoey. "You know what you're doing. Are we taking the car to England?"

"No. We'll leave that in Cherbourg. Having French plates would make it too recognizable. We'll pick up a rental when we get to Portsmouth."

"Sounds like a plan," said Zoey. "What's on the cards for today?"

"Well, we walked along the Seine last night. There's no shortage of things to do here. We're within walking distance from the Louvre and the Eiffel Tower. We're not far either from the Arc de Triomph."

"So, tourist things?" replied Zoey.

"Easy ways to get a look at the city while not being seen yourself," replied Sascha. "And the walks are beautiful."

"I've been meaning to ask. Why haven't you been wearing any disguises? You were when you were in Charles de Gaulle and on the train. Aren't you worried about being recognized?"

"A bit, but I've stopped using them for now for your benefit. I'd rather you were able to see me and recognize me if you needed to. Plus, I've seen you staring. You're not subtle."

Zoey gave an embarrassed grin. "No point denying it, I suppose. You're very good-looking. I can't help myself."

"You can keep stroking my ego our entire day of sightseeing if you want," chuckled Sascha.

"Can you show me where you used to live?" asked Zoey. She bit the inside of her cheek. Even now, she hadn't learned much about Sascha or where he came from.

Sascha's expression faltered. "No. Where I used to live is gone. The building was demolished a few years back."

Zoey glanced away. Maybe it had been wrong to try and pry. "Oh . . . I was just hoping to . . . I don't know."

Sascha gave another quiet laugh, and Zoey saw him incline his head a fraction. He paused, seeming to debate with himself. One of his hands fiddled with the bedspread.

"Slovenia," he said after a moment of silence.

"What?"

"Where I was born. Slovenia. My father was Slovene, my mother was German." He sighed and adjusted the way he lay, flickers of tension gathering behind his eyes. "I know I haven't given you much about my history, but that's because I can't tell much. It's easier to have nothing to tell a person rather than try not to tell something."

"Do you think I might be questioned about you?"

"Yes. And I think the person who questions you will be Maxwell."

"Sasch," said Zoey, sitting more upright. "I'm going to stop you there. We're having a good time. We're having a good conversation. We're still in bed. Can we please not invite my father into it?"

Sascha laughed and the tension left his expression. "I think I can do that. Now, think you can bear to disentangle yourself from me long enough to get up?"

~ ~ ~ ~ ~ ~

The day passed in an amicable way. In spite of the looming danger of OMNI searching for them, Zoey found that she was actually able to relax. There was something unerringly safe about Sascha's presence beside her. The irony in that was almost tangible.

They'd stopped on the Pont des Arts bridge overlooking the Seine, each of them holding a disposable coffee mug. Boats passed up and down the river, their paces languid and calming. Green trees lined each side of the river avenues. A few evening pedestrians walked across the bridge, never batting an eye at them. Yellow streetlamps turned on, bathing the city in a soft light and accentuating the pale stone. Zoey pressed a little closer to Sascha, their shoulders touching. They were a few miles from their hotel. Afternoon was gone, evening pushing in, the sky turning lavender and the air cooling.

"What do you think of Paris now?" Sascha asked, breaking the quiet.

"I can see why you love it," replied Zoey, taking a last sip of her coffee as she took Sascha's empty cup and tossed both into a nearby trash bin. "This is much better than the first time round."

"In your defense, you didn't see much of the city the last time you were here. Still haven't. I wish we had more time here. A day isn't nearly long enough to see Paris properly. So now that you have seen a bit of it, what was your favorite part?"

"What kind of a question is that?" she asked, grinning. "The Paris Opera Ballet School, obviously. I've always wanted to see it."

"It's a shame they didn't have any performances when we got there."

"I'm just happy I got to see it. It's a beautiful building. And what about you?"

"Tuileries Gardens. Sorry for my predictability, but I've always loved the gardens in Paris."

"No surprises there," said Zoey, fighting the urge to squeeze into the space under his arm as the evening grew colder. "Have you ever been to the Catacombs?"

"No, dead people scare me."

"Oh, shut up."

Sascha laughed. "The answer's still no. I never really felt the urge. Something about being surrounded by the dead doesn't particularly appeal to me."

Zoey tilted her head and started to form a reply. Then her heart skipped a beat in her chest. There. Beyond Sascha's shoulder. Zoey's breath caught in her throat. At the far side of the bridge. Her knees went weak. She placed a hand on Sascha's upper arm to steady herself.

He caught her around the waist, supporting her. "Zoey, what's wrong?"

Heart juddering, Zoey couldn't speak. Weeks. She'd waited weeks to see that face, more than just in the mirror.

The words left Zoey's mouth in a whisper. "Rona."

Across the bridge, Zoey saw Rona stop and stare at her. Zoey stared back, unable to move. They locked eyes. A face identical to her own. Hair so dark it was almost black. It *was* Rona. She was certain of it. Rona was here. *Why* was Rona here?

Then Rona was moving, sprinting along the slats of the bridge. "Zoey!"

Breath left Zoey's chest in a sob. Her sister. Here in Paris. She shifted her weight forward to run to her. Sascha's arm barred her way. Zoey looked up at him, confused. Why was he stopping her? He gave a marginal shake of his head, and Zoey stayed herself. The sharp look was back on Sascha's face. His jaw was tense. She looked back at Rona, desperation clawing at her chest. Rona had stopped a few meters away, looking stricken. Her face had drained of color.

Zoey rested a hand on Sascha's forearm and stared at him. "Sascha, that's my sister."

He dropped his arm and leaned down, his voice low, the tone dangerous. "We don't know why she's here or how she got here. Go carefully. I'm behind you."

Go carefully. Zoey couldn't. She sprang forward, closing the distance between her and Rona. Then her arms were around Rona. She dropped her chin to Rona's shoulder, a few dry sobs taking hold of her chest.

"You're here," whispered Rona, her voice shaking.

Zoey leaned back, holding Rona's shoulders. "Rona. What are *you* doing here?"

"Looking for you. Maxwell sent me," replied Rona. "You're really here. I can't believe it. And you're okay! I thought . . ."

Zoey turned as Rona's gaze shifted over her shoulder, landing on Sascha. Emotion clouded Rona's face. Anger. Fear. Disgust. Zoey shook her head, confused. Sascha and Rona didn't know each other, so why . . .? How had Rona found them? Maxwell had sent her? Zoey turned to Sascha. His jaw was tight, his shoulders stiff. His eyes had gone cold. She made eye contact with him. Settling herself, Zoey caught his meaning. On edge. Something wasn't right.

Zoey took hold of Rona's shoulder. "Rona, what's going on? I need to know right now. How are you here? How did you find us?"

Rona blinked at her, her relieved expression faltering. "What? I thought you'd be happy to see me, not interrogate me."

"I *am* happy to see you, but, Rona, please, what is going on? You shouldn't be here. It's too dangerous."

"We followed you," said Rona. She sounded lost, and Zoey's heart constricted. Rona shook her head and took a step back. "Flynn and I, we came all this way looking for you, Zoey. Me, Maxwell, Simon, and Flynn have been watching security cameras and traffic cams since you vanished. We picked you up on CCTV yesterday, coming into Paris. Maxwell's on his way."

"Wait, slow down," said Zoey. "Who's Flynn? Who's Simon?"

"They . . . they work for our dad . . ." Rona jerked her chin in the direction she'd come from. "That's Flynn, he's Maxwell's intern."

Zoey looked in the direction Rona had indicated. The only person she saw was a bespectacled man at the far end of the bridge. He flashed a quick, nervous smile and raised his hand in a wave. Zoey looked at Sascha. A muscle in his jaw twitched, his eyes knife edges. She inhaled, steeling herself for *something*. Exactly what though, she didn't know. Her chest ached as she heard Rona make a small, confused sound and reach out after her.

"What do we do?" she asked, taking a step back to Sascha.

Blue eyes darted back and forth for a second, as though Sascha himself was grappling for an answer. Zoey felt her pulse speed up. She'd never seen Sascha confused.

He shook his head and stared at Rona. "Did you fly into the country?"

"What?" snapped Rona. "Yes, of course."

Sascha didn't seem taken back by her tone. "Using your own passport?"

"What other passport would I use?" Rona snarled. "What does it matter?"

Zoey swallowed as Sascha's eyes flashed and he inhaled with a hiss. She scanned his eyes for something, anything, as he turned to her. He took a breath, and Zoey caught the smallest flash of fear in his eyes.

"What is it?" Zoey asked.

"OMNI operatives are watching for the name Blackmore. Her passport will have been flagged at the airport. They know she's here, and they'll assume she's come to meet you."

Cold rushed over Zoey's body. The air tensed. She heard the unsaid part of Sascha's statement. OMNI knew they were in Paris. Not just in Paris, but most likely also knew their exact location, here and now. It wouldn't take much for them to close in on four people. Two was difficult, but four . . . their chances of being spotted had just doubled.

"Zoey," said Rona, taking a step forward. "Let's *go*. Let's get you out of here."

Zoey felt Rona's hand close over her wrist but held her ground as Rona tried to pull her away from Sascha. She wasn't leaving his side. Not now, not like this. Not with the situation this precarious.

"Rona, stop. I'm not going anywhere. Not yet," said Zoey, jerking her wrist from her sister's grip. She turned back to Sascha, opening her mouth to say something – anything. But she didn't know what to say. Any words stuck in her throat. This had put all of them in danger. This had put *Sascha* in danger.

"Zoey, what are you *doing*?" hissed Rona. Zoey watched as her sister's glare lifted to Sascha. "Don't you know *who* that is? *What* he is?" Unprecedented anger flared in Zoey's chest. It wasn't that she was unhappy to see Rona – not at all. She was elated. But now, she felt all too aware of the danger pressing in around them. Rona had let OMNI know where they were, where they all were. They'd all been exposed. Cold fear crested. Rona, for all her love, for all her desperation, had shifted the entire, razor balance.

"I know who he is. I've been with him for the last month." Zoey stepped back, returning to Sascha's side and looked up at him. She forced herself to ignore Rona's horrified expression. "What do we do?"

Sascha shook his head, as though clearing his thoughts. "Get packed. We're leaving tonight. Before OMNI has the chance to close in. Rona, you and your companion will have to come with us."

Rona stepped forward, shaking her head. "No way. Zoey, you can't leave. Maxwell's on his way here. He's going to get us back to England."

Zoey glanced over as Sascha stiffened beside her. She grappled for anything. Plans were unravelling. Falling apart. If Sascha and her father crossed paths, she didn't want to think about what might happen. If she and OMNI crossed paths, the outcome was inevitable. Two parties now converged on Paris, two parties who both wanted Sascha dead. She took a deep breath, trying to calm her racing pulse. She looked at Rona, watching her sister carefully.

"I'm with Sascha. I'm staying with him. He knows what he's doing."

"Zoey . . ." said Rona. Zoey caught the pleading note in her voice. "Come with us. Come with me. *Please*."

Next to her, Sascha froze. Zoey moved to turn to him. Then his hand settled on her wrist. His jaw was clenched. "We need to go. Right now."

"Rona," said Zoey. "Come with *us*."

Rona shook her head. "But –"

"Please, Rona," said Zoey, falling into step beside Sascha, and relief swamped her chest as Rona turned to walk beside her.

Zoey matched Sascha stride for stride as they walked down the steps at the end of the bridge. The street peddlers from earlier had vanished. There wasn't even a trace of them left. Zoey paused as she got her first good look at the man who Rona said had come with her. Flynn. He was a slight man, equally as tall as Sascha, but narrower, with wild, hazel eyes behind his glasses.

"You're with Rona?" asked Sascha, his voice more clipped than Zoey had ever heard it before.

Flynn seemed to shake himself and nodded, not uttering a sound.

Sascha nodded once. "Then you're with us now. We're going back to the hotel."

"You're insane if you think we're going anywhere with you," snarled Rona, stopping at the bottom of the bridge and edging closer to Flynn. "Zoey, this is nuts. Just come with us. We're going home."

Zoey heard Sascha as he sighed in the back of his throat. Frustration. "We can talk this out when we're safe."

"No. We're going home."

"Stop! Everyone stop. Just let me think for two seconds." Zoey pulled away from Sascha. Space. She needed space.

Inhale.

Exhale.

With Sascha or with Rona? She and Sascha had everything planned. Cherbourg. Portsmouth. England. Rona and Flynn . . . had blown any cover they'd had. Rona was her sister. Sascha was her . . . she didn't know what he was, but he was important, too. She shook her head. Err on the side of safety. If she went with Rona and Flynn, she could risk exposing all of them, and she didn't fancy their chances against OMNI without Sascha. He'd kept her safe this long. He'd keep Rona and Flynn – or at least Rona – safe, too.

"We'll go back to my and Sascha's hotel. We've obviously got a lot to talk about. There are things me and Sascha know that you and Flynn don't, Rona. And I'm sure there are things you know that we don't. But we can't talk properly unless we're safe."

Chapter 31

The white gossamer curtains did little to block out the light from the street. Zoey couldn't help feeling exposed, more exposed than she had in a month. She sat on the bed, sitting cross-legged and attempting to make herself look smaller, undetectable to the world outside the window. Rona sat on the far corner of the bed, and Flynn perched on the edge of the hotel room chair, looking more uncomfortable than words could describe. Sascha leaned in the bathroom doorway, silent. Zoey could feel his wariness. This had to go against everything in him.

Break the silence. Zoey cleared her throat. "How did you find us, Rona?"

"I told you. Me, Flynn, Maxwell, and Simon watched everything. Street cameras. Social media. Websites. Everything." The side of her mouth pulled downward. "We waited weeks to see any sign of you, Zoey. We saw you vanish at Gare de l'Est. Gone. Zoey, I thought you were dead. Then I got your voicemail, and I had to keep looking for you. I just didn't know how, aside from watching the cameras. I didn't know where to start, so we focused on Paris. It was the last place we knew that we saw you. Then you cropped up on a camera. With *him*. And I knew I needed to try and help. Maxwell bought me and Flynn the tickets to fly into Paris and directed us through the city until we found you. I wanted to bring you home. Like I said, he's on his way, but he wanted me to get here first. He isn't . . . he's . . ."

"I already know that part," said Zoey. Her voice was quieter than she'd imagined it would be. "Sascha told me."

"Which begs the question. How did you two get tangled up together?" asked Rona, venom creeping back into her tone. "Did he *buy* you?"

"No." Zoey had to fight to keep the snap out of her voice. "Sascha saved my life. I told you in my voicemail that I had a friend, and, well . . . that's him. I owe him everything. My life twice over."

"Wow. A murderer saving a life," said Rona, sarcasm bleeding thick into each word.

"Don't," replied Zoey, catching Sascha's sharp breath. "At least I landed on my feet with an assassin at my back. You came with an intern. That's like bringing a paperclip to a gunfight."

Flynn's head jerked up. "Hey! I'm not just an *intern*. I'm Maxwell's field operative. I'm in the SAS, too."

"Stop it, Zoey," sighed Rona. "Flynn's been invaluable. I couldn't have gotten this far without him."

"And I couldn't have escaped from the men who kidnapped me without Sascha. If it wasn't for him, you would never have seen me again, not even on cameras, so stop hounding him."

"Okay!" snapped Rona, raising her hands up to shoulder height. "But if you've been with him for this long, what took so long for you to get back to Paris?"

"Rona, we're being hunted," said Zoey. Rona's brow furrowed, a question in her eyes, and Zoey continued. "OMNI, the human trafficking group you thought Sascha bought me from, is tracking me. Maxwell shut down some of their operations, and they're after us. You, me, and Hailee. Sascha managed to get me a false passport so that I could get home without tipping OMNI off to where I was, but we couldn't move until we got it."

"Wait," said Rona. "Does that mean that this OMNI thing will be looking for me now, too?"

Zoey didn't know how to reply. She knew the answer, but she couldn't bring herself to say it. She turned to Sascha. Gray eyes met blue, then Sascha nodded once. He cleared his throat and adjusted the way he leaned against the wall. Zoey watched him. He was the only one in the room who knew what to do.

"Yes. OMNI will –" started Sascha.

Rona's upper lip curled. "I wasn't talking to *you*."

"Rona," snapped Zoey. "He's my friend. He's done nothing wrong." "He's a murderer," said Rona, still glaring at Sascha. "He's killed *children*, Zoey."

Zoey took a breath, seeing Sascha's expression turn stony in her peripherals. "He's our only hope of getting out of here. I trust him."

"*I* don't."

Zoey closed her eyes. She was going to pull her hair out. "Then trust the fact that I trust him."

Across from her, Rona sighed, but Zoey thought she caught the tiniest bit of give in her gaze. Then Rona shrugged, and Zoey turned back to Sascha. He was more unpredictable tonight than she'd ever seen him. Tense and pensive. On edge.

Sascha looked toward the windows. "OMNI will know you're here, Rona. They'll be looking for you, Zoey, and myself now. Perhaps you, too, Mr. Edmunds."

Flynn stared in silence, as though gathering words together, then he swallowed. "You know my name."

Sascha breathed a very quiet, dangerous laugh. "I keep track of Maxwell's field operatives. Past and present."

Flynn went white, and he nodded in silence, but Sascha said nothing more.

"Why is OMNI looking for *you*?" Rona asked Sascha. "You're working for them, aren't you?"

"No," replied Sascha. He glanced at Zoey, and she caught the flicker of warmth in his eyes. "They wanted me to, but I refused their offer."

Zoey felt Rona's eyes on her and, feeling a little too conspicuous, she adjusted the way she sat on the bed. "Sascha, what do we do?"

"The three of you are going to stay here for a minute. I'm going to go and check the car. Before I do, Zoey, can you help me with something, please?"

"Okay," replied Zoey, standing up.

An uncomfortable kind of silence fell over the room as Sascha stepped into the bathroom, turning on the light. Zoey followed. The light's glare off the tile was harsher than she remembered. Everything seemed harsher right now. She swallowed, seeing the seriousness in his eyes.

"Phone," he said.

Furrowing her brow, Zoey passed her phone to him. His fingers lingered a moment too long on her hand, then he pulled away. There was something unsaid there, but she wasn't sure what. Sascha flashed a humorless smile and ran the sink full of water before pulling out her phone's SIM card. He placed the phone on the tile floor, screen down, then braced against the sink and stamped down hard on it, his heel impacting the plastic back. Zoey hissed through her teeth as she heard the screen shatter. She'd always been protective of any phone she'd had. To see one deliberately broken struck her in a different kind of way.

He stooped to pick up the broken phone. "Leave the phone and the SIM in the sink until I get back."

"Why?" asked Zoey. "I thought it was a burner."

Sascha straightened, dropping the SIM card into the sink, too. "It is. But I'm not taking any risks."

"What about yours?"

"It'll get the same treatment when I get back."

Zoey nodded. "How long will you be?"

"Fifteen minutes. No more than twenty. I think you and your sister need to talk. Without me."

Zoey nodded, watching him turn toward the door without a word. She narrowed her eyes as he opened the door, his hand straying toward his pocket and pulling his phone free. Zoey paused, then shook her head. She exited the bathroom, too, just in time to watch the main hotel room door close.

"What was all that noise about?" asked Rona.

Zoey shrugged. "Nothing to be worried about. He's just taking precautions."

"He doesn't scare you? You know what he is."

"I know. I'm not afraid of him," replied Zoey, shaking her head. "Not anymore."

"If you've been free this whole time, why didn't you come home?" asked Rona.

Zoey's heart constricted. Rona sounded so lost. "I couldn't. I tried. Me and Sascha both wanted to get me home a long time ago, but Ro, I got shot. We had to give me time to heal."

"You got shot?!" yelped Rona, snapping upright on the bed. "Was it Sascha who shot you?"

"No," replied Zoey. She was fighting now to keep the shortness out of her voice. Everything felt like such a mess. Two worlds had collided, and neither one made sense.

"Rona," said Flynn, cringing. He sounded less tense now that Sascha was gone. "Keep your voice down. Might not be a good idea to broadcast that to the hotel."

Zoey breathed a small laugh and glanced out the window. A light drizzle had started. "It wasn't Sascha. It was an accident. Bouncer shot me by accident during a car crash. I think I caused it. Sascha got me away from them after that."

"Bouncer?" asked Rona.

Zoey grimaced. "That's what I mentally called one of my kidnappers. He's long dead now, though."

"Sascha actually did help you, didn't he?" asked Rona. Her voice was quiet. Tight.

"Yeah. Sascha's the reason I'm still alive. He knows what he's doing, Rona. He and I had a plan to get me back to England. We were going to cross the channel on a ferry tomorrow. I think our plans have been skewed a little now though."

"I thought you needed saving," said Rona. "We saw you with Sarajevo, and we thought he was going to kill you. Or that he'd bought you. Or something. I thought you needed help."

Zoey sighed and sat next to her sister as Rona's gaze dropped to the bedclothes. She thought she'd seen a few tears gathering at the corners of Rona's eyes. "I love you, too, Rona-Bell. I would have done the same for you. I just wish you'd waited two or three more days."

"What should we do?" asked Rona.

Zoey rested a hand on Rona's shoulders. "Sascha will figure something out. He's clever, and he's used to this. Where have you been staying?"

Flynn perked up. "A little place across the river. Not far from here. We've got Simon to thank for finding the place."

"Speaking of, who the hell is Simon?" asked Zoey.

"Oh my God. Of course. You don't know. Zoey, we've got godparents. Two former coworkers of Maxwell's. They picked up me and Hailee after you vanished, and we've been camped out on their farm in Wales ever since. Simon's our godfather."

"You're joking?" sighed Zoey, leaning forward.

"I wish I was. Charity, our godmother, used to work for Maxwell, too. Well, both of them did."

"Have we got any *fairy* godparents in there, too? Maybe a wicked stepmother?"

"At this rate, it wouldn't surprise me."

"Christ," replied Zoey, shaking her head. "Not a single thing Maxwell told us about our lives is true, is it? Either that, or he neglected to tell us anything at all."

Rona laughed. "I'm not even entirely sure my name's Rona. For all I know at this point, you, me, and Hailee could be aliens he smuggled in from another planet."

"Rona, I have to ask," said Zoey. "Why did Maxwell send you ahead of him?" Rona hesitated. "He said that if you saw him approaching, you might run. You'd feel less threatened by me and might listen to reason. Guess that didn't work so well. He also said that if you were with Sascha, it might get dangerous for him to be here. I wanted to help however I could. By the way, Flynn . . . ?"

"Already reported in," he replied.

"Reported in?" asked Zoey.

"Maxwell asked us to give updates when we found you. That way he could help us back to England."

"Have you heard from him since you told him you'd found me and Sascha?"

Flynn shook his head. "The message doesn't show that it's been read. But that could mean he's on his way here."

Blood ran cold in Zoey's veins. It was bad enough that OMNI knew they were here. If Maxwell was closing in as well . . . Zoey couldn't help glancing at the window. Sascha.

"Where is he?" Zoey's voice was harder than she'd thought it would be. "Where *exactly* is Maxwell, Rona?"

Rona shook her head. "I don't know. Honestly. Flynn and I left England only yesterday. Maxwell said he'd follow us. He didn't say when, and he didn't say where he'd be. I don't even know for certain that he's really coming."

Zoey shook her head. Did Rona know about the real nature of Maxwell and Sascha's relationship? Unlikely, since she herself hadn't known until recently. Zoey swallowed hard. She didn't want to think about what might happen if Maxwell and Sascha crossed paths.

She changed the subject. That was safer. "How's Hailee? I don't have the words to say how much I've missed you both. I thought about both of you every day since I was taken."

"She's doing ok. Shaken up by everything, but she's okay. Probably a lot more traumatized than she lets on."

Zoey shook her head. "That's Hailee though. Does she think I'm . . . ?"

"Dead?" asked Rona.

"That."

"I think she's afraid that might be the case. I was, too. I thought you were dead until I got your voicemail. Then I thought you were worse than dead because you were with *him*."

"How did you find out about Sascha?" asked Zoey.

Flynn cleared his throat. "Maxwell recognized him the moment he saw him on the cameras. He's been on Maxwell's watch list for years. Since Sascha was about your age. He's someone Maxwell wants dead or put in prison. He's tried to get his hands on Sascha several times in the past. Clearly, he's never been successful."

Zoey opened her mouth to speak, the urge to reveal the true nature of Maxwell and Sascha's association rising in her chest, when the door to their hotel room opened again, and Sascha stepped back inside. He was drenched, blond hair sticking to his forehead. It had to be raining harder than she'd thought. His expression was unreadable, but in his eyes, there was something pained.

"What is it?" asked Zoey, standing and ignoring the way Rona stiffened on the edge of the bed.

Sascha shook his head and looked instead at Flynn, folding his arms. "Where are you staying?"

Flynn balked, his face paling a fraction. "Across the river." "You're staying here tonight. There's a room open on the next floor up. I've paid for it for you and Rona."

Zoey reached out and touched Sascha's forearm. "What's going on?"

"Two tires slashed. Brake lines cut. I had a look through some of my media sources. They know. Trains, the metro, and buses are too risky. Too much wait time and too much margin for error. We can't leave." Sascha clenched his jaw, and Zoey saw a muscle twitch. "We'll regroup and see what we can do in the morning."

The floor seemed to fall away beneath Zoey's feet. "There's nothing we can do?"

Sascha shook his head. "Not right now."

~ ~ ~ ~ ~ ~

Restless. Anxious. Zoey took a deep, shuddering breath as she stared out the window. She and Rona had talked for hours. They'd talked about everything and nothing. The Roost in Wales. The discovery of Simon and Charity. Their father's lies. and yet, Zoey couldn't settle. She adjusted the way she stood and tore her gaze away from the rain-soaked street below. Sascha's phone had joined hers in the bathroom sink. Sascha lay on his back on the bed, eyes on the ceiling. His face was unreadable. Zoey swallowed and glanced up. Rona and Flynn were in the room above theirs. Rona had tried to argue for Zoey staying in the same room. Sascha had refused with a coldness that had made even Zoey feel a touch of wariness toward him.

"Any ideas?" asked Zoey, unable to keep quiet. Break the tension.

Sascha blinked, as though coming out of a reverie, and sat up a fraction. He sighed. "Other than renting another car, no. And we still can't get one until tomorrow."

Zoey crossed the room and sat down next to him on the bed. "Why did you keep me and Rona in separate rooms? I'd thought you'd have wanted us in the same place."

"You're both targets now. It's better to keep you away from each other. I'd rather that OMNI have to try and strike two separate rooms than just strike one and get you both. Keep them guessing as much as we can."

"Are you worried?" asked Zoey. She settled down, leaning on one elbow and setting herself on the same level as Sascha.

"Yes." Sascha opened and closed his mouth, as though he was fighting to say or not say something. "I promised I would get you home. Safe."

"There's no reason we won't still get back to England. It's just got a bit more difficult," replied Zoey, offering a small smile.

Sascha propped up on an elbow, facing her. Blue eyes locked on hers, and Zoey felt herself still. She didn't want to move. He was reading her. A glimmer of apology crept into the corners of his eyes, and Sascha leaned in. Zoey threw caution to the wind. Laying back, she rested each palm on the sides of his face and pulled him down, kissing him with all the words she couldn't say. There was something overwhelming in this. Something visceral in the way Sascha smelled of gunmetal and fresh cut flowers. Something agonizing in the emotions bursting in Zoey's chest with each beat of her heart. As his lips moved against hers, she felt the faintest hint of a smile and couldn't help reciprocating. The expression fell quickly from her lips though. This was one of their last nights together. They broke apart, and Zoey didn't resist the urge to pull him back once more, their bodies flush together. Their last days together. She pressed her forehead to his and closed her eyes. A rush flooded through her chest. Intense. Powerful. Potential. Her throat felt as though it was going to close.

"I may have to part from you sooner than I had hoped," said Sascha.

Zoey opened her eyes. "What? Why?"

"OMNI knows you're travelling with me. If we make it through Paris tomorrow, we will part at Cherbourg. I might be able to keep up the façade that you're with me long enough for you, Rona, and Flynn to get back to England safely. At the least, it would force them to divide their assets. One group to hunt me down and one group for you."

She moved closer, if that were even possible. "I don't want to do this without you. It's bad enough that I'll never seen you again. I . . . I want to know you've made it."

"That's my concern, Zoey. Don't worry about me."

"That's only going to make me worry more."

"I know." He sighed and closed his eyes. They seemed to stay closed a moment longer than usual, and he leaned further forward. Zoey felt his lips brush her forehead. "I wish I could think of another way."

"We could run away," said Zoey, a humorless laugh escaping her.

"And where would we go?" he asked.

"Somewhere isolated. Somewhere that has mountains and eagles. With a dance studio for me and a flower shop for you. Somewhere you can point out Altair and Aquila and tell me about all the constellations until I beg you to stop. We could go now. Run off quietly into the night."

Sascha smiled and leaned in a second time. "Of course, we could."

The fragile smile fell from Zoey's face. "In another life."

"In another life, I'll point out every star and flower that I know and bore you with their details," Sascha said softly, and Zoey's breath hitched as his lips brushed hers. "But in this one, I'll do whatever it takes to get you safe."

Zoey was moving before she'd even thought about it. One hand lifted, coming to rest on Sascha's jaw. She could feel the start of stubble under her palm. She pressed her lips to his, closing the distance between them again. Sascha's hand came up, settling on her waist and pulling her flush against him for a second time that night. Zoey inhaled, parting her lips as Sascha adjusted, rolling them over. She was under him now, his body half-covering and pressing against hers. Chest to chest. Hip to hip. His forearms braced on either side of her head. There was something desperate between them, some heated, frantic energy that thrummed in the air, radiating into and out of her very skin. Zoey didn't know what it was. She didn't care. Whatever it was, she wanted it to stay, to embrace it tonight. Tomorrow was uncertain. Tonight was immediate. Tonight was given.

To have this moment, this time, with Sascha meant more than words would ever say. She'd known she would never see him again when they parted, but the idea of losing him even sooner than she'd anticipated – that was almost too much to bear. Zoey's left hand fell to his chest and rested against his shirt. Her eyes opened as Sascha pulled back a short distance. There was an expression in his eyes. Unveiled. Exposed. Emotion he was showing her. Unexpected tears welled up in Zoey's eyes. These were the beginnings of something more. Things that could never be said. Should never be said. Things that had to remain unsaid for both of their sakes. Sascha's hand settled on top of hers, pressing her palm flat. Zoey could feel the even, steady beat of his heart. It seemed to match the rhythm of her own.

Chapter 32

Predawn moved in; gray, overcast, and humid. Heavy. Zoey could feel the weight of tension in the air before she even opened her eyes. She took a breath and pressed closer into Sascha's arms, wishing away the morning, willing back the stars and the night. But no amount of hope could drive away the lead-bellied clouds outside.

"Morning," said Sascha.

Zoey tilted her head up, resting her chin on his bare chest. She'd fallen asleep in his arms. Waking up here, like this, struck a chord somewhere deep inside her. All the emotion she'd seen in his blue eyes last night was gone, replaced with a calculating hardness that she recognized. She'd seen it in Innsbruck and in Merano.

"Morning," replied Zoey. "What time is it?"

"Just gone five o'clock."

"It feels earlier. Any ideas?"

"Don't beat around the bush, do you?" A humorless smile flitted across Sascha's face. "We go to Rona and Flynn's hotel, get their passports, rent a car, swing back here, and get out of Paris. It's the best I can come up with."

"Shouldn't we get our things from here first? It would cut out a step."

"There are some things I have with me that would not do to be found. If we're intercepted by OMNI or your father, I'd rather I didn't have any of those things with us. If we're caught, my presence will be incriminating enough without illegal items."

"You mean things that you hide in that black duffel bag of yours?"

"The very same," replied Sascha.

"What's in there, Sascha?"

"Mostly orders. Job reservations. Ghost guns. Tools of the trade. They're mine, but they're things I can't allow to be found."

Zoey glanced away, not sure how to respond. It was easy to forget what Sascha did outside of this, that his morality was gray at best. Easy to forget that he wasn't what most people would think of as 'good'.

Sascha shifted beside her. "Ready?"

Words failed again, and Zoey nodded, getting out of bed. It was cooler in the room than she'd anticipated, and a shiver worked its way across her skin. She wasn't ready. Not really. Hours now. She had *hours* left with him. This assassin, this man, that she had spent the last month getting to know. The reality that she would never see him again. Why, *why* did it hurt so much? She should have been happy to be almost home, and she was, in a bittersweet kind of way. It had to be the situation. She wanted to be home, but she didn't want to part from him. The fact remained though, that they were running now, crashing forward with almost no plan. Subject to wild desperation.

"Zoey," said Sascha.

She looked up, pausing as she shuffled through her bag for fresh clothes. Draped over one arm was his bulletproof vest. He extended it toward her. Zoey's heart constricted in her chest. His meaning was clear. He really *was* worried.

"It's your only one," she said.

"That doesn't matter. This is replaceable. You are not. I want you safe today."

"It'll be too big. It won't fit," replied Zoey.

Out of the corner of her eye, she caught Sascha's lips curling into a smirk. Realization of what she'd said dawned on her. She turned to stop whatever he was going to say.

"Sascha, please –"

"You said the same thing last night, and we made it work," he said.

Zoey flushed bright red. She could have sworn steam left her ears. "You know, Sasch, if The Czarina doesn't kill you, I will."

"Of course, you will." Sascha's smile faded, leaving only a softness in its wake. "It's adjustable. Please, Zoey. Put my mind at ease."

"What about you?"

"I've spent the last ten years avoiding bullets, Zoey. I'll be fine."

There was that familiar ache. It settled further down now, and Zoey felt her entire body tense. Thumbing the fabric covering, she forced a smile.

"Thank you."

She swung the vest over her head and tightened the Velcro straps at the sides. It was still a little oversized on her, but all things considered, it fit better than she expected. Sascha approached and reached out to her, fingers landing on the Ursa Minor necklace, where it had somehow landed on the outside of the vest. Zoey stepped a little closer to him. He took the pendant in hand for a moment, thumb resting on the North Star. There was something incredibly tender in his gaze. Zoey inclined her head. Then Sascha flashed a quick smile and dropped the pendant into the gap between the vest and her shirt.

"I should have got you one of Aquila, too," Sascha murmured. Then he cleared his throat. "I'll go and get Flynn and your sister. We need to get moving. I don't want to waste any time."

Zoey glanced out the window as Sascha left the room. The street below was quieter than it had been yesterday morning. Maybe it was just due to the time. But . . . something about it unsettled her. Was OMNI out there, lying in wait? She swallowed. Were they laying a trap, waiting to spring it? Zoey readjusted the Velcro straps at her waist and thought back on the words she'd heard over The Czarina's prerecorded video. *'I'll feed you to my dogs.'*

~ ~ ~ ~ ~ ~

Paris's streets were quiet. There were fewer cars than there had been in the evening. Less activity. Zoey couldn't help but feel uneasy. A few dark vans swept up and down the streets. Vendor vans, moving vans. Early people going about early business. But on the street, a group of four looked odd at this hour. If that worried her, she knew Sascha would be on a tight hair-trigger because of it. Zoey lengthened her stride, now half a pace behind him. Zoey wanted to reach out to him, to set her hand in his. But she didn't quite dare. Not in front of Rona and Flynn. Not now, with Sascha so tense. If he needed to reach for a firearm, she knew he'd want both hands free. She exhaled hard, feeling the weight of the one against her own hip. Rona's hand touched her arm.

"You look worried," said Rona.

"I am, and you should be, too," replied Zoey. "This is . . . a very charged situation."

"Yeah, I'm starting to believe you," sighed Rona, her eyes darting this way and that.

Steps ahead, Sascha paused at a pedestrian crossing. "We're almost at the river. Would any of you care to take the lead?"

Flynn stepped forward, and Zoey couldn't help feeling struck by how different he was from Sascha. Less at home, yet less on edge. Zoey took a few steps closer to Sascha as they, together but not together, crossed a main road. Then she watched as Rona moved closer to Flynn.

"It's on Boulevard Raspail," said Flynn, glancing over his shoulder. "I don't know if that's much help –"

"I know where Boulevard Raspail is," said Sascha.

Zoey resisted the urge to flinch away. Sascha's voice was sharper than she'd ever heard it before. Sascha's bulletproof vest under her jacket restricted her movement a fraction, and she reached for her necklace. He was worried, grasping at straws to pull everything back together.

"When we go across the river, we'll split up."

"Why?" snapped Rona.

Zoey saw the tension at the corners of Sascha's eyes and spoke before he could. "You and me can't be in one confined area together. If OMNI is behind us, a bridge is a perfect place for an ambush. If we cross in two different places, they'll have to split up."

"So why are we using bridges at all?" asked Rona, sounding terse.

Sascha pressed his lips together hard. "It's our quickest option, and . . ."

"Sascha?" Zoey asked, turning to him. But his gaze was over her head, his focus on something she couldn't see.

"We have to go. Rona, you and Flynn cross at Pont du Carrousel," hissed Sascha. "Zoey, stay with me. Pont Royal. We'll meet at Boulevard Raspail. Move, now!"

Zoey moved in the same instant as Sascha. Shifting from a standstill to a run. Sprinting. The rhythm of the city shattered. Sascha was already a few steps ahead of her, racing beside the low wall bordering the river walk alongside the Seine. She lengthened her stride, fighting to keep up with him. He was taller than her, his strides longer. Zoey slowed without meaning to and looked back, eyes scanning for Rona and Flynn. There. They'd doubled back to the other side of the road.

A gunshot split the morning, and the broken city rhythm fragmented into dust. Small chunks of concrete flew up just to Zoey's right.

A hand closed around her wrist. Familiar grip. Sascha. He'd stopped. Zoey slowed, a question on her lips. A question she didn't ask. Sascha shoved her in front of him and onward, and she stumbled a step. Sascha's vest was heavier than she'd realized. Behind her, another shot echoed through the streets. Zoey couldn't not turn. Sascha was at her shoulder. Metal flashed in his right hand. She lunged forward as she felt him press at her back, urging her on.

"Stay with me!"

Zoey nearly slipped as they turned onto Pont Royal bridge. Keep moving. Once they were across the bridge, surely, they'd be home free. Surely, then. Just keep running. Ignore how her chest ached. Ignore how her legs burned. Keep going.

Another gunshot cracked through the morning.

Stars flashed across Zoey's vision as her breath left her chest. She gasped, winded and stumbled. Had she been shot? Any breath she'd had left crushed out of her chest as Sascha knocked her down, crashing against the pavement. Her cheek burned. Her palms slapped the bridge, skinned and bleeding. She spun, rolling onto her side, heaving for air. She cast around. Why didn't this feel like it had when Bouncer had shot her? Sascha braced over her. Zoey lashed out trying to throw him off her, to keep moving. Panic sunk in.

"You're alright. They hit the vest," said Sascha, resting his free hand on her arm. His gaze was fixed over his left shoulder, watching the end of the bridge. Zoey raised her head, gasping. Air rushed back into her lungs. Movement flickered at a crosswalk. Sascha whipped around. Raise. Aim. Fire. He swore.

"OMNI?" Zoey asked. Her voice was hoarse.

Sascha met her gaze and lurched to his feet. "Get up, Zoey."

Zoey scrambled up. She was hurting. She knew she was hurting. But she couldn't feel anything. Then she caught sight of Sascha's face. Bloodless. Stricken. She followed his line of sight. Two black vans pulled in, blocking off one end of the bridge. There was no way back.

Sascha whipped around, sprinting toward the far end of the bridge. Zoey fought to keep up with him, running a few steps behind.

"OMNI?" she gasped, her breath ragged in her throat.

"No," replied Sascha. The word was hardly more than a raspy whisper.

Her father. Zoey knew it with certainty. She knew it with the same conviction that she knew Sascha was afraid. There was no forging that look in his eyes. The way they showed more whiteness around the edges than they ever should have.

Three more vans closed off the other end of the bridge. Cut off.

Trapped. She'd been right. A bridge *was* the perfect place for an ambush.

Sascha skidded to a halt. Zoey stopped half a pace behind him. She wasn't leaving him now. Not now. Men poured out of the vans. The vehicles must have been filled to capacity. All armed. Cold horror ran through Zoey's blood. Sascha had one weapon. Two counting the one pressed to her own hip.

Beside her, Sascha moved, lunging toward one side of the bridge. Zoey dashed after him, fear fueling her movements. There was nothing to guarantee that these men wouldn't shoot her, too. Beyond Sascha's shoulder, she could just make out two figures racing across a bridge further downriver. Rona and Flynn. It had to be.

Two shots.

A chunk of pavement between Sascha and the bridge wall flew several feet into the air. Sascha made a strangled noise high in his throat. Something desperate. Frenzied. Zoey moved to go to him. Gunshot again. Another chunk of the bridge's surface directly in front of her feet flew into the air. A warning. Zoey stepped backward. She couldn't get to him. She couldn't close the distance between them anymore.

"Sascha –"

"It's okay. You're okay."

Cold ran over Zoey's skin as Sascha's mouth lifted in a snarl, and at his side, his finger twitched to the trigger. His eyes though, weren't on her.

Zoey froze as a new voice broke across the bridge. A voice she knew. A voice she'd grown up with.

"Weapons down. Hands up."

She couldn't stop herself from turning. The armed men at each end of the bridge had drawn closer, trapping them. And in the center of the closest line, Maxwell. She froze, staring at him. There had to be something she could do. Something she could say to convince him to let Sascha go. She opened her mouth to call to him, to beg him. But no sound left her mouth.

The line of men to either side of Maxwell lifted their weapons higher. The movement was so uniform that it was almost audible. Zoey gaped at her father, silently mouthing words that wouldn't come. There was a clatter from Sascha's direction. Zoey turned and stared at him as he kicked his handgun away. She didn't think she'd ever forget the sound of metal grating against stone.

"Do as he says, Zoey," said Sascha, raising his hands and placing them behind his head. There was a strange expression on his face. Something almost calm.

"What about you?" Zoey could hear the pleading concern in her own voice. Sascha. His freedom. His life. All in danger. Because of her. Because he'd chosen to help her.

Sascha smiled, the expression tight, blue eyes sparkling. "That's your father, Zoey. Regardless of what happens now, you're safe. I've done what I promised I'd do."

Zoey stared at him, her eyes burning as they filled with tears. She shook her head. There had to be something. She turned back to Maxwell, still walking slowly toward them.

"Let him go!"

But the advance did not stop.

She'd drawn before she really knew what she was doing. Dimly, she heard a shouted command in her father's voice, but it sounded far away. As though it had been called from another world. Zoey's hands trembled, but she tightened her grip and lined her father up in her sights. The air felt thick.

She shouted again, her voice stronger than she felt. "Let him go!"

Slowly, Maxwell, head tilted marginally, stretched one hand out to his side. A ripple of movement spread through the men to each side of Maxwell as they lifted their weapons higher.

"You don't want to do that, Zoey," said Sascha.

She glanced at him, Maxwell still in her sights. Sascha came a few paces closer, hands still behind his head. He reached out slowly and settled one hand over hers, pulling her aim down away from Maxwell, starting to disentangle her fingers from the grip.

"You need to go," she whispered with tears in her voice.

Sascha offered a tiny smile, and his fingers tightened gently over hers. "You need to put this down. You'll get yourself killed if you don't, and I don't want to see that happen. They're tense enough. Now let me take this."

From the corner of her eye, she caught a short, sharp movement from Maxwell, and she felt rather than heard running feet. She knew Sascha couldn't bear to see her killed, as much as she couldn't bear to see him caught. She started to turn back. She'd shoot. Do anything to buy Sascha some time. But Sascha didn't budge. His hand clamped down tight on her wrist before she could move, holding her fast. Her finger pulled the trigger, and a single shot escaped the handgun.

The weight of Sascha's hand on her wrist vanished.

Everything stopped. The world fell deaf to ringing in Zoey's ears. Nothing and no one moved. Zoey stared, weapon falling from her hand in slow motion and landing on the bridge with a sound she barely registered. Sascha knelt on the bridge a few paces from her. He bared his teeth in silence, one hand braced on the stone ground, the other clamped down over his side. Red seeped up between his fingers, dripping down and spattering the pale stone. Dampness spread across his shirt in a dark stain.

"Sascha," Zoey whispered, her voice trembling.

He hissed through his teeth and looked up at her, agony written in every line of his expression. Trembling, he grimaced, muscles in his jaw flexing. "I told you, you needed better trigger control."

Words left her mouth in broken sobs. "I'm sorry. I'm sorry. I'm so sorry."

"Zoey, it's okay. I promise. It's okay. I'm fine. Everything's okay." He breathed out through gritted teeth in a sound that gave way to a low groan. "I'm okay. It's just a bullet. I'll be fine."

Zoey spun to look at her father, making eye contact and pleading with him in silence to stop now. Wasn't this enough? Wasn't getting his daughter back more important? It was just one man. Couldn't he let Sascha go?

Maxwell's chin lowered a fraction.

A scream tore from Zoey's mouth as human bodies rushed, pressing from all sides. Indistinguishable. The world crushed in. Breaths too sharp. The air stung her lungs like needles. Every sound pounded on her eardrums. Black uniforms. Faces covered by plastic shields. The men her father had brought. She stumbled, trying to keep her balance. Gloved hands pulled at her wrists, drawing them behind her back. Plastic zip ties tightened around them. She reared back, kicking and flailing. Fight. Shake them off. Panic sank its claws in. Get away. Get back to help Sascha. Sascha needed to go to the hospital. He needed help. Over her own struggle, she could hear Sascha shouting.

"Maxwell, stop! Let her go! She has nothing to do with –!"

"That's enough," Maxwell snarled, his voice ringing out over the bridge. Zoey thought she could hear a touch of amusement in his voice. "She was armed, wasn't she? Aiming at me. She's dangerous. Just as much as you are."

Fighting, Zoey craned her neck to see Sascha. If he could run, he needed to go *now*. She caught a glimpse of him. He was still on his knees, hands back behind his head. Red spread across his shirt as her father focused solely on him. What was Sascha doing? This was his last chance. Zoey stumbled as she was both pushed and pulled forward, toward the end of the bridge. Ushered, hauled away. Leaving Sascha alone in the center of the bridge. Not now.

She caught the sound of Sascha's voice again. "Maxwell, she's –"

Thud. Something hard impacting something soft. Digging her heels in, Zoey craned backwards. Sascha righted himself where he knelt. An angry, red mark formed at the side of his mouth. Scarlet trickled down his chin.

Fury. Panic. A combination unlike anything she'd ever felt broke in her chest, and she fought to pull away. He was injured. Bleeding. Don't separate them yet. Not yet. Let her help him. Let her say what she hadn't been able to the night before. Just don't pull them apart like this. Not like this.

"Stop!" Zoey's voice broke in a sob. "Get off me! Just let me –!"

She struggled to get free. Just let her say goodbye. Let her say goodbye before Sascha ran. He had to run. He had to. He valued his freedom too much. He was the most resourceful man she knew. Even hurt, there had to be something he could do. If he ran now, he could get himself over the side of the bridge and into the Seine before they could aim and fire. *Do* something. Why didn't he do something? Through a gap in her father's men, she saw Sascha nose to nose with the muzzle of her father's handgun. Talking. They were talking. Working something out. Some compromise. Please. The gap closed. Zoey plunged, searching for another glimpse of him. There. Sascha was looking in her direction now, as though he could see her. Zoey's eyes clouded with tears. She didn't know how their farewell was supposed to have been. But it wasn't supposed to be like this. Not. Like. This.

A shot broke the air.

No.

Breath caught in Zoey's throat.

No. No.

One of Maxwell's men moved, and a second gap between them opened. Let Sascha have gotten away. Made some miracle escape. Let that be why the shot was fired. Don't let . . .

Tears streamed down Zoey's cheeks. The final gap was here. She looked through, desperate. Her father's hand lowered back to his side. And . . . Zoey stopped, her body frozen. She couldn't move. Sascha lay on the bridge. Legs folded beneath him. His back to her. Motionless.

Get up.

He had to. Zoey's throat closed.

Get up.

Everything stopped. She stopped. Autonomy left.

Get up.

But darkness pooled beneath him, spilling across the pavement, and Sascha didn't get up.

Chapter 33

Gray. That was all this place was. Gray. One room. A bed along one wall. One heavy metal door. No windows. Just gray. And a single, fluorescent light overhead. That was it. Zoey pulled her knees to her chest and pressed herself into the corner. The wall behind her was cold. She didn't know whether it was metal or concrete. She closed her eyes and buried her face against her knees. It didn't matter. She didn't know how long she'd been here – wherever *here* was. While Maxwell figured out what to do with her.

What did "here" and "there" matter when Sascha was . . . Zoey forced herself to stop. Dangerous. That was what Maxwell had called her on the bridge. But neither she nor Sascha had been dangerous. He'd just been trying to get her home. She'd been trying to keep him safe. And in doing that, she'd got him . . . Zoey shook her head, feeling the fabric of her jeans rub against her forehead.

All she knew was that after she'd been dragged away, she was loaded into one of the vans. One of her father's men had given her water. She'd refused. Did she sleep? She didn't know. She didn't care. The world had fallen away behind a screen. Her senses had been dull. Numbed out. Her father's men hadn't spoken to her. She hadn't spoken to them. There had been a shuffle as they'd crossed back over the English Channel. Zoey hadn't paid it attention. Her mind had been too drained. Then she'd been brought *here* by her father's men – his subordinates, she assumed – zip tie handcuffs removed, and Sascha's vest taken. Even her shoes had been taken. God only knew why. Then she'd been left. Alone. Crushingly alone. Her only consolation was the silver constellation around her neck. Ursa Minor. The constellation with the North Star. The guiding light.

She hurt. Now that she'd stopped moving, now that the adrenaline was gone, her body told her where it hurt. Her back hurt. Where she'd been shot. Where Sascha's vest had saved her life. She lifted her head and glanced at her hands. Her palms were still skinned from where Sascha had knocked her down. She could still feel the weight of him as he leaned over her. The red rings around her wrists were starting to fade now. Her cheek throbbed where the skin had been scraped away. She drew a shuddering breath and leaned her head back against the wall. Her entire body was damp with sweat. She needed a shower to wash off the grime, the blood . . . blood on Sascha, his body, the ground . . . under him.

Stop.

Don't think of it.

But she couldn't stop her mind replaying the image of him lying on his side, facing away from her, the first traces of blood seeping through his blond hair. Over. And over. And over. She closed her eyes and clenched her jaw, wishing she had more tears to shed. The only reprieve had to be that he had fallen away from her. To have seen his eyes dull in death . . . she didn't think she could have survived that. Her eyes burned. She'd cried herself out before she'd even arrived here. Her chest still ached from the sobs that had wracked her body.

Her friend.

The man who had meant more.

The man who'd made her chest ache and her heart pound.

Gone.

And she was to blame.

He could have got away had it not been for her. And the bitter, sick truth was that she'd got him killed.

Zoey wrapped herself in a hug, grappling for comfort. She felt nausea slicking the back of her throat. Sascha was gone. And it was her fault. She fisted a hand in her hair and inhaled with a dry, shuddering sob. There was no comfort here. But what comfort could come? She only wanted him. To apologize him. To hug him once more before they parted. A grinning afterimage of him danced behind her eyes, a stalk of harebells tucked behind his ear.

Breathing hurt. It felt wrong. Zoey inhaled and exhaled with a sob. Sascha had done far more for her than anyone she'd ever known. She shook her head, her eyes stinging again. There were no more tears.

The harsh clang of the door to the room unlocking made Zoey jump. Could it be Rona? Hailee? Every nerve lurched onto high alert, and she stood up, socked feet just hitting the floor as the metal door swung inward.

Maxwell. Face to face for the first time in over a month. Not on a bridge now, but inches apart. Why she'd expected anyone else, she didn't know. He stood there in silence, gray eyes unreadable. Zoey swallowed and set her jaw, pushing aside the crushing disappointment in her chest. Why did she and her father have to look so alike? There was something stomach-churning about it. Even their eyes were the same shade of heather gray. Had he looked so cold when he'd shot Sascha? Had their so-similar eyes been the last thing Sascha had seen? Silence stretched between them, hanging like an unfilled noose.

"Zoey," said Maxwell, folding his arms.

"Hello," she replied, mirroring him.

"'Hello'? That's the best you can do?" he asked, a cold smile crossing his face. "No hug? No smile? That's gratitude for you, I suppose."

"For killing my friend? For hauling me off here?" Her eyes flickered up and down him. He still wore the same clothes from the bridge. Small mercy that his hands looked clean. Truth be told, no matter how clean they were, they would always have blood on them. Sascha's blood. "You shot any gratitude I had."

Maxwell laughed very quietly. "To be fair, I didn't shoot him first, did I? I should thank you, really. I would never have been able to get that close to him without you. You brought him down for me. Couldn't have done it without you."

A slow breath left Zoey's throat. She'd expected goading. She'd expected tears to prickle the backs of her eyes. What she didn't expect was the furious, hot wave of anger that swept through her chest. It was all she could do to not lunge across the remaining space and punch Maxwell.

"I want to see Rona," said Zoey, looking up and tightening the fold of her arms.

"No."

"Where is she?"

"She's here. We picked her up a moment after you. A lot less dramatic than you were, thank God. I don't think I could have taken any more hysterics. She's upstairs."

"What is this place? Where are we?"

"Near the Kent Downs. That's all you need to know."

"Why am I here? Why are you keeping me here?"

"This is protective custody. I thought you'd be glad to have it. There are a lot of people still looking for you. Not all of them good. And a lot of people have worked very hard to find you. Rona among them. You've been troublesome these last weeks, Zoey. I hope you know that."

"You act like this is my fault. Like I asked for this to happen."

Not in a thousand years would she have wanted this.

A small laugh slipped from Maxwell's mouth, and he smiled, showing far too many teeth. "No. You'd have never imagined something like this. Though, I am surprised."

Zoey reset her jaw, grinding her teeth now. "About what?"

"That Sascha would involve himself. It's a bit pathetic. Well. Annoying. Your trail went cold after he cut across it. That's not the most surprising thing, though."

"What would that be? I know you're dying for me to ask," said Zoey, the words tasting like arsenic on her tongue.

Maxwell bit one of his nails, expression bored. "You. Of all things, who would have thought *you* would have been his weakness. A woman. I thought I taught him better than that. Thought *he* knew better. I overestimated him."

"I was his friend," snapped Zoey. "Not a weakness."

"Friend, weakness. Same thing. If I'd have thought you would have been Sascha's undoing, I'd have thrown you in his path years ago. We might have caught him sooner." Maxwell's gray eyes hardened. "What did he have with him?"

"What do you mean?" asked Zoey.

"What was he planning to bring into England aside from you? Drugs? Arms? Munitions? Orders? You can't have been his only motivation."

"I don't know," replied Zoey. Sascha hadn't spoken about his work with her. She'd never asked. She was glad of it. Now there was nothing to tell. "We never talked about it."

"Why are you bothering to protect him? If the situations were reversed, he wouldn't do the same."

Zoey shook her head, thinking of the pensive look, the emotions, that had come across Sascha's face in Merano, after The Czarina's threat. Some instinct, something deeper than logic, told her that Sascha would have done the same that she was doing now. He would have protected her. He had protected her from the first day she'd known him.

A dry laugh leaped from Zoey's mouth. Unexpected. "You didn't know him at all, did you? The Sascha I know would keep me safe."

"Know him? *Know* him? Zoey, I raised the bastard. I pulled him from the gutter myself and made him become the man you think you know. I know him better than you could ever wish to know him. Sascha only showed you the side of himself that he wanted you to see. He didn't show you the man who was willing to cheat, steal, and kill without remorse to get what he wanted."

But she had seen that side of Sascha. She'd seen it the first day she'd known him. "That's not who he really is."

"Then who is he really, Zoey? Enlighten me." Maxwell sneered, taking a few steps closer. "A *kind* man? A kind man wouldn't do the things he's done. There's no point in you protecting him, and he doesn't deserve it. Where did he keep you the month you were with him?"

"Do you mean where did we stay?" asked Zoey. She wanted to back against the wall.

"*Where*, Zoey?"

Zoey sighed, looking away. They'd emptied the safe house. Her father would only find a shell if he decided to search it. "Germany."

"Damn. I was close. I was watching Slovenia. Germany. Clever."

"What?" asked Zoey.

"He had properties all over Europe." Maxwell sounded distracted. "We were trying to track down where exactly. Doesn't matter now, I suppose. Just a shame we had to waste him before we got some answers. Do you know who he was working for when he picked you up?"

"He wasn't working for anyone," replied Zoey. She wished Maxwell would leave. Everything was worse with him here. So much worse. She would rather be alone again than be in this tiny, confined room with him.

Maxwell hummed in his throat and didn't reply.

Zoey took a breath. "When were you going to tell us?"

"Tell you what?" asked Maxwell. There was a new, razor's edge in his voice.

"What you really are."

"And what *am* I?" he asked. Again, that overly toothy grin settled on his mouth. Savage. Menacing.

"An SAS operative."

"I'm a specialist more than an operative, really. Do me some justice, Zoey. I take high-profile affairs like this. I'm normally a bit more subtle than I was today, but it was nice to give Sascha a worthy send off, international boundaries and decorum be damned."

"When were you going to tell us?" Zoey asked again. As usual, Maxwell had spoken around the point.

"Why would I have needed to tell you? There was no reason for you to know."

"No reason? No reason?!" The dam in Zoey's chest burst. She snapped upright. She'd crossed the room before she realized she was moving. "I was kidnapped! OMNI had all of my information! All of it! Every piece of information the internet could provide. They have mine! They have Rona's! They have Hailee's! None of us knew how much danger we've been in. I didn't know a thing until Sascha told me. And you weren't going to breathe a *word*."

Maxwell tilted his head. He looked unruffled. "No."

Zoey stopped. Her chest was heaving. "What did you do to make them want to come after you? After *us*?"

"Shut down some operations of theirs. Helped with intelligence and provided firepower." He quirked a smile. "Cost them a lot of merchandise. High profile people."

"And you never thought they might strike back?" She gritted her teeth and took another step toward her father. "You didn't think they might attack the one thing that might make any *normal* father's skin crawl?"

"I was counting on it," snarled Maxwell, his voice low, just above a whisper.

The room seemed to slant. Zoey backed down half a step. There was only her father and his frigid, gray eyes.

"What?" she breathed.

"For years, my team and I have been closing in on OMNI. Closing, but never catching. We've shut down cells, websites, caught some minor leaders. But until we find their operation heads, we don't stand a chance at beating them. Shut down one cell and six more appear the next day. I knew I had to do something major to flush them out. Get them to make a move. Throw something in their way that they just couldn't resist. You and your sisters? Package deal? Perfect bait."

"We're your *children*."

"And?" He breathed a beat of laughter. "It made you all the more tempting."

Far away, Zoey could have sworn she heard the rapid beat of a drummer. She was wrong. It wasn't a drum. It was her pulse.

"No. You're lying. You wouldn't . . . you didn't –" Zoey spat. Maxwell always lied. He had to be lying now. He had to be.

"A liar, am I?" He leaned forward, that savage smile catching him again. His grin slid into a snarl. "Tell me, Zoey, who do you think released your information?"

This couldn't be true. It couldn't be. Random chance was better than this. Calculating, cold design. But even as she stared at her own father, Zoey knew he was telling the truth. There was no forging that delighted viciousness in his eyes. Maxwell had deliberately released their information in the hopes of OMNI finding them. Just to further his organization's agenda. Searing anger reared in Zoey's chest. His own daughters. Her sisters – the perfect bait.

Blood boiling in her veins, Zoey stared at Maxwell. He could throw her in the way of as many criminal organizations as he wanted. He could rage and storm at her as much as he liked. He could keep her in as many of these cold, gray cells as he wished. He could do whatever he liked to her. Until he touched her sisters. Until he betrayed *them*. Until he put *them* in danger. Zoey stepped in. One hand pulled back. She bared her teeth and planted her foot. In the back of her mind, she nearly heard Sascha's bright laugh, nearly heard him talking again about stars and constellations. Could practically *feel* him at her shoulder.

She swung, catching Maxwell square on the side of his mouth. A knuckle in her hand popped, and her hand throbbed, the skinned patches on her palms burning where her fingernails had dug in.

But it was worth it.

Zoey stood inches from him, trembling. "You. Are. Foul."

She held her ground as her father's expression contorted with rage. He touched the side of his mouth, fingers coming away bloody. His shoulders tensed. A sneer worked its way onto his face, and he tucked his chin ever so slightly. A look she could only describe as loathing entered his eyes. Zoey balled her fists at her sides, preparing for him to lunge at her. She was ready. It would give her some outlet. Internally, she begged him to swing back at her. Somewhere, anywhere for her anger, for her hurt, for her guilt to go. A red welt started to form on the side of his face. Maxwell leaned forward ever so slightly. Zoey adjusted her weight into the balls of her feet. An alarm sounded from beyond the tiny room. Maxwell exhaled hard and shook his head, turning on his heel, jerking the door open.

"Get her out of here," he snapped.

Then he was gone, the door falling shut. Before it slammed against the jamb, a hand shoved it back open, and Rona plunged inside. Zoey's breath caught as she spotted someone else enter just a step behind Rona. Could it –? Was it –? Then she realized who it was. Flynn. Not Sascha. Because Sascha was –

"Zoey!"

Rona's voice broke her trance. Breathing a sob, Zoey dashed forward, wrapping her arms around her sister. She dropped her head to Rona's shoulder and broke. Dry sobs caught her aching chest, and she felt Rona's arms pull tight, supporting her. She heard Rona draw a shuddering breath and exhale hard.

"Are you okay?" asked Rona.

Zoey laughed desperately, the sound bordering on manic, and shook her head, pressing her forehead fast against Rona's shoulder. Rona seemed like the only solid thing in a world that had turned to inconsequential nothingness. From a world away, she felt her sister's hand settle on the back of her head. Just holding. Zoey gasped for breath. For air. For an explanation that wouldn't come. Words failed now. Emotion held her again, pressurizing. She'd been cast out into empty space, dark abyss opening around her. Distant stars watched from lifetimes away, unable or unwilling to pull her back into orbit. Air refused to pass her lungs. The North Star flickered and died, swallowed away into a black void, its guiding light extinguished. Zoey's legs buckled beneath her, and a universe away, she felt Rona lower them both to the floor. Maxwell had betrayed them. Nothing would ever be right again. Not the way it used to be. Sascha was dead. Night closed in. A whining scream tore Zoey's chest and throat, a weak, strangled thing. The Ursa Minor pendant hung like a tightening noose around her neck, and her mind's eye, Aquila fell, ripped from the sky.

Sneak Peek

To be continued

    Read on for a "Sneak Peek" of what's ahead:

Unseasonably cold September air tore through Zoey's thin jacket as she walked behind Simon. She wished she'd grabbed her heavier coat from her duffel bag at the bed-and-breakfast in Kinloch Rannoch. But going back to get it wasn't an option. Kinloch Rannoch, the warm bed-and-breakfast, and her coat were hours away, over the mountains. She shivered and pulled her jacket closer, quickening her steps to catch Simon.

"Where are we?" she asked, peeking over his shoulder at the map in his hands.

"South of Loch Ericht," he replied, passing the map to her. "We've crossed Sawnton Manor's property line already."

Zoey turned the paper map over in her hands and laughed. "I was never much good at reading these. We came on a hiking trip to Scotland when I was younger, and Maxwell put me in charge of the map. I got us hopelessly lost. He was furious. I was lucky Mum was there."

"Your dad's always furious," laughed Simon, taking the map back. "I hope you're braced for it when we get back to Wales. He's going to go nuclear. It'll probably measure on the Richter Scale."

"I can hardly wait. He does realize that we're only out here *because* of him, doesn't he?"

"Maxwell? Take responsibility for something he caused? You'd be lucky to see that happen, Zoey." Simon glanced at the map again, then nodded uphill. "When we reach the summit of Sgairneach Mhor, we should be more or less on top of Sawnton Manor itself. It's not much further of a climb. Think you can do it?"

Zoey nodded, a grim smile forming on her mouth. "I have to. It's too important not to do it."

"Not really," replied Simon, a tiny, nervous grin breaking across his face. "We shouldn't be smiling about this, you know. It's indecent."

"I don't think there's anything indecent about trespassing on some billionaire's land. Particularly when said billionaire has done the awful things *he* has."

Simon's smile fell away. "Well, when you put it like that . . ."

Zoey took a deep breath of the chill air as she watched Simon stride ahead. Maybe smiling as much as she had been *was* indecent. But it felt so gratifying to finally be *doing* something. Just taking some kind of direct action was liberating. She felt like she could breathe again. Make a difference. It was the kind of thing Sascha would have done.

Sascha . . .

She swallowed, again looking ahead at Simon. If she squinted hard enough, imagined hard enough, she could almost see attributes of Sascha in Simon. Almost. But not quite. That bitter, sinking sensation of defeat opened in her chest for what felt like the thousandth time. Sascha was dead. She'd never see him again. And no amount of squinting at other people would bring him back. Dead people tended to stay dead.

Trying to distract herself, she pulled her phone out of her pocket and tapped the screen. She sighed, seeing two disheartening but familiar words. No service.

A low buzz interrupted her thoughts, and Zoey looked up, slipping her phone back into her pocket. A drone hovered overhead, swinging and fluctuating in the air before zipping away over the mountains.

"Simon!" she called. "We've got a drone!"

Simon turned, and Zoey caught the concern that flashed across his face.

"I don't like the looks of that! Let's get in and get out while we can!" called Simon.

She quickened her stride and ignored the burn in her legs. They'd ache tomorrow. Panting, she crested the rise of Sgairneach Mhor's summit and stood beside Simon. Taking a moment to catch her breath, a tiny smile formed at the corners of her mouth. Below, the world sloped away, down and down and down, giving way eventually to a gray expanse of water.

"Loch Ericht," said Simon quietly. He glanced at the map, then pointed to a building made of pale stone on the far bank. "And that is Sawnton Manor."

"That's where Lord Marion lives?" asked Zoey.

"Some of the year, yeah," nodded Simon. "Records say that he stays at Sawnton during the autumn."

"So, what now?" asked Zoey.

"Well," said Simon, glancing at the map again, before folding it. "They hold scheduled tours throughout the first two floors of Sawnton Manor. Apparently, it's one of the most haunted manors in Scotland. If we could get ourselves onto one of those tours, I can cause a distraction, and you can slip off and search the private rooms. Without getting caught, mind you. We'll need solid proof that Lord Marion's actually here and has committed a crime if we're going to convince Maxwell to come up here – and not tear our heads off in the process. Lord Marion's a member of the British aristocracy. Maxwell hardly even wants to consider him as a potential head of OMNI, let alone investigate him or storm one of his properties."

Zoey sighed sharply. "He bought me. Isn't that proof enough?"

"Not really," replied Simon, grimacing. "Lord Marion is the name we've *heard* several times, but we can't find any tangible evidence that he has anything to do with OMNI, let alone with buying you this past summer. There's no paper trail. Nothing. Maxwell's going to take some serious convincing if he's going to even consider coming up here."

"So, Varek threatening me in broad daylight only a few days ago isn't enough?" snapped Zoey. "What he's got *inside* that manor isn't enough?"

Simon gave her a long, sympathetic look. "Not for Maxwell."

"I should have known," sighed Zoey, her shoulders falling forward. "Can't we just smash a window or something? Get in that way? It would be so much easier."

"I think that's called breaking and entering, Zoey. And you didn't factor in that Lord Marion still has Varek and a whole private security team at his disposal. It'd be like trying to break into a place protected by Sascha."

"So, we've hiked out here for nothing?"

"Not nothing. It's given both of us a good look at the place. Which I wanted before we signed up for one of the tour groups. There's a lot you can learn about a property you're trying to, again, *legally* break into."

"Oh, yeah?" asked Zoey, turning to him. "Like?"

"Well, look at the terrain –"

An echoing bang split the mountain air. Simon choked off the last half of his sentence, his eyes flying wide with shock. He swayed on his feet, the map fluttering in tatters from his hands and landing in shreds on the grass. He fumbled at his side, hand coming away bloody. Moving slowly, he turned to her, eyes focusing and unfocusing behind his glasses. Zoey stared at him in horror.

"Simon?" she asked in a whisper.

He didn't respond. Then, in slow motion, Simon slipped down sideways, landing with a devastating *thud* against the hard ground. Zoey stared, utterly frozen. An image of Sascha on the bridge in Paris, gripping his side flashed in front of her eyes. Simon sucked in a breath through his teeth, then he curled into a ball and stifled a low scream. It jarred Zoey into motion. This wasn't Sascha. Sascha hadn't screamed. This was Simon. And Simon *was* screaming. She rushed to his side and knelt, hands pressing down on top of his, applying what pressure she could. A horrified whimper left her throat as her godfather's blood welled up between her fingers.

Simon drew a few quick breaths, panting heavily. His eyes flickered behind his glasses, as though searching for something only he could see. Zoey stilled as he made eye contact with her. She stared back at him, a horrible numbness sweeping over her.

He hissed and groaned through gritted teeth, pushing her hands away. "Get out of here, Zoey. *Now.*"

"I can't leave you," she said, her voice alarmingly calm.

"It's you they want. Go!"

"Simon –" started Zoey, the terrible sensation of panic starting to set in.

Zoey yelped as Simon grabbed her arm in a death grip. His blood seeped into the fabric of her jacket. Simon shoved her hard, sending her sprawling backwards in the heather. Zoey scrambled to her feet only seconds later, adrenaline pounding through her veins.

"Get out of here! Just go!" hissed Simon between clenched teeth before his voice gave way to another strangled scream.

Zoey almost shook her head. But the low buzzing of the drone was back in the air. She had to get help. She couldn't fail Simon. He'd die if she did. She couldn't lose anyone else. She gave him a last, desperate look and bolted, dirt and scree scattering underfoot as she ran.

Printed in Great Britain
by Amazon